"Sandra McDonald knows the Navy, what makes a ship run well, and what can make it run badly. Lieutenant Jodenny Scott is the sort of tough, smart but thoroughly human officer we'd all like alongside us in an emergency. She and the other vivid characters in *The Outback Stars* propel forward a great story combining military fiction and criminal investigation in space."

—John G. Hemry, author of *Against All Enemies* and
(as Jack Campbell) *The Lost Fleet: Dauntless*

"*The Outback Stars* takes a number of interesting ideas and weaves them into a fast-moving page-turner—rivalry aboard a large naval vessel, surviving a terrible accident, mysterious deaths, among other things. But what really sets it apart is the introduction of Australasian Aboriginal myth and cosmology as an integral part of the ways and means of interstellar travel. The author shows intimate knowledge of the nuts and bolts of what *really* makes big ships tick—and her careful attention to the elements of Aboriginal culture makes this even more worthy of a reader's time."

—Walter H. Hunt, author of *The Dark Ascent*

"Lots of folks write military science fiction, but most of them you can spot as civilians who are just faking it. Sandra McDonald gets the social interaction that makes it possible for people to live in ships. She gets the petty politics, the sexual tension, even the reasons an officer will make a big deal out of badly shined shoes. It's that realism that makes *The Outback Stars* an unusually absorbing read."

—James D. Macdonald, coauthor of *The Price of the Stars*
and *Land of Mist and Snow*

THE
OUTBACK
STARS

SANDRA
McDONALD

A TOM DOHERTY ASSOCIATES BOOK
NEW YORK

This is a work of fiction. All of the characters, organizations, and events portrayed in this novel are either products of the author's imagination or are used fictitiously.

THE OUTBACK STARS

Copyright © 2007 by Sandra McDonald

Edited by James D. Macdonald

A Tor Book
Published by Tom Doherty Associates, LLC
175 Fifth Avenue
New York, NY 10010

www.tor.com

Tor® is a registered trademark of Tom Doherty Associates, LLC.

ISBN-13: 978-0-7653-5555-3
ISBN-10: 0-7653-5555-8

First Edition: April 2007
First Mass Market Edition: February 2008

Printed in the United States of America

0 9 8 7 6 5 4 3 2 1

To my parents, for everything.
And to Stephanie, Terry, and JPK,
for everything else.

ACKNOWLEDGMENTS

A novel is never created in a vacuum, not even the vacuum of outer space. My thanks for this book's Big Bang go first to the extraordinary men and women of the United States Navy, including Kathy Harris, James Goudreau, Robin Allen, Linda Hutton, and Jay Munninghoff. They taught me how to be (and not to be) a military officer.

My gratitude also goes out to the faculty and students of the Viable Paradise workshop on Martha's Vineyard, especially James Patrick Kelly, Steven Gould, and Debra Doyle. May there always be midnight strolls to the beach to gaze at the stars. Fond thanks to the folks at the Strange Horizons workshop in New Jersey, where Mary Anne exclaimed, "Don't tell me what happens next! Get it published so I can read it then."

I am grateful to Patrick Nielsen Hayden and James D. Macdonald for making these adventures better, and to Teresa Nielsen Hayden for believing in me. Many thanks also to my agent, Jeff Kellogg, and that rainy day in a Boston bakery when we became partners. His comments and insights have been amazing.

Most important, thank you and much love to Wilfred and Carol McDonald, Eric McDonald, David Bruno, Brian McDonald, Stephanie Wojtowicz, Terry Berube, Terry Odell, and the spouts. Every sailor needs a port to call home, and you've been mine.

THE
OUTBACK
STARS

PROLOGUE

Despite the protective suit shielding her from flames, Lieutenant Jodenny Scott expected to die very soon. The prospect should have alarmed her, but on some dim, exhausted level, she supposed it was only fair. So many of her shipmates were already dead or dying, cut down by unexpected violence in the middle of what should have been routine operations. Why should she be any different? She fought her way through the fire, her damaged lungs laboring, her gloved hands groping for the control panel that would put an end to this inferno.

"Lieutenant," said the voice over her commset. "Report!"

She would have been angry—how did they expect her to talk when she could barely even *breathe*?—but all her energy was focused on her mission. If somehow she survived this disaster, she would direct her fury toward the people who had caused it. The murderers who'd killed her friends and coworkers. Very briefly she thought of the man she loved, and how she had last seen him: burned, bleeding, unable to even hear her final farewell.

Jodenny's hands closed on what she hoped was the control panel. She bent forward so that her visor was flush against the metal, but ash and smoke made it impossible to see. In her mind's eye she imagined the panel: the sensors, the indicator lights, the override. Her gloves were too bulky to feel fine details. She pulled one off, ignoring the noisy alarm in her helmet that indicated a suit breach. She touched searing hot metal and recoiled with a cry. But then her fingers brushed against the lever she needed, and she wrapped her burning, blistered hand around its handle.

Here goes everything, she thought, and pulled with all her strength.

A new alarm started to screech. With violent speed, smoke and debris and corpses and anything that wasn't lashed down, including Jodenny herself, rushed toward the vacuum outside the ship. She felt herself lifted and carried toward the stars, her lungs collapsing, her suit unable to protect her. But she had done it. She had saved her ship. *This time . . .*

CHAPTER **ONE**

If Jodenny spent one more day on the planet Kookaburra she might try to kill herself again. *Not funny,* she told herself, and not true, but morbid humor was her only defense against the prospect of spending the next eight hours stuck in a cubicle, routing invoices that nobody at Fleet gave a damn about. Nearly dying on the *Yangtze* was one thing, but bureaucratic suffocation promised to be no less fatal. First thing Thursday morning she headed to the Assignments building, but as she drew near she saw that Matt Lu had beaten her to it.

"Forget it." Lu shaded his eyes against the sun. "No requisitions came in and the Survey Wing didn't post any new jobs."

"What about the *Aral Sea*?" Jodenny asked. The freighter, with its complement of five thousand crew and colonists, had been in orbit for a week.

"Leaves today for the Alcheringa. Trapped for another day in paradise, that's us."

He gave her a jaunty salute and headed off toward the mess hall, circling a miniature sculpture of Wondjina Spheres as he went. With the cadets on holiday, Alice Training Base's peaceful air was broken only by the hum of robots cutting the grass on the soccer fields. Beyond the main gate, a lush eucalyptus forest stretched all the way to the pink sandstone of the

MacBride Mountains. Earth must have looked like that once, back before the Debasement, but Jodenny had no time for beautiful landscapes and instead went inside the cool, ink-scented lobby of the building behind her.

Before Jodenny could ask, the ruddy-faced sergeant on duty said, "No, Lieutenant Scott. Yes, I'm sure. Yes, I remember you'd be eternally grateful if I called you the moment anything came in. So would Lieutenant Lu, Lieutenant Armstrong, Lieutenant Bell—"

"Quit your blabbering, sailor." Chief Pau came to the counter with an armful of files. "Take these down to Processing and shove them up their asses, why don't you? Goddamned paperwork."

As soon as they were alone, Pau leaned over and gave her a conspiratorial wink. "Thirty minutes ago the *Aral Sea* sent out a priority call for a supply officer. The requisition is in the commodore's queue."

"Chief, I love you," Jodenny blurted out. She regretted the inappropriate words immediately, but Pau only grinned.

"Better get over there before everyone else smells blood in the water, Lieutenant."

She slipped out the back door, brazenly cut across the V.I.P. parking lot, and reached the commodore's suite thirty seconds later. The cold, quiet offices were carpeted in blue and curtained in gold. Models of starships and a massive Team Space pennant provided the proper military decoration. Campos's aide, busy on a link, held up a hand to forestall her from barging in on the commodore. From behind closed doors, Jodenny could hear an angry voice.

"Do you really think I'd throw everything away?" a man was saying. "Fifteen years in, pension on the horizon, and I'm going to take up with an able tech half my age? I'd be an idiot!"

Campos's reply was too low for Jodenny to distinguish any words. A moment later the door was wrenched open and a lieutenant commander, his face red, stormed past Jodenny and out of the suite. Jodenny kept her gaze averted. She waited a respectful moment and then knocked on Campos's door.

"Good morning, ma'am," Jodenny said.

Campos was standing behind her desk, her expression grim. "Lieutenant Scott. What brings you here?"

"I came to talk to you about that requisition. On the *Aral Sea*?"

"News travels fast."

"Consider me packed."

"Come in and sit down, Lieutenant."

Jodenny resisted the urge to rub her right thigh. Most days she forgot entirely about the new bone there, but every now and then too much exertion would set it throbbing. She sat in a straight-backed chair and focused on a pink gymea lily on Campos's desk. The commodore came from authentic Aboriginal ancestry, and she'd decorated her office with art, sculpture, and weavings from Old Australia.

"I don't think you're ready to go back into space," Campos said.

"I passed my physical—"

"With a moderate duty recommendation for six months. I don't think that means jumping into the middle of a deployment."

Jodenny lifted her chin. "I'm cleared for reassignment, ma'am, and there's nothing for me to do here."

"There are dozens of other officers waiting for jobs to open up, and five of them are supply types like yourself."

"But I'm the best one for the job. You know my record, ma'am."

"I do." Campos gazed at her squarely. "I know what you did on the *Yangtze* and I know what you did afterward."

Jodenny didn't flinch. The scars on her wrists had been hidden so well by plastic surgery that even she couldn't see them anymore. "I've earned this."

"Maybe. But I've decided to send Lieutenant Lu instead."

"Commodore—"

"I just pinged him," Campos said. "He's going to have to hustle to get on the *Aral Sea*'s last birdie at noon. Don't worry, Lieutenant. The *Alaska*'s due to arrive in a few months. Maybe they'll have something."

"Yes, ma'am."

Jodenny waited until she was outside before she pulled out her gib and pinged Fleet. Commander Taymore appeared on the screen wearing a distracted expression.

"Good morning, Lieutenant. How are things?"

"Fine, sir." Jodenny squared her shoulders, knowing that what she was about to do was highly irregular. "I was hoping the admiral was in."

Taymore scratched his chin. "He's stuck in a meeting. Something I can help you with?"

"It's about the *Aral Sea,* sir. I don't think it can wait."

"I heard they had a last-minute billet open. Did the commodore choose someone else?"

"Yes, sir. But I want it."

"I know what the admiral told you," Taymore said. "Promises made during the award of the MacBride Cross aren't taken lightly. But are you sure? The *Aral Sea* isn't a happy ship."

And I'm not a happy lieutenant, Jodenny thought, but it didn't matter. Unlike the *Yangtze,* the *Aral Sea* was intact and functional. Her bulkheads hadn't been ripped open to the stars. Her decks weren't stained with blood nor fused with flesh, and if any ghosts haunted her passageways at least they didn't whisper Jodenny's name.

"Yes, sir. I'm sure," Jodenny said.

"Then you'd better go pack, Lieutenant. The admiral will authorize your transfer."

If he waited only thirty more minutes, Terry Myell would miss the birdie and be officially AWOL. It wouldn't be the first detrimental entry on his service record but it would be the last, because if he started walking, he would keep going—up over the mountains, straight past Sydney Harbor, and all the way to the back of beyond. No more closed-in starships filled with filtered air and recycled gossip for him. He would live in a tent on the open range, cook over open fires, maybe even get a dog. A Labrador retriever. And it would all be perfect and

THE OUTBACK STARS ✳ 7

peaceful until military police showed up to haul him away in handcuffs.

"Hey, Terry!" a woman called out happily. Myell turned, but the woman went into the arms of a businessman in a blue summer suit. He should have known. Although he'd once had friends on the *Aral Sea,* people who might be happy to see him, that had all changed since Fortune. No one but Team Space security would care if he disappeared over the hills.

Something flickered at the corner of his eye, and he focused on a small brown gecko that had crawled up onto the slat of his bench.

"What do you think?" Myell asked it. "Stay or go?"

The gecko didn't answer. A dozen Sydney United fans poured out of a van, boisterous after their weekend victory. A sullen group of Manchester South supporters watched them from across the median. Three do-wops with guitars slung over their backs strolled past a woman teleconferencing on her sunglasses. A young girl beside her played with a toy robot. The girl resembled Myell's niece, and he reminded himself that when the *Aral Sea* made it to Mary River he'd at least have some downtime with Colby and the family.

If he survived the trip to Mary River.

Maybe going AWOL wasn't such a bad idea after all.

"Hey, donger," a voice called out. "Forget where the ship is?"

Myell stood up. "Fuck you, too, Spallone."

Tony Spallone gave him a smile that did nothing to improve his puffy features. Behind him, Joe Olsson paid off a cabdriver and shouldered his bag. Both men were Chiba's dogs, and Spallone, at least, was as much a bully and thief as his boss.

"Sure you don't want to head north and put all this shit behind you?" Spallone asked. "It's not like people are going to forget, Myell. Space is big but Team Space is fucking tiny."

Myell said, "Only two people know what really happened, and you're not one of them."

"But Wendy told us everything. So you'd better stay in your little dark corner and don't come out, you understand?"

Olsson started inside. "I'm not missing the birdie for this."

Spallone cuffed Myell on the side of the head and followed Olsson. Myell stood rooted to his spot with his fists clenched until a female lieutenant approached him. She had dark blue eyes, glossy brown hair pulled back into a regulation-style braid, and a pretty face marred by dark circles under her eyes. Her nametag read Scott and she wore the same supply insignia he did. For a moment he felt a faint sizzle of recognition, almost as if they were old friends unexpectedly reunited, but the feeling passed almost immediately.

Myell saluted. "Good morning, ma'am."

"Good morning, Sergeant. Do you know which gate is for the *Aral Sea*?"

"Number twelve, ma'am."

"Thank you." She scrutinized his uniform. "You need to polish your boots."

Myell glanced down at his scuffed heels. "Yes, ma'am."

Lieutenant Scott started inside. She wore her uniform quite well, and her slacks showed off her long legs and shapely rear. He might never be able to date a commissioned officer, but that didn't mean he couldn't appreciate her assets. After a moment she turned as if sensing his attention and asked, rather crisply, "Do you intend to miss the flight?"

So much for appreciation. Myell picked up his rucksack, resisted one last look at the mountains, and followed her inside.

Jodenny had hurried to her quarters, crammed her gear into a bag, and rented a P-train. She spent two hours reviewing data about the *Aral Sea* as the unit whisked her south and looked up only when the local triad of Father, Mother, and Child Spheres appeared near Point Elliot. The Spheres stood enormous and regal in the sunshine, ancient sentinels from another age. A busload of tourists posed for pictures, even though dozens of Spheres, always in the same grouping and same alignment, dotted every continent in the Seven Sisters. The orphanage in which Jodenny had grown up had been right across from the most popular triad on Fortune.

Traffic was heavy, and by the time she reached Sato Spaceport she only had a few minutes to spare. She asked directions from the first crewman she saw, a sergeant with an *Aral Sea* nametag and ten years' worth of patches on his uniform.

"Number twelve, ma'am," Sergeant Myell told her.

He had short brown hair and brown eyes to match. Handsome, with sturdy muscles in his forearms and a bit of sunburn in his cheeks. The outdoorsy type, probably, as much as any man could be when he spent most of his life on a starship. She pushed down a pull of attraction and told him he needed to polish his boots.

"Yes, ma'am," he said.

Jodenny gave Myell a nod and started inside. He didn't follow. "Do you intend to miss the flight?" she asked, more sharply than she intended. Myell's only answer was to pick up his sack and follow her at a respectful distance.

Inside, Sato was an oasis of cool air and well-tended gardens that stretched along concourses filled with tourist shops. Gate twelve was crowded with friends and family who'd come to bid farewell to the crew already beyond the barriers. Given what had happened to the *Yangtze,* security was tighter than usual. Jodenny had to pass through two scanners to get to the manning desk, where a civilian security guard checked her retinal scans and said, "You're not on the access list, Lieutenant."

"I just got reassigned. Check again."

"Salter, Sbrizza, Seabaugh—no Scott."

The comm announced boarding for the *Aral Sea*'s birdie. Myell, who'd already moved through his line, glanced back over his shoulder at her. Jodenny insisted, "Admiral Cartwright authorized the transfer himself."

The guard called a coworker over. The two of them conferred while the *Aral Sea* crew filed up a ramp. Had the admiral changed his mind, or something gone wrong with her records? Jodenny tried not to fidget.

"I need to get on that birdie," she said.

"Yes, ma'am," the second guard said. "Know you from someplace, don't I?"

Surely he'd seen the media reports. "Maybe. Can you check again?"

The first guard let out a triumphant noise. "Ha! Here you are, Lieutenant. Just came through. You'd better hurry."

She rushed into the nearly empty lounge and started for the ramp. After two steps her legs locked, her mouth went dry, and her heart began to pound out a staccato beat. Only three months had passed since the bombing. Ninety days of injury, recovery, sleepless nights, and continuous regret. Jem was dead. Dyanne was dead. Jodenny could have requested a planetside job and Team Space would have given it to her; she could have asked to terminate her contract and not even the admiral himself would have refused.

"Lieutenant?" Myell stood at her elbow with a crease between his eyes. She hadn't even noticed him hang back while others went ahead. He asked, "Something wrong?"

Last chance to turn around, she told herself. To be free. The *Aral Sea* is not a happy ship, Taymore had said. But her life wasn't about happiness. It hadn't been for a long time.

"No," she said. "Nothing's wrong. Let's go."

They walked up the ramp together.

CHAPTER **TWO**

Jodenny took the last remaining aisle seat beside a sailor whose nametag and insignia identified him as Able Technician Cardoza. Myell maneuvered into the window seat of a row up ahead, and she was disappointed that they couldn't sit together. As a member of the Supply Department he could give her all the most current gouge. Cardoza, who wore an Ops patch, wouldn't know much gossip at all.

"Would you like the window, ma'am?" Cardoza asked. "I can move."

"I'm fine, thank you." The window wasn't real anyway, just another vid.

The sailors on the birdie ignored the prerecorded safety announcements and talked right over the launch countdown.

As the engines roared to life Jodenny gripped the armrests so hard her fingers went numb. Kookaburra receded beneath their wings and the artificial gravity kicked in. A DNGO rolled down the dirty carpet of the aisle to sell refreshments. Jodenny paid for a bottle of marsala tea and some onigiri to settle her stomach.

"How long have you been aboard, AT Cardoza?"

"About a year. This is my first run." He eyed her patches. "You've done three, that's great."

Two and a half, actually. She'd earned her first two Alcheringa patches the hard way, each run taking about ten months. Jodenny's third trip down the Alcheringa had been brutally cut short, as had the lives of seven hundred forty-nine sailors and civilians. The terrorists of the Colonial Freedom Project had seen to that.

Cardoza adjusted the vid screen. "Is this okay? I always like that first glimpse of the ship. Kind of reminds you how big she really is."

The image of the *Aral Sea* grew larger. She was identical to the *Yangtze,* both of them built in Fortune's orbital shipyards, each freighter twelve decks high and longer than three soccer fields. Attached to Mainship by an umbilical shaft was the ship's promenade, and attached to the promenade were twenty cylindrical towers, each a self-contained cargo hold crammed with colonists, equipment, supplies, and families of the *Aral Sea*'s crew. Most of the towers were destined to be towed away and replaced at one of the Seven Sister planets farther down the Alcheringa.

"You don't think there's going to be any problem, do you, ma'am?"

"Everything will be fine," Jodenny said. "It's not going to happen again."

Halfway to the *Aral Sea* she went to wash up in the head, and when she came out she bumped into another sergeant from the Supply Department. "I'm Tony Spallone, ma'am," he said, a smile pasted on his face. "You must be here because of Lieutenant Commander Greiger. Too bad about him, eh?"

"What happened?"

He grimaced. "Car accident. A shame, really. I hope he makes it."

Jodenny heard sympathy in his voice but Spallone's gaze was shifty, insincere. She saw that Myell had stood up to stretch and had his eye on the both of them. "What division do you work in, Sergeant?"

"Maintenance/HazMat, ma'am. Great place. All the divisions are straight up except for Underway Stores. That was Lieutenant Commander Greiger's division. Not his fault, mind you, he got stuck with some bad apples. Dicensu, Ishikawa, Myell—I shouldn't say any more."

"No, you shouldn't." Spallone had no doubt watched her and Myell board together. "I'll see you around, Sergeant."

She returned to her seat. Myell had sat down again, and the back of his head told her nothing. Jodenny unwrapped her onigiri and ate her way to the marinated kelp at its center. The ship's Supply Officer had the discretion to put anyone he wanted in charge of Underway Stores. Surely he wouldn't fill it with a junior officer such as herself. With any luck at all she'd be put into Flight Support, which was much more exciting and interesting. Underway Stores sounded like a troubled division, and she didn't need any more problems than the ones she already had.

That first whiff of the *Aral Sea*'s air—clean but recycled, cool and faintly scented with machine oil—should have kicked her in the stomach. She expected it to, and stepped off the birdie in the Flight Hangar braced for a flood of memories. To her surprise Jodenny felt only a bit of disorientation as the other passengers cleared a temporary security barrier and began to disperse. The hangar was large and well organized, busy with equipment and Flight personnel, and not conducive to casual lingering. Once past the barrier Jodenny decided to head for the Supply Flats, but a blond ensign with pale skin blocked her way.

"Hi, I'm Clara Hultz. You're Lieutenant Scott, right? I'm supposed to show you around. First stop's the bridge, because the captain wants to see you. Then I'll take you to the Flats and you can meet Commander Al-Banna. He's the new SUPPO. Well, not so new now. Are you hungry? Nothing's really open on Mainship but I'm in charge of the vending machines, so I know where the best ones are. Oh, and we're going to be working together. Isn't that great?"

Hultz stopped to take a breath.

"I need to drop off my things," Jodenny said.

"I'll have someone take it down. Hey, Sergeant Spallone, could you—"

"Never mind." Jodenny tightened her grip. "I'll keep it with me."

"You're sure? Okay. Let's go. I hardly ever get to go to the bridge—"

Jodenny followed the chattering ensign down the passage. The *Aral Sea*'s black and gray color scheme was similar to the *Yangtze*'s, but the matting on the decks was a little darker, the lettering on signs larger. The ship's air and drive systems hummed in the background, punctuated by occasional comm announcements. She noticed that the *Yangtze* was the one thing that Hultz wasn't talking about, and was grateful.

"—and I'm supposed to be done with my quals already, but things have been busy since the Commander Banana came onboard—"

"Commander who?"

"I mean, Commander Al-Banna. He took over after that big problem with Commander Matsuda. They say the department's having a bad run of luck and I guess Reggie proves that—poor guy went off the road and was trapped for hours before someone found him. Dave Quenger's excited, though, because he's going to get the DIVO job. The commander practically said so."

The parade of names was making Jodenny dizzy. "Did you say we're going to be working together?"

"Unless they give you Quenger's old job in Maintenance, but you don't want that."

"How about Flight Support?" Jodenny asked. "Who's in charge there?"

Before Hultz could answer, the lift doors slid open to a bridge identical to the *Yangtze*'s. Dozens of consoles formed a semicircle around the towering mainscreen. Twice as many personnel monitored every aspect of Mainship and the Towers. Back at Alice Base, almost everyone had been appallingly young. The *Aral Sea*'s bridge was full of seasoned sailors, crisp and serious as they readied the ship for launch. Overlooking the bridge were the captain's office and, high in the domed overhead, a totem in the shape of a gum tree, a naval tradition since Captain Jackie MacBride and her heroic crew first slid down the Little Alcheringa.

A swarthy Master-at-Arms confronted them, checked their badges, and inspected Jodenny's bag. Only then were they allowed to cross a gangplank toward the captain's suite. Below them, a swarm of techs gathered to fret over an Ops station. Someone at Drive ordered new specs. When Jodenny stopped to let a regular technician roll a unit past she saw a tall, dark-haired, and regrettably familiar figure standing down by the Data Department consoles.

Sam Osherman. Shit and spice. Of all the goddamned bad luck in the universe—

"Something wrong?" Hultz asked.

Jodenny had studied the ship's roster on the P-train and Osherman's name hadn't been on it. What had she ever done to deserve such malign fate?

"Lieutenant?" Hultz asked. "You okay?"

Quickly, before Osherman could look up and see her, Jodenny forced herself forward. The captain's inner offices were guarded by a round-faced aide who took her bag and said, "The Executive Officer's not in, but Captain Umbundo wants to meet you."

The modular furniture in the captain's office was strictly shipyard design but autographed ASL soccer balls and framed jerseys from the Kookaburra World Cup provided a bit of color. Umbundo sat behind his desk, a sturdy man with dark skin and more than a dozen Alcheringa patches on his jacket. The only decoration on his desk was a Wondjina Sphere paperweight, and the only vid on the wall showed a live relay from the bridge.

"Lieutenant Scott reporting for duty, sir."

Umbundo didn't stand or smile. "Sit down, Miz Scott."

She sat, and told herself not to wipe her sweaty palms on her slacks.

"My condolences on the loss of your friends and fellow shipmates," he said. "You can imagine our shock when we arrived last week and learned the news. It's a terrible tragedy, one that will have repercussions for years to come."

"Yes, sir," she said. Information traveled one way down the Alcheringa, no faster than the ships that carried it. The news about what the Colonial Freedom Project had done to the *Yangtze* had yet to reach Fortune. "I'm sure you knew people aboard as well, Captain."

"I did." He didn't elaborate. "How was your stay on Kookaburra?"

"There are worse places to convalesce, sir."

"And better places?"

The wallvid's volume was turned down, but Jodenny could see a group of officers suddenly cluster around the Data panel. She said, "I'd rather not have needed to convalesce at all."

"You'd rather have been killed?"

That stung, but Jodenny had expected something like it. "I'm not suffering from survivor's guilt, Captain."

"That ship was your first posting. You had good friends onboard. Friends that became family."

"Yes, sir," Jodenny said. Osherman was in the middle of the vid now, explaining something with an expressive wave of his hand. She forced herself to look away. "The orphanage on Fortune where I grew up was my first home. Team Space was my second, and my last ship was my third. But the CFP can't make me afraid to go back into space and I'm not going to let the past interfere with the present."

Umbundo gazed at her steadily. "I want you to take over Underway Stores."

Her stomach knotted. "Sir?"

"The position is usually billeted for a lieutenant commander, but we don't have any to spare. Someone's got to straighten out that mess down there. Do the job right, and it'll be a solid step toward lieutenant commander. You up for it?"

The vid forgotten, Jodenny reviewed what Spallone had told her about bad apples and Hultz mentioning someone else already being promised the job. "I believe the SUPPO has another replacement in mind."

"I'm not interested in the SUPPO's idea for a replacement."

There was really only one answer he wanted to hear, and Jodenny knew it. "Yes, sir. I'm up for the job."

The comm pinged. The captain's aide said, "You're needed on the bridge, sir."

Jodenny stood. Umbundo rose, shook her hand with a grip like iron, and said, "Good luck."

"Thank you, sir."

His gaze caught on her jumpsuit. "Where's your MacBride Cross? Don't tell me you forgot to put it on."

"Sorry, sir," Jodenny said. She didn't tell him that wearing the decoration made her feel like a fraud. She'd been told about her heroic actions, had listened to an admiral speak highly of her bravery, but her memory was a muddy collection of images and sensations: fire, pain, thick choking smoke. The doctors blamed a head injury, and had told her she might never fully recall what had happened. "I'll make sure it's sewed on properly."

Osherman was standing by the aide's desk when Jodenny stepped out of Umbundo's office. He blinked at her in surprise.

"Lieutenant Scott," he said, with a trace of Kiwi accent in his voice. His dark hair was a little shorter than she remembered, with strands of silver every here and there. Of course he wouldn't color it. He was a few centimeters taller than she, with strong, handsome features and a freckle under the tip of his chin. She remembered other freckles as well, and the little birthmark on his shoulder blade.

Jodenny said, "Commander. You look well."

"As do you." Osherman's gaze slipped to Umbundo. "Good afternoon, sir."

Umbundo brushed past them. "This isn't high tea, people. Get back to work."

Osherman opened his mouth and closed it again. That had been cute, before—his tendency to start something and then think the better of it. Now it made him look like a fish suddenly bereft of oxygenated water. Osherman followed Umbundo down to the bridge and the captain's aide said, "Call if you need anything, Lieutenant Scott. Welcome aboard."

Jodenny thanked him, took her bag back from Hultz, and headed toward the gangplank.

"So what did he say? I heard he's strict—"

"Ensign Hultz, have you ever heard that silence is golden?"

Hultz frowned. "Do you really think that's true?"

They went down to the Flats on D-Deck. Immediately beyond the lift was Ship's Services, which included the mess decks, laundry rooms, barbershops, and other stores. Across the way was the division that oversaw the ship's cleanliness, maintenance, and waste disposal. Standing at the crossroads of two passages, Jodenny also identified the offices for the officers' wardroom, chief petty officer mess, and Colony Stores. Her own office, Underway Stores, would be down on G-Deck. Fronting the Supply Officer's suite was a lobby manned by RT Bartis, who had bloodshot eyes and a wide nose.

"Welcome aboard, ma'am," Bartis said. "Sorry about the *Yangtze.*"

Jodenny stiffened. "Don't you know it's bad luck to say the name of a lost ship?"

He didn't even blink. "Sorry, ma'am."

"Is Commander Al-Banna available?" Hultz asked.

"Hear the yelling? Any minute now he'll start throwing those Customs agents up against the bulkhead."

"Commander Matsuda was never that loud," Hultz said. "How about Miz Wildstein?"

"She's refereeing." Bartis brought out a ship's gib and had Jodenny sign for it. "Your agent's waiting for you to set up your preferences. I'll let him or her know when the commander can see you. Here's your check-in list—you have two weeks to visit each department and make sure they sign off. Your quarters assignment is cabin D12."

A dark-haired lieutenant with a thick mustache and bright blue eyes was waiting for them when they stepped out of the SUPPO's suite. He asked, "Clara, is this our new addition?" and without waiting for an answer reached out to shake Jodenny's hand. "David Quenger, welcome aboard the best ship in the fleet."

That was his first mistake. She had already served on the best ship in the fleet. "Jodenny Scott. Pleased to be here."

"Wait until you've been onboard awhile," said the redheaded man at Quenger's side.

Quenger slapped his shoulder. "This is Kal Ysten. Unhappiest ensign you'll ever meet."

Ysten shook Jodenny's hand. "That's not true."

"Wait until you hear him start complaining, Jo," Quenger said.

"Jo's not my name," she replied.

Hultz giggled. Quenger smiled even brighter. "Clara, if you're busy, we could show Jodenny around for her check-ins."

"It's okay, David," Hultz said. "I'm not busy."

The constant and improper use of first names in public set Jodenny's teeth on edge. Just as she was about to tell *Mr. Quenger* that she and *Miz Hultz* would do fine, he reached over and touched her shoulder.

"Let's do dinner tonight," he suggested.

She removed his hand. "I'll be dining in the wardroom tonight. Good day, gentlemen."

Jodenny couldn't resist a look at Quenger's face as they moved away: still a smirk, but a confused one at that. He obviously wasn't accustomed to being turned down. Once out of earshot Hultz said, "You should get to know him. He's really a great guy."

"I already know his type."

Jodenny followed Hultz to Supply officers' country. She could have found her own way, but Hultz's presence at least distracted her from the double vision that had started to bother her eyes. *Yangtze. Aral Sea.* Two ships, two fates.

"So what's the story with Ysten?" Jodenny asked.

"Oh, I don't know, he's always miserable about something. Nobody likes him."

Jodenny's knees weakened when they passed what would have been her stateroom on the *Yangtze*. The doorplate read A. FRANCESCO. Hultz continued to jabber on, and the image of the ensign wavered in Jodenny's vision. She took a deep breath and refused to faint.

"Lieutenant? Jodenny?" Hultz sounded worried. "Spacesick so soon, eh? Don't worry. I used to puke all the time. Here's your cabin."

Jodenny forced herself to focus on the hatch. The sign J. SCOTT was already in place. She logged her thumbprint and voice into the door lock and walked inside to a small cabin filled with standard blue and gray furnishings.

"Dump your stuff and we can go grab a snack," Hultz said.

"No, thanks. I think I'll stay here for a while, get myself oriented."

"You sure?" At Jodenny's nod Hultz said, "Okay. I'll come and get you for dinner. See you at eighteen hundred hours."

After the ensign was gone, Jodenny began unpacking. She tried to remember everyone she'd met. Captain Umbundo. Clara Hultz, with her short hair and unfocused enthusiasm. That bloodshot tech who worked for the SUPPO—Bartis, that was his name. David Quenger, so incredibly full of himself. His unhappy friend Ysten. And Osherman, on the bridge. Jodenny went to her desk and accessed Core.

"Good afternoon, Lieutenant Scott," a male voice said. "Would you like to set up your agent now?"

"No. Tell me when Commander Samuel Osherman reported onboard."

"May first."

Eight days earlier. "Where did he report from?"

"Alice Training Base."

Nonsense. She had never seen him at Alice. Jodenny sat back in her chair. After a few minutes she leaned forward to check her imail. Standard messages had already started pouring into her queue. Rules for quarters, emergency procedures, boring bureaucracy . . . Where had Osherman been since the accident? Definitely not at Alice. She logged onto the ship's message boards and scanned the several dozen listed topics. Thousands of messages from strangers, the chorus and chaos of a ship she knew so little about—

An alarm shrieked through the cabin, making her jerk away from the desk. General Quarters. The alarm that had started the nightmare on the *Yangtze*.

It was starting all over again, all over, all over . . .

CHAPTER **THREE**

Myell's gib beeped as soon as the birdie landed.

"Get yourself over to T6," Chief Nitta said. "Ishikawa's sick and I need someone in the tower for launch."

Myell was a sergeant and Ishikawa was an able tech. Underway Stores had twenty personnel assigned to it, and almost any of them could have babysat the DNGOs in Tower 6. But there was no use arguing about it. He dropped his rucksack off in his cabin and took a tram from Mainship to the Rocks. The access ring to T6 switched him around to the tower's gravity orientation and six minutes after Nitta's page he was relieving Ahmed Lange in the command module. Lange had his feet up on the counter and was playing Snipe.

"What's wrong with Ish?" Myell asked.

"Who knows?" Lange gestured toward the windows. "Your dogs missed you."

Myell gazed out at the tower, which measured fifty decks from base to dome. DNGOs darted silently and efficiently in the zero-g of the central shaft, their guide lights glimmering like stars. Directly beneath the command module, Loading Dock 6 received deliveries from the DNGOs and sent them over to Mainship via a mag-lev Direct Conveyance System.

"Anyone else around?" Myell asked.

"Strayborn and some others are down securing the dock. I'm off to a security watch."

"Right, then. See you."

Myell locked down the command controls and took the lift down to the base of the hold. Dim down there, cold as hell, but the gravity shell kept him rooted to the deck. Ishikawa had left three DNGOs at his workbench and a log of what she'd done while he was on Kookaburra.

"Again, Castalia?" He patted the Class III's round surface and took a look at her damaged thruster. "What have you been banging against?"

Although DNGOs couldn't feel emotions, he fancied a certain glumness in her eyes. Beside her, Boann, a Class IV, had damaged her camera while retrieving items in the slots. The Class I, Isis, had stopped responding to recalls from the control module. He could probably fix the latter two but Castalia would have to go to the Repair Shop. When he went to attach her leash, she rose swiftly from the bench and hovered in place ten meters above him. The damaged thruster made her wobble dangerously.

"Damn it," Myell said. Ishikawa knew better than to leave the unit on standby. He switched his gib to the DNGO command channel and ordered her down. Castalia spun hesitantly, listed to the side, and descended with an air of resignation.

"Sorry, girl." Myell slid in a restraining bolt. "It's an unfair universe."

He tugged Castalia into the lift, up to level twenty-five, and across the access ring to the Rocks. The restaurants, shops, and other businesses along the kilometer-long promenade were closing up in preparation for launch. Electronic ducks cruising the winding stream began to tuck their heads under their wings, and similarly artificial koalas retreated to the upper branches of a live eucalyptus tree. The overhead dome offered a stunning view of Kookaburra but after they dropped into the Alcheringa, holograms would simulate blue skies or starry nights. In a month or so they would emerge at Mary River, and after a week or so continue down the Alcheringa to

Warramala and Baiame. He didn't mind Warramala so much. He had no intention of stepping foot on Baiame.

"Launch minus two hours," the comm announced. "All passengers return to quarters."

A tram stopped at a nearby station. Inside it, a dozen youngsters jumped up and down in excitement while red-robed nuns tried to calm them. An elderly couple smiled at the children and stroked a pair of puppies squirming in their laps. As the tram started to slide away Myell saw something he never expected to see on a starship, even one full of immigrants and travelers: a naked Aboriginal man, dusty and short, standing at a set of doors with a wooden spear in hand. He wore a belt of knotted hair, and his skin had been painted with swirling white designs from forehead to hips. He was scowling at Myell with such a fierce expression that Myell took an involuntary step backward.

All the trams were equipped with cameras, and Security would never let anyone wander around naked and armed. Yet no one on the tram even seemed to notice him. Throat suddenly dry, Myell told himself it was some odd trick of the light, maybe a prank by someone with a hologram projector. He forced himself to look away for a few seconds. When he turned his head back the tram was far down the boulevard and the Aboriginal was gone.

Pushing down a sense of unease, Myell tugged Castalia over to the Repair Shop.

Pug-ugly RT Engel, who nobody much liked anyway, said, "We're closed."

"Says who?" Myell asked.

"New rules. We close two hours before launch."

"Why?"

"He said we're closed, swipe."

He knew that voice. Had listened to it almost every day during the bad months, when Greiger had been the DIVO but everyone in Underway Stores understood who was really in charge. Myell turned to Chief Chiba. "I heard him."

Chiba had at least six centimeters and ten kilograms on Myell, and spent two hours a day weight lifting. Myell had seen him once put his fist through a barracks wall in a fit of pique. It was hard not to step back when he approached, or beg for mercy right away to avoid being hurt. Myell stood his ground anyway, despite the cold sweat beading on his palms.

Chiba said, "You heard him but you don't listen, Myell. You never listen."

"Two hours is ridiculous—" Myell said, and made the mistake of glancing toward Engel. Chiba grabbed his shoulder, spun him around, and shoved him up against the bulkhead. Something jabbed him so hard in the lower back that he gasped. Chiba's arm went across his throat, choking off most of his air supply.

"You have a lot of problems," Chiba growled, his face so close Myell could smell onions on his breath. "But I will always be number one on your list. Understand?"

Myell tried to pull Chiba's arm away but couldn't. The Repair Shop grayed at the edges as the pressure against his throat grew stronger. How would they explain his body if they killed him? Maybe they'd shove his corpse out an airlock, or stow it in a tower until someone found it by accident.

"Understand, swipe?" Chiba asked.

"Yes," Myell ground out.

The crushing pressure eased away. Chiba stepped back. "Good. Get the hell out of my shop."

Myell grabbed Castalia's leash and left as quickly as he could. His face felt hot and his fists shook. He should have gone AWOL, he should have never joined Team Space, he should have—

The General Quarters alarm started shrieking. Passengers who'd been dawdling on the Rocks jerked in surprise. A tram that had started across the gulf to Mainship ground to a halt and reversed direction. Fire and radiation hatches slammed shut as comm orders squawked overhead.

"Crew to emergency stations. Power Plants into standby. Lifepods, prepare to launch."

Myell's lifepod was back in Mainship. He'd never make it. He leashed Castalia to a lamppost and sprinted toward T6. Twenty seconds passed. Thirty. The alarm blasted against his eardrums. He reached a crew ladder and scrambled down to the station below the access ring. The press of his thumb opened the hatch and registered his location with Core. More than a dozen men and women had already crowded inside, some from his own department, the others from Maintenance or Tower Support. All the lights on the boards shone a steady green.

Myell pushed his way forward. "What's going on?"

Only Gordon Strayborn, as immaculate and straight-shouldered as ever, deigned to answer. "When I got here, Engineering was lit up like a Christmas tree. But everything switched back. It must have been a screwy sensor."

Chardray Nagarajan slapped the panel. "Maybe it's this shitty machine, and the whole ship is going to hell around us."

"Like the *Yangtze*," someone said.

Strayborn ordered, "Don't say that name."

Although the module was well ventilated, Myell smelled the dank odor of fear. Nearly eight hundred people had died on the *Yangtze*. The board lights remained green, the comm silent. He asked, "Can you get the bridge channel up?"

Strayborn shook his head. "It's locked out."

An able tech from Maintenance raised her hand. "Sometimes I listen to the Repair channel. It's simplex, but they forget to lock it."

Strayborn punched it up. They heard a fast clicking sound, then a man's irritated voice. "That's a big fat zero. I double-checked. Nothing looks out of place."

"They're looking for sabotage," Strayborn said tightly.

Or maybe a CFP bomb. For thirty minutes they listened to the one-sided conversations. The GQ lights and tones finally faded and the comm announced, "All conditions normal. All personnel report back to duty. Passengers are restricted to quarters. T-minus two hours and holding."

Myell approached the tech who'd spoken up about the Repair line. "That was a good suggestion, AT Holden. What else can you hear?"

She gave him a nervous smile. "Almost all the B channels. Not Security, not Medical, but you can listen to Tower Support bitch about passengers and hear what the captain's ordered for lunch."

Myell grinned. "You don't want to be caught eavesdropping on the captain." Everyone knew his punishments were swift and severe.

"You're right about that." Her smile widened, but then she focused on his nametag and all good humor fled. "You're Sergeant Myell?"

He said, "Last time I checked, yes."

"Oh." This time her voice was filled with ice. "I've got to get back to work."

Myell watched her go. Her reaction reminded him of Chiba and the swipes back in Repair Services. He trudged back to the Rocks to retrieve Castalia, but she was no longer attached to the post where he'd left her. Myell tipped his head back, wondering if she'd floated off, but the dome was stark blue with no sign of the DNGO. He opened the command channel on his gib but she didn't come when called, and in fact made no response at all.

"Shit," he said. Something else to be blamed for.

Jodenny had fled her cabin blindly, with no idea where she was going. On the *Yangtze,* her emergency station had been on H-Deck. On the *Aral Sea,* it could be on any of a dozen others. Flummoxed, she came to a complete halt on the ladder she was climbing. A hand shoved her ass indelicately and she stumbled out to the nearest deck. The GQ klaxon screamed into her brain as it had so many nightmare-soaked nights in the Alice barracks.

T6 lighting up like a supernova. Parts of its shredded hull shattering the Rocks and ripping into Mainship. Thick smoke all around her, the wounded screaming in pain and panic, the pulsing fear that something terrible had already befallen her friends—

"Them's the breaks, boot," Jem would have said, had he lived.

Jodenny blinked. Damn it, this wasn't the *Yangtze.* She

hauled herself down the ladder and made for her old station. A slim, short chief named Vostic was supervising as personnel rushed past.

"You don't belong here," Vostic said to Jodenny.

"I don't know which one—"

"We're full. Try J-Deck."

Nonessential personnel from Supply, Medical, and Ops pushed their thumbs to the wallgib and hurried inside the life-pod. Jodenny said, "No! They might not have room."

"Try D—"

"Chief, nothing in this universe is keeping me from getting into that pod," Jodenny said, and meant it. Something in her expression must have convinced the chief of her desperation, because Vostic grabbed Jodenny's thumb, pushed it to the gib, verified it with her own print, and shoved her inside the pod.

Tears threatening to blind her, Jodenny staggered down the row to one of the last remaining seats. She pulled the safety bars down over her body and sat on her violently trembling hands. The crew around her tactfully ignored her shaken state.

"If this is a damn drill, I'll kill the lunatic who planned it," an ensign said.

Someone answered with, "I'll help you dispose of the body."

Jodenny squeezed her eyes shut. Jem's corpse had been lost in space. Dyanne had been crushed between bulkheads until only a mangle of bones and flesh remained. Voices swam around her in debate, some fearful, some petulant. Campos had been right. She should have never left Kookaburra.

"You know what I think?" a sergeant said. "I think whoever decided naming these ships after environmental disasters back on Earth ought to have a psych consult."

For several minutes Jodenny forced herself to exhale and inhale through her nose. The *Yangtze* had been lost. The *Aral Sea* was still intact. The longer the lifepod stayed in dock, the more likely it was that the GQ was either a false alarm or a test of crew readiness. There was no way that the fanatics of the Colonial Freedom Project could have successfully planted another bomb. When the comm clicked to life, Jodenny's head shot up.

"All conditions normal," a voice said.

Complaints and conversation drowned out the rest of the announcement. Jodenny stood up and was nearly crushed by a swarm of bodies. By diligently keeping her eyes on the hatch she was able to keep from panicking, and after an interminably long period of pushing and pulling she broke free into the passage.

Vostic was there, in conference with a commander. Embarrassed by her overreaction, Jodenny tried to slink off unnoticed but didn't get far.

"Lieutenant Scott!" The commander came her way. He was short and compact, with steel-colored hair. He squeezed her hand like a vise. "Fayid Al-Banna. You ready to check in with me?"

"Yes, sir," she replied, but he had already walked away.

Al-Banna brushed past the line forming at the lift. "Bet this scared the hell out of you."

"A little, sir."

"Piss on that. I was scared, and I didn't just come off the worst wreck in TS history." The lift arrived and Al-Banna boarded immediately. "Goddamn drills. Probably delay us at least two hours. What do they think on the bridge, that we've got nothing better to do down here?"

Jodenny didn't think he was setting a good example, complaining in front of the crew that way, but she tried to make a diplomatic response. "Maybe it was a mistake."

"Whoever made it should get his ass demoted."

On the Flats, people scurried to get out of Al-Banna's way. He led Jodenny past Bartis's counter and into his office, which was small and immaculate and located in the middle of a desert. The grammed walls showed bleached sand and pale blue sky in all directions. She wondered if he considered himself a direct descendant of the nomads of ancient Egypt or a reincarnation of some mighty pharaoh.

Al-Banna gestured for her to sit and then dropped into his own chair, his back ramrod straight. "There have to be dozens of supply lieutenants down on Kookaburra, just waiting for an assignment like this. How'd you land it?"

"I was lucky, sir."

"Piss on luck. Did you pull strings? Call in a favor or two, use your fame with the higher-ups?"

She almost denied it, but that seemed pointless. "Some might say so, sir."

"Nothing wrong with that. But if you ever try jumping over my head, I'll slap you down so hard they'll have to scrape your career off the deck with a spatula. Understood?"

"Yes, sir."

"Good. I'm putting you in Food Services. Try not to poison anyone important and we'll get along fine."

Jodenny took a deep breath. "The captain put me in charge of Underway Stores, sir."

Al-Banna stared at her. "He did what?"

"He said I'm replacing Lieutenant Commander Greiger."

"Goddamn it! Who the hell is running this department?" He stabbed his comm button. "Larrean, this is Al-Banna."

An administrative aide replied, "I'm sorry, sir, the Executive Officer is unavailable. May I tell him you called?"

Al-Banna hung up. "Fuck it all. Go ahead and take over Underway Stores. It's the worst division I have. If Greiger hadn't run himself into a mountain I would have fired his ass. You'll piss off Quenger, who was supposed to get it. Wildstein, too. She's his mentor. But those are your problems now. Have fun."

Jodenny left as quickly as she could. Out on the Flats, the air was cold and dry and oppressively thick. On rubbery legs she forced herself past blurry strangers and toward her quarters. No one stopped her, which was a relief.

She certainly didn't want her new shipmates to see her sobbing like a baby.

At seventeen hundred hours the *Aral Sea* engaged aux drive and left Kookaburra. The haul to the Alcheringa drop point would take five days. An hour after launch, sequestered in his favorite booth at the No Holds Barred, Myell peered into the depths of his beer. His roommate Mick Timrin sat beside him. Some of the overvids displayed girls gyrating to music but most were replaying the Dunredding soccer game.

"Fucking idiots." Timrin glared at the soccer players. "I would have won a hundred yuros on that game, you know."

Myell appreciated Timrin trying to distract him from the loss of the DNGO. He'd filed a report and knew that someone from Security would be by to interview him within twenty-four hours. "How do you lose a robot?" some snarky chief would ask, as if Myell should have dragged a DNGO to the emergency station.

"There's always another game," Myell told Timrin.

Three Ops techs, each with one or two Alcheringa run patches, sidled up to the bar. Above their heads, the dancers faded away as the nightly news came on. Two virtual hosts, Hal and Sal, addressed the camera with vapid smiles.

Hal said, "Good evening. In today's news, departure was delayed by two hours and ten minutes after a General Quarters alarm."

Sal added, "The five-minute response rate was ninety percent, a new ship's record."

"Notice they're not saying why," Timrin said. "Some Ops swipe probably pushed the wrong button."

One of the Ops techs glared their way. Myell nudged Timrin. Timrin grimaced. "So what?"

"Departure went smoothly," Hal said. "All systems are go for a safe flight."

Safe. Since the *Yangtze,* nothing about spaceflight seemed particularly safe. Myell had heard more than one rumor that the CFP was somehow responsible for the drill. The idea of a bomb somewhere on the ship made him gulp at his beer.

"In other news," Sal said, "the Medical and Supply Departments both announced new appointments. Lieutenant Mitchell Moody has been appointed to Crew Medicine, and Lieutenant Jodenny Scott has taken over the Underway Stores Division."

"Supply spaz," said a tech wearing a Kiwi patch. "She freaked out during GQ."

"What did she do?" another tech asked.

"Went to the wrong pod, got all hysterical. They almost had to sedate her."

A third tech popped a peanut into his mouth. "They say you're never the same after a spacewreck. She was on the *Yangtze*."

The one with the Kiwi patch said, "Supply types always fall apart when there's trouble. Look at the old SUPPO. Ran off like a jackal, didn't he, rather than take it like a man?"

Timrin finished his drink. "You know where to find an Ops tech during an emergency? Under a desk, pissing his pants."

The Kiwi tech pushed back his stool. The bartender, a bald civvie with wide shoulders, came out from behind the counter and warned, "You want trouble, you take it outside."

"We don't want trouble," Myell said.

"Not unless there's a girl to hold down," the Kiwi tech said.

Myell changed his mind. He did want trouble, the kind that would result in the satisfying thump of his fist against the Kiwi tech's nose. But Timrin's barricading arm kept him from lunging forward. Timrin said, "They're not worth it."

"Sit your asses down before I call Security," the bartender said to the Ops techs.

Public brawling could land the offenders in the brig and leave black marks on service records. Better to fight in private and explain the injuries as work-related accidents—fingers caught in a hatch or ribs bruised by a ladder fall.

"Ignore them," Timrin said when they reached the passage outside. "Fucking idiots."

Myell's temper cooled down on the ride to Supply berthing. A half-dozen people were sprawled in the lounge playing Izim on the large-screen vid. Someone had spilled beer on the carpet again, and popcorn had been scattered on the sofa. Chris Amador, in charge of the Izim siege, said, "Jesus fucking Christ! Where did those moths come from?"

Timrin's gaze swept disdainfully over the screen. "Izim's for slomes."

"Heard you lost a dingo, Myell," Nagarajan said, snuggling close to Amador's side.

Amador asked, "How do you manage that?"

"Not so hard," said Mike Gallivan, who was sprawled in a corner chair with his guitar in hand. Gallivan had checked onboard at the same time as Myell, and for a while they'd been good friends. "Little buggers get into all sorts of shit."

"Or get put there," Nagarajan said.

Myell clenched his fists and didn't answer. Fuck them all if they thought he'd meant to lose any equipment put into his care. He followed Timrin down the noisy passage past a dozen half-open hatches. In cabin nine, Ben Chang was competing with the volume of his Snipe game as he relayed a story to Sergeant Tisa VanAmsal, who stood in the doorway.

"—so Chief Vostic told her she was at the wrong station, and Scott told her to get out of the way, and Vostic told her to try another lifepod, and Scott told her to go to hell."

That encounter must have spawned dozens of imails and message threads, either through Core or on individual pocket servers. Myell wondered why the hell people didn't have anything better to worry about.

"Quenger must be pissed she's taking over," VanAmsal said, unpinning one of her braids. She was older than most in Underway Stores but still one of the more attractive sergeants on the *Aral Sea*. Myell respected how she kept a cool head and ran Loading Dock G with a firm hand.

"Quenger's a swipe," Timrin said.

Chang scored a direct hit. "Nitta will put her in her place."

Myell tried to put in a good word. "Lieutenant Scott seems sharp enough."

VanAmsal gave him a frosty look. "It's not a fresh start for you, Myell. Already you're screwing up again."

He turned away at the unexpected sting. The lost DNGO he could live with. Equipment was always disappearing on the ship. But no one was ever going to forget what Wendy Ford had said. Myell went inside his and Timrin's cabin, yanked off his shirt, and threw it down the wash-chute.

"Christ," Timrin said behind him. "What happened to you?"

Myell turned and glimpsed, in the mirror, a bruise darkening his back. "Nothing."

"If Chiba's fucking with you again, you should let someone know."

"Who would I tell? Al-Banna? DiSola?" He pulled on a T-shirt, ignoring the protest in his back. "I don't care anymore."

Timrin let the hatch close and leaned against his locker with folded arms. "You care. Too much. Honor, commitment, all that recruiting bullshit—they really got it when you signed up. Your trouble is you want to fight Chiba on his terms. You have to be smarter than him, not tougher. Next time something happens, get some proof."

Proof. Wendy Ford had claimed the bruises on her body were Myell's doing, when they both knew it had been Chiba. Gritting his teeth at the memory, he lifted his rucksack from his bed and went to shove it into his locker. Something small fell on his bedcover.

"Christ," Myell said. "There's an omen for you. A dead gecko."

Timrin bent close to it. "I don't think it's dead."

"Of course it is," Myell said, but under Timrin's urging he put the gecko in a cup near a lamp and it flicked its tail. It was small and brown, like the one that had crawled up on the bench outside Sato Spaceport. It peered up at Myell with beady black eyes.

Timrin grinned. "I always wanted a better roommate than you."

Myell didn't need a pet. He didn't need to be responsible for anyone or anything else on the ship. Hell, he couldn't even take care of a DNGO. But he couldn't very well let it run loose or flush it down into the ship's sewage system.

"What are you going to call him?" Timrin said.

"Kookaburra," Myell decided. "Koo for short. And it's a her, not a him."

Timrin rolled his eyes. "Like you haven't had enough trouble with women."

"Welcome aboard, Koo." Myell bent close to the cup. "I hope you don't regret it."

CHAPTER FOUR

"T-minus thirty minutes. All off-duty personnel and passengers report to quarters."

Sitting on her rack with her knees pulled to her chest, Jodenny tried to empty her mind of fear and doubt.

"T-minus ten. Towers secure. Engines to speed."

Somewhere back at Alice Training Base, Matt Lu was probably cursing her name. Going over Campos's head to Admiral Cartwright had probably made the commodore an enemy as well. Though she'd only been on the *Aral Sea* a few hours, Jodenny had already managed to annoy her boss, make a less than favorable impression on the captain, and embarrass herself in front of countless members of the crew. The *Yangtze* dead, lying in row after row of tidy graves, bitterly watched her from their dark repose.

A slight, almost imperceptible jolt beneath her. The thrill of increasing acceleration. No other fanfare, no blast of trumpets, but the deed was done. Jodenny closed her eyes just as the comm came to life with, "Attention, attention, this is the XO speaking. We have departed Kookaburra and bid farewell to those we leave behind. Resume normal operations."

Jodenny didn't move. She could venture forth from the cabin and do her check-in rounds, but what was the point? The ship had departed without incident but in five days they would reach the Alcheringa and the horror would begin all over again. Maybe she should find some broken glass and lay waste to her wrists again—

No. That had been a onetime aberration, a dark time she barely remembered. She would not succumb again. And to fear that the *Aral Sea* was doomed when it reached the Alcheringa was foolishness itself. Team Space would have never authorized the next leg of her journey if there was a serious threat from CFP fanatics.

Someone pinged the door. The wallvid flickered to life. "Lieutenant Scott? I'm from the chaplain's office."

For a moment she considered pretending she wasn't in, but then she wiped her face and opened the hatch. Her visitor was slim like a willow, with commander's bars on one collar and a chaplain's pip on the other. She held a large wicker basket in both hands.

"I'm Kath Mowaljarlai. Call me Kath or Chaplain Mow. Can I come in?"

Jodenny stepped aside and let the chaplain enter. Mow handed her the basket and said, "The official welcome-aboard kit from the Religious Service Office. Flowers-in-a-jar, two movie passes, a copy of our religious activities schedule, and a vid of me giving inspirational sermons. No, just kidding about that last bit. Chocolate biscuits. Much better than sermons."

"Chocolate's always welcome around here." Jodenny took the jar out, opened its lid, and watched a handful of fresh daffodils spring to full flourish. They reminded her abruptly of funerals and she stepped into the head.

"Sorry." Jodenny splashed water on her face. "Allergies."

"I suffer from them myself." Chaplain Mow favored the flowers with her full attention but didn't remove them. She let Jodenny compose herself and then said, "The *Aral Sea* isn't what you're used to, but I hope you'll learn to like her. We've got some good people here. People who'll listen to whatever you want to say."

Jodenny knew this game, and was relieved Chaplain Mow had slipped into it without wasting any time. "Alice was full of people who wanted to listen. Doctors, therapists, grief counselors, chaplains—they were lined up outside our doors. I've done more talking in the last three months than in twenty-eight years."

Chaplain Mow smiled. "You never know when the urge might strike again. My office is up on C-Deck. Come by tomorrow and I'll sign your check-in sheet. Should I put you down as Unitarian, Gagudjun, New Denominationalist, Muslim, Mormon, Catholic, Jewish, Buddhist, agnostic, atheist, or something else altogether?"

"Something else altogether."

"Can do. And remember, you're not alone here. Have your agent call my agent and we'll have lunch, okay?"

After Mow left, Jodenny mustered enough energy to take a hot shower. The prospect of dinner depressed her all over again. Walking for the first time into the sea of strangers that had been the *Yangtze*'s wardroom had been nerve-wracking enough, but at the time she had been merely a new ensign. Now she carried the weight of tragedy and the day's humiliations on her shoulders. She rubbed away a smudge on her shoes, buffed the gold buttons on her jacket, braided her hair, braided it a different way, changed her earrings, and changed them back. Maybe she could plead a headache and prolong everyone's inevitable discovery that she wasn't fit to be back in space, never mind in charge of the Supply Department's worst division.

The ship's bells rang at eighteen hundred but Hultz didn't appear. Jodenny paced the cabin and passageway. Five minutes later, just as Jodenny was about to strike out on her own, Hultz rounded the corner.

"You're late," Jodenny said.

"No one ever goes on time," Hultz said. "Is it true you're in charge of Underway Stores? Al-Banna must really like you."

"Liking me has nothing to do with it. Let's go."

On her way down the passage Jodenny wiped her sweaty palms on the sides of her uniform.

Hultz squeezed her arm. "Relax. Everyone's great. Here we are."

Jodenny followed Hultz through the hatch and stopped. The supply wardroom had the same design and layout as the one on the *Yangtze*, but where she expected to see plaques and trophies she saw only empty shelves. The bulkheads were smooth gray parasteel, unmarked by anything as sentimental as pictures or murals. Empty stools stood against the darkened bar. The dining table had been set for ten people.

"—and the guy next to me in the pod had the worst farts ever," said a swarthy, dark-haired man on the sofa. "Clara, you're late."

Hultz said, "Since when? Jodenny, this is Mike Zeni."

"Pleased to meet you." Zeni wore sub-lieutenant's bars, and his cologne smelled strong and clean. "Did you like our friendly welcome-aboard alarm?"

Obviously he hadn't heard what a fool she'd made of herself. "Immensely."

Beside Zeni was Lieutenant A. J. Francesco, who was slender and dark-skinned. They both worked in Ship's Services—Francesco ran the Disbursing Division and Zeni was in charge of Colony Berthing. Ensign Leanne Weaver, with extremely short hair, worked in Flight Support. Jodenny had already met Kal Ysten.

"Let's eat," Weaver said. "I'm starving."

"Shouldn't we wait for everyone else?" Jodenny asked.

"No one else is coming," Ysten said gloomily.

Francesco pulled out his chair. "Congratulations on your new job, Jodenny."

Zeni lifted his beer. "And good luck. You never hear anything good about Underway Stores."

"You'll do fine if you can get along with Chief Nitta," Weaver said.

Ysten grimaced. "That's if you can get a single moment's work out of him."

On the *Yangtze,* no one had dared miss wardroom dinner unless they were on watch or in Sick Berth. Jodenny sat down reluctantly and shook out her napkin. AT Ashmont, the lithe young steward, started the soup course.

Weaver said, "Chief Nitta's the least of the problems in Underway Stores. Dicensu's dumber than a rock. They say that new girl, Ishikawa, she's doing kasai. And don't forget Myell."

Jodenny remembered the handsome sergeant with the scuffed boots. "What about him?"

Ysten said, "He raped a girl."

Raped? On the *Yangtze* Jodenny had supervised a sailor accused of trying to kill his roommate, but she'd never worked with a rapist. She tried to imagine Myell pinning down a woman and forcing himself into her, but the idea didn't make sense.

Francesco said, "Shut up, Kal. You don't know what happened."

A no-good chief and a purported rapist. No wonder Al-Banna despised her division. The conversation moved on to the gossip about an ensign in the Navigation Department who had been seen, of late, sneaking in and out of chiefs' berthing.

"Let the captain catch wind of that, and she'll be out an airlock," Weaver said.

"It's probably nothing," Francesco said.

Weaver downed more of her wine. "They say that's where Matsuda went, you know. Airlock. Not on a birdie at all."

"Idiot talk," Zeni said.

"I don't understand," Jodenny said.

Francesco told the tale. "Commander Matsuda was our SUPPO. He was two years into a three-year tour, and I won't say he was popular or good at it, but we were getting the job done. We left Fortune as scheduled, no problem. Got to Kiwi, some people take shore leave, Matsuda says he's on his way to visit family. Forty-eight hours before launch, he's due back, no one can find him."

"Disappeared completely," Hultz said. "No trace whatsoever. No one could even prove he went down to the surface."

"Not true." Zeni waved his fork. "Data showed that his flight pass had been used as scheduled on one of the birdies."

Weaver shook her head. "Anyone could have used it. The security vids were all corrupted up, none of the other passengers remembered seeing him, and Kiwi Customs couldn't prove he passed through. Even his family said they hadn't seen him."

"Half the ship believes he deserted, for whatever reason, and his family was covering for him," Francesco said. "There are rumors he was under investigation for dereliction of duty, but no one knows much about it. The other half think maybe he stayed onboard, hiding, until we reached Sundowner—he always said he wanted to retire there. Maybe he got off there. And yet another half think maybe he was a victim of foul play."

"That's three halves," Zeni said.

Francesco said, "I never did like fractions."

"We had to wait four whole days at the Alcheringa drop point off Kiwi before they sent us a new SUPPO," Hultz said. "Then there was the incident with Myell and the girl, and poor Reggie ends up in a big car accident on Kookaburra—so you can see, the Supply Department's got a reputation for being cursed. Now you're here—"

"Clara," Francesco said sharply.

"I didn't mean it negatively!" Hultz protested. "She'll bring us good luck. She survived."

Jodenny stared down at her dinner plate. Survived. Yes, she had survived when so many others had not. But that was a curse, not a blessing.

"I hear the General Quarters today was a CFP bomb threat," Weaver said into the sudden quiet. "The captain had to take it seriously. Otherwise why be so crazy to pull a drill right before launch?"

Francesco said, "It was probably just a hoax."

Further conversation was halted as David Quenger strolled in, clad in expensive civilian clothes and smelling strongly of cologne. "Evening, everyone," he said. He came up behind Jodenny and squeezed her shoulder. "I understand congratulations are in order."

She imagined breaking his fingers. "Thank you."

"You're not annoyed?" Zeni asked, mischief in his eyes.

Quenger didn't take the bait. "Underway Stores is a mess, and Al-Banna must think Jo's the gal to clean it up."

Maybe she'd break his entire hand.

Quenger gave a sloppy salute. "Good night, then. Try to keep the noise down, won't you? The neighbors complain."

After dinner had been cleared, Ysten settled in to watch the evening's ASL soccer game in the lounge, Weaver and Hultz decided to go nightclubbing, and Zeni and Francesco invited Jodenny to play Hachi-Hachi. She rolled a five and became oya. Francesco dealt seven cards to each of them, left six faceup on the table, and put the rest in the stockpile.

"You'll have to ignore Hultz and Weaver and all the naysayers," Francesco said. "Our department's no more screwed up than any other on the ship."

"That's not saying a whole lot," Zeni said.

Jodenny matched two butterfly cards. She couldn't do anything about Matsuda's disappearance, nor Greiger's car accident, but Myell was one of her men, now. "What happened with Sergeant Myell?"

"It was right after we left Fortune," Francesco said. "Security found him and RT Ford in the hydroponics forest. She said Myell forced her. Myell was arrested but never charged. This was while Matsuda was still onboard. I wouldn't say the commander gave him much support. After Al-Banna came aboard, he told Security to either drop it or clear it, and the case died."

"Is Ford still onboard?" Jodenny asked.

Zeni matched two deer cards. "She got to bail out of the deployment at Kiwi. Some said maybe that's why she said it, just to get out, but you never know. She was dating Myell's boss at the time, the Underway Stores chief. Big ugly guy named Chiba. You don't want to cross him or his little Japanese yakuza."

"None of that," Francesco said sharply.

"What, I can't say it? Him and Nitta, Matsuda—"

"You can suspect anyone you want," Francesco replied. "But if you're dumb enough to say it aloud, you better have proof."

There had been rumors of Japanese mafia on the *Yangtze* as well, though Jem had told Jodenny to pay them no mind. "Everyone's in some kind of gang or another," he'd said. But having a chief and sergeant seeing the same woman in a division was bound to cause trouble, and the situation sounded bad all around.

"Do you think Myell did it?" she asked.

"Sure he did," Zeni said.

Francesco studied his cards. "The man's innocent until proven guilty."

Zeni won the game after twelve rounds. They wanted her to play crazy-seven next, but Jodenny excused herself, returned to her cabin, and changed into off-duty clothes. After a half hour of staring at the bulkhead she climbed downladder toward the Underway Stores office. The decks were empty at that time of night, with only the hum of the air units to keep her company. As she approached Underway Stores she heard voices, and when she rounded the bend she saw Quenger and a tall man exiting the office. Quickly she pulled back around the corner.

"Let me know how that goes," Quenger was saying.

"Oh, you'll be hearing lots, I'm sure," the tall man replied.

They headed off in the other direction. Jodenny considered confronting Quenger but held back. When she was sure they were gone she pressed her thumb to the lock. Inside the office were two desks for the admin clerks. One was tidy and organized, the other cluttered with paperwork. Windows overlooked Loading Dock G, the heart of the distribution system that moved supplies through Mainship. The Direct Conveyance System connected the loading dock to T6, the laundry, the galley, the Flight Deck, two maintenance hangars, and four issue rooms. It operated twenty-four/seven, and she could see smartcrates arriving and being shipped out again under the DNGOs' vigilant care.

She peeked into Nitta's office, which was neatly decorated with plaques from his previous tours of duty. A gram showed him accepting an award, and she recognized him as the tall man who'd been accompanying Quenger. Reggie Greiger's office, right next door, resembled the aftermath of a tornado. Jodenny cleared a pile of clutter off his chair and accessed the databases, rosters, schedules, and reports for the division. By midnight she'd read enough to know if Greiger hadn't driven himself off a mountain, he would have lost his job during the next inspection cycle. She was surprised someone as no-nonsense as Al-Banna had put up with him.

She activated the comm. "Chief Nitta, please."

After two rings Nitta's agent answered. "He's not available. May I take a message?"

"This is Lieutenant Scott, his new DIVO. Tell him to report to my office at oh-seven hundred tomorrow."

"Yes, ma'am."

Jodenny remembered that she hadn't set up her own agent

yet, but that could wait. She went through Greiger's desk and discovered a bottle of brandy. The liquor burned the back of her throat. She had the wallvid bring up a live shot of Boyne, Kookaburra's moon, and after several minutes the *Yangtze* began to come around from the dark side.

From a distance, the ship seemed as beautiful and invulnerable as she had the day Jodenny first boarded her. Only as the ship lifted higher in orbit did the gaping wounds on her starboard side become visible—black, ragged holes where huge chunks of tower shrapnel had slashed through the hull. She imagined herself drifting along the *Yangtze*'s pitch-black passages, her noncorporeal self passing through bulkheads and decks. Her cold breath sent dust swirling through compartments. The touch of her hand made ice crystals scatter like diamonds. She glided ever so silently to her cabin and to the familiar comfort of her bed. The blankets and sheets held no warmth yet as she wrapped herself up and let the blackness take her—

Jodenny blinked. She was no longer inside the *Yangtze* but instead watching it from her new office. She raised her glass. To the Wondjina, who had made the Alcheringa and the Seven Sisters and all things good and beautiful, she asked for release. Hers was no longer a ship of tragedy and doom. She belonged to the *Aral Sea* now, where men and women needed her.

She waited for a long time, but felt no peace.

CHAPTER **FIVE**

Chief Nitta wasn't in the Underway Stores office at oh-seven hundred hours. Neither were the two administrative aides. The first one, a gangly woman named RT Caldicot, came in at oh-seven-twelve with coffee and doughnuts in hand. "We're not open yet, Lieutenant. You want to come back later?"

"We're open," Jodenny said. "I'm your new DIVO."

"Oh." Caldicot didn't look impressed. "I was expecting Lieutenant Quenger."

Jodenny didn't believe for one second that Caldicot had somehow missed the news of her appointment. "Where do you usually hold division quarters?"

Caldicot took a bite of her doughnut and spoke with her mouth full. "In the crew lounge. We had one last week."

"They're supposed to be held daily."

"Lieutenant Commander Greiger didn't see the need."

"I do. Page all our people and have them in T6 in fifteen minutes. Anyone who isn't there will be locked out and earn two demerits."

"Ma'am! That's a little extreme for your first morning, isn't it? We don't start work around here until oh-seven-thirty."

"Ship's regs say oh-seven hundred."

"If you walk down the Flats you won't find a soul—"

"Fifteen minutes, RT Caldicot. Be there."

Jodenny left the offices and boarded a tram to cross the gulf. She told herself she wasn't superstitious, but doubt rode with her. Assembling her entire division at the base of T6 was an invitation to disaster. She hadn't been in the *Yangtze*'s T6 when the CFP bomb detonated, but instead up on the bridge turning over duty. The first alarm had started shrieking right after she signed out of the log. Only the luck of the watch schedule had kept her from being vented into space or crushed between steel or burnt alive . . .

So lost was she in grim memories that Jodenny almost missed getting off at the first stop on the Rocks. A group of DNGOs was moving in tandem down the boulevard, watering plants and sweeping up litter. Advertisements played silently on overvids and sidewalks. Jodenny crossed T6's access ring and descended to the base of the hold. She peered up the shaft at the twinkling lights of DNGOs and when she looked down the alleged rapist was standing a few meters away.

"Good morning, ma'am," Myell said.

"Good morning, Sergeant." Jodenny told herself she was safe, that he'd never been proven guilty. Then again, many guilty people got off scot-free. Casually she said, "I see you polished your boots."

"You were right. They were dirty."

His gaze was level and, on the surface, untroubled. But there was something about the way he held his hands flat against his legs that made Jodenny think he was nervous about her being there. She asked, "How long have you worked down here?"

"Since we left Kiwi, ma'am."

Since Al-Banna had come aboard. The new SUPPO might have gotten the charges cleared, but he let Greiger shove Myell to the bottom of the tower to do shitty jobs far below his rank. Not much of a punishment if he was guilty, but an injustice if innocent.

The arrival of four able techs interrupted them. "AT Ishikawa," Jodenny said. "Start taking a roster. That lift gets turned off at oh-seven-thirty precisely."

"Yes, ma'am!" The young sailor unnecessarily saluted. She was a pretty girl, with fine features and neatly braided hair. It took a second for Jodenny to remember the wardroom talk about Ishikawa being a kasai girl. Accepting gifts for companionship was a tradition from old Japan, not exactly legal under Team Space regulations, not exactly illegal either.

Jodenny turned to Myell. "Show me your spaces, Sergeant."

Two DNGOs sat inactive in Myell's workshop, with tools and spare parts hung neatly beside them. A quick glance at Myell's maintenance log and she knew she wouldn't have to worry about him doing his job. One entry did catch her eye, however. She asked, "What's this about a missing dingo?"

"A Class III disappeared during the GQ yesterday," Myell said.

"Disappeared in the slots?" Jodenny asked. DNGOs were always getting lost in the maze of bins on each level. Sometimes they broke, sometimes they powered down by accident. Jem had claimed they were sneaking off to fool around and make baby DNGOs.

"No, on the Rocks. I was taking her to Repair. I notified Loss Accounting and they're coming later to investigate."

She would have to follow up on that further. Jodenny inspected Myell's bench, which was almost painfully neat. The only personal touch was a gram of a tropical beach. In it, a woman with an easy smile held back her long hair and squinted at the camera. She wore a bright yellow dress, and the blue-green surf swirled around her ankles.

"Is that Baiame?" she asked.

"No, Earth. Before the Debasement." He sounded a little wistful. "Someplace called the Gold Coast."

"A friend?"

"My mom," he said. "She died a long time ago."

"I'm sorry." Jodenny didn't tell him that her own parents had died when she was a toddler. She studied him in profile. Handsome, yes. He had a faint scar above his eyebrow that would be easy to fix, but for some reason he hadn't bothered to. Her impression was of an intelligent if not a cheerful man. But who would be jolly, stuck in the bottom of a cold cargo hold for months on end with only DNGOs for company?

"Lieutenant Scott," a man said, and she turned to see a dark-skinned sergeant approach. He was shorter than Myell but twice as wide, his immaculate uniform stretching over thick muscles. Maori, maybe, though most of them had stayed back on Earth. "I'm Strayborn, ma'am, your leading sergeant. I'm in charge here in T6. Welcome aboard."

"Thank you."

"The troops are assembled and eager to meet you."

Fourteen people had assembled in ragged rows. Strayborn joined the front line and Myell melted into the back. No sign of Chief Nitta, but Caldicot had managed to get herself there on time. Jodenny checked her watch and made sure Ishikawa shut off the lift.

"Underway Stores, atten-hut," she ordered.

She had seen better military posture among schoolchildren. Half of them were in standard coveralls with scuffed boots, soiled cuffs, or worn elbows. Others wore working trousers and blue shirts that had clearly seen better days. At least two of the men had hair past the edge of their collars and one woman had cascades of blonde curls pinned in a sloppy knot.

Jodenny began calling names off her gib. "AT Amador."

"He's on watch, ma'am," Strayborn said. "So are AT Lange and Sergeant VanAmsal."

"AT Amir."

Strayborn grimaced. "Transferred last month."

"AT Barivee."

"He's in the brig, ma'am." RT Gallivan, standing in the front row, gave her a cheeky smile. "Keeping AT Kevwitch and AT Yee company, no doubt. There's a bartender in Red Arrow with a beef to settle about some broken furniture."

Jodenny continued steadfastly down the list. AT Chang was present and wearing an Alcheringa Soccer League T-shirt under his jumpsuit. AM Dicensu was missing, and at his name someone chuckled. Young AM Dyatt, in the back row, was at least seven months pregnant. AT Nagarajan's hair was completely out of reg, but RT Minnich could have been a poster boy for a Team Space brochure.

Gallivan spoke up again. "You forgot AT Lund, ma'am. No doubt at Sick Call again."

"Thank you." Jodenny added Lund to her list and put her gib away. "Division quarters will be every morning at oh-six-forty-five until further notice. Tomorrow morning we'll have a uniform inspection, blue jumpsuits. That means clean clothes, required patches, and regulation haircuts. Working hours begin here at quarters, lunch is from eleven-thirty to twelve-thirty, and knockoff is at seventeen hundred or until work is done."

Ishikawa made a startled noise. Jodenny ignored it.

"Let me tell you what I know about Underway Stores." She gave them a steely appraisal. "It's not as glamorous as Flight Support. It's not as interesting as Ship's Services. If you want a steady career, you work in Disbursing. If you like to cook, you work in Food Services. For everyone else it's a choice between Underway Stores or Maintenance—telling a dingo to retrieve a broom or telling it to sweep the deck. Not very exciting at all."

Gallivan snickered.

Jodenny said, "Sergeant Strayborn. Two demerits for the next person who can't keep quiet."

"Yes, ma'am."

Gallivan's smirk disappeared.

"Most people don't realize how crucial Underway Stores is," she continued. "When our team doesn't deliver supplies to the galley, people can't eat. When our team doesn't issue bleach to the laundry shops, nobody gets clean underwear. Customer service is our first priority. We're going to reduce our backlog, improve our satisfaction rating, and treat every single customer we get with the utmost professionalism. Is there any question about that?"

Silence.

"Let's get to work," Jodenny said. "Underway Stores, dismissed."

Her new division quickly departed. Strayborn said, "Miz Scott? Thank you for calling inspections for tomorrow. It's been a while."

Jodenny glanced at his shiny patches and spotless boots. "How close are you to being promoted to chief?"

"I've got my hopes set on the ECP—the list should be out soon."

The Enlisted Commissioning Program made officers out of sailors who had earned their university degrees through Core. The process was grueling and the standards high. She made a note to check out his application and was giving him more orders when the lift returned with three people onboard, including Chief Nitta.

"Someone turned off the goddamned lift!" he said, his expression mottled.

"I did, Chief."

"We were on time!"

"Let's have a talk, Chief." Jodenny started climbing the nearest ladder. "Sergeant Strayborn, lock down level one for us."

She didn't look to see if Nitta followed, but after a moment his footsteps rang out behind her. Jodenny checked the indicator lights to make sure traffic on the level was disabled and swung off the ladder. A Class I DNGO stood nearby, paralyzed, a smartcrate in its claws. Behind it, the slots stretched out in dark and complicated patterns. Slot stories had become

Team Space folklore—ghosts in the maze, techs who went in to retrieve DNGOs and got lost forever.

"Do you know what's on this level, Chief?" she asked.

"Agroparts."

"Uniforms. Do you know our backlog status on uniforms? Three weeks. Three weeks to get some apprentice mate a new set of coveralls."

Nitta spread his hands. "Everything's been backlogged since we deployed. We loaded a thousand uniform items at Kookaburra."

"Then you better make sure they start getting distributed. This division is in serious trouble. Our COSAL reports are overdue to Fleet and we missed two data calls. We've got a five-week backlog on common parts for Housekeeping, six weeks for the galley. The March inventory showed a fifteen percent error rate and April's numbers should have been turned in last week. I also can't find the semiannual evals for able techs, which were due last week."

Nitta glared at her. "Just hold on a minute, Lieutenant. You don't know what it's like on this ship. You can come in and make all the value judgments you want, but you don't know how things work around here."

"I know how things work around here now. You've got until the end of the day to get that inventory on my desk. And you'll be right beside me at the uniform inspection tomorrow morning, so you'd better see to your own uniform first. Your pants are too long."

He wagged a finger at her. "First off, I didn't get your message because I was on watch in Flight Ops all night."

Amazing that he could stand watch and still visit the Underway Stores office with Quenger, but she didn't contradict him.

"Secondly, you can have the inventory done right, or you can have it done by the end of the day, but you can't have both."

"Why not? If you've been doing the daily and weekly reconciliations, all you have to do is compile everything and check the discrepancies."

Nitta folded his arms. "If you'd ever worked in Underway Stores before, you'd know it's more complicated than that."

She didn't tell him that she had, in fact, worked in Underway Stores, for Jem. "No, it's not. We take on provisions at every port. Core tells the dingoes where to store items and the dingoes do it. When someone onboard requests something, they transmit the requisition, Core approves it, and the dingoes deliver the items to the issue rooms or to the loading docks. All you have to do is match the records and balance the money."

"We're a little behind in the dailies."

"How far behind?"

"Don't worry about it. You'll get your inventory." Nitta stalked off without permission.

Jodenny made herself count to fifty before she followed him down the ladder. Ready to reprimand anyone who gave her a cross-eyed look, she trammed back to her office and found Caldicot in conference with a civilian woman who was old enough to be Jodenny's grandmother. Beside them stood an apprentice mate with wide blue eyes and pimples on his chin.

"Miz Scott!" The AM hurried to her side. "I'm Peter Dicensu. I'm sorry I wasn't at quarters. I got called for a Sweet test!"

Caldicot warned, "Peter, leave Miz Scott alone. She's busy."

Jodenny said, "It's all right. AM Dicensu, what's your job?"

"I help Mary, when she lets me. And I move things. And I can play Snipe."

"You don't play Snipe at work, do you?" Jodenny asked.

Dicensu ducked his head. "Only when there's nothing else to do, ma'am."

Caldicot handed him a gib. "You always have something to do. Sometimes you forget. Take this to Sergeant Strayborn. Get him to sign it. Then to RT Gallivan. He'll sign it, too. And RT Minnich after that."

"No problem!" Dicensu said, and dashed off.

The women watched him go.

"Before you ask," Caldicot said, "he's related to some three-star admiral on Warramala."

Jodenny shut her mouth.

The civilian woman offered her hand. "Lieutenant Scott, I'm Liddy Mullaly. I'm sorry I wasn't on time—my husband was late returning from watch in Engineering, and I wasn't sure how to get here. It's my first day."

"Mine, too," Jodenny said. "Is that an American accent I hear?"

Mrs. Mullaly beamed. Not only did she have the accent, but her face bore the kind of skin damage that came from living on a planet with a dangerously thinned ozone layer. "Born and bred, all my life. Then I decided, what the hell, time to see the universe. I met Mike on Fortune and we got married and here I am, at my age, in deep space. I've never worked for the military before. Is that a problem?"

Mrs. Mullaly's expression seemed so eager and cheerful that Jodenny gave her the benefit of the doubt. "I'm sure it will be fine."

Jodenny retreated to her office and rubbed her temples. Employing civilians for nonessential jobs was one tactic Team Space used to keep military spouses occupied during the long Alcheringa deployments, but did she have to get one so green behind the ears? And an American, to boot. Jodenny had never been to Earth, but she'd heard wild things about the kinds of people who roughed out a living in what was left of the United States. That Mrs. Mullaly's husband worked in Engineering was an additional concern. Any indiscreet word or action on Jodenny's part might easily spread—it wasn't oil that kept Team Space lubricated, it was the damned gossip.

With a sigh she turned to her deskgib. Imail had already begun to pile up in her queue. Somewhere in the bowels of Core, a demonic subroutine had started assigning her all of Greiger's old collateral duties. Cultural Diversity Committee. Voting Information Officer. Shore Leave Recommendations Board. Meanwhile the Public Relations office wondered if she would like to participate in a roundtable discussion about the *Yangtze*. Not at all. A civilian wanted to know if she thought the explosion had been caused by invading aliens. Delete. A barely coherent message placed blame for every death in the universe on the state of New Palestine on Fortune.

"Configure agent," she told Core. "Female, random name, no sense of humor."

A voice said, "Good morning, Lieutenant. My name is Holland."

"Start sorting my mail, Holland. Delete anything with a subject or message text that references my last ship, regardless of originator."

"Do you mean the *Yangtze*?"

"Yes."

"Understood, Lieutenant."

Jodenny pinged Bartis and tried to get on Lieutenant Commander Wildstein's schedule. Bartis said, "She's very busy this week, Lieutenant. I'll call your agent when there's an opening."

"I appreciate it." Jodenny wondered if Wildstein would be as busy if someone else was calling—her protégé Quenger, for instance. She pinged Security and reached the office of the Assistant Security Officer, Lieutenant Commander Senga. He was a slight but intense man, with a noticeable tic in his left eyelid.

"I'm told I have three sailors in the brig," she said after introducing herself. "Kevwitch, Yee, and Barivee."

Senga checked his gib, one hand drumming restlessly on his desk. "Bar brawl. They already went to mast. Three weeks in the brig and docked pay. Captain's very strict on that."

Jodenny changed the subject. "One of my dingoes disappeared during the GQ yesterday. Any chance of recovering it?"

"The Loss Accounting Division will take a statement, poke around, but you know. Kids or pranksters, probably. That dingo could be in a hundred pieces by now, souvenirs of the trip."

"Kids or pranksters during a General Quarters?"

He sounded glum. "You'd be surprised what disappears on this ship."

"The dingo was with Sergeant Myell," Jodenny said. "I understand he's been in trouble recently."

Senga straightened immediately. "He should have been court-martialed for what happened."

The vehemence in his tone surprised her. Jodenny asked, "So why wasn't he?"

"The girl didn't want to testify. Myell probably got to her, intimidated her. Him or his friends. The captain could have gone ahead and had Myell charged anyway—should have, just to keep him from attacking some other poor tech. If you've got missing equipment and he was the last person to use it, there's your thief."

Jodenny had already considered the idea. "He works with dingoes all the time. If he wanted parts, he could probably find a more subtle way to steal them."

Senga's frown deepened. "Unless that's what he wants you to think."

"He doesn't seem like the type."

"I've known him longer than you. He's exactly the type. If he's stealing Team Space property, we'll nail him for it. That's a promise."

His eagerness disturbed her. Jodenny signed off and leaned back in her chair. She couldn't see Myell stealing a DNGO, and had to trust that if he hadn't been brought to court-martial there was probably a good reason. "Holland, retrieve the personnel files on the following division members: Kevwitch, Yee, Barivee, Lund, Ishikawa, Myell, and Dicensu." She might as well get to know the more troubled members of her division through reports filed by her predecessors. But she would start with the most troublesome. "Open Myell's first."

CHAPTER SIX

Sergeant Rosegarten, a diminutive woman with curly red hair, was the leading sergeant for Loss Accounting. She interviewed Myell about the loss of Castalia at the base of T6, taking notes on her gib but obviously entranced by the lights of the DNGOs operating in the shaft above them.

"You said the Repair Shop was closing?" she asked, her head tilted back.

"Yes."

"And this was two hours before launch?"

"Yes."

"Are you sure it's safe to stand under them like this? What if one drops something?"

Myell pulled a wrench from his toolbelt and tossed it upward. It bounced harmlessly off the clearshield and clattered into the corner. "There's no gravity in the shaft, so nothing can fall. But if the gravity somehow got turned on, you could drop an asteroid on that shield and it would still hold. It's the same technology they use on the Flight Deck to protect against the vacuum of space."

Rosegarten lowered her gaze and rubbed her neck. "So why did you take the dingo over there if they were closing?"

Myell went after the wrench. "I didn't know their hours had changed."

Rosegarten consulted her gib. "So there you were, on the Rocks, the General Quarters alarm went off, and you did what?"

Myell hung the wrench back in its proper slot over his bench. Some of the other wrenches were in the wrong places. Every time he let Ishikawa near his things she managed to rearrange them. "I tied her to the post. She had a restraining bolt that wouldn't have let her go off on her own, but I wanted to make sure. After we were cleared to return to quarters I went back to the Rocks and she was gone."

"Doesn't each dingo have a positioning transceiver that allows it to be tracked by Core?"

"I've tried several times. She's not showing up on any scopes. Either the transceiver's not working or Core's misreading her signal." Myell adjusted the magnetic strips holding his screwdrivers in place. He realized Rosegarten might interpret his action as nervous fidgeting and stilled his hands. "I've seen both situations before."

"Have you lost dingoes before?"

Myell tried not to sound annoyed. "I didn't lose this one."

Abruptly she pocketed her gib. "I agree. I don't see any blame in this for you, Sergeant, except for not knowing the Repair

Shop was closed. I'll file your statement and my review. Who knows? Maybe the dingo will show up on its own."

She sounded optimistic, but Myell doubted he'd ever see Castalia again. She was probably torn down to her frame by now and stripped of anything that could be sold or swapped. After Rosegarten left, Myell began work again on Isis, who needed a new transceiver. He took off her access plate and was wrist-deep in her frame when Strayborn came by.

"Lieutenant wants the inventory done today," Strayborn said.

Myell took back every nice thing he'd ever thought about Jodenny Scott. "That's crazy. The reconciliations are overdue, the dingoes are nowhere near uploaded—"

Strayborn held up a forestalling hand. "Orders."

Myell blew out a noisy breath and patted Isis. "If I finish fixing this one, it'll go faster."

"No time. I need you up in the command module with Ishikawa. You recall the dingoes, Hosaka and I will handle the uploads. Send this one over to the Repair Shop."

He wouldn't, but there was no use arguing about it. Instead Myell said, "There's no way we can finish the whole inventory today."

Strayborn clapped him on the shoulder. "What Lieutenant wants, Lieutenant gets."

Evaluations from Myell's earlier ships portrayed a serious, dedicated sailor who'd enlisted on Baiame the day he turned eighteen. He had earned high marks and two achievement awards on the *Kashmir,* where his chiefs and division officers had noted his reliability and initiative. Those same traits were cited in his early promotion to sergeant on the *Okeechobee,* where he had been in charge of two issue rooms and later a loading dock. For his first few months on the *Aral Sea,* under the supervision of Lieutenant Commander Ellithorpe and Chief Mustav, things had gone well; it was only after Greiger took over and Chief Chiba moved in that Myell's scores dropped. Chiba's first review stated, "Surly and uncoopera-tive. Shows no leadership potential and is a detriment to the division."

Jodenny had seen good sailors turn bad for various reasons. Sometimes they got addicted to Sweet or some other drug, or fell in with the wrong crowd, or let an unhappy romance influ-ence their professional lives. Having met Chiba and witnessed firsthand the results of Greiger's management style, she was inclined to go with her gut instinct on Myell.

"RT Caldicot," Jodenny said, pinging her. "Update the divi-sion roster by noon. Get those AT evals started. Set up a meet-ing with the chief and all the sergeants for sometime tomorrow, here in my office. And schedule yourself too so we can go over office procedures."

"Yes, ma'am." Caldicot didn't sound enthused.

She put the service records aside and concentrated for the rest of the morning on overdue COSAL reports. When lunch-time rolled around Jodenny considered eating out of the vends but braved the mess deck instead. Inside the entrance she hes-itated, caught by bittersweet longing for the company of the officers she had eaten with so many times. She imagined the *Yangtze* galley now, twisted and dark and cold, bone embed-ded in metal—

A Drive tech bumped into her arm, almost toppling her tray. "Sorry, ma'am."

Jem's voice:"Where would you rather be, boot?"

Jodenny forced herself into line and picked out selections from the salad bar. Decorations for the week centered around the celebration of Mother's Day in several nations, and she ig-nored the callousness of the organizers in thinking everyone had a mother to celebrate. She went to the wardroom seating area and saw three clusters—one large group of Data officers to port, some Drive officers straight ahead, and a rowdy table of Flight officers to starboard. Closer at hand was a young en-sign with a Data patch munching on a kofte burger.

"May I sit down?" she asked.

His nametag said Cartik and he wore the pinched expression

of someone trying hard to look as if he didn't mind eating by himself. "You don't want to eat here."

"Is the food that bad?"

"Not here. I mean, here here. It being your second day and all, you probably want to meet more people."

"How do you know it's my second day?"

"You're all over the vids, Lieutenant." Cartik started to rise. "If you'll excuse me—"

"Sit down, mister. That's an order."

Cartik blinked. "That's illegal. You can't order me to have lunch with you."

"In that case, I'll give you a yuro to stay."

He didn't smile, but his shoulders relaxed a little. "Five."

"Five," she agreed. Cartik took his seat again. Five yuros would barely buy a candy bar in the ship's store. Jodenny added, "With negotiating skills like that you should be in the Supply Department."

The smile dissolved into a frown. "Couldn't be any worse."

"What's wrong with Data?"

Cartik glanced at the Data Department officers sitting at the next table. Jodenny changed the subject and asked him about life on the *Aral Sea*. He'd been onboard a year but couldn't recommend much for recreation except the occasional Mystery parties from Drive. He didn't play Snipe or Izim, but on his pocket server he ran several soccer discussion groups. He seemed reasonably intelligent, able to carry on a decent conversation, and she could discern no reason for his being an outcast from the Data Department. But he was definitely an outcast.

"Hi!" Hultz slid into the chair next to Jodenny. With her were Quenger, Zeni, and a man Jodenny didn't recognize. "I called your office but your agent didn't pick up."

"Speaking of leaving . . ." Cartik rose again.

"Don't go on our account," Quenger said. "We don't mind slumming."

Quenger missed the look that remark earned him but Jodenny didn't. After Cartik left, Hultz introduced Sub-lieutenant Cully Gunther.

"Glad to meet you!" Gunther reached for the rolls and nearly knocked over his water glass. "What do you think of the ship? Did you ask for this posting? Big mistake. I'd have asked for one of the new probes, I hear they're the ticket to adventure, not these milk runs—"

"Cully, shut up," Hultz said kindly.

Quenger said, "How's it going? They say Greiger left Underway Stores in a real mess."

"Not at all," Jodenny said. "A few loose ends. Nothing we can't take care of."

Hultz and Gunther launched into a story about something Greiger had done at a party several months previously. Although Jodenny tried to stay interested she felt Quenger staring at her. She wondered if he was plotting revenge for taking the job he wanted. She was so focused on ignoring him that she failed to notice Osherman coming up the ramp with his lunch tray.

"—and he denied everything, threatened everyone to never say a word about it, and wouldn't drink beer for the next month." Hultz finished as Osherman stopped beside their table with a lunch tray in hand.

"Miz Scott," he said.

Jodenny was acutely aware of everyone's eyes on her. "Mr. Osherman."

Their gazes locked. Jodenny tried not to think about the vacation they'd spent at a tropical resort on Kiwi, how it had been to wake up in his arms in a sunlit bed. He had a swimmer's body, long and lean and made for distance. He'd given her snorkeling lessons in the ocean, their bodies spooned together in the warm current, his knees nudging her legs open.

No, she wasn't going to think of any of that.

Osherman nodded abruptly, said, "Good day," and moved on to sit at another table.

Gunther asked, "That's the new guy in Data, isn't it? Do you know him? You look like you know him, that's why I ask—"

"We were on the same ship." Although Jodenny wanted to flee, she forced herself to stay for the next twenty minutes to spite Osherman. Let him think she was settling in fine, the belle of the ball. When Jodenny finally returned to the Underway Stores office, Mrs. Mullaly was studying the division roster.

"Why do they call them able technicians and regular technicians?" Mrs. Mullaly asked. "It doesn't sound glamorous."

"In the old Australian navy, the ranks were called able seaman and leading seaman. 'Seaman' was changed to 'technician' when we moved into space, and 'leading' became 'regular.' Now people start out as apprentice mates, move up to able techs, go on to regular techs, and then get promoted to sergeant, which was more of an army designation."

"Is everything based on the old Australian military?"

"Not everything. The Australians got first dibs because they discovered the Little Alcheringa near Mars."

"Yes, but Americans reached the moon first," Mrs. Mullaly said. "We started it all."

Jodenny was fairly sure the Russians had started it all, but she wasn't about to start debating history. "If anyone needs me, send me a ping. I'll be back in a bit."

She went directly to Issue Room 4, which was closed even though the hours of operation were clearly posted and eight techs were waiting in line. Jodenny used her thumbprint to enter the compartment. She waded past a stack of fallen bedsheets and jerked the gate open.

"What do you need?" she asked AT Abagli, the first tech in line.

He blinked a few times. "Medium coveralls, ma'am. But I can wait."

The last person to use the deskgib had been playing Izim. Gritting her teeth, Jodenny cleared the game and keyed in her request. RT Mauro came down the passage just as she was searching through a messy shelf.

"Miz Scott!" he said. "You shouldn't have to do this!"

"You're right, but no one else was here. Where did you put the medium coveralls?"

"I'm all out. The issue log's out-of-date."

Jodenny went back to the counter. "AT Abagli, someone will deliver your coveralls to your cabin before dinner. Will that do?"

His eyes widened in surprise. "Er, yes, ma'am."

Several minutes later, after the passage was clear of customers, Mauro said, "Honestly, ma'am, I couldn't help being late—I was up in Disbursing."

"You were up in Disbursing while people were in line for you?"

"I had to get my pay cleared up!"

"I see you were also playing Izim."

Mauro winced. "I was only looking—"

"Games are for your rec time, not work time. Who else works here with you?"

"Barivee, ma'am. He's in the brig."

"Then you'll have to carry on by yourself, and do the best you can," Jodenny said.

She went to IR2 next, up in officer country, where Gallivan and Chang were standing bright-eyed at the counter with no customers in sight. Jodenny asked, "Slow day, gentlemen?"

"No, ma'am," Gallivan replied. "We're just very efficient."

The two of them were much more organized than Mauro, although they couldn't produce a current F-89. They didn't think that was a significant deficit on their fault and neither did Jodenny. She asked them how long they'd been onboard and learned that Chang had recently passed the one-year mark. Gallivan was at the end of his contract, and would rotate off the *Aral Sea* when they reached Warramala.

"I'm going into music." Gallivan drummed his hands on the counter. "My band plays on the Rocks every Friday."

"How hard has someone tried to talk you into staying?"

"Very hard. Extremely hard. Can't be done, ma'am."

Jem probably could have done it. Jodenny made a note to try and persuade him herself, congratulated both of them on doing good work, and trammed over to T6. Strayborn and Hosaka sat clustered in the command module. Three upsynching DNGOs hovered in the zero-g outside.

Strayborn popped out of his chair. "Ma'am!"

"How's it going, Sergeant?"

"Absolutely fine," Strayborn said.

She couldn't tell if he truly meant it or was merely exhibiting a can-do mentality. Hosaka, with her platinum-colored hair and dark eyes, peered intently at her datastream. Jodenny said, "I need a set of medium coveralls delivered to AT Abagli in Ops berthing within the hour. And make it known that playing games is not acceptable while on duty. I'm going to take away the gib of the next person I catch."

"Yes, ma'am."

"Who else is working with you on this inventory?"

"Myell and Ishikawa are up in the observation module. Su and Lange are down below."

She had wanted to talk to Myell about AT Ford, but would rather they get the inventory done. "Carry on," Jodenny said. On the tram back to Mainship she checked her imail. Twelve new messages had arrived, including a friendly note from A. J. Francesco asking how her day was going. Jodenny decided to swing by the Supply Flats and see if she could drop in on Lieutenant Commander Wildstein. She arrived in time to see Dicensu, who was hurrying down the passage while scribbling in a notebook, plow into the perpetually unhappy Ensign Ysten. Both men crashed to the deck.

Ysten shoved Dicensu off him. "Why the hell don't you watch where you're going?"

"Sorry, sir!" Dicensu's face screwed up as if he were about to cry.

Jodenny grabbed the AT's arm and hauled him up. "It's all right. No one's hurt."

"Fucking baka," Ysten spat out, climbing to his feet. "You're a goddamned menace—"

Jodenny swung on him. "Mr. Ysten! That's enough."

"He shouldn't even be—"

"That's enough!" Jodenny turned to the techs who had gathered to watch the spectacle. "Everyone back to work."

Ysten stalked off. Tear tracks marked Dicensu's cheeks and blood streamed from a cut on his lip. Jodenny picked up his notebook and steered him into the nearest dual-gender head.

"Minor injury alert," she called to the medbot perched high on the bulkhead. The unit, no larger than her fisted hand, swooped down with a series of beeps. "Check patient's mouth."

Dicensu giggled as the medbot scanned his lips, teeth, and gums. Jodenny told him to hold still while the medbot sprayed a tiny amount of sealant on a lip cut.

"No further medical attention necessary," the medbot said.

Jodenny said, "AM Dicensu, why don't you go back and ask RT Caldicot for something to do."

"Okay, Miz Scott."

"Don't forget your notebook." As Jodenny started to hand it back, a drawing of a DNGO caught her eye. "Did you do this?"

"Yes, ma'am. Do you want to see some more?"

Dicensu flipped through the pages for her, and Jodenny saw manga sketches of Caldicot, Strayborn, Loading Dock G, the plant on Bartis's counter, and a small gray cat.

"These are very good," Jodenny said. "Can you draw something for me?"

"Sure, ma'am. What?"

Jodenny told him. Dicensu promised to do his best. Once he was gone, she went down to the Admin office and saw Ysten sitting in a chair outside Al-Banna's hatch. The glower he was aiming at the bulkhead switched focus to her. He said, "You had no right to reprimand me in front of those techs. Dicensu is a menace."

"Dicensu is a member of this crew who deserves to be treated the same as everyone else."

"He's more trouble than he's worth."

"That's what they say about ensigns. If you're thinking about crying on the commander's shoulders, remember that what happened reflects more on you than on me or Dicensu."

Ysten's cheeks turned red. The hatch beside Jodenny opened. Lieutenant Commander Wildstein, a stocky brunette with a Fortune homeworld patch, gave both Jodenny and Ysten a stern look. "Don't either of you have work you could be doing?"

"Yes, ma'am." Ysten scampered off.

Jodenny squared her shoulders. "Good afternoon, ma'am. We haven't met yet—"

"I know who you are. RT Bartis will get you on my schedule."

"Thank you, Commander."

"I heard you couldn't find your lifepod."

Would it have killed the Wondjina to give her a supportive superior officer? Jodenny said, "I know where it is now, ma'am."

Wildstein didn't look impressed. "How reassuring. You're excused, Lieutenant."

As Jodenny walked through the Flats reconsidering her decision to stay in Team Space, she saw Nitta talking with Master Chief DiSola and the notorious Chief Chiba. DiSola was a lanky man with bushy eyebrows and an easy smile. Chiba was tall and wide, not quite bald, and looked strong enough to bench-press a birdie.

"Miz Scott." DiSola had a deep voice and a strong handshake. "Welcome aboard."

"Best ship in the fleet," Chiba said, squeezing Jodenny's hand a moment later. She had no doubt he wanted her to feel how strong he was. So this was the man who'd made Myell's life miserable. Part of the ship's yakuza, or so Zeni had said.

"You work for Lieutenant Quenger, don't you?" Jodenny asked.

"Lieutenant Commander Zarkesh is the DIVO. Lieutenant Quenger and I work side by side." Point made, Chiba gave Nitta a smirk. "Too bad you're stuck with the lot you've got. Underway Stores was a much different division when I ran it."

Jodenny bit back a retort and asked, "How's the inventory going, Chief Nitta?"

"Looks good," Nitta said. "I was just at T6."

"So was I. Too bad I missed you."

Nitta took a judicious sip from his coffee cup. DiSola said, "I'd love to sit down and chat with you, Miz Scott. Is now a good time?"

Jodenny had known that was coming. "Now's great, Master Chief."

DiSola's warm, cozy office had been grammed to look like a wood-paneled cabin of an old sailing ship. Nautical charts and reproductions of brass antiques hung on the bulkheads.

He said, "I've been on this ship for three years. Since coming aboard I've seen two SUPPOs come and go, as well as twenty officers and three hundred enlisted. Our turnover rate is thirty percent. Helluva way to maintain a status quo."

"I don't think there's such a thing as a status quo."

"But it would be nice to have a little stability once in a while, don't you think?"

"*'Anyone can hold the helm when the sea is calm,'* Chief," she said.

DiSola laughed. "I prefer Epicurus over Syrus: *'Skillful pilots gain their reputation from storms and tempests.'* May I offer some advice? There's lots of personalities in this department. Lots of inflated egos. It's real easy to annoy the wrong people. You might want to get a feel for how things work around here before you start making big changes."

"That's good advice. When you have the benefit of calm weather."

"You're going to liven this department right up, aren't you, Miz Scott?"

"It's not my goal, but I don't think I can avoid it."

DiSola lifted his coffee cup. "To be honest, neither do I."

CHAPTER **SEVEN**

Myell had known Lieutenant Scott was in T6 because Hosaka had left the comm open. He and Ishikawa heard her order Strayborn to deliver a set of coveralls to some apprentice mate and marveled at how enthusiastically Strayborn snapped, "Aye, aye, ma'am."

Ishikawa asked, "Are we doing home deliveries now?"

"Lieutenant's a big believer in customer service," Myell replied. And Strayborn was a big believer in sucking-up. Granted, Team Space wasn't usually kind to Maori and Strayborn was notoriously ambitious. Myell suspected much more ass kissing to come.

"This is boring." Ishikawa plopped into a chair and spun around lazily. Outside the observation module's windows, a DNGO was busy uploading its data. "How much longer is it going to take?"

"All day and maybe half the night." The Class IV and Vs could upsynch from wherever they were in the slots. The other classes had to be retrieved and plugged into Core so that their data could be downloaded to the master database. Once the comparison was run, all discrepancies had to be corrected or justified. If the job had been done daily, per regulations, the task would have only taken a few hours.

"I can't stay half the night." Ishikawa slumped dramatically. "I have a date."

Myell wondered if it was kasai. He realized that he and Ishikawa were alone in the module without anyone else to observe them and remembered Timrin's lecture on proof. Ish was an okay kid but like Ford she could make any accusation she wanted and people would listen. With a slight flick of his left hand he turned on the recording log.

"The dingoes can't go faster," he said. "The reconciliations are to make sure no one's stealing anything. Everything that comes in or goes out has to be accounted for."

Through the comm they heard Lieutenant Scott warn Strayborn about people playing Snipe or Izim. Ishikawa asked, "Can she really take away someone's gib?"

"Sure she can," Myell said, although it would be a drastic step to take.

Lieutenant Scott departed. Strayborn sent Hosaka off to deliver the coveralls while he and Myell resumed pulling DNGOs from the slots.

"Sarge, you know my roommate, right? Shevi Dyatt?" Ishikawa asked.

"Sure," he said. Dyatt worked for VanAmsal over on Loading Dock G. She'd transferred from Ops back on Fortune, already pregnant.

"She's having a problem with Joe Olsson."

"What kind of problem?" he asked, against his better judgment. Olsson had been in Underway Stores until he transferred with Chiba to Maintenance. He wasn't as bad as Spallone, but he could cause trouble when he wanted to.

"I think she wants to break up with him, but he won't take no for an answer."

"She should report it to Sergeant VanAmsal. Or to Security."

Ishikawa pushed her black bangs away from her eyes. "She doesn't want to make it official. Could you talk to him or something? Guy to guy?"

"VanAmsal's her boss."

"You could tell him—"

"No. I'm not getting involved."

Ishikawa sulked for the rest of the afternoon. Myell concentrated on retrieving the DNGOs and gathering their data. By seventeen hundred hours they had most of the job done, but a Class III named Circe failed to respond when summoned.

"Myell, go in and get her," Strayborn said over the comm.

"How about you, Ish?" Myell asked. "Want to have a go?"

"No, sir."

Myell said, "That's 'No, Sergeant.' Watch your attitude."

"You hear me up there?" Strayborn asked.

"We hear you." Already he could tell that Lieutenant Scott's attention was going to Strayborn's head. "Give me five minutes."

Myell started pulling equipment from the gear locker. He kicked off his boots and zipped himself into the EV suit. Ishikawa, apparently done with her sulking, helped him check the oxygen supply, heating unit, and maneuvering thrusters. The bubble dome gave him a wide range of vision but made him feel as if his head were in a fishbowl.

Ishikawa said, "I hate zero-g. Doesn't it scare you?"

"No," he said, but he wasn't mad keen on it, either. As he waited for the airlock to decompress, he decided the worst part was always looking down from the ledge at a thousand meters of horrifying emptiness and forcing himself to step away, in defiance of all logic and self-preservation, from the haven of safety.

Ishikawa said, "Radio check. Can you hear me?"

"No problems." Myell's voice sounded unnaturally loud in his own ears.

"The tower's all locked down," Hosaka said. "Not a creature stirring, not even a mouse."

Myell demagnetized his boots, squeezed his eyes shut, and pushed off. One pulse-pounding second passed, then another, and when he was sure he wasn't going to plummet to his death he opened his eyes again. He used his thrusters to maneuver toward level forty-six. Over the commset Ishikawa asked, "Why do all the dingoes have strange names?"

"That was Chief Mustav's idea," Myell said. "He named them after ancient Earth goddesses."

Ishikawa said, "Oh." A moment later she asked, "Can we send out for dinner? I'm dying of starvation."

Lange, down at the bottom of the shaft, chipped in with a sour comment. "I bet the lieutenant's enjoying her dinner."

His friend Su added, "How come officers never do any of the hard work?"

"Shut up," Strayborn said. "This is our job, not hers."

Myell reached the level he wanted and peered inside the slots cautiously. DNGOs could sense each other but weren't as good with soft human flesh. One could easily crash into him or crush him against a bulkhead.

"You're sure everything's locked down?" he asked.

From the command module Hosaka said, "Absolutely."

Myell pulled himself inside. He coasted along on momentum for a few seconds and then used the thrusters to propel himself past the bins. The headlights on his helmet provided illumination in the cold darkness. Among other things, level forty-six housed weapons and ammunition in case the Security Department was ever needed to augment local Team Space forces in times of civil unrest, like they had during the Separatist uprisings on Warramala. He could feel the weight of violence and death surrounding him, the never-ending prospect of war.

"We're tracking you at 46-340-Bravo," Hosaka said. "Is that right?"

Myell read the address on the nearest bin. "Perfect."

Something flickered at the edge of his vision, but when he swung around he saw only crates lashed into place behind the metal gratings. Newsvids of the *Yangtze* disaster rose in his mind. No one knew why their T6 had exploded. One moment it was all whole and intact, the next a horrific outrushing of shrapnel and burning cargo.

"Haven't you found anything yet?" Strayborn asked.

"I don't see it," Myell said. "Are you sure—no, wait."

Another flicker of motion, gone almost before he could register it. Goose bumps ran across the back of his neck. Maybe someone was playing tricks on him. Maybe this was an elaborate setup for some new prank by Chiba. Or maybe someone—something?—was in the slot with him, crouched behind the crates. Something cold and alien, sinuous and malevolent. The fact that no alien life had ever been discovered in the Seven Sisters did nothing to calm him.

"Terry?" Hosaka asked.

"It's okay." Myell hoped they didn't hear the crack in his voice. "I thought I saw—"

Something large darted by at the corner of his eye. "Christ!" he said. "Something's moving down here!"

"Stay exactly where you are," Strayborn ordered.

"Don't move," Hosaka echoed.

Myell ignored them both. He swung his flashlight down the slots and maneuvered closer to the bins. Strayborn and Hosaka were chattering on, reading off lists of DNGO whereabouts, double-checking that no strays had slipped through Core's lockdown. With each eliminated possibility he heard doubt edging into their voices and knew, with a sinking feeling, that this would be another bit of gossip held against him—nut job Myell, imagining monsters in the slots and under his bed.

"There's nothing on the scopes," Strayborn finally said, which was a polite way of questioning his sanity.

"Maybe it's Circe," Hosaka said. "You should get out of there until we make sure."

"No," Myell said. He had calmed down a little, and was beginning to doubt whether he'd really seen anything at all. "I'll get her."

He moved deeper into the slots gingerly, hyperaware of every shadow. Ten minutes later his beam caught the silver-gray of Circe's hull. The DNGO hung adrift with her lights out. She didn't look damaged, but nothing happened when Myell tried to reset her manually. "She's not responding."

"Batteries must be dead," Strayborn said.

"I doubt it," he replied. The rechargeable ion cells had a shelf life of several hundred hours, and the DNGOs were programmed to charge themselves during off-hours. More likely Circe had burned out a thruster or lost her navigation sensors, but neither problem should have made her shut down so entirely.

Strayborn said, "Doesn't matter. Haul her out of there."

Myell fitted the DNGO with a restraining bolt in case she decided to wake up and finish the last task remaining in her cache. Like an oversized silver balloon, she drifted as he pulled her out of the slots. Focusing on the DNGO's motion took his mind off the creepy feeling of being stalked, but he was still appallingly glad when they exited the maze into the free space of the shaft. Hosaka sent down another DNGO to tow Circe to the command module, and Myell made his own way back up to level fifty.

By the time he'd processed himself through the airlock, Hosaka had plugged Circe into the ship's power supply and had ordered a reboot. Hosaka said, "I hope the data's still intact."

Ishikawa helped Myell out of his suit. "Then can we go eat?"

No one said anything about his meltdown in the slots. Myell rubbed his arms until they'd warmed up and hoped the subject never came up again. He *had* seen something, hadn't he? He sat down and saw that Ishikawa had been fiddling with the control panel while he was gone.

"What were you doing?" he asked.

Ishikawa's nose crinkled in confusion. "You mean with the synch log? Trying to figure out more about how it all works. Sounds important."

She was more likely to be cruising the ship's message boards than actually taking the initiative on anything, but Myell's suspicions were distracted by the flashing tally from Circe's newly synched memory. "Crap," Hosaka said from the command module. "We're never getting out of here."

The comparison between transactions recorded by Core and transactions recorded by Circe scored only a seventy-eight percent match. Date of request, requisition number, quantity ordered, quantity retrieved, quantity delivered—a deviation in any of a dozen categories was enough to kick the record onto the discrepancy list. It was the worst number from any of the DNGOs, and would drag down the monthly score to an unacceptable level.

"We're going to have to justify each record manually." Strayborn didn't sound happy. "Myell, Ish, you take the first hundred and fifty. Lange, Su, you take the second batch."

Myell heard heartfelt groans over the comm.

"How about we take a dinner break first, Sarge?" Su asked. "We're starving down here."

"Just a half hour," Lange added.

While they tried to persuade Strayborn to let them go, Myell skimmed over the data. "Jen," he said, "sort the discrepancies by date."

"Why?" Hosaka asked. "Oh. I see it. Most of the mismatches are in the last twenty-four hours. If her batteries were going, it might have affected her data collection."

Myell said, "We don't know it's the batteries. I'll have to test it."

"If it wasn't the battery, we'll be sitting here all night trying to figure out why Core says the galley got a thousand spoons while Circe says it only got ten," Strayborn said. "It'll take us until at least midnight, and that's not counting all the other records we have to justify before we can think of getting out of here and preparing for tomorrow's uniform inspection."

Hosaka said, "It's the battery."

Lange and Su agreed.

"Myell?" Strayborn asked

Myell squeezed the bridge of his nose. "We can't write off three hundred transactions without justification."

"We've got justification," Strayborn said. "They're all glitches. I'll write up a paragraph or two and make sure the chief and Lieutenant Scott are okay with it."

Ishikawa's hopeful gaze did Myell in. He already felt like a fool for imagining something in the slots. He wouldn't be the jerk who kept everyone at work all night long.

"All right," Myell said. No use fighting about it. "It's probably the battery."

On her way to dinner Jodenny passed Quenger boarding a lift.

"You shouldn't waste too much time in our wardroom," he said. "The real action's elsewhere."

She replied, "I'm not interested in real action. I've seen enough of it."

"That's obvious." Quenger nodded toward her MacBride Cross. "Flaunting it, are you? You weren't wearing that when you first came aboard."

The lift doors closed before she could tell him to go screw himself. Jodenny fumed all the way to the wardroom, where Ysten and Weaver were mixing drinks and Francesco was watching the ship's evening news.

"You look ready to rip someone in pieces," Weaver said.

"I am." Jodenny considered pouring herself a strong drink but went to the table instead. "AT Ashmont, what time is it?"

"Ma'am? It's top of the hour."

"Start serving," Jodenny ordered.

"We usually wait," Weaver said.

"I'm the senior officer here," Jodenny said, "and I'd like to eat."

Francesco might have been senior to her, depending on his commissioning date, but he only scratched his ear and took a seat without comment. Ysten and Weaver both sat down with cautious expressions. Zeni and Hultz wandered in ten minutes later and look startled to see the first course under way. "What happened?" Zeni asked.

"It's a new tradition," Jodenny said. "Dinner starts promptly at eighteen hundred."

Ysten didn't come to dinner at all, which prompted Hultz's bit of gossip. "I hear Dicensu knocked him unconscious on the Flats."

"They bumped each other in the passage," Jodenny said. "Nothing more."

Weaver reached for her beer. "He's in big trouble with Vu, anyway. Keeps bad-mouthing the food on the mess decks. Not too smart when your own boss is in charge of it, right?"

Jodenny couldn't have said what dinner that night tasted like. The minor victory of eating on time was far outweighed by Quenger's cutting remarks. A heavy depression swung over her, a pitch-black shadow that encompassed the terrible condition of Underway Stores, the encounter with Osherman at lunch, and her problems with Nitta and Ysten.

"Is anything wrong?" Francesco asked when she went to check her queue after dinner.

"No," Jodenny said. "I'm waiting for a report."

"No talk of paperwork so soon after eating. Come play Seven Up."

Jodenny partnered with Hultz. Zeni cut for the deal and Francesco showed the highest card. He dealt out six cards to each of them and turned up the next for trump. Hultz begged, Francesco dealt out more, and Jodenny wondered if Nitta had at least had dinner delivered to the crew working over in T6.

"You weren't even trying," Hultz said when they lost the hand.

"I'm sorry." Jodenny stood. "Excuse me. There's something I need to go do."

She couldn't pretend to be in the tower for some casual reason. She would have to betray herself as someone who didn't trust her own people. Even as the tram crossed across the gulf from Mainship, she told herself to turn back. But she ignored her own advice and crossed the access ring to T6's control module.

The lights were down, the displays dim. Perplexed, her pulse beginning to pound against her temple, Jodenny went to the Underway Stores office and saw Nitta at his desk.

"I'm routing the inventory to you right this minute. Ninety-two percent." Nitta leaned back in his chair to beam at her. "We did a damn fine job."

Jodenny didn't return his smile. "I look forward to reading it. Don't forget that uniform inspection in the morning."

"Come on, Miz Scott. Don't you think we could forego that? Everyone worked late."

Jodenny glanced pointedly at the clock. "Not that late."

"I think it'll go over well if you postpone it."

"No."

He chuckled. "Then I better go hem my trousers."

Jodenny watched him go. In the fourteen or so hours that she'd known him, she hadn't thought he was capable of a good mood. She went to her desk and activated Holland.

"Take a look at the monthly inventory sitting in my queue," Jodenny said. "Run all the standard fraud and irregularity checks. Double-check the ID numbers, purchase orders, accounts receivable, issued goods, and dingo retrieval rates."

After a moment Holland said, "I've detected no anomalies, Lieutenant."

Ninety-two percent. Not bad. She could think of one or two of her supply school classmates who would be happy to score that high.

Maybe her job wasn't going to be as difficult as she had feared.

CHAPTER **EIGHT**

Myell woke earlier than usual from nightmares. First he'd been in the slots, lost in the dark maze while something sinister and cold ruthlessly tracked him down. Then he'd been back on Baiame, running from his older brother's wrath across an immense field of rotting crops. Black vines reached for his ankles and tried to drag him down to the dirt. "Come take your beating!" Daris yelled, his voice booming across the steel-gray sky. Legs numb, chest laboring,

Myell fell to his knees. Just before Daris's unseen fist rammed into the small of his back (he couldn't see it but he knew it was coming, with the odd prescience of dreams) a voice commanded, "Stop!" The same naked Aboriginal he'd seen on the tram appeared on a nearby hill. The circles and swirls on his body were silver in the odd light, and his spear pulsed with unnatural power. He was a shaman, Myell realized. A medicine man fallen out of Aboriginal history.

"Begone!" The shaman stabbed his spear at a point over Myell's shoulder. The spear turned into a multicolored snake that arched through the air with a hiss like falling rain. "You are not welcome in this world!"

Lightning; thunder; the heavy smell of ozone. Myell blinked his eyes and found himself curled up in his rack. Koo stared at him from the perch of a rock he'd placed in her terrarium. He could feel his heart thudding in his chest like a thing gone wild.

"Shit," he said, and Koo skittered off her rock to burrow under some grass.

Timrin was away on watch. After a few minutes Myell snapped on the light and got dressed. He went up to the E-Deck gym and did a half hour on a treadmill, but not even a brisk run could drive away lingering feelings of doom. The terror he'd felt in the slots was just the result of an overactive imagination. Daris was a demon he'd long put to rest, or so he'd hoped. And what was his subconscious doing, mucking around with that weird shaman? Myell had no Aboriginal ancestors that he knew of, and certainly didn't need any defending him in his dreams.

He returned to Supply berthing downladder into the lounge, which was littered with leftovers and empty beer cans. Erickson was asleep on one of the sofas, no doubt kicked out of his cabin so Chang could have a girlfriend over. Joe Olsson was waiting for the lift. It would have been easier to pass him by, and smarter, too, but Myell stopped anyway.

"Olsson," he said.

"What do you want?"

"You still seeing Shevi Dyatt?"

"What's it to you?"

"Wanted to make sure she's not unhappy about it."

Olsson stabbed the lift button. "Fuck off, Myell."

"No need to get hostile," he said, and wished he had a way of recording the conversation in case Olsson got physical.

Olsson's lips thinned. "She say something to you?"

"No. And I'm not getting involved. Just be careful."

"Yeah, like you were with Wendy Ford." The lift doors opened and Olsson stepped inside. "Find that dingo you lost on the Rocks? No, and you're not going to. Keep asking questions, and you'll lose a lot more."

As Myell watched the doors close he imagined the stupefied expression on his own face. He had toyed with the idea that Chiba's dogs had taken Castalia, but why would they? Just to mess with him? Dumbfounded, he returned to his cabin, showered, and donned his neatest uniform. He still had an hour before Lieutenant Scott's inspection began and was heading for the mess decks when Security pinged him.

"Report to Lieutenant Commander Senga's office," he was told.

He went, his throat tight. The Security offices were open twenty-four/seven, but the day shift had yet to come on duty. A regular tech directed him past empty desks to Senga's office, which was grammed in black tile and smelled like burned coffee. Sergeant Rosegarten was standing with Senga, an unhappy expression on her face. Senga, who'd been Wendy Ford's staunchest supporter, gave Myell a cold look.

"Sit down, Sergeant," Senga said. "Tell me what you really did with that dingo you reported missing."

Myell sat. As evenly as possible he said, "I left it on the Rocks and it disappeared, sir."

"On its own," Senga said, and there was no missing the sarcasm. "It just flew away."

Rosegarten's frown deepened.

"No, sir," Myell said. "It was fitted with a restraining bolt."

Senga hammered away at his story. Why did he take the DNGO to the Rocks if the Repair Shop was closed? Why didn't he leave it there when the alarms sounded? How hard had he tried to retrieve it? The insinuation that he'd stolen it was clear, but Myell refused to be baited. He tried not to look at the clock, but the minutes ticked away toward division quarters.

"You know what I think?" Senga said. "I think you'll say anything to cover your ass."

He wasn't about to repeat what Olsson had said in the lounge, and he certainly wasn't going to show them the bruises that Chiba had left from the manhandling. Senga would probably blame him for fighting and get him thrown into the brig again.

"I don't have any reason to lie to you, sir. But I do have to be at division quarters in ten minutes."

Senga smiled for the first time. "Well, Lieutenant Scott will understand. She's the one who called me, after all. She wanted to know why you weren't charged for raping AT Ford. She's worried more equipment might go missing."

Myell had expected Jodenny Scott to hear about the mess, but had held on to some faint hope that she might give him a chance to have his say. "If you suspect me of something, I demand written notification of my legal rights and want a lawyer present."

"You *demand*?" Senga leaned forward, fists curled.

"Sir," Rosegarten said, "may I speak with you outside?"

"How about you go outside and Sergeant Myell and I talk about his *demands*?"

"*Sir,*" she insisted, an edge in her voice that even Myell couldn't miss. Senga and Rosegarten left. Myell watched the clock. Oh-six-forty-five came and went. He couldn't do anything about it, not unless he bolted from the room without permission. Finally Rosegarten returned alone.

"I apologize for the lieutenant commander," she said, her expression stoic. "You're free to go."

Myell left. The trams were running slow, and it was several minutes before he was crossing the access ring to T6. He hesitated at the command module, wondering if it was better to miss quarters altogether than show up late, but duty compelled him to ride the lift down. The division was still assembled in ranks and Lieutenant Scott was inspecting Ishikawa with Chief Nitta beside her. Nitta smirked at Myell's tardiness. Jodenny gave him the briefest glance and said, "Into line, Sergeant."

He did as told and fixed his gaze on the back of Chang's head. The hold was very quiet, with only an occasional shuffle of feet and Lieutenant Scott's low murmurs of approval or disapproval. "You need a better haircut," she told Lange. "Nice boots, AM Dicensu," she said a moment later. When she reached Myell she gave him a thorough scrutiny from top to bottom. He didn't dare break attention to meet her eyes, but knew they were full of disappointment. "Satisfactory," she told Nitta, and with a soft beep the judgment was entered into Nitta's gib. "Two demerits for being late." Then, louder, she said, "Underway Stores, dismissed."

The assembly broke up quickly. Jodenny and Nitta left without a word, but Myell didn't imagine he'd escape so easily and he didn't. "Where the hell were you?" Strayborn asked.

The tone of it grated on him. "I got delayed," Myell said, and headed for his workbench.

Strayborn followed. "What kind of delay?"

"Don't worry about it. I can handle—" Myell broke off when he saw the empty places where he had left Circe and Isis. "Jesus. They did take more."

"What, the dingoes? I had Ish bring them to Repair Services."

Myell's temper rose. "I told you I could fix them!"

Strayborn put a hand out as if he were a pedestrian crossing guard. "Stop right there. I don't know what's gotten into you, but calm the hell down."

"I could have fixed them," was all Myell trusted himself to say. Isis he didn't mind so much, though it would have taken only a few more minutes to get her working. But Circe was over on a stranger's bench, probably in pieces, at the mercy of Chiba's men and with the mystery of those erroneous records wired into her data core.

"What's the drama?" Strayborn said. "The inventory's done and the dingoes will be back in a few days. If you tell me why you were late, maybe I can get the lieutenant to drop your demerits."

"Forget it," Myell said. "Just let me work, all right?"

"But, Terry—"

"Go away, Gordon," Myell said, and Strayborn did.

Jodenny went straight from the morning inspection to a division officer meeting on the Supply Flats. Fifteen minutes early, she sat in the drab conference room and rehearsed good things to say about Underway Stores. The inspection had at least gone well, except for Myell's tardiness. She would confront him later about that. No sergeant of hers was going to stroll in late without a damn good reason.

"Didn't they tell you?" Lieutenant Commander Vu from Food Services entered the room. She looked like an Asian elf—petite, slim, with cropped hair and delicate features. "The most junior DIVO always brings breakfast. Commander Matsuda was big into muffins, but Commander Al-Banna's a doughnut man through and through. He'll be furious if there aren't any."

Jodenny replied, "Well, it wouldn't be the first time I've pissed him off."

Vu laughed and extended her hand. "I'm Margaret. Congratulations on your new position. Or condolences. Depends on how you look at it."

A male lieutenant commander with jet-black hair entered. "What, nothing to eat?"

Vu said, "Jodenny, this is Sam Zarkesh. Complain to him when your decks aren't clean."

"Decks on this ship are always clean," Zarkesh replied loftily.

Wildstein arrived next. "The SUPPO's in a foul mood. Let's make this short and sweet."

"Short and sweet, aye," Vu said.

Al-Banna walked in, his uniform impeccable and shoes spotless. He growled, "What, no doughnuts?"

"My fault, sir," Jodenny offered.

"Damn right." Al-Banna sat down, leaned backward, and drummed his fingers on the table. "Where's Tony? Can't anyone get to a goddamned meeting around here on time?"

"We're here, sir," Wildstein said, turning her attention to her gib.

"Thanks, Grace." Al-Banna didn't sound appreciative. "Zee, you first."

Zarkesh leaned back in his chair. "The Flight wardroom's complaining that their air-conditioning keeps going on and off. I've sent mechbots through their vents and checked the programming, but I think they're mitzi. We'll keep working on it. I've got sixteen dingoes in the shop, most of them fixable. One went missing from Underway Stores during the GQ."

Jodenny sat up straighter. "Yes, sir. A Class III."

"How did you lose it?" Al-Banna asked.

"One of the sergeants was on his way to the Repair Shop when the alarm went off, sir. He couldn't take it with him so he left it on the Rocks."

"Which sergeant?"

"Myell."

Jodenny didn't miss the frown that passed over Vu's face, or the way Wildstein glanced up, ever so briefly, from her gib. Immediately she said, "I don't believe he's responsible, sir."

Al-Banna's expression didn't change. "Security will figure it out. Anything else, Zee?"

"No, sir," Zarkesh said.

"Anything from Underway Stores?" Al-Banna asked.

"The monthly inventory came in at ninety-two percent, sir."

Wildstein didn't look impressed. "Maybe you could spend some time on the backlog. I've got requisitions that are over a month old sitting in your division."

"Yes, ma'am. I'll get that backlog down." Jodenny turned to Zarkesh. "And I can tell you exactly what's wrong with the a/c in the Flight wardroom."

Zarkesh's eyebrows quirked upward. "Can you, now?"

"There's an auxiliary data storage closet above it that only gets used if Core takes a cold drive offline and needs some-place for temporary backup. When the closet gets turned on, the a/c in the wardroom gets diverted."

In an admiring voice, Vu said, "Clever, isn't she? I say we keep her."

The hatch opened. Lieutenant Commander Rokutan, the division officer for Flight Support, came in with three gibs in hand. Tall and freckled, with brown hair and a handsome face, he was strangely familiar to Jodenny. After a moment, she remembered seeing his pictures hanging in the sports gallery back at the academy. He was a College Cup Champion soccer player, twice over.

"Sorry I'm late." As Rokutan sat down, one of his gibs fell to the deck. He nearly slammed his head on the table as he bent to pick it up. Jodenny fetched it for him and passed it over. He smiled crookedly, and she felt herself warm a little.

Al-Banna ignored Rokutan. "Margaret, what's going on in your department?"

Vu reported on the state of the galley, upcoming special meals, the service division's profit for the month, and a rash of petty thefts from the ship's laundry. When his turn came, Rokutan said that the Flight Department was still doing train-ing operations. Wildstein reminded everyone that AT evals were due on Friday.

Al-Banna grimaced. "Let's not be too generous about how great they are. Who got stuck with Greiger's job on the Cul-tural Diversity Committee?"

"I did, sir," Jodenny said.

"Be sure you attend all the meetings. Smile and make sure you say the right things."

She couldn't help herself. "Don't you approve of the cul-tural diversity, sir?"

He gave her a dour look. "I think we have too much cultural diversity, Lieutenant. What Team Space needs is more unity and less celebration of every single difference between us."

"A nice enemy to fight would be helpful, too," Zarkesh added. "A hundred years in space and still not a single alien to shoot at."

Al-Banna harrumphed. "What about the Hail and Farewell?"

Vu said, "I'm helping getting it organized. Jodenny and six others are getting hailed, and five are getting farewelled. The captain wants it on the Flight Deck."

"How special." Wildstein gave Jodenny a pointed glance.

Rokutan spoke up. "I've got a question. What are we doing about getting people qualified? All of my assistants are pulling watches, but I never see Hultz, Sanchez, or Ysten on the schedule."

"We need a training officer," Vu said. "Every department's supposed to have someone who reports to Commander Calinder."

Silence for a moment. Jodenny kept her head down. She'd risked enough with the cultural diversity question. The last thing she needed was to be put in charge of shepherding whiny ensigns through their qualifications.

"I'll do it," Wildstein said, with a martyr's sigh.

"No, Lieutenant Scott will do it," Al-Banna said. "Meeting's over. Go get some work done."

Jodenny considered a protest—Training Officer would be her eighth or ninth collateral duty—but Al-Banna was already leaving with Wildstein on his heels. The rest of them stood and gathered their gibs. Zarkesh asked, "Where did you come up with that bit about the data closet?"

"I worked in Maintenance for a year," she replied. "It took us weeks to figure out the wardroom problem."

"If that's it, I'll buy you dinner."

Vu squeezed Jodenny's arm. "Not before I take her to lunch. Women in this department have to stick together."

Rokutan introduced himself with a warm, firm handshake. "Congratulations. I did Underway Stores on my last ship. Come over to Flight sometime, and I'll show you around."

Jodenny felt suddenly shy. "I will."

Back in Underway Stores, Nitta and Caldicot were slogging through the AT evals. Jodenny scanned their preliminary list and asked, "Where's Ishikawa's?"

"She's only been onboard for three months," Caldicot said.

"We still have to grade her," Jodenny said.

"No, ma'am," Nitta said. "There was an all-fleet message that changed the eval requirements. You must have missed it."

Jodenny shut her mouth. The *Yangtze* tragedy hadn't stopped the flow of rules, regulations, and assorted electronic paperwork in Team Space—it had merely caused it to hiccup for a few minutes. "Send me a copy of the message for my records," she said. "Good work on getting these evals done. Mrs. Mullaly?"

"Yes, Lieutenant?" The American aide appeared at the hatch wearing a bright blue sweater. Her wardrobe, Jodenny had decided, consisted entirely of slacks and blue sweaters.

"I picked up another collateral duty. Can you set up a folder for Training Officer and pull the watch qualifications on all the officers and chiefs in the Supply Department?"

Mrs. Mullaly looked blank for a moment. "You mean like Fire Watch, Security Watch, those things?"

"Yes, but those are junior watches," Jodenny said. "Chiefs and officers pull different ones—Assistant Officer of the Watch, Officer of the Watch, Assistant Command Duty Officer, or Command Duty Officer. We usually stand them on the bridge, but sometimes in Drive or Flight."

"I don't understand why everyone has so many extra duties," Mrs. Mullaly said.

Nitta said, "Too much work and not enough people."

Fifteen minutes later VanAmsal and Strayborn showed up for the meeting Jodenny had told Caldicot to arrange. VanAmsal reminded Jodenny of Dyanne in some ways—same height, same neatly coiled braids—but unlike Dyanne, humorless and stern.

"Is this going to take long, Lieutenant?" VanAmsal jerked her head to the window that overlooked LD-G. "I hate to leave them on their own for too long."

"It takes as long as it takes," Jodenny said.

Nitta asked, "Should we meet in your office or mine?"

"Mine, just as soon as Sergeant Myell arrives."

Nitta blinked. "Why Myell?"

"He's a sergeant in this division, isn't he?" Jodenny turned to Caldicot. "Didn't you notify him?"

Caldicot shot Nitta a quick glance. "I didn't know you meant Myell, too."

"He's not in charge of anything," VanAmsal said.

Strayborn said, "I'll ping him, Lieutenant."

Ten minutes later Myell showed up, obviously bewildered at being included. When the five of them sat in Jodenny's office, Strayborn sat beside Myell but VanAmsal turned so that she couldn't see him. Nitta didn't look at any of them as Jodenny ran through the list of concerns she'd prepared: the late COSALs, the requisition backlog, the outdated MSSL, RIP drops, poor FIFO methods, inaccurate Q-Cost logs.

"I realize the division is undermanned," she said. "After the Alcheringa drop, we're going to have to look at some organizational changes. Maybe I can get us more people, or we can move shift positions around."

Strayborn leaned forward. "It's not how many people we have, it's how good they are. Some aren't pulling their weight. Kevwitch is in the brig more often than he's out of it. Lund spends all of his time in Sick Berth. Dyatt's good but she can't work on the dock—"

"She does fine in the command module," VanAmsal said.

"Soon you're going to lose her to maternity leave," Strayborn continued, undeterred. "Gallivan's leaving without a replacement. We're supposed to have twenty-five people, we're at twenty-two right now, and that'll leave us with twenty. Nineteen if I get picked up for ECP—"

"*If* you get it," VanAmsal said.

Staffing was always a problem, and Jodenny had expected it to top their list of complaints. She watched as VanAmsal and Strayborn bickered back and forth. Nitta wore a distracted expression, as if he was trying to remember something he'd forgotten to do. Myell intently studied his gib.

"I'll talk to Commander Al-Banna about getting more people," Jodenny said. "In the meantime, we deal with what we've got."

VanAmsal said, "Caldicot could be reassigned. You don't need two administrative assistants, do you, Lieutenant?"

She heard the challenge in VanAmsal's tone. "I don't know.

It's a possibility. Maybe AM Dyatt could come up here to work, or you could take over T6 if Sergeant Strayborn gets promoted."

Myell blinked. VanAmsal's face tightened and she said, "I like where I work."

"Everyone should start thinking about possible changes," Jodenny said. "Now, what else is a problem besides staffing?"

VanAmsal complained about erroneous requisitions and difficulties getting Core to reboot malfunctioning DNGOs. Strayborn added the problem of too many ship's departments demanding priority placement on their orders. Nitta bitched about last-minute paperwork that Data kept dumping into the queues, which VanAmsal agreed was a problem. Strayborn opined that too many low-bid contractors were delivering shoddy goods that wore out faster than usual and required unexpected replacements.

"What about you, Sergeant Myell?" Jodenny asked. "Do you agree with all that?"

Myell folded the cover on his gib and fixed his gaze on a spot behind Jodenny's head. "Departments keep requesting priority routing because our backlog is so bad they think routine ones will get overlooked. We can't stop some admiral's aide somewhere from putting out a data call—all we can do is answer as quickly and accurately as possible. Contractors are something else we have no control over. And Core's so overburdened that it's no wonder it takes an hour to reboot one dingo."

The temperature in the room dropped several degrees, but Jodenny kept her eyes on Myell. "So what do you recommend?"

He shrugged, as if it wasn't really his problem after all.

Jodenny tried to hide her disappointment. "Let's focus on what we can control and fix it. Make sure your people are in the correct uniform of the day. Counsel them if they're late, rude to customers, or slacking off. Make sure they're studying for their exams or working toward qualifications. Don't bitch in front of them, don't let them bitch in front of you, and make sure they know you care about them, this division, and this ship. What we say in here stays in here; you're the leaders of Underway Stores, and you need to be one hundred and ten percent professional."

The dirty look VanAmsal shot Myell as they stood to go was anything but professional and Strayborn was noticeably silent. Jodenny didn't worry too much about their hurt feelings but did say, "Sergeant Myell. Hold on a minute."

When they were alone she said, "I expect you to set a good example. Your tardiness to quarters this morning shouldn't be repeated."

"Yes, ma'am."

"Did you oversleep?"

"No," he said. "It won't happen again."

Jodenny waited for him to say more, but it was clear he wasn't going to elaborate. "Very well. Carry on."

Holland spoke up, reminding her that she still had to work on her check-in list. Jodenny went up to Safety, where a department rep signed off her gib with the instruction to read all the procedures in Core and contact her with any questions. The Morale Department was closed for a luncheon. Jodenny took the opportunity to grab a bite to eat at a snack bar. From there she went to Security, where sad-faced Sergeant Polson stared at her MacBride Cross and advised her about staying out of restricted areas such as Operations and Tower 14.

"What's in T14?" Jodenny asked.

"It's a penal colony. Four hundred convicts on their way to Warramala."

He was still staring at her MacBride Cross.

"Is something wrong, Sergeant?"

"No, ma'am. My sister—well, she died."

In the explosion. Or maybe later, from burns or injuries. Jodenny said, "I'm sorry."

"Maybe you knew her? Pamela Polson. She worked in Drive."

Jodenny hadn't known her. She fled Polson's grief and was standing at the lift when another Security sergeant approached her. "Lieutenant? I'm Sergeant Rosegarten. I wanted to explain about this morning."

"What about this morning?" Jodenny asked.

Rosegarten grimaced. "I told Lieutenant Commander Senga that there was nothing more to the case. Things disappear on this ship all the time. But he has this thing, ever since Fortune. He wanted to ask the questions himself. So it was our fault Myell was late."

It took Jodenny a moment to figure out exactly what Rosegarten meant, and another few minutes to get the whole story. She almost stormed over to Senga's office to confront him, but decided to let her temper cool first. Besides which, she couldn't figure out who she was more angry with—Senga for pulling such a stunt, or Myell for not telling her. Muttering, Jodenny went down to the E-Deck gym, which was equipped with a swimming pool, sauna, steam rooms, cardiovascular and weight equipment, and three studios for yoga, aerobics, and martial arts.

The energetic civilian at the front desk said, "Most of the officers prefer to use the officers' gym, ma'am. It's about half the size, and there's no pool. But then you don't have to mingle with anybody but other officers."

"I'll be fine down here," Jodenny said.

She had saved the worst for last. The instant she stepped inside Sick Berth, the faint smell of antiseptic swept her back to unhappy memories of Alice Naval Hospital. A medical tech with cold hands took her vital statistics and escorted her to a cubicle to wait for Lieutenant Moody, the physician on duty. Jodenny couldn't sit still on the exam table, so instead she studied the wallgib that listed the department ping numbers. Sick Berth serviced Team Space military personnel. Civvie employees, passengers, and family members used the hospital over in T1. She was amusing herself by memorizing names when a lieutenant with gray hair entered.

"I'm Mitchell Moody. Nice to meet you."

"New to the service?" Jodenny asked. Team Space often recruited civvie doctors to fill the ranks of its medical corps.

He chuckled. "You can tell in two seconds?"

"Your insignia is upside down."

Moody patted the item. "One day I'll get this all right. How's your leg doing?"

"Only hurts when I laugh."

"Why don't you scoot up there on that table?" Moody ran a scanner over her thigh. "Still giving you twinges?"

"Not really."

"Your chart says you weren't sleeping well at Alice. How's that now?"

"Better."

"Any other complaints or concerns?"

"No."

Moody shut off the scanner and asked, "Do you always become monosyllabic when the topic is your well-being?"

" 'Better' has two syllables in it," Jodenny said. Moody raised his eyebrows. She added, "I don't like to talk about my injuries. They're all healed now."

"Do you know we have several other *Yangtze* survivors on-board? I'm starting a support group that meets twice a week. Sometimes it helps to talk to other people who went through the same thing."

"We all went through something different." Some people had escaped in their lifepods without incident. Others had been trapped for days until collapsed decks could be pulled apart. Jodenny preferred not to dwell on her own experiences extinguishing fires, freeing trapped victims, and ushering the wounded to safety despite her own injuries. Much of it was a jumble anyway. She had only done what she was supposed to do, what any officer should have done. And afterward, what she had done in the hospital—well, that wasn't going to ever happen again.

"Keep the invitation in mind," Moody said. "That's all I ask."

On her way out of Sick Berth, Jodenny was met by a civvie with a Science Corps patch on his arm. He was young and earnest, with Asian features and long dark hair held back in a ponytail.

"Lieutenant Scott?" he asked. "I'm Dr. Ng. I've been trying

to reach you. Space Sciences Department. I wanted to sit down with you for ten or fifteen minutes."

"About what?"

"The *Yangtze*. I could buy you lunch or dinner—"

"Dr. Ng, I can't help you."

Jodenny moved away. *How does it feel, having survived the death of your friends and crewmates?* the reporters on Kookaburra had asked. *What's it like to face death in the line of duty?* She considered herself lucky that base security had kept the media away, and that their imail inquiries had dwindled to a trickle.

Ng followed her, saying, "I have a theory about the accident—"

It was hard to keep her voice even. "It wasn't an accident, Doctor. It was the deliberate destruction of Team Space personnel and property by the Colonial Freedom Project." And of that, what could she say? She'd never given much credence to separatists. Any colony that thought it could do without Team Space was crazy. The explosion proved that the separatists were not just crazy, but also more dangerous than anyone ever expected. She hoped that the people responsible were apprehended and sent to prison for the rest of their miserable lives. "I have nothing more to say about it."

She started up a crew ladder. To his credit, Ng didn't follow. On the next deck Jodenny stopped to rest her burning face against the bulkhead. When she could breathe easier she boarded a tram and headed straight for T6's gloomy silence.

Myell met her at the bottom of the lift and asked, "Can I help you, ma'am?"

"No, Sergeant." With horror Jodenny realized that she wanted to bury her head against his neck and let his comforting arms hold her tight. She told herself it was a natural response to stress and not specific to Myell himself. "I just came to check out something."

Jodenny climbed up to level one and sat on the cold deck with her back against a storage bin. The slots had always been Jem's favorite retreat when he needed to get away from it all.

"Lieutenant?" Myell's voice drifted up the ladder.

"What is it, Sergeant?"

"I locked down the level for you."

She had forgotten. Easy way to get killed, that. Some DNGO on a mission from Core might career around the corner and flatten her like a pancake. "Thank you, Sergeant."

His footsteps receded. Maybe he would forget she was there. She could hide forever in the lower slots, foraging for food out of the galley supplies, sleeping on mattresses destined for crew quarters. She would recruit the DNGOs to serve her and create her own private autocracy in the dark fortress of T6.

Or she could wait awhile until she felt strong enough to face them all—Al-Banna, Wildstein, Dr. Ng, Osherman, ghosts, the Wondjina.

A kingdom of DNGOs sounded better.

Myell wondered what Jodenny could possibly be doing up there. He tried to concentrate on Leto, a Class II with a broken video relay. He popped in a new one and tested the unit, but the display still came up fuzzy. For a half hour he fiddled with it, listening for any stray sounds from level one. His only interruption was a call from Chang.

"Did you get it?" Myell asked.

"Working on it. You sure you want top-of-the-line?"

"Absolutely." If he was going to get a pocket server with built-in audio and video sensors, he might as well splurge.

Chang promised to do his best. He was the division's go-to guy, able to procure any number of legal and illegal items on the ship. Not Sweet or other illegal drugs, but computer equipment was his specialty. After Chang hung up, VanAmsal pinged from Loading Dock G.

"You left a message?" VanAmsal asked.

"Is Dyatt with you?"

"No. She's on watch. Why?"

"I heard she was having problems with Olsson."

VanAmsal glared across the link. "You stay out of my division, Myell."

"I will if you take care of your people," he said.

If she could have reached through the screen she would have probably strangled him. "Got the lieutenant wrapped around your finger and now you think you're running things, is that it?"

"She's not wrapped anywhere," Myell said. "I don't want to see Dyatt get hurt."

"Like Ford?" VanAmsal asked, and cut out before he could answer.

Myell had expected her to be annoyed after the meeting in Jodenny's office, but the strength of her bitterness caught him off guard. He hadn't asked to be invited and it had been a surprise when Jodenny took his opinions seriously. In retrospect he supposed he should have told her about Lieutenant Commander Senga, but what had Senga said? Jodenny had raised suspicion first. It was her fault, then, that he'd been late to quarters and set a bad example.

Despite his disappointment and resentment over that, he couldn't bear the silence anymore. Myell went over to the ladder and asked, "Miz Scott?"

Her boots appeared on the top rung. Myell moved aside so she could climb down.

"Everything looks good," she said, as if she'd been conducting an impromptu inspection. Her eyes were slightly red but her voice was calm. "What are you working on?"

"Repairs. Nothing too urgent."

Jodenny started walking toward his bench. "The SUPPO asked about the missing dingo. What do you think happened to it?"

He worked hard not to sound defensive. "I don't know."

"Is that what you told Security?"

She wasn't looking at him. Myell folded his arms. "You talked to them."

"I talked to Sergeant Rosegarten. When I see Mr. Senga, I'm going to tell him that under no circumstances is he ever to question members of my division without letting me know."

Myell was confused. "No. I mean, you told Lieutenant Commander Senga that you suspected me. That's why he called me in."

"Sergeant, if I had suspected you of anything, you would have heard it from me."

Abashed, he said, "Yes, ma'am. I'm sorry I didn't tell you about it this morning."

"Why didn't you?"

He shrugged.

Jodenny peered down at the DNGO on his bench. "What's the story on this one?"

Myell was grateful that she'd changed the subject. "This is Leto. She has a broken relay."

"Did you name all the dingoes?"

"Not me. There was a chief who was working here when I first came into the division. Chief Mustav. He did it." Myell showed her the inscription underneath Leto's registration tag. "The repair techs hate them and keep scrubbing them out."

She ran her fingers over Leto's hull. "I used to help fix these."

Myell offered her a wrench. "Be my guest."

For the first time since he'd known her, she smiled. Myell liked her smile. It made her eyes less haunted and brought color to her cheeks.

"Maybe later," she said.

"Anytime. It's usually just me and the dingoes down here— your secret will be safe."

So would her other secret. If she wanted to come down and cry in the slots, that was nothing that had to be shared with the rest of the ship. Because of the separation in their ranks he would never be able to comfort her, but he could protect her in at least that small way.

Jodenny gave him a speculative look. "When do you take the chief's exam?"

"I'm not." Myell took the wrench back and plugged the broken relay into a testing unit. "I wasn't recommended for promotion on my last evaluation."

"You'll get a new eval in a few months."

"I'm getting out at the end of this contract."

"If you make chief, you might change your mind."

Damn her for making him say it. "There was an accusation."

She didn't blink. "Was it true?"

"No."

Jodenny stared at him for a long moment. He guessed she would take Ford's side. She had no choice, really. When a young woman cried rape she always got the benefit of the doubt, and whoever had his pants down at the time was guilty as charged. But then Jodenny said, "I believe you," and something that had been frozen inside him began to thaw.

"Thank you," Myell said. And there, he felt it again; sadness that they would never be able to get to know each other the way a man and a woman could, regret that rank would always keep them separated. He would have to work hard to keep his feelings locked away, but he was accustomed to that. A starship was no place to share one's heart.

"Take the chief's exam," Jodenny said. "You never know what's going to happen."

"Yes, ma'am," he said, but just to see her smile again.

CHAPTER NINE

Forty-eight hours before the *Aral Sea* dropped into the Alcheringa, Jodenny called Commander Calinder and explained she'd been tasked to be the watchbill training officer for the Supply Department.

"Good luck to you," Calinder said. "I turned the job over to Commander Osherman last week."

"Thank you, sir. I'll contact him." Jodenny hung up and buried her head in her arms. After several minutes she mustered enough strength to ping Osherman.

"Jodenny," he said when he answered his gib.

"I've taken over junior officer training for the Supply Department. I didn't know you were in charge of the program."

"I'll send you the meeting schedule."

"Thank you, sir."

"Jo—" Osherman leaned closer to the vid. She remembered the tenderness of his touch, the way he sighed sometimes in his sleep. "Are you sure you're ready to be back in space?"

"As ready as you are, Commander," she said, and cut the connection. Her health and well-being certainly hadn't been a priority for him when he had so abruptly broken off their relationship on the *Yangtze*. She was still glaring at the comm when Caldicot pinged her to say Lund had arrived. He came into her office with a pained expression.

"Ma'am. You wanted to talk to me?"

"Sit, sit," Jodenny insisted. "I'm worried about you. You've been to Sick Berth twelve times this month."

"Irritable bowel syndrome. Chronic indigestion. My headaches—you wouldn't believe my headaches."

She offered him a bottle of water from her refrigerator. "It's criminal that none of the doctors onboard have helped you."

Lund looked pitiful. "They try, ma'am."

Jodenny shook her head. "They're not doing enough. I'm going to complain to Commander Al-Banna on your behalf. The staff is obviously incompetent."

"I wouldn't go that far, ma'am. They do a lot of tests."

"Tests are nothing without results. I've scheduled you to see some specialists at Fleet when we get to Mary River. And if they can't help, specialists on Warramala. Everywhere we go, I want you to see physicians until we get you proper treatment."

Lund's face was almost comically indecisive. "*Everywhere* we go?"

"Everywhere," Jodenny said. "And every test there is, every procedure, no matter how arduous—you need to undergo it."

"Arduous?" he squeaked out.

"But this is the hard part, AT Lund. Even though you're ill, even though you may not feel your best, I need you in this division. We're falling apart without people like you who know how to do their jobs. Will you promise me that you'll do your best to come to work, even though you might feel ill?"

"I'll try, ma'am," he said, his voice faint.

"Good," Jodenny replied. "Thank you."

Twenty-four hours before the countdown to the Alcheringa expired, Jodenny pinged Ensign Sanchez in Ship's Services and said, "Commander Al-Banna put me in charge of watch-bill training. We're having a meeting tonight, at twenty hundred hours, in the wardroom. Why don't you come to dinner first?"

That night the wardroom table was full. Sanchez, a dour older woman with a pin for prior enlisted service, had joined the usual complement of Hultz, Francesco, Zeni, Ysten, and Weaver. Also joining them was the ever-talkative Cally Gunther, who dug into roasted eggplant and papita.

"I should eat here more often," he said around a mouthful of food.

"I hear you've been working out at the main gym, Jodenny," Zeni said. "Didn't anyone tell you there's an officers' gym on F-Deck?"

"Isn't E-Deck bigger? More equipment." And less chance of running into Osherman, Jodenny thought.

"Aren't you worried about being all sweaty in front of your troops?" Hultz asked.

Francesco smiled. "I think it's a fine idea. If more division officers worked out with their crews, there might be fewer people in the obesity program."

After coffee and dessert, Jodenny gathered Hultz, Gunther, Sanchez, and Ysten in the lounge. She said, "The four of you are all overdue on your watch qualifications."

"I've tried, honest!" Hultz protested.

Ysten had obviously not forgiven her for the Dicensu incident. With a sneer he said, "It's hard getting the quals done when you have other duties, Lieutenant."

"I understand," Jodenny said. "That's why we're going to help each other. Every night after dinner we're going to get together right here and study. The only time you're excused is if you're on a training watch—I'll schedule you for those—or you're in Sick Berth."

Sanchez folded her arms. "I've got a husband and kids in the Towers. My evenings are for spending with them, not studying here."

"As soon as you get qualified, you go on the watchbill. Then your evenings will be up to the watchbill coordinator."

Sanchez stood up. "I'm going to talk to Lieutenant Commander Vu."

"Sit down, Ensign," Jodenny ordered. After a moment Sanchez sat with a glower. Jodenny continued. "Any of your division officers can call me tomorrow if they have any questions. In the meantime, I've pulled the quals each of you still have to finish, as well as my own. Let's take a look."

Four hours before they reached the Alcheringa, Jodenny got out of the bed in which she'd spent most of the night staring at the overhead. She brought coffee to the security guards on duty at the base of T6.

"Thank you, ma'am. There's nothing to report here." That came from Polson, whose sister had died on the *Yangtze*. He had volunteered for this duty. It had been the captain's decision, to tighten security and cancel normal routine in T6 as the *Aral Sea* made her final approach. Jodenny didn't agree with the fuss, but she didn't disagree, either.

Ten minutes later the Security Officer, Commander Picariello, made his appearance. He had a noble face of Mediterranean ancestry and mismatched eyes. One was bright blue, like a robin's egg. The other was as brown as milk chocolate.

"How are you holding up, Lieutenant?" Picariello asked.

"I'll be a lot happier once we're in the Alcheringa," she admitted. "How about you, sir?"

"You can tell yourself there's no way the CFP could have planted anything onboard—and I'm here to guarantee it—but I wouldn't want to be the CO right now." Picariello made sure none of the guards were within eavesdropping range. "I heard you had a discussion with Lieutenant Commander Senga. A rather energetic discussion."

"Yes, sir," Jodenny said. *Discussion* was a polite way of labeling it. She had clearly articulated what she thought of him whisking Myell away before regular working hours for an impromptu interrogation. He had expressed his adamant belief that Myell was guilty as hell of rape and theft. Only the presence of Sergeant Rosegarten had kept things civil.

"I'll be keeping my eye on things," Picariello said. "Call me if you have any more problems."

Three hours before the *Aral Sea* was scheduled to drop, Mrs. Mullaly came into Jodenny's office and burst into tears.

"What if something goes wrong?" she asked.

Jodenny handed her a tissue. "Nothing's going to go wrong. One minute we'll be in normal space, and the next we won't. It's like dropping a stone into a river."

Mrs. Mullaly blew her nose. "Sure. That's what they all say. When we left Fortune, I thought it was hardly worth the fuss. You wouldn't even notice if you weren't looking out a porthole. But it went wrong for the *Yangtze*, right? It could go wrong again."

"That was because of the CFP, not the Alcheringa," Jodenny said. "The Wondjina built it very carefully. If we don't approach the drop point at the right speed and trajectory, we just keep going in normal space."

Mrs. Mullaly seemed satisfied by Jodenny's explanation, although her nose was still dripping as she returned to her desk. Jodenny almost gave her the rest of the day off, but most offices and services were open for business and every department was under orders to maintain routine. She checked her queue for messages. No one had sent her anything in the last ten minutes. Jodenny reviewed the minutes of the Garden and Soil Committee twice before realizing none of the words were making any sense. When she scanned for the wreck of the *Yangtze,* it was too far out of range to display.

Her gib beeped. "Scott, this is Al-Banna."

"Yes, sir?"

"Report to the CO's briefing room on C-Deck."

What had she done wrong? "Sir?"

Al-Banna didn't mask the displeasure in his voice. "Now, Lieutenant."

Jodenny hurried to the lift.

* * *

Because T6 was closed, Nitta told Myell to make himself useful in IR4 by helping Mauro straighten out his logs. The issue room had seen better days, but after a few hours of Mauro working the counter and Myell matching receipts, a small modicum of order was restored.

"You've got to stay on top of this stuff," Myell said.

"I try," Mauro said, "but it's a lot of work."

Myell checked the clock. Just about an hour until they dropped into the Alcheringa. He wondered how Lieutenant Scott was holding up under the pressure. He was trying to invent a pretext for visiting her office when Nitta pinged and said, "Mauro, get down here to LD-G and explain what the hell kind of COSAL you sent VanAmsal yesterday."

Mauro grimaced. "Yes, Chief."

Business died down after Mauro left, and Myell started restacking boxes of boots. He heard a shuffle behind him but swung around too late to prevent someone's fist from driving into his side. The shock of it drove the breath from his lungs and sent him to his knees. Surging sideways, he tackled his attacker at the waist and knocked him against the shelves. Spallone. The bastard. A second attacker grabbed Myell's shoulders, dragged him backward, and threw him facedown to the deck. A terrible weight pressed against his spine.

"Stay out of Olsson's business," Engel said, malicious glee in his voice.

Spallone crouched low beside Myell. "You make the same fucking mistake over and over, Myell. Curiosity killed the—"

"Medbot activate!" Myell ordered.

The flying robot swooped in to be of assistance. While Engel's attention was momentarily distracted, Myell bucked him off. Spallone made a grab for him, and the two of them slammed against the shelves again. A sharp pain spiraled along Myell's left ribs but he kept swinging his fist at Spallone's face.

"Hey! What's going on in there?" someone shouted.

"Fuck off!" Spallone said.

Three apprentice mates burst into the issue room and separated them. Spallone's nose was bleeding, Engel had cut his head against a shelf, and Myell's right hand throbbed as if he'd been hitting a brick wall. The medbot fluttered in indecision before zeroing in on Spallone.

"Please stand still," it said to him.

Spallone twisted away. "Get the fuck away."

AM Loudermilk, baby-faced and indignant, asked, "You hurt, Sarge?"

Spallone tried to free himself from Loudermilk's grip. "You should goddamn mind your own business."

"You want us to call Security?" Hoefer asked.

"No," Myell said. "They're not going to cause any more trouble."

It wasn't true, but it was expedient. Spallone and Engel shrugged themselves free and left the issue room. The apprentice mates gave Myell reproachful looks. He knew that in their eyes he was chickenshit, a coward, one damn poor excuse for a sergeant.

"Did you have some requisitions?" he asked, ducking his head.

Loudermilk answered for all of them. "Nah, we'll come back later."

His rescuers departed. Myell locked the door that Mauro had neglected to secure and closed the gate on the counter. He sat on a stool in the back until the worst of the shakes passed and he could hold his hands steady. When Mauro came back he didn't say anything about the closed gate or Myell's disheveled condition.

"Chief said you can go back to T6 once we drop into the Alcheringa," Mauro said, his eyes averted.

"Yeah." Myell slipped a hand into his pocket and touched the thin, flat server that had recorded the whole incident. "I bet he did."

The captain's briefing room was guarded by a security tech who opened the hatch for Jodenny. Once inside she saw several high-ranking officers and civilians as well as Chaplain Mow and Osherman. Most people were picking food from a buffet table or sipping morning cocktails. The ship's Executive Officer, Commander Larrean, came over to introduce himself.

"Sorry I wasn't available when you checked onboard." He was a short man with round checks and a kind smile. "I'm glad you could come this morning."

"Does the captain throw a party every time we drop, sir?" Jodenny asked.

Larrean's smile widened. "Not always. Let me show you around."

She shook hands with the governor of an Aboriginal colony in T9, the warden of the penal tower, and the Bishop of Baiame, who was returning from the Vatican on Fortune. Larrean didn't tell them she'd been on the *Yangtze,* but more than one gaze lingered on her MacBride Cross. When she couldn't bring herself to mingle anymore she stood by the vids and looked at the stars. The Alcheringa was out there, invisible, twisting, waiting to carry them down the line or herald their destruction.

Osherman appeared at her elbow. "I heard you're shaking up Underway Stores."

Jodenny deliberately kept her gaze on the vid. "I held a uniform inspection. That's as far as shaking up goes."

His voice was dry. "Challenging the status quo on this ship might not be the wisest course of action to take."

"What would you suggest? Leaving things the way they are?"

"There's some benefit in keeping under the radar."

"It doesn't benefit my people," she replied.

"If you can't be persuaded, at least take care," Osherman said. "The stress can pile up on you in ways you don't expect, make you do things you regret later."

The hairs on Jodenny's neck stood up. Her records were sealed. No one but Commander Campos was supposed to know what had happened. She turned to him and said, "I never saw you at Alice. Weren't you there for temp duty?"

"Only on paper. Mostly I was doing odd jobs over at Fleet."

He stared at the vid. "It's not going to happen again, you know."

Their relationship or an explosion? The first was a given, but the second was still to be determined. Osherman drifted off to mingle. With ten minutes left on the clock, Jodenny rehearsed the number and location of her lifepod. She plotted a mental map on how she was going to get there. She watched the countdown clock and realized that she should be with her people, wherever they were. She turned to tell Larrean she was leaving but he was deep in conversation with a commander from Drive. Why wasn't he on the bridge, where he belonged? Why weren't they all already in their lifepods, ready to launch?

Chaplain Mow caught her gaze and came straight over. "Don't worry. Dropping into the Alcheringa is as routine as brushing your teeth."

"It wasn't last time I did it." Jodenny started to shake. "We should go to our lifepods."

Chaplain Mow steered Jodenny back to the vids. "What do you see out there?"

"Nothing."

"*Focus,* Lieutenant."

The snap in Mow's voice helped. "The universe," Jodenny replied.

"Imagine Jackie MacBride and her crew on that first accidental slide down the Little Alcheringa. One minute they're approaching Mars and then—nothing! Sensors dead, no external data. They had no idea of what had happened or where they were going. Did they panic?"

"No."

"But as far as they knew, they were already dead."

"She held them together."

"How?" Chaplain Mow asked.

"Faith." Jodenny took a steadying breath. Back at the academy, the cadets had been required to read the crew logs from that fateful trip. Books, movies, and popular songs had immortalized the story. A picture of Jackie MacBride had hung in her room for years. "Discipline."

"And what happened?"

"They reached Fortune, turned around, and came home safely."

Chaplain Mow smiled. "As will we."

The countdown expired. Without any sense of transition at all, the ship dropped into the stream and the vids went dark.

"We're in," Chaplain Mow said, and gave her a friendly squeeze around the shoulders.

In. On the circuit. Sliding down the Big Alcheringa. And alive, for now.

CHAPTER TEN

Myell's gib beeped late the night the ship dropped into the Alcheringa.

"I'm sorry they hurt you," Shevi Dyatt said, her eyes puffy. "Ish shouldn't have said anything. Forget it, okay?"

Timrin was on watch again. Myell sat in the darkness with three pillows wedged behind his sore back and over-the-counter painkillers taking the edge off. On the desk, near a heat lamp, Koo amused herself in her splendid terrarium. He wondered how old Dyatt was—eighteen, nineteen?—and asked, "Is Olsson giving you problems?"

Dyatt wiped her nose. "I don't want anyone else to get in trouble. I'll be okay."

Christ, to be so young and so alone on a ship of five thousand people. He tried to remember where her cabin was. Past the lounge, past Gallivan's place, near the lift somewhere. Near Olsson and Spallone. "Are you safe right now?"

"I think so. They're at the shop."

"At this hour?"

"I can't tell Sergeant VanAmsal." Dyatt's shoulders hitched up as she started to cry. "And I can't tell Security, it'll just make it worse. I'm sorry you got hurt."

"Meet me in the lounge," he said. "Dress in civvies."

"But it's so late—"

"Just do it."

Ten minutes later, standing alone in the dirty lounge with his head throbbing, he wondered if she'd changed her mind. When she came down the passage she was dressed in trousers and a maternity soccer shirt. One of her hands clutched tissues.

"Where are we going?"

"Chaplain's office," he said.

"But I'm not religious."

"Doesn't matter. Everything you say will be confidential and they can't report any of it if you don't want them to."

He walked her up to C-Deck. The chapel adjacent was open twenty-four/seven, and while Dyatt sat trembling in a back row he pinged the Duty Chaplain.

"You don't have to put up with it," he said while they waited.

Dyatt averted her gaze. "I can take care of myself."

"Shevi—"

"You know what really sucks about being an apprentice mate?" she asked. "Everyone above you gives you orders you don't want to follow and advice you plain don't want."

Myell closed his mouth. The nondenominational chapel had been painted in soft pink and yellow tones and smelled like sandalwood. Myell didn't believe in holy places, especially in the middle of starships sliding down the dark void of the Alcheringa, but he had to admit that the colors and warm air soothed him, made him less skeptical about religion than usual. When Chaplain Mow arrived she looked sleepy but had a gentle expression on her face.

"I'll take it from here, Sergeant," she said as she led Dyatt toward her office. "Come back and visit sometime. It's been a while."

Myell nodded in acknowledgment but not promise. Back in his cabin he tried to sleep but rest was elusive, filled with Dyatt's tears and Spallone's fists and pain in his ribs every time he shifted on the bunk. What were Olsson and the others doing in the Repair Shop at such an hour? Long before ship's dawn he got up, checked his imail, and surfed the ship's message boards. A gym workout was out of the question but instead of going to T6 early he lingered on the Rocks. He didn't want to see Nitta, who had set him up for the altercation in the issue room. But he wasn't about to miss quarters, either. With just moments to spare he slipped into his spot in the back row. Dyatt's place was empty.

"AT Lund." Jodenny pulled Lund out of the lineup to confer off to the side.

"What's that about?" Gallivan asked in a loud whisper.

Jodenny asked Lund something. He shook his head, but she insisted and in a moment he was sitting in a chair that Ishikawa pulled over from Myell's workshop.

"Good grief," Chang said.

Lund sat unhappily in his chair as Jodenny returned to the front of the assembly.

"Listen up," Nitta said, reading from the plan of the day. "If you know a civvie looking for a job, have them contact Outsourcing during work hours. The Garden and Soil Committee's looking for volunteers and the MWR Department still has slots open for field trips on Mary River."

After standing in place for several minutes Myell's vision began to gray around the edges, but then quarters was over and he was free to go to his workbench. Gallivan followed him.

"Are you okay?" Gallivan asked.

"Never better." Myell pretended to be busy fixing a circuit tester.

"Why didn't you report it to Security?"

"Report what?"

"You were always stubborn, but I didn't think you were stupid."

"Leave it alone. When we get to Warramala you won't have to worry about a thing."

Gallivan grabbed his wrist and forced Myell to look at him. "You think you don't have mates here but that's not true. You shut us out."

"Let the fuck go," Myell said, and Gallivan released his grip.

Myell turned back to the DNGO and set to work on the access plate even though his hands were trembling. Maybe he did shut them out, but they'd shut him out first and some hurts were still too raw to be forgiven. He said, "I've got work to do."

Gallivan left with a muttered curse. Myell put down the screwdriver and closed his eyes at the approach of more footsteps.

"Myell," VanAmsal said. "What's going on with Dyatt?"

"How should I know?"

"Because you tried to tell me yesterday and I didn't listen."

"I don't know. Go ask her."

"Terry—" VanAmsal started, but when he didn't respond she too walked away. Finally, some peace. He sat on his stool and braced himself for the next visitor, Strayborn, who apparently shared the same grapevine as everyone else in the goddamned division.

"I heard you fell in the issue room," Strayborn said. "You should go to Medical."

"If I hear one more piece of advice I'm going to shove someone out an airlock," Myell said. "That's a promise, Gordon. So if you have some words of wisdom, if you think you know my situation better than I do, if you have some miracle cure for all the ills of this ship, do me a favor. Write a memo."

On her way to T6 that morning, Jodenny had received a ping from Chaplain Mow. Mow said, "I'd like for you to excuse AM Dyatt from quarters. She's with me."

"Is she all right?"

"She's going to be fine."

At quarters, Jodenny sensed an odd undercurrent in the division. Myell was grim-faced and VanAmsal seemed more tense than usual. Even Gallivan had lost his good humor.

"Sergeant Strayborn," she said after quarters was over. "Is something wrong?"

"Ma'am?" he asked.

"Something going on I should know about?"

"No, ma'am. Everything's fine."

He was probably lying, but Jodenny decided to let the situation stew until something arose out of it. She went up to the Rocks and to an apparel shop that sold sports shirts. The proprietor listened to her request and gave her a quote that didn't seem unreasonable.

"I'll get back to you," Jodenny said.

She trammed back to Mainship and tackled paperwork until the ASUPPO called her that afternoon. Jodenny went up to the Flats wondering what she had done to merit Wildstein's attention and found Master Chief DiSola in Wildstein's office.

"AM Dyatt is going to Ops," Wildstein said without preamble.

"Why?" Jodenny asked. "Is she unhappy with Underway Stores?"

Master Chief DiSola said, "It's a department thing. I already let Chief Nitta know."

A department thing. Jodenny wondered how much Chaplain Mow had confided in either of them. She said, "I'll need a replacement. While we're at it, I could stand a few more ATs. Ship's Services is ten percent overmanned but I've got three billets empty."

"Take it up with Lieutenant Commander Vu," Wildstein said.

"I think I could reduce that backlog if—"

"That's all, Lieutenant."

"Actually, ma'am, I have a request. I'd like to use some official funds to buy shirts."

"Shirts?" Master Chief DiSola asked. "For who?"

"For my division."

Wildstein said, "They get a uniform allowance. Let them buy their own."

"I was thinking of something special, ma'am," Jodenny said. "Something to build unity. Maybe something with the Underway Stores logo on it."

DiSola laughed. "Underway Stores has a logo?"

"I don't care if it has a logo and a theme song." Wildstein

rose and grabbed a pile of folders. "You can't use ship's money for optional clothing."

Deterred but not undefeated, Jodenny went to LD-G and watched from the command module while VanAmsal supervised Amador and a small contingent of DNGOs. The sergeant stomped up to the module saying, "Lieutenant, this is ridiculous. Lund's in Sick Berth, Dyatt's not here, and I'm getting two hundred shipments an hour coming through."

"Pull Chang out of IR2," Jodenny said. "Gallivan can handle it alone. You're not getting Dyatt back—she's going to Ops. Any idea why?"

"How should I know? No one tells me anything."

"Take a moment and review your attitude, Sergeant."

"Lieutenant, I can't run my loading dock if you want to stand around and chitchat."

With an attitude like that, VanAmsal might soon not be running a loading dock at all. Jodenny said, "Why are you so angry, Sergeant? It's not Dyatt and it's not the shipments, so if it's me then we have a problem."

VanAmsal stormed out of the module. Jodenny watched her get halfway down the stairs before reason took hold. On the loading dock floor, Amador sent two DNGOs to the conveyer belt and shouted a question Jodenny couldn't hear over the rattle of machinery. VanAmsal waited another minute before doing an about-face and coming back.

"I apologize," she said with a face as hard as stone. "I was out of line."

Jodenny closed the hatch. "Tell me what's going on."

"I think Dyatt's been having trouble with her boyfriend. AT Olsson. Works in Maintenance. Myell tried to tell me about it but I wouldn't listen. She's a good kid and I haven't done right by her."

"Maybe you have or maybe you haven't. You'll have to ask her. What else?"

"I don't think you're handling the situation with Lund correctly. You can't coddle him, Lieutenant. It's what he wants."

"Observation noted. Next?"

A muscle spasmed in VanAmsal's cheek. "Lieutenant Commander Greiger had his faults but he didn't interfere down here."

"Maybe he didn't care as much as I do," Jodenny said.

"Lieutenant, caring is only going to end up making you disappointed. I've been here two years. I should know."

"I can deal with disappointment. So can you. It's the achievements we have to focus on."

VanAmsal shook her head. "Being short another person isn't an achievement. Hearing that I might be sent over to T6 isn't a big thrill either. You can't listen to everything Nitta and Strayborn tell you."

The shrill ring of a DCS alarm ground operations to a halt. Jodenny left VanAmsal and Amador to deal with breakdown and went to her office. She almost pinged Myell to ask what he knew of Dyatt's problems but decided she had enough of her own and simply forwarded the personnel file to Ops. When Nitta showed up she said, "You told me you were going to run a spot check on the agroparts. Where is it?"

"Still working on it, Lieutenant. You didn't say you were in a hurry."

She allowed herself an uncharitable thought or two about how he'd ever gotten promoted, which reminded her of something else he'd neglected. "Strayborn's got his hopes pinned on the ECP, but VanAmsal and Myell should be signing up for the chief's exam. Double-check that their paperwork is in order."

"I don't think encouraging Myell is a good idea."

"Why not?"

Nitta leaned back in his chair. Sweat gleamed on his forehead. "You know. He's had some problems. People on this ship have long memories."

So did she, and it occurred to her that Security had yet to route her a copy of the Loss Accounting report on the DNGO that had disappeared in Myell's care. She made herself a note to have Holland call over and get it.

"And he's not doing a spectacular job down there in T6," Nitta added. "There's been trouble with the dingoes. He tries to fix them himself and won't take them to Repair Services."

"Maybe he's trying to show some initiative."

"You're not thinking of doing anything rash, are you?" Nitta asked.

"Such as?"

"Like putting him in charge of anything. Morale will suffer if you started giving him preferential treatment."

"Make sure he signs up for the exam," was all Jodenny had to say. "I'll worry about morale."

Now that the ship was safely cruising the Alcheringa, Jodenny made a list of improvements to make in her division, and brainstormed several ideas on how to change the Supply wardroom for the better. In the meantime she set up an exercise schedule for herself and started working out before breakfast each morning.

After flipping through the treadmill hologram choices she settled on a tropical beach routine. Palm trees tipped toward her in the salty breeze and golden sand kicked up from her every step. The vista was supposed to represent the North Island on Fortune, but she could have just as well been on pristine Earth, back before it had been ruined. She heard birds and the pounding of the surf but as she passed the two-kilometer mark all else was quiet—no overhead announcements, no ATs clambering for her attention, and no indication whatsoever that she was really in the middle of the E-Deck gym.

At the five-kilometer mark an alarm pulsed against her wrist. She took off the hologram glasses and earphones, slowed the machine, and took a long sip of water.

"Lieutenant." Dr. Ng climbed on the treadmill beside her.

"Doctor." Jodenny plugged herself back into the program for another two kilometers. She pushed herself until her thigh started to ache in earnest. When she disengaged Ng was still there, red-faced and gasping as he attempted one of the more difficult inclines.

Jodenny stepped down. "You don't work out much."

Ng wiped his face. "I hoped that if we had something in common, you might talk to me."

She went off and showered in the women's locker room.

When she emerged, Ng was slumped on a bench with two water bottles in hand. He offered her one.

"Truce?" he asked. "I'm sorry if I upset you last time we met. I'm not some kind of ghoulish nut. I'm simply not convinced the *Yangtze* disaster was caused by the Colonial Freedom Project."

"I disagree." Jodenny made her way through the rows of machines to the exit, Ng at her heels.

He said, "The CFP haven't claimed responsibility, which they usually do. They had to know that destroying an entire freighter would harm their cause more than help it. The bad publicity will last for years to come. Team Space has yet to release any information on what kind of bomb was planted in the cargo hold, or explain how the CFP got around standard security. Those facts alone should make any reasonable person suspicious."

Jodenny pressed the lift button. "Information on the investigation is classified. People a lot smarter than you or I are working on it, and I'm sure they've considered those factors."

Ng's gaze was intense. "But perhaps it wasn't a bomb at all. I've been doing simulations, re-creating the *Yangtze*'s course and speed. The explosion occurred at a particular point in space that can be correlated back to a set of Wondjina Spheres on Kookaburra."

The damn lift was taking its time. "Correlated how?"

"There are fourteen triads of spheres on Kookaburra. That includes the ones at Point Elliot, just south of Alice Training Base. Like all Spheres, when mapped from center to center, they form a perfect triangle." Ng drew an imaginary line on the bulkhead. "If you extend a line from the center of that triangle to the coordinates of the Alcheringa drop point, it forms a track the *Yangtze* crossed at the same moment her tower number six exploded."

So he was one of those Wondjina conspiracy nuts, sure that the Spheres and Alcheringa were all part of a grandiose alien conspiracy to enslave mankind. That no actual aliens had ever been discovered was irrelevant to their belief system. The lift doors opened and Jodenny stepped inside with relief.

"Don't call me, Dr. Ng," she said. "Don't send me imail, don't come to this gym, don't even come near me on the mess deck. You're as crazy as any of the dingbats back on Kookaburra, maybe even more so, because you're supposed to be a scientist. If I hear from you again I'll file a complaint for harassment."

The doors closed on his crestfallen face, and she hoped that would be the last of him.

CHAPTER **ELEVEN**

Remember, Lieutenant," Holland said the next Saturday afternoon as Jodenny trammed over to the Rocks. "The wardroom Hail and Farewell begins in ninety minutes."

"I know." Jodenny had been considering ducking out on the affair, but as she disembarked and made her way across T6's access ring she couldn't think up a good excuse. Two hours, she promised herself: enough time to make an appearance, then escape back to the peace and quiet of her cabin.

Once in T6, she saw Strayborn and Hosaka upsynching in the command module. Someone in an EV suit was tugging a DNGO toward the docking cradle. Jodenny went straight down to the base. Lange, who was supposed to be manning the lower safety controls, was sitting with his feet up playing Izim.

"Miz Scott!" He pushed back and nearly caused the chair to fall over. "You scared me."

"Give me that gib."

Lange grimaced and did as ordered. She killed the program.

"Hey—" he said. "I mean, Miz Scott—that was my best game yet."

Jodenny said, "You can get this gib back after you go see Chief Nitta and get a counseling chit. Now go up to the control module and send someone else down here."

Lange stormed away. Jodenny pinged Nitta and told him what she'd done.

Nitta asked, "You sure that's a good idea, taking someone's gib away?"

"He'll get it back. When he comes to see you, tell him he has to write a five-hundred-word essay on 'Why I Shouldn't Play Games on Duty.' "

"Ma'am?"

"You heard me." Jodenny cut the connection.

Ishikawa came down from the command module wearing a wary expression. She saluted. "Ma'am!"

"AT Ishikawa, you don't salute onboard ship unless you're wearing your uniform cover. Where's Sergeant Myell?"

Ishikawa gestured upward. "One of the dingoes got stuck in the slots again."

Jodenny craned her head. She could barely see the glimmer of Myell's EV suit. "How are things going for you?"

"Ma'am?"

"Is your job what you expected it to be? Are you enjoying your off-duty time?"

"My job's okay, Lieutenant. I didn't really expect having to do so much drudge work. But don't get me wrong—it's better than a lot of other departments."

"And off-duty?"

Ishikawa shrugged.

"There's talk that you might be doing kasai."

"Oh, Lieutenant." Ishikawa rolled her eyes. "People say that because I go out a lot. There's nothing wrong with that, right? Sometimes my dates buy me stuff because they like me."

"That's more or less what kasai is all about."

Ishikawa turned bashful. "Lieutenant, it's not like that."

"It's not against regulations to do it," Jodenny said, "but people will still look askance at it. Think about the long-term consequences to your career."

"Oh, I don't plan on having a career," Ishikawa said earnestly. "I'm getting out of Team Space as soon as my contract's up. Who would want to do this all their life?"

Jodenny watched Myell's efforts to retrieve the lost DNGO for as long as possible. His communications were terse and unhappy-sounding. She wondered if he was the kind who got nervous in the slots. Finally she went back to her cabin, dressed in her formal uniform, and trudged over to the Flight Deck. Lines of birdies and Fox fighters had been neatly parked against the bulkheads to make room for banquet tables, three large buffets, two wet bars, and a deejay. The launch doors were closed and decorated with flags and streamers. Most of the ship's four hundred officers were already circulating with wine and hors d'oeuvres in hand. Music played from the Flight Ops booth overhead. Francesco, Zeni, Hultz, and Weaver were admiring a large blue and gold cake.

"It's about time you showed up, Jodenny," Zeni said. "We thought you had a hot date."

"With who?" Jodenny asked.

Hultz smiled. "How about Commander Rokutan? He's very cute, though maybe not so smart."

"All elbows and knees." Weaver sipped from her wineglass. "How about the SUPPO? Man of mystery—"

"Enough," Jodenny said. The last thing she needed was a rumor of anything between her and Al-Banna, who had a wife living over in T2. Rokutan was a different matter, though. His awkwardness was appealing, those elbows and knees charming. Funny how a man so fluid on the soccer field could be so klutzy off it.

Hultz gave her a wicked grin. "Quenger."

"More than enough," Jodenny warned.

"Where is our Davy boy lately?" Zeni asked. "He's hardly ever around."

Weaver shrugged. "I think he's still dating that teacher."

Zeni lifted some sushi from a tray. "I think he's still sulking over not getting Greiger's job."

Quenger showed up a half hour later and circulated through the room, shaking hands and slapping shoulders. He didn't look like he was sulking at all. Jodenny stayed by the bar and sipped her beer. The old Jodenny—the predisaster Jodenny, her younger and untainted self—would have been eager to make friends and connections, to start establishing the ties that might make or break her career on the *Aral Sea*. But having a mentor hadn't saved Jem from losing his life. Being respected by her peers hadn't saved Dyanne from being crushed.

At nineteen hundred hours the captain arrived. Umbundo asked, "How's Underway Stores, Lieutenant Scott? You've had an entire fortnight to clean the place up."

"It's fine, sir. I'm enjoying it very much."

"She's a great addition to the department, sir," Quenger added, appearing at Jodenny's elbow as if by magic. "We really enjoy having her."

Umbundo's gaze narrowed. "Quenger, is it?"

"Yes, sir," he replied.

"I hear good things about Disbursing," Umbundo said.

"Yes, sir," Quenger said, though A. J. Francesco ran Disbursing.

A ringing bell announced the beginning of the evening's festivities. Seven officers were being hailed, including Jodenny, Osherman, and Dr. Moody. Five others were being farewelled, ready to disembark at Mary River for new duty assignments or civvie jobs. The hails came first, with the honorees sitting on stage. Umbundo himself spoke for Osherman.

"Commander Sam Osherman comes to us out of tragedy, but we're extremely lucky to have him. Ever since he put on his lieutenant's bars, he's made a career of terrorizing junior officers."

Laughter from the assembly. Jodenny didn't smile. When it was her turn, Al-Banna spoke without jokes.

"Lieutenant Jodenny Scott graduated from the academy in the top one percent of her class. She earned her Supply pin two years later, and worked in Underway Stores and Maintenance on the *Yangtze*. For her heroism and quick thinking during the disaster, she was awarded the MacBride Cross."

Respectful applause followed. Jodenny kept her eyes locked on the far bulkhead. The last hail was a lieutenant from Ops, and once that was over she followed Osherman off the stage so quickly she nearly tripped into him.

"Steady," he said.

Jodenny pulled her arm free. She didn't need his help or his touch. "I'm fine."

"Let me buy you a drink," he said. "God knows I need one."

She didn't want anything from him, but Osherman was already ordering two Scotches from the bartender. Osherman's gaze swept the crowd. "I should have scheduled myself for a watch."

Jodenny couldn't resist. "You know you love this."

"You really think so?" he asked.

On the stage, Umbundo gave a faux leather briefcase to a departing commander from Flight. Jodenny tried not to brood over the fact that Jem's and Dyanne's farewells had been funeral services. She pictured the *Yangtze*'s flight decks as they currently existed—dark, stripped bare, ice-cold.

"There's a scientist onboard who's been asking questions," she told Osherman. "He thinks the explosion had something to do with the Wondjina Spheres."

Osherman's lips thinned. "Dr. Ng?"

"He talked to you?"

"I told him he's full of shit."

"Here you are!" Vu hooked her arm around Jodenny's. "Come cut the cake."

After the cake-cutting, Jodenny told Vu she was going to the head. Instead she went straight back to her cabin. She stripped off her uniform, curled up in her bunk, and tried not to think about the *Yangtze* even as her mind circled back to blood and death. She wished she had Greiger's bottle of brandy from her office. She wished she had gone down with her ship. No. She wished instead that the ship hadn't gone down at all.

The door pinged. Jodenny threw on a robe and opened it.

"You skipped out early." Quenger waved a bottle of champagne and two glasses. His tie was loose, his shirt unbuttoned to reveal a smooth chest. "Thought you might like a private celebration."

"With you?"

"We got off on the wrong foot." Quenger's gaze dropped to the top of her robe. "I just want to be friends."

"I have enough friends."

"You can always do with more." He leaned closer, his dark eyes intent. "Maybe the tension you feel when you're around me is romantic. Maybe we should try it and see how we could be good with each other."

She leaned forward and said, "If you try to kiss me, I'll grab your balls and twist them until they break off."

Quenger laughed but backed away. He waved the champagne bottle at her. "Oh, Jo. You don't know. How far we could go—"

Jodenny shut the hatch.

The next day was Sunday. Jodenny slept late and ran into Francesco in the E-Deck gym. He was working out on a treadmill beside a blonde woman in green shorts.

"I took your advice," Francesco asked. "It is nicer working out down here than the officers' gym. Have you met my Chief Vostic?"

"We met the day you checked onboard," Vostic said.

Jodenny remembered the lifepod incident all too well. "Nice to see you again."

She did five kilometers on a machine, and after showering went to Underway Stores. Sunday routine didn't shut the ship down, but working hours were reduced and Mrs. Mullaly, for one, had the whole day off to spend with her family. With Caldicot on watch, Jodenny had the whole office to herself and uninterrupted stretches to wade through paperwork. The AT evals had come back from the SUPPO's office with a few corrections to be made. Sergeant Rosegarten had sent an imail saying the Loss Accounting report on Myell's DNGO was still waiting to be signed by the Security Officer. It occurred to Jodenny that it was taking an abnormally long time. Around lunchtime Holland said, "Lieutenant, I was talking to Ensign Hultz's agent and she said someone had queried her about you."

"Who?"

"Dr. Ng from Space Sciences. He had queried me, but I refused to answer."

"Why didn't you tell me before?"

"Your security setting is medium, Lieutenant. You asked not to be disturbed—"

Jodenny's hands fisted. "Set it to high and ping the bastard."

Dr. Ng answered with a distracted air. "Yes?"

"Dr. Ng, I'm filing that complaint I warned you about."

"Complaint?" Ng blinked owlishly. "But why?"

"Do you deny trying to get information about me out of my agent?"

"It's not what you think—okay, look, here. Watch this, will you?" An animation flickered on the screen. She recognized the Point Elliot Spheres. Ng said, "Point A is the center of the triangle they form. If we zoom out to Point B, that's the Wondjina drop point. If you draw a line from A to B—and look, here comes the *Yangtze* on its standard approach, which means you've got to maneuver a little, since you have to hit the drop at the right angle or skip over it entirely—okay, here! T6 swings around into the path of the Point Elliot track first— watch this. T6 explodes, parts of F-Deck are breached—"

Jodenny closed her eyes, unable to bear looking at it. "It's a coincidence. It doesn't prove anything. Even if your data is correct, ships have been using the Alcheringa for several decades now. I'm sure sometime, somewhere, ships departing Kookaburra have crossed this ludicrous track you've drawn."

"They have!" Ng said. The animation on the screen had frozen. "I've re-created at least ten journeys where ships cross lines between the Alcheringa and a set of Spheres, and none of them have ever resulted in an explosion until the *Yangtze*. Maybe something in her T6 was different or special— something in the hold, or the ammunition or explosives, or maybe something that wasn't even on the official manifest. Team Space just wants us to *think* it was the CFP."

The animation rewound on the screen and started to play again.

Unable to speak anymore, Jodenny hung up. The animation vanished into the milky darkness of her deskgib, leaving behind only the memory of a tiny ship on its way to destruction.

CHAPTER **TWELVE**

AT Kevwitch, returned from the brig, had to bend over to keep from hitting his head on overheads. Jodenny decided he might be handy to have around if she ever needed someone to rip open a bulkhead with his bare hands. AT Barivee had a coiled tenseness that made her uneasy. AT Yee looked mortified when Strayborn reprimanded him for scuffed boots at morning quarters.

"Sorry, ma'am," he said to Jodenny.

"They're just boots," Barivee muttered.

Jodenny gave him a hard look. "There will be no sloppy uniforms in this division."

Strayborn went through the roster. Nitta read the list of daily announcements and told everyone to get their requests in for Mary River liberty. Her thoughts on Ng and his crazy theory, Jodenny almost missed it when Nitta gave a pointed reminder about not playing games at work. She ignored Lange's glare and signaled for Amador and Ishikawa to haul out the boxes she'd brought down with her.

"When I first came onboard, I told you that we're a team doing a job together. I thought it would be nice if we had something that illustrated that. I'm not telling you that you have to wear these, but I hope you do and remember who your teammates are."

Amador and Ishikawa started handing out the T-shirts. The sports shop had done a good job with the Underway Stores emblem and she'd made sure that everyone's name was spelled correctly on the back. The sizes had been easy to pull from the uniform records.

"Are these dingoes?" Chang asked, holding his shirt up to scrutiny.

"Never saw robots with muscles like that," Gallivan said. "Or shit-eating grins!"

"Dicensu drew it," Jodenny said.

Dicensu blushed. "It wasn't too hard."

Myell took his with a blank expression. Nitta, who had told her he didn't see the point, threw his over his shoulder and said, "I'm off to a Menu Board meeting, Lieutenant. See you."

Jodenny saw Lange hold out his shirt and mutter something to Barivee. Both of them snorted in private amusement. Dicensu might have overheard the comment, because his expression fell. Caldicot patted his arm and said, "I think they're great, Peter. Will you autograph mine?"

Bless Caldicot's heart. Dicensu perked up immediately. Jodenny decided to ignore Lange and Barivee. As the division drifted off to work, she asked Strayborn and Myell to stay behind.

"I like them." Strayborn held his shirt at arm's length. "No other division has them."

"That's what I thought," Jodenny said. Myell stayed silent and inscrutable, which annoyed her. "How's the May inventory coming?"

"The numbers are going to be good," Strayborn said. "Ninety-four, maybe ninety-five."

"Good," she said. "Every month, we're going to do better."

Later that morning she went off to the Shore Leave Briefing, where she was pleasantly surprised to see Danyen Cartik.

"You still owe me five yuros," he said.

"I've been looking to pay you off but you're never at lunch."

"You know how Data is," he said, but didn't sound convincing about it. "I've been swamped."

After the room had filled with representatives from the various departments, Lieutenant Commander Senga from Security got up to give a review of restricted areas in Mary River's capital city of New Christchurch. His gaze slid coldly past Jodenny as he detailed bars where drugs or venereal diseases were known to be prevalent, shops that sold illicit material, neighborhoods where unsuspecting crew members might find themselves at the wrong end of a knife. The review took exactly thirty seconds.

"Not a very exciting place, is it?" Cartik said to Jodenny.

"Not if you like fun."

His eye twitching, Senga said, "Tell your people to remember to dress appropriately. They shouldn't get drunk or rowdy in public, and be careful of public displays of affection."

"What's the punishment for spitting on the sidewalk?" someone drawled.

Senga grimaced. "Don't ask. Homosexuality is legal, they can't do anything about that, but it's frowned upon. Last time we visited, we had four instances of TS crew being harassed. I don't want anyone missing movement because they're stuck in jail for fighting or on some trumped-up morals charge."

"What about demonstrations?" someone asked.

Senga smiled humorlessly. "We don't think the CFP will dare. They're strong on Mary River, but there's still a lot of backlash. They don't want the media attention."

Jodenny let her mind drift to Ng's rubbish theory. She drew the Point Elliot Spheres and a small picture of the *Yangtze* on her gib. When the meeting broke up she asked Cartik, "Are you going planetside?"

"Wouldn't want to risk a morals charge," he said with a trace of bitterness.

She wondered if that was the cause of his disenchantment with Data. Some departments were less tolerant than others, despite strict rules about sexual orientation harassment. "Well, then, how about lunch on Friday? I know a good café on B-Deck."

"I'll be there," he said.

On her way back to the office she swung by Supply crew berthing aft of the Flats. The rug in the lounge had seen much better days. The big-screen vid was cracked at one corner and the sofas had stains of suspicious origins. No one had emptied the garbage recently. Jodenny went down the passage to Lund's door and rang the bell.

He answered wearing his pajamas. "Ma'am!" he said. Behind him, Jodenny could see Izim open on his deskgib.

"You weren't at quarters, so I brought you this."

Lund examined the T-shirt she handed him. "Thank you, Lieutenant. I have a chit from my doctor for bed rest. I sent you a copy."

"I understand. You need your rest. I think you'd better scoot yourself into bed, though. You don't want eyestrain, do you?"

"No, ma'am," he said.

"I'm going to send Sergeant Strayborn around this afternoon to make sure you're all right," Jodenny said. "And Sergeant VanAmsal at dinnertime. Maybe I'll ask her to bring you some soup."

"I don't want to bother anyone."

Jodenny patted his arm. "You're not a bother. You're a member of this team. Oh, and before I forget, I've set you up with three highly recommended doctors on Warramala."

"Three?"

"We have to pinpoint your ailments," Jodenny said. "You need help."

Back in her office she tried not to gloat too much over the memory of Lund's crestfallen expression. She sent Nitta an imail telling him to schedule berthing inspections for the end of the week. No sailors of hers were going to live in squalor. When she turned on her gib she saw the Wondjina Spheres she'd sketched.

"Holland," she said, "pull up the navigational logs from my last ship and plot its last flight for me. See if you can establish any relationship to the Point Elliot Spheres on Kookaburra's surface."

"In accordance with Dr. Ng's theory?" Holland asked.

"Have you been eavesdropping?"

"It's not a secret, Lieutenant. Dr. Ng is not held in high esteem by his peers in the Space Sciences Department. Though this is only the first of three deployments he signed on for, there's speculation his contract will be terminated at the end of the deployment."

"Re-create the data on your own and run a comparison against his," Jodenny said.

A few seconds passed before Holland filled the deskgib with data. "My projection of the *Yangtze*'s track matches Dr. Ng's. But in the absence of other evidence, his hypothesis is illogical. Just because the ship crossed such a hypothetical track does not mean the explosion is somehow related."

The animation stayed in Jodenny's thoughts. She was re-watching Holland's version the next morning before the DIVO meeting when Al-Banna walked in and said, "I hope you're not playing Izim, Lieutenant."

Vu coughed. Wildstein squinted at Al-Banna as if trying to decide if he were joking.

"No, sir." She put her gib aside.

Wildstein asked, "Was it really necessary to confiscate RT Lange's gib?"

"Yes, ma'am," Jodenny said. "The whole division was warned, and he was playing while there was a hazardous operation under way in the tower."

"Bet he took it well," Vu said.

After the meeting Al-Banna said, "Lieutenant Scott. Wait one minute."

Both Al-Banna and Wildstein had grim looks on their faces. She braced herself, expecting more bitching about Lange's gib, but after the room was clear Wildstein said, "Did I or did I not tell you that you couldn't spend your division funds on T-shirts?"

"I didn't, ma'am," Jodenny protested.

"You bought the shirts," Wildstein said. "I saw two of your people wearing them on the Rocks last night. How did you pay for them?"

Jodenny was happy to hear at least someone was wearing them. "I'd rather not say."

Al-Banna tapped his fingers impatiently. "Answer the question, Lieutenant."

She supposed there was no avoiding it. "I asked the Morale Department for the funding, but they said no. So I did it myself."

"You paid for all of them?" Wildstein asked.

"Yes, ma'am. While I was in the hospital, I was still pulling space pay—anyway, it's just a small gesture from me to the division. But I thought you might like your own, too."

From the bag she'd brought she pulled out the shirts personalized for Al-Banna and Wildstein. Wildstein grimaced, but Al-Banna unfolded his and held it to his chest.

"Good fit," he said. "But you're not paying for mine, Lieutenant. I'll transfer the yuros to your account. Ten? Fifteen?"

"No, sir," Jodenny said. "It's a gift."

"You don't give gifts to your superior officers," Al-Banna said. He walked out admiring his shirt. Wildstein said, "I heard you wanted to conduct berthing inspections."

"Yes, ma'am. I asked Chief Nitta to schedule them."

"Berthing cleanliness isn't your concern. Some of the other officers have complained about the prospect of you inspecting their sailors."

Who had complained? Quenger, she bet. Jodenny squared her shoulders. "The cleanliness of the common areas directly affects my people, ma'am. Last time I walked through there, the lounge was a pigsty."

"It's still not your jurisprudence," Wildstein said. "If there's a problem, I'll see to it. I'll inspect the lounge Friday at oh-eight-hundred."

"Yes, ma'am. Thank you."

"I'm not doing it for you." Wildstein passed back her T-shirt. "And you can keep this. Give it to someone who'll wear it."

Myell rose early, worked out for an hour, and swung by the mess deck for breakfast. Judging by the posters, overvids, and other colorful displays, it was time to celebrate Dragon Boat Week. Gallivan, Minnich, and Amador were in one booth, laughing at a joke. Chiba was in another, guffawing with some of his dogs. Myell sat far from all of them and skimmed over the May inventory while shoveling through his oatmeal. The numbers were definitely better than they'd been for April. As he forwarded them up to Strayborn a shadow fell across his table.

"Trouble in Underway Stores?" Spallone asked with a smirk. "Poor little things having their gibs taken away by Miz Scott?"

"Only if they're dumb enough to get caught playing Izim on duty."

Spallone leaned forward. "I hear it's all your fault, anyway. Scott only got pissed because you were in the shaft when she caught Lange. You're her favorite. Are you fucking her? The two of you sneaking off to the slots to fool around?"

To go from being the department scapegoat to Lieutenant Scott's favored child would be too ironic. Myell brushed past Spallone and took his tray toward the scullery. When he turned the corner Chiba was blocking his way.

Chiba said, "Sit down. Let's chat."

Sitting meant listening to old threats and new crap. "Get out of my way."

"I just want to talk. Maybe admire your brand-new T-shirt."

"You can kiss my ass," Myell said.

Chiba shoved him off his feet. The breakfast tray went flying and Myell landed with a solid thwack against his tailbone. Worse than the physical shock was the humiliation as people turned toward the commotion and a DNGO whirled their way, intent on claiming dirty silverware and sweeping up crumbs. He decided he didn't care anymore what they might do to him for assaulting a chief, and scrambled to regain his footing and swing a punch. But then Chief Roush, the Assistant Food Services Officer, wedged himself between Myell and Chiba and demanded, "What's going on here?"

"He lost his balance and fell," Chiba said. "Floor must be wet."

"Sure it is," Roush said. "Get out."

Chiba wagged a warning finger. "Careful. You wouldn't want to slip, too."

"Out," Roush repeated. Chiba left with his dogs in tow. Roush asked Myell, "You hurt?"

"No." Myell brushed bread crumbs from his coveralls. He could feel something wet on his backside and hoped the stain wasn't too obvious. Fucking Chiba, fucking all of them.

Roush patted his shoulder. "They're assholes. Best thing to do? You take Chiba down below and beat the shit out of him."

"Great idea, Chief. I'll look into that." Myell left before Roush could offer any more helpful advice. He went to T6 for morning quarters and hid until the last minute, unable to bear seeing Gallivan or the others who had witnessed his humiliation. Jodenny made some announcements, Nitta added something irrelevant, and Strayborn said that the ASUPPO would be inspecting the lounge at the end of the week. Stupid, stupid, stupid, he thought. Didn't anyone on the ship realize there were more important things to worry about than inspections?

After quarters, Gallivan snagged his arm. "Chiba's a swipe. You know that, right?"

"He's a swipe who people believe."

Gallivan grimaced. "Not him. They believed Ford."

Her name still caused Myell's gut to churn. Before her, he had never known exactly how much trouble a man could get into based on one woman's accusations. "You believed her."

"No," Gallivan. "I never believed her. But for a while . . . well, for a while it seemed safer to mind my own business. No one knows what really happened to the old SUPPO, right? And with Chiba and Greiger running things . . . I'm sorry. It was the wrong decision."

He sounded contrite, but Myell wasn't so eager to forgive. Before he could say so, Jodenny called his name. How she had already managed to hear about the fracas was beyond him, but as Gallivan slinked away and Jodenny approached he steeled himself for questions or a lecture.

"Yes, Lieutenant?" he asked.

"How's the inventory going?"

"It's in Sergeant Strayborn's queue, ma'am. Looks like ninety-five percent."

"Good. Anything else exciting going on?"

"No, ma'am," he said. "But I don't think the ASUPPO should inspect our lounge. Officer berthing doesn't get inspected. Why should ours?"

"Because the officers are keeping their common areas clean." Jodenny cocked her head. "When I walked through yours the other day, it was filthy."

Abrupt weariness washed through him. Fuck Team Space, anyway. "Yes, ma'am."

After everyone had cleared out of his tower he settled down

in the control module for a few hours of upsynching. Circe had come back from the shop with a new battery and showed no errors at all, but as a Class II named Hera synched he saw a thousand duplicate records. Myell traced the glitch back to Core, reported it to the duty techs, and waited for them to reboot the appropriate subroutines. Lunch was a cold sandwich from a vending machine. His only visitor was Strayborn, who showed up with the leave roster in hand and took an interest in Hera's problem.

"How long have you been waiting for the reboot?" Strayborn asked.

"Two hours."

"Data techs. All they do is sit around on their asses." Strayborn studied the roster. "Is this right? You're taking a week when we get to Mary River?"

"Yes."

"Going hiking?"

"Visiting family."

A beep on the deskgib alerted him to the reboot. Hera came back online and began uploading again. Strayborn stuck around to watch the datastream.

Myell said, "The duplicates have cleared, but now she's missing ten minutes of her log."

"Ask for another reboot," Strayborn said.

If Jodenny hadn't made her new rule, Myell might have wasted the next two hours playing Snipe. He almost did it anyway. Instead he skimmed practice questions for the chief's exam he didn't intend to take. No doubt VanAmsal had already spent months in preparation, but as he keyed through questions about regs, procedures, and more procedures he scored moderately well. When Core signaled that the subroutine was reset, he ordered Hera to upsynch again. She dashed up and away into the slots.

"Get back here," he said, but she didn't respond to his orders. He checked Core, but no tasks had been sent her way. He turned on the tracking monitors but she didn't register, and when he pinged her transponder he got no response. "Where did you go?"

After several minutes he had Core reboot her. Hera's transponder began blinking on level ten. He recalled her to the command module and she floated up to hover outside the window. Myell upsynched her and saw that the records matched Core exactly.

"That's pretty convenient," he told her.

Myell had Hera report to the base of the tower. He locked her down with a restraining bolt and tugged her to his bench. There were fresh scratches on her hull, but that was no surprise. DNGOs were always scraping themselves against the bins. Her access plate was also loose. That was an easy fix, but didn't explain her vanishing act.

"Time for a full diagnostic," he told her.

His gib beeped. "Go over to IR2," Nitta said. "Chang's sick, Gallivan's gone off to stand watch, and there's no one else to cover. Lieutenant's really pissed."

Myell hesitated. It was possible that Nitta was setting him up again for another assault. He fingered his pocket server and went over full of trepidation, relaxing only when he saw Jodenny herself manning the issue room. She looked irritated, though not at him. She said, "I need you to deliver these orders, Sergeant. The uniforms are for Lieutenant Deven, these boots are for Lieutenant Coswell, and the sheets go to Lieutenant Pearson. Don't dawdle."

Dawdle. Myell never dawdled. He did, however, keep his eyes down as he hurried through the passages. He remembered stumbling into officer country by accident on his first cruise and the tongue-lashing he'd received. A former shipmate had been court-martialed for being caught in Ops officer berthing. Of course, the man had also been having an affair with an ensign, and so he was also court-martialed for fraternization. The ensign had been, too.

No one was home in Deven's cabin. Coswell was sleepy-eyed and took his new boots with a grumble. Myell was approaching Pearson's cabin when a tall officer barreled out of a cabin without looking and knocked Myell backward. His head slammed into the bulkhead.

"Damn it!" the officer said. "Are you all right?"

Myell's vision filled with stars. Beneath the domed sky, a harsh desert stretched far and flat to the horizon. A snake as large as a mountain flicked its massive tongue to the beat of ancient drums and consciousness faded, faded, faded away.

CHAPTER **THIRTEEN**

Myell woke to find an unfamiliar shape bent over him. *Daris,* he thought, and almost lashed out with his hands and feet. Then he saw commander's bars and a nametag that said Osherman. His patches included several Alcheringa runs and a memoriam badge for the *Yangtze.*

"Stay still, Sergeant," Osherman ordered sternly. "I'll call Medical."

"I'm fine." Myell sat up to prove it. He rubbed the side of his head and touched a hot spot where his cheek had slammed into the deck. "What happened?"

"I knocked you down. I apologize. Can you stand?"

He could, and did, and though he himself was steady the passageway swayed like a boat on an ocean. Osherman wanted to walk him down to Sick Berth but Myell convinced him that going back to the issue room was a better idea. Jodenny blanched when she saw the two of them.

"What happened to you?" she demanded, reaching as if to touch his cheek.

Myell deflected her hand. "An accident."

"My fault," Osherman said. "Should I call Medical?"

"Sit down." Jodenny steered him toward a stool. Her fingers were remarkably soft, and felt warm against his skin. "Medbot activate."

"I don't need—" Myell started to stay, but the unit was already honing in on him with a flashing light. "It's nothing, Lieutenant."

"Did you lose consciousness?"

The medbot hovered around his right ear and swung to his left. "No," Myell said.

"Yes," Osherman said. "Only for a few seconds."

Jodenny shot Osherman a gaze. In it Myell saw something old, maybe something bitter. He knew they had both served on the *Yangtze*. It didn't take much to imagine them attending the same meetings, or sharing a cozy rendezvous in officer berthing.

Osherman added, "You were trying to say something, Sergeant."

Myell tried to remember, but nothing came to him. The medbot announced, "No emergency medical assistance required. Please report to Sick Berth at your convenience."

Lieutenant Quenger appeared at the counter. He was Chiba's boss, as much as any officer could be said to be. Almost as much trouble, though far less powerful. Myell had never liked him. Quenger said, "So, what happened here? Blood and guts. Looks interesting."

Osherman ignored Quenger completely. "Again, Sergeant, my apologies. If you'll excuse me, I'm late to an appointment."

He strode off. Quenger said, cheerfully, "I can come back, if you two need a moment or two."

Myell didn't like the tone in Quenger's voice, but Jodenny's expression betrayed nothing. She said, "Go get yourself checked out, Sergeant. I'll have Nitta send someone else up."

"I can keep working—"

She gave him a forced smile. Maybe she was ashamed of him in some way, or maybe she just wanted to talk to Quenger alone. "You'll scare the ensigns, looking like you do. They'll think I'm abusing my crew."

Myell nodded unhappily. He left the issue room and rounded the next corner, then stopped to eavesdrop.

"What do you need?" Jodenny asked.

"That's a pretty open-ended question, isn't it, Jo?"

"What do you need from the issue room?"

"New jacket. Lost my other one."

Myell envisioned her taking the requisition and pulling down a jacket from the shelves. The prospect of Quenger ogling her while she bent over or reached up made his fists clench. Quenger asked, "When are you going to let me take you to dinner?"

"Is that what you had in mind the other night?"

"You should have let me in."

"I don't date fellow officers."

Quenger laughed. "Dating wasn't on the agenda."

"Here's your jacket." Jodenny didn't sound amused. "Good-bye, Lieutenant."

"Jo, Jo, Jo," Quenger chided.

The approach of footsteps made Myell climb down the nearest ladder and head back to his quarters. A cold cloth eased the bump on his head and aspirin started to work on the headache. He lay in his rack trying not to think about Quenger putting his hands on Jodenny. After several sleepless minutes of replaying the accident with Osherman he checked officer berthing assignments in Core. Osherman had knocked him down while coming out of quarters assigned to Lieutenant Anzo, who worked for him in the Data Department.

Myell called up Anzo's biography and picture but didn't recognize her. There could be a very innocent reason for Osherman visiting one of his subordinates' cabins during working hours—maybe Anzo was sick in quarters, or just coming off a watch—but Myell found it curious she hadn't noticed the accident in the passage just outside her door, or hadn't come to check. Or had she?

The pocket server, programmed to activate at any impact, had dumped data right into an encrypted account. Myell played it back and heard Osherman saying, "Damn it!" A thud. A rustle as Osherman bent over him. "Sergeant? Sergeant?" he asked, somewhat frantic. A cabin hatch clicked open.

"What happened?" a woman's voice asked.

"I'll take care of it," Osherman said.

"You want me to call Medical?"

"No. Go back inside."

The hatch door closed. Osherman said, "Sergeant, wake up," and then Myell's own voice murmured something too low for him to hear on the replay. He upped the volume.

"Uru . . ."

Osherman asked, "What, Sergeant?"

"Oolu . . ." Myell mumbled, then silence. A few seconds later he had woken up.

Myell stared at Koo, who was busy sleeping in her terrarium and no help at all. Though Osherman had told Myell he would call Medical, and had again offered in front of Jodenny, it was obvious he didn't want anyone else involved. His trip to Lieutenant Anzo's cabin didn't look so innocuous after all. Suddenly weary, Myell downloaded all of the pocket server's data to his personal ship's account and climbed into bed. Sometime later cloth rustled and he woke up swinging.

"Hey, hey!" Timrin backed away with a blanket in hand. "Just trying to be nice."

Upright, dizzy, Myell dragged a hand across his eyes. "Sorry."

Timrin peered at his cheek. "Jesus. Chiba do that to you?"

"Got knocked down." The past and present blurred, and Myell wasn't sure who he was making excuses for. Timrin's thoughtful if incautious move had tumbled him back to Baiame, the fall of a shadow in the doorway, Daris's calloused hands.

"Terry? You with me?"

He shook himself back to the present. "What time is it?"

"Almost time for the game, and I've got my money on East Enfield." Timrin threw the blanket aside and pulled off his coveralls with quick, efficient tugs. "Someone should teach fucking Chiba a lesson."

"I told you. This wasn't Chiba."

"Don't cover for him. I heard what happened. Did you record it?"

Myell sipped some water. "You're not listening."

"I hear what you're not saying." Timrin slid into a new shirt and buttoned it. He was a thin man, bony in all the wrong places, unlucky when it came to women. He paid for sex, usually, either directly or through kasai girls. "So why does the side of your face look like raw hamburger?"

The anger in Timrin's voice made Myell feel a little better. "Someone rushed too quickly out of a hatch while I was in berthing. Satisfied? Drop it."

Timrin peered into the mirror and combed his hair. "Officers. Can't live with them, can't push them out an airlock."

Myell's chest tightened. Don't be paranoid, he told himself. "I didn't say it was an officer."

"It would have to be, wouldn't it?" Timrin grimaced. "Clumsy dongers, the whole lot."

Myell leaned back and turned his face to the wall.

After dinner that night Francesco pulled Jodenny aside. "I hear there was a scuffle in the mess this morning. Chief Chiba and Sergeant Myell."

And here she had thought the highlight of Myell's day had been getting flattened by Osherman. "Did you see it?"

"Not personally."

"I'll talk to Myell," she said.

That night she tossed and turned in bed. Osherman hadn't volunteered to make a safety report after his accident with Myell, which was uncharacteristic. The officer she remembered from the *Yangtze* had been meticulous about regulations and paperwork. Osherman had also been in a decided hurry to leave once Quenger showed up. Myell, meanwhile, should have told her about the mess deck incident with Chiba. The man had a definite problem with asking for help. The next morning she went to quarters early to discuss it with him and came across Strayborn and Myell arguing.

"You should have asked me," Myell was saying.

"I don't need to—" Strayborn stopped when he saw Jodenny.

"Is there a problem?" she asked.

"No," Myell said.

Strayborn said nothing. Jodenny eyed the two of them. "Sergeant Myell, I'd like to speak with you in private for a moment."

He shook his head. "Can't, Lieutenant. I'm due on watch in ten minutes. I only came to leave notes for Ishikawa."

Jodenny couldn't interfere with his watch schedule. She conducted quarters and reminded everyone about the rules regarding shore leave on Mary River. Afterward Strayborn accompanied her back to Mainship. As they waited for a tram she asked, "Was there an incident yesterday between Myell and Chief Chiba?"

Strayborn grimaced. "I heard there was. I didn't see it."

"Why didn't he report it to Security?"

The tram pulled into their station with only a few passengers aboard. Jodenny and Strayborn retreated to a corner and held on to poles as it slid into motion again.

Strayborn said, "Anyone tell you about AT Ford, Lieutenant?"

"I heard a thing or two."

"Myell was in the brig for a while while they tried to sort through everything."

That information had most definitely not been in his record. "Was he?"

"Part of it was for his own protection. The girl who said he raped her was dating Chief Chiba. He runs a pretty mean crowd."

"So I hear." The tram began to slow as it approached Mainship. "Do you know that for a fact?"

Strayborn raised an eyebrow. "Don't tell me you believe the official position that there are no gangs on Team Space ships, ma'am."

No, she didn't believe that. No matter how much she might prefer otherwise, gangs were a fact of life on Fortune, Baiame, and Warramala. Crew who came from rough neighborhoods didn't lose their allegiances when they signed up. If anything, the long Alcheringa runs strengthened the ties that cut across rank, rate, and position.

"So Myell was in trouble with Chiba and his people," she said.

"Yes, ma'am. Meanwhile, a lot of people who didn't know better were already convicting him. The charges were dropped but there are hard feelings all around. That's what breakfast was probably about. If I know Myell, he'd rather cut off his arm than go to Security."

The tram slid into the first station on Mainship. Jodenny paused in the open doorway. "When were you going to tell me all this?"

Strayborn's expression gave away nothing. "I wasn't. No disrespect, but there's never been a reason around here to get the DIVO involved in anything. Not until now."

Jodenny accepted Strayborn's backhanded compliment with silence. She returned to her office, stared at her deskgib for a while, and went to a scheduled meeting with Lieutenant Commander Vu regarding purchase orders. The mess decks were empty but for two RTs trying to lower a dragon boat from its mount high on the bulkhead. Vu grabbed two cups of horchata and slid into a booth opposite from Jodenny.

"I hear you're causing all sorts of trouble," Vu said, her eyes sparkling. "Uniform inspections. Taking away people's gibs. Making the ensigns study for watch. You're not going to win the vote for Most Popular DIVO."

"I figured as much," Jodenny said.

The comm sounded. "Attention all crew and passengers. Mary River transition commencing. Five, four, three, two, one."

The slightest of bumps indicated that the *Aral Sea* had dropped into Mary River's solar system. The distance between the Alcheringa drop point and Mary River was much shorter than back on Kookaburra, and in just a few hours the *Aral Sea* would start releasing towers for local freighters to tow away. The first shore leave birdies would depart in the morning, each of them jammed full with sailors seeking to escape the ship for recreation and relaxation.

"Popular or not, you've got Grace Wildstein in a fit of jealousy. She thinks you're Al-Banna's new darling," Vu said.

"That's silly."

Over by the salad bar, one of the RTs trying to fix the dragon boat lost his grip. The boat slid down several centimeters before its safety wire caught with a loud snap.

"Careful!" Vu warned them.

"Sorry, ma'am," the RT said.

Vu turned back to Jodenny. "Grace can be a little silly, I suppose. Ever since Matsuda disappeared back when we were leaving Kiwi, she's been a little insecure. You heard that story? About our old SUPPO?"

"I heard it," Jodenny said. "What do you think happened to him?"

"I could give you a different theory for every day of the week. My favorite is that Team Space pulled him at the last minute as part of a criminal investigation. He was slippery that way, you know? Slimy under the surface. Grace is a good officer, runs everything by reg, but stains spread pretty wide on this ship. If he was involved in anything shady she might be held accountable for not catching on to it."

"Shady like what?'

"Kickbacks. Bribes. Had himself quite a nest egg, but apparently didn't hide the data trail very well." Vu watched the RTs finish their work on the boat and retreat to the kitchen. "I don't know for sure but he disappears, Al-Banna shows up out of nowhere, Umbundo puts you in Greiger's job—it's no wonder Grace is feeling undermined."

Jodenny didn't want to talk about Wildstein anymore. "You should come to dinner in the wardroom tonight—we could do with some fresh faces."

"I think my husband would miss me."

Jodenny looked for a wedding ring, but Vu waved her hand and said, "I don't wear one. Neither does Mike. He's the master chief for Data."

"You're married to a master chief?"

"You don't have to look so shocked," Vu said. "It does happen, you know. More often than commanding officers like to admit. The decent ones overlook it. The uptight ones, they can make an issue of it, but they can't force you to get a divorce."

"When I was in Supply School on Fortune, one of the ensigns in my class married a regular tech she'd known from childhood." Jodenny sipped at her coffee. "They took away her commission."

"An ensign at Supply School? Of course they'll come down hard on her. Too visible for Team Space's comfort, and they figure they can nip it early. A lieutenant commander and master chief married for ten years now, both of them on one Alcheringa run after another? No captain wants to take that on. Come over to our place for Sunday brunch and meet Mike. You'll like him. Bring a date, if you'd like."

"I'm not seeing anyone," Jodenny said. Her last date had been four months earlier with an easygoing pilot. They had walked around the *Yangtze*'s Rocks and eaten ice cream and then returned to her cabin, where they'd made fumbling love. Weeks after the accident, when she finally dared to look, she read his name on the list of disaster victims.

Vu smiled mischievously. "I hear Quenger's interested."

Jodenny shuddered. "I'm not."

"Oh, Dave's not so bad. A little full of himself. That's what happens when you get everything you want with the snap of a finger. How about someone else?"

Jodenny didn't have to think hard to come up with the name of someone she did find attractive, but a personal relationship with Myell was unthinkable. Despite Vu's personal story, regulations against fraternization existed for a good reason and deserved to be upheld.

"No," she told Vu. "There's no one else."

CHAPTER FOURTEEN

It took some creative maneuvering to avoid Jodenny, but Myell suspected she must have heard about the confrontation with Chiba by now and he didn't want to talk about it. Come morning he'd be sitting on a birdie and two hours after that would have the firm ground of Mary River under his feet. Until then he was satisfied to eat dinner alone on the mess decks long after most people had finished. He was reviewing message boards on his gib when VanAmsal slid into his booth.

"Did you do it?" VanAmsal asked.

"Do what?"

"Ford."

"No." Myell went back to his dinner of potatoes and beans.

"She said you did." VanAmsal took his butter knife and scratched it along the table's surface. "One of you is lying."

"It's not me."

She gazed at him steadily. "Why's your face all bruised?"

Myell touched his cheek. "This wasn't—"

"Everyone knows you were ambushed the day we dropped," she said. "Shevi Dyatt went to Sick Berth this morning with a black eye that she claims she got from walking into a door. Someone needs to teach Chiba's men a lesson."

"Tisa—"

"I'd stay in my cabin tonight if I were you," she said, and walked away.

Myell went back to Supply berthing. The lounge was empty and Gallivan didn't answer his gib. His uneasiness increasing, Myell trammed over to the Rocks. Music spilled out of storefronts, colonists ate sumptuous meals under the starry dome, and children darted in and around their parents' legs. The evening's game, Dunredding vs. Notting Bay, played out in every bar and on the Rocks' main vids. An exceptionally bad call by a referee caused a riot of boos and heckles. Myell checked the clubs where Gallivan's band played and the theater where old Earth films were shown on an old-fashioned flat screen. He ran into Lieutenant Francesco from Disbursing at the popcorn counter.

"Something wrong, Sergeant?" Francesco asked. "You look worried."

"No, sir," Myell said. "Have a good evening."

On his way out he saw Chief Vostic duck into a corner. There were rumors about Francesco and Vostic, but he had no interest in seeing if they were true. For the next hour he scoured the Rocks but returned to his cabin in defeat. Timrin, standing a Fire and Security midwatch, pinged him at oh-three-hundred.

"There was a fight down near the Flight Deck," Timrin said. "Security's sorting them all out now. Your guys and Maintenance."

"Shit," Myell said. "Does Lieutenant Scott know?"

"She's on her way down."

"Should I come, too?" he asked.

Timrin gave him a humorless smile. "If I were you, I'd go crawl under a rock. The less anyone sees of you, the better for everyone."

Jodenny had spent most of her afternoon attending meetings, answering COSAL data requests, and reviewing the final May inventory, which held at ninety-five percent. After work, she popped aspirin for a headache and had dinner in the wardroom. Then she gathered Hultz, Gunther, and Ysten to tell them any liberty they'd been granted for Mary River was canceled because their watch qualifications were unfinished.

"That's not fair!" Gunther said.

"I've been planning a trip on Mary River since deployment began," Ysten said.

"If you'd finished up like Sanchez did, you wouldn't be in this predicament," Jodenny said. "Besides, you're not liberty-starved. You all had time off on Kiwi and Kookaburra."

"Can't you talk to Commander Al-Banna and change his mind?" Hultz asked.

"It was my idea," Jodenny said.

Hultz threw herself back on the sofa. "But it's all so dumb! Ship's velocity, Alcheringa coordinates—I mean, really, when will I ever be in charge of the bridge when there's not seventy people who know what they're doing better than I do?"

"When those seventy people are dead or dying," Jodenny snapped.

That night she had a nightmare in which she could hear Dyanne telling her not to be so hard on the ensigns. In her dream Dyanne was standing right behind her. "Turn around and see," Dyanne said, but Jodenny wouldn't. She knew the thing behind her wasn't human anymore, but instead a monster of crushed bone and flesh. The buckled decks of the *Yangtze* stretched all around her, the bulkheads burning and ripping apart—

Holland's voice said, "Lieutenant, please wake up. Security has informed me that RT Gallivan, RT Chang, AT Kevwitch, and AT Ishikawa have been taken into custody for fighting."

Jodenny stared at the ceiling for a moment, unsure if she was awake or still dreaming. She asked Holland to repeat what she had said and then called the duty sergeant, Sergeant Timrin. He told her that sailors from the Maintenance division were also involved in the fight. He said, "Lieutenant Quenger's been notified, and Chief Chiba's on his way. Do you want me to call the SUPPO?"

"No, don't bother him. I'll be right down."

The situation was bad enough without the added detail that Osherman was the Command Duty Officer, and his grim expression was the first thing Jodenny saw when she arrived in Security. Her four sailors were sequestered in one cell sporting a variety of bruises and cuts. In a separate cell sat Spallone, Engel, and Olsson, each of them equally banged up. Chiba had already arrived and acted mad enough to throw a few punches himself.

"Your people started this," he said to Jodenny.

Jodenny ignored his accusatory tone. "Commander, what happened?"

"They claim it's something about the soccer game," Osherman said.

"I lost some money myself," Sergeant Timrin volunteered from the corner.

Osherman gave him a withering look. "I don't believe them."

"My men are clean." Chiba glared at the holding cells. "They know my rules about fighting and they know what I'd do to them after a thing like this. If anyone started it, it was Underway Stores."

Jodenny appealed to Osherman. "Fighting is a serious offense, sir, but this looks more like a scuffle—"

"Have you seen Engel's eye?" Chiba demanded.

Jodenny kept talking. "What if we agree to handle it in-house? I'm sure Commander Al-Banna would be happy to address it within the Supply Department. Less paperwork and bloodshed all around if we don't have to do captain's masts."

"It's not up to Commander Al-Banna," Osherman said, but she noticed that he didn't entirely disagree with the suggestion.

"I think Underway Stores should pay for starting trouble," Chiba said.

Jodenny turned to Timrin. "Was there any property damage, Sergeant Timrin?"

"Not at all, ma'am."

"That's not what I meant," Chiba fumed.

"And no civilians saw what happened," Timrin added helpfully.

"Release them and we'll make sure this doesn't happen again," Jodenny said to Osherman.

Osherman didn't look entirely convinced. "Do you agree, Chief, or do you want to muddy up both divisions in front of the CO?"

For a minute Jodenny thought he was going to be an asshole about it, just because he could. Then Chiba blew out a noisy breath. "Looks like I'm outvoted, doesn't it?"

Osherman went off to consult by gib with Senga and Picariello. Chiba glowered at everyone and everything. Jodenny decided not to try to reason with him. When Osherman returned he said, "All right. They're yours. No complaints will be filed for the time being. But the incident's in the log, and next time this happens, they'll face double charges."

"There won't be a next time," Jodenny promised, and went to collect her sailors.

"Lieutenant!" Gallivan stood up with some excuse ready on his lips, but she wasn't in the mood to hear it.

"Go back to your cabins, lock the doors, clean yourselves up, and get into your best dress uniforms," she ordered. "We're all going to be in the SUPPO's office at oh-seven-hundred."

Gallivan asked, "Don't you want to know what happened?"

"They started it," Chang said.

"I don't want to hear excuses," Jodenny said. "The one thing I told you all when we first started working together was that I expected you to be professionals. This is so far from the definition of professional that I guess I was speaking some foreign language."

"But we did it for Underway Stores," Gallivan protested.

She retorted, "I thought it was about soccer."

Chang swallowed hard. "It was for the honor of the division, ma'am. You can't let them push people around."

"Who did they push around?" Jodenny asked, although she already had a good idea.

Kevwitch kept silent. Ishikawa, who had said nothing since Jodenny entered the cell, studied the tips of her boots. Chang turned immediately to Gallivan, who cleared his throat and said, "It doesn't matter, ma'am. We've all worked out an understanding."

"Do as I told you," she said. "And if you so much as ping someone from Maintenance I'll have you back here so fast you'll think you never left."

"Ma'am," Gallivan said, but she pointed toward the lift and he plodded off with a hangdog expression.

"AT Kevwitch," she said, commanding him to stay. "Do you have a keen wish to spend the entire cruise here in the brig?"

"No, ma'am."

"You would think a man your size could stay out of trouble."

"It's because I'm this size that I'm always in trouble," he said glumly. "Everyone wants backup, or to prove a point, or to make a show of force."

"Is that what you were doing tonight? Making a show of force?"

His cheeks colored. "Shevi Dyatt never treats me like an ogre. Sergeant Myell always talks to me like I'm smart."

"Did Dyatt or Myell ask you to do this?"

"No!" he said. "They don't know anything about it."

"So you just decided to defend the division's honor. I can

see Chang and Gallivan in such a harebrained scheme, but Ishikawa? You took an eighteen-year-old girl into a fight?"

Kevwitch blinked in surprise. "Oh, no. She was there with Spallone and such. Hangs out with them sometimes, you know."

Jodenny hadn't heard that, but she wasn't surprised that Ishikawa was less than sensible about who she hung out with. "You're dismissed, AT Kevwitch."

She pinged Nitta, informed him of what had happened, and told him to conduct morning quarters. At oh-seven-hundred she had her four sailors standing at attention outside Al-Banna's door, much to Bartis's amusement. When Al-Banna came in fifteen minutes later he snapped, "Just you, Lieutenant. Inside. Now."

Jodenny took a deep breath and followed him. Al-Banna had turned off his decor since her last visit, leaving in place only the gray parasteel and a few framed commendations.

"Do I look like some kind of goddamned babysitter?" he asked once the hatch was closed. "You should have let them rot in the brig!"

"I figured the department doesn't need any more bad publicity—"

"I'll decide what this department does and does not need. *Not you.* Understood? If our sailors are dumb enough to get caught fighting, they deserve to be hauled in front of the captain! And what's this bullshit about it being about a soccer game?"

Jodenny said, "Dunredding vs. Notting Bay, sir. I had a hundred yuros on it myself."

Al-Banna scowled. "Get out of here and send your people in."

A half hour after they went in, her four sailors emerged looking thoroughly shaken. Ishikawa had tear tracks on her face, Kevwitch's armpits were soaked with sweat, and Chang was so pale she almost had him sit down. Even the normally insouciant Gallivan had to roll his shoulders a few times.

"Commander's got quite a temper," he said.

"Yes, he does," Jodenny said.

"Get me Zarkesh, Quenger, and Chiba!" Al-Banna bellowed, and Jodenny ushered her errant sailors out the door as Bartis scrambled to obey.

Myell noticed that Gallivan, Chang, Ishikawa, and Kevwitch were all absent from morning quarters. Speculation ran rampant: Al-Banna, most agreed, had probably thrown them in the brig. Nitta, acting hungover, had nothing to say about it. He read off a few announcements before letting everyone go off to work. By oh-eight-hundred, just as Myell was heading off for shore leave, Ishikawa showed up in T6. Her visit to Mary River had been canceled and Al-Banna had ordered her to do fifty hours of extra duty.

"I only went to help!" Ishikawa broke into tears. "I didn't mean to hit anyone."

Myell left Hosaka to console her. Though time was short, he trammed over to IR2 to ask Gallivan, "Why?"

"Why what?" Gallivan asked, fingering his cut lip. "Why did we teach those dongers a lesson? Easy enough to figure out."

"Explain it in little words," Myell suggested.

Gallivan started stacking boots onto a shelf. "I told you, Terry. You have mates here. So does Dyatt. Chiba and his dogs know now that we've got our eyes on them, and that we're not going to stand for any messing around with our people."

"It's just going to make things worse," Myell said.

"Sergeant Gloom, that's you. Always looking at the worse angle of things."

Myell wanted to argue more, but he didn't dare miss his flight. "We're going to talk about this later," he promised Gallivan.

"Whatever you say, Gloom. Give my love to Mary River, won't you?"

CHAPTER **FIFTEEN**

Myell stayed firmly buckled in his seat for the journey to New Christchurch and tried not to dwell on trifling details such as gravity and acceleration. He didn't mind death so much as the prospect of the minutes that would lead up to it, the shuttle full of screams and burning metal. *You've watched too many disaster vids,* he told himself. Adding to his general uneasiness was the presence of two ATs from Maintenance, both of them sitting a few rows behind him. Not Engel, Olsson, or Spallone, thank goodness. They had all had their leaves canceled. But the two ATs had a mean look about them that he didn't trust. If Chiba meant to start trouble with Myell's family, the bastard would regret it for the rest of his short life.

"You all right, Sarge?" asked the apprentice mate sitting beside him.

Myell forced his hand to unclench the seat rest. "Fine."

The AM peered at the vid. "Were those our towers?"

Myell glanced over at the cargo being towed off by local freighters. "Ten, twelve, and fourteen."

"Do we get 'em back?"

"The *Alaska* will pick them up in a couple months. We'll be picking up any left by the *Chernobyl*."

The AM settled back in his seat and drummed his fingers restlessly. "Are there any nice girls down on Mary River?"

An RT across the aisle said, "Hell, most of the girls on Mary River are frigid. You'd have a warmer time sticking it into a bucket of ice."

Rowdy laughter. The AM blushed and didn't ask any more questions. The Rocks offered more lively entertainment than Mary River did. The planet's lures were fresh air, true blue skies, and the chance to escape the ship, though you might have to put up with a sermon or a separatist lecture in the meantime.

Myell closed his eyes until final approach, during which

time he squeezed them shut even harder and hoped to just die quickly. After the birdie was safely docked he was first in line to get off. The port had a spare, utilitarian look to it, with low ceilings and plain furniture and crucifixes emblazoning every sign. It took until another hour to clear Customs and Quarantine. Myell followed the ramps outside to blazing summertime heat and a curb crowded with minicabs, flits, and public buses. Beyond the glinting roofs of prefab warehouses, jagged green and white mountains soared back into the sky he had fallen from.

"Boring but beautiful," was how Colby described it.

Myell took a bus to a discount lot and rented a cheap flit. It levitated well enough, but the fins were scratched and the engine was a little loud. Within minutes he was following a wide boulevard past New Christchurch's handful of skyscrapers. Traffic flowed evenly and without snarls. Bright, well-tended flower gardens lined the roads. The announcer on the city's official radio station reminded Myell twice to thank the Lord for His Blessings, and billboards of happy, devout families beamed proselytizing commercials into his flit.

"Not today," he said, and snapped the radio off.

He drove to the Bethlehem Parkway North and started toward Colby's farm. A mag-lev train, silver and bright in the sunshine, kept him company much of the way before veering east. If he'd spent more money on an upgrade, he could have turned on the flit's autopilot and napped for the rest of the trip. Instead he rolled down his window, stuck his elbow out, and tried to keep his thoughts from circling around and around to the *Aral Sea,* orbiting so high overhead. He hadn't asked anyone to intervene on his behalf, and was still mad at Gallivan and the others for doing so.

Ninety minutes after leaving New Christchurch he turned off the parkway into a rich forest of pine and oak trees. When he stopped the car the pervasive quiet of nature wrapped around him like a blanket. He could hear insects in the bushes, the flap of birds' wings, and the wind in the leaves, but no comm announcements. No Snipe vids. He heaved his rucksack over his shoulder and started up the lane toward the barn.

Colby had built a long, low addition to the farmhouse and planted another vegetable garden. The old clunky housebot— Erma? Rema?—was hanging clothes on the line. Two broken speeders were parked by the horse stable and a few chickens pecked at the dirt.

A burst of mazer fire sent his heart racing.

"Space Patrol! You're under arrest!" a voice yelled.

Myell obediently raised his hands. "I surrender."

Giggles, and the sound of bodies jumping from the tree branches to the ground behind him. Something jabbed him in the back. "State your name!"

"Myell, Teren A. Sergeant, *T.S.S. Aral Sea*."

"State your business!"

"I've come to kidnap small children," he admitted, and swung around to grab Jake and Adryn and hoist them into the sky. The toy mazers shot more bursts of light into the sun-dappled trees. They fell into the bushes, the children squirming with laughter. They ganged up together to start tickling him.

"I surrender!" Myell shouted, twisting away from their devilish fingers. "Get your presents!"

Eight-year-old Jake groped for the bag. "What did you bring us?"

"Anything expensive?" Adryn pushed her long bangs from her forehead and joined her brother.

"Exquisitely expensive. And rare and unique."

Jake unwrapped a square white package. "Wow," he said, his eyes widening. "A basebot! Dad said I couldn't have one until Christmas." He grinned wildly. "Thanks, Uncle Terry!"

Adryn unwrapped her gift and asked, "What is it?"

"The Best of the Universe, honey." Myell sat up and turned it on. An image of Fortune's most famous Spheres sprang up in the center of the glass triangle. "You can visit hundreds of the most beautiful places in the Seven Sisters without ever leaving your room."

"Oh." With a distinct lack of enthusiasm she added, "Thanks."

"Let's go play basebot," Jake proposed, jumping to his feet.

The kids ran off to the field with the hologram left forgotten in the grass.

"There's nothing harder to please in the universe than a little girl," Colby's voice said behind Myell. "Unless it's a little girl's mom."

Myell squinted up at his older brother. "Don't let Dottie hear you say that. She already calls you one of the great last chauvinists."

Colby pulled him to his feet and they spent a few seconds in mutual appraisal. Colby's face was deeply tanned, his fair hair beginning to thin. He still had the strong, rugged look he'd picked up during his years on Mary River but his clothes hung loose on his medium frame.

"You're getting skinny," Myell said.

"You're getting fat."

Myell patted his stomach. "Muscle."

"Between your ears." Colby gave him an unexpected hug. "Welcome back."

When they broke apart the sun seemed brighter to Myell, the farm more familiar. "How's Team Space treating you?" Colby asked, picking up the rucksack and Adryn's discarded gift. "Make admiral yet?"

"Not yet."

"Lieutenant?"

"I'd be lucky to make chief. I don't have the right tickets."

"Get your degree, there's a ticket."

"In what? Agrofarming?" The last wasn't meant to open old wounds, but university was still a sore subject. If Colby noticed the testiness he didn't comment on it, and Myell didn't have time to apologize before the front door swung open.

"Terry! It's been so long!" Dottie said.

Myell stared at her enormous stomach. "At least nine months, I'd say."

Dottie patted her tummy. She had always been pretty, but the pregnancy had brought a new fullness and pinkness to her cheeks. "Give me a hug anyway."

He did, surprised at the bulk of her, able to smell the rose shampoo in her hair. Dottie pulled them into the cool, sunlit living room and shut down her deskgib. "Sorry the place is a mess—Erma's been acting up and Colby hasn't managed to fix her properly."

"Not fair," Colby protested. "Every year I try to get a new housebot, but no. 'She's one of the family,' is all I hear. Thing's ready for the rustpile."

Dottie wanted to get them drinks but Colby did it instead, insisting she rest and put up her feet. Myell sat on the comfortable sofa and let his eyes soak in the homey atmosphere of thick braided rugs, real wooden furniture, and hand-sewn pillows. A calico cat sat in the warm sunlight of a windowsill, her eyes opening only slightly to consider the stranger before her. From beyond the open windows Jake shouted for Adryn to get her hands off the basebot.

"Boy or girl?" he asked Dottie.

She beamed. "Boy. We're going to name him Terry."

"Not after you." Colby returned with the drinks. "Some other Terry we know."

The tart lemonade was refreshing after the long drive. Myell leaned back and caught up on the details of their lives that would have been dull in an imail. The crops were less than anticipated but profitable, the kids were doing well in school, Dottie was due in twenty-two days, and Mary River was becoming more religiously conservative than ever imagined.

"There's talk the bishops want to ban women from work," Dottie said, a worry line between her eyes.

"They couldn't do that," Myell protested. "It's against the Assembly Constitution."

Colby said, "They could withdraw from the Assembly."

"Pull out of the Seven Sisters?" Myell asked. "That's nuts. There's too much at stake—shipments, tourism, trade—"

Dottie's gaze locked on her husband, although it was ostensibly Myell she was speaking to. "Some people feel the disadvantages wouldn't be so bad."

"Colby?" Myell felt a sudden chill. "Have you joined the CFP?"

"No. Of course not. But not all their ideas are bad ones—"

"They blew up a Team Space ship!" Myell said.

Colby held up his hands. "I'm just saying that maybe Mary River would be better off by herself, cut off from the worst of Union politics."

"And how far are you willing to go to support that?" Myell could no longer hear Jake and Adryn playing in the field, only the hum of insects and the tick of an old-fashioned clock. The cat rose from her perch and picked her delicate way across the sofa arm to the floor.

Colby shook his head. "It's all just talk, Terry. Nothing's ever going to come of it. For better or worse, the Seven Sisters will always stay together."

Myell wondered if he should leave. He couldn't stay in that house if Colby really did support the CFP. Erma called them all to lunch in the airy kitchen, and he decided to let the subject go for the moment. The kids entertained him with stories about school and their hobbies, and after lunch he helped them set up the basebot. The sun and a full stomach soon had him ready for a nap. He stretched out on the guest-room bed, which was twice as large as his rack on the *Aral Sea*. When he woke the sun had dipped and Adryn was shaking his shoulder.

"Mom says you should get up now or you won't sleep all night."

"Okay, honey." Myell rolled over. Sleeping all night sounded like a good plan.

"And she says I should tell you I really like my gift, because you're a bachelor and shouldn't be expected to know what kids like anyway." Adryn circled the bed and gave him a wet kiss on the cheek. "Thanks, Uncle Terry."

"You're welcome," he murmured. He fell into a dream filled with images of Jodenny and Strayborn and that commander who'd knocked him down, Osherman, and in the dream they were all drinking cocktails at the No Holds Barred with an oversized gecko sitting on the table. The shaman, naked as always, stood behind the bar serving drinks. Gallivan was playing a grand piano with Wendy Ford draped across the top like a chanteuse. "I'm not who you think I am!" Myell heard himself shout, over and over, but Jodenny snuggled closer to Osherman and didn't seem to hear him. The shaman nodded wisely and slammed his staff against the counter. The thunder of it sent Myell bolting upright in his bed. The room was dark and very quiet, and as he navigated to the bathroom and the kitchen he had the strange, lingering conviction that he was still dreaming, not awake at all.

A glass of water helped clear his mind. Outside the windows Mary River's moon bathed the fields and far mountains in cool sheets of silver-white light. Colby was sitting out on the porch, wrapped in a sweater. Myell fixed himself a tomato sandwich and brought out another one to Colby, who shook his head.

"Sleep okay?" Colby asked.

"Yeah. Well enough."

"I want you to know I have nothing to do with the CFP. I didn't mean to upset you."

Myell tore off the crusts of his sandwich and chewed the soft middle. "Yeah. Whatever."

Colby sighed. "So how are things going for you? You wrote something about getting out next year."

He shrugged. "It's not the place for me anymore."

"Ten years is a lot of time to throw away."

"I won't be throwing it away. I'll be getting it back."

"You're not happy?"

Since when did happiness matter? It hadn't mattered when they were children. It hadn't mattered when Colby went off to college and left Myell with Daris to contend with. He'd been happy on his first ship and his second, but those were jobs and positions he'd left behind. All that mattered now was surviving the *Aral Sea* until his contract expired.

Just as Myell was ready to go back to bed, Colby stood up and made his chair squeak. "Something I want to show you. Out in the barn."

The horses blinked and stirred when Colby lit a lantern. Yellow light pooled on the straw and dirt floor. Colby reached up to a shelf and pulled down a small traveling trunk. It was well worn, but the weatherproof lining was intact and the contents well protected. Myell touched only what he could see— a red blouse, a green and blue flannel shirt, a teak jewelry box.

He held up the blouse and smelled a faint, fruity perfume. Old memories woke in him, accompanied by old grief.

"Where did you get these?" he asked, keeping his voice even.

"Daris. Came through here almost a year ago, just after your last visit."

Myell stared down at the trunk, his eyes stinging but dry.

"He'd sold what was left of the farm and was on his way to Warramala. Wanted me to have this and share it with you. Said you didn't take anything with you when you left, just the clothes on your back."

"Not true," Myell said. Then again, Daris had always been comfortable bending the truth any old way he wanted to.

"He's got a job now, in Waipata. Works at the port." Colby fingered the blouse. "He's a changed man, Terry. Gave up the liquor and all. He's very . . . sorry. About everything. He apologized."

"Apologized?" A laugh bubbled out of Myell, propelled by incredulity. "Jesus."

Colby's face was grim. "He said he's been working on his temper for a couple of years now. He sounded genuinely sorry."

Myell stifled a set of giggles. He was sure if he kept on with the merriment Colby would think him insane. Still. *Apologized.* He rubbed his hand over his eyes and smelled his mother's perfume on his fingers.

"He wanted to know how to reach you," Colby said.

The discussion was no longer funny. "If you ever tell him, I'll break your neck."

"Terry, it's okay to put this in the past—"

"It's not okay." Myell shut the trunk firmly and turned away. "The past isn't far enough away."

He didn't sleep for the rest of the night. Izim killed a few hours, and browsing sample questions for the chief's exam took care of the rest. When pale light showed at the horizon he put his gib aside with relief. He made sure Colby was up and out of the house before he ventured to the kitchen, where Dottie was making pancakes.

"Good morning, sleepyhead," she said.

"Sit down," he told her. "I can do that."

She eased herself into a chair and let him cook breakfast. Jake and Adryn wolfed down their portions before they logged into their remote classrooms. Dottie folded her hands over her belly and gave Myell a long look.

"Colby says you're going to settle down."

"I'm getting out of Team Space," he said. "Maybe not the same thing."

"You could get your own farm. Colby and I can help. There's plenty of young women around here who'd throw themselves at a handsome and eligible man. There's a dance Saturday night that we've promised to go to. Not that I'll be much on my feet, but it's Colby's chance to hang around with other men. If you come, I can guarantee you'll be more popular than you can imagine."

"I thought you were an engineer, not a dating service."

Dottie smiled. "Don't you want to get married and have kids?"

He did, eventually. Myell imagined himself on a farm with Jodenny, raising kids, sharing a marriage bed. But that was the route his parents had taken. His mother had withered under Baiame's sun, and his father had broken under the weight of failure. Maybe he and Jodenny would live in a skyscraper on Fortune, with a bedroom overlooking a shining city of light and commerce. They could settle in a beach house somewhere, the ocean waves crashing on sand as they made love. Or maybe somewhere in the desert, where they could always see the stars.

Utter fantasy. Ridiculous. She was no more likely to give up Team Space than she was to stop breathing oxygen, and would probably marry a commander or admiral someday, someone more on par with her rank and ambition.

"I came here for rest, not romance," Myell said. "Trust me. There are no women in my immediate future."

CHAPTER SIXTEEN

All week long they took on deliveries, and not even Saturday morning brought rest for Underway Stores. Jodenny pulled herself out of bed and went down to LD-G, where VanAmsal had things well in hand. When she got to her office Lange was waiting for her.

"I routed my essay to you," he said. "Can I get my gib back now?"

"Let's see what you wrote first." Jodenny opened her queue and pulled up the imail. Well formatted, well written, good topic sentences, requisite number of words. "Better yet, why don't you tell me what you wrote?"

"Ma'am?"

"Tell me, in your own words, what you wrote in this essay. How does it start?"

Lange fidgeted. "I worked on it all night, ma'am. It's kind of fuzzy now."

"You can paraphrase."

He clenched his jaw.

"RT Lange, you didn't write this, did you?" Jodenny asked.

"I did! Most of it, anyway. Maybe I had some help."

"Which parts?"

Lange waved his hands helplessly. "You shouldn't ask me to do what I can't do, Lieutenant!"

"Why can't you write an essay?"

He turned red. "Because I'm not good at it. I never got much schooling."

Jodenny opened up his record. He had grown up on Kiwi and had graduated from high school, but that didn't prove a standard of literacy. Schools on Kiwi were notoriously understaffed and underfunded. "RT Lange, if you need assistance with writing or reading, there's help available right here onboard."

"I'd need my gib to access it," he said bitterly.

"You can do it from the library. I'll have Sergeant Strayborn show you the tutorials. After that we'll talk about getting your gib back. You're dismissed."

She was all set to return to LD-G when AM Dyatt appeared at her door, as pregnant as ever. "Can I talk to you, ma'am?"

"Certainly." Jodenny had her sit down. "How's Ops?"

"It's okay, I guess. I miss my mates here in Supply." Dyatt fidgeted with the hem of her maternity shirt. "I didn't come here for me, though. I was wondering if you had a job for my boyfriend, AT Olsson."

Jodenny remembered him. "Wasn't he in that fight the other night?"

Dyatt picked at a hangnail. "It wasn't his fault, ma'am. People in Maintenance . . . well, it's not a good place to work. Nobody's happy, and there's things going on that Joe doesn't like, but there's nothing he can do about it. Him just being an AT and all."

"What kind of things?" Jodenny asked. "Things involving Chief Chiba?"

Dyatt shrugged.

Jodenny leaned back in her chair. "To be truthful, I don't know if I want AT Olsson working here."

Dyatt gave her a wounded look. "Won't you at least talk to him? He wants to do the right thing, honest he does."

"I heard you went to Sick Berth with a black eye the other day," Jodenny said. She'd checked into it after the fight between her division and Maintenance. Dyatt told everyone she had walked into a door, but no one really believed her.

"That wasn't Joe," Dyatt said firmly. "I swear it wasn't. And you don't have to worry, because it's not going to happen again. I'm not lying to you."

Jodenny sighed. She couldn't be sure if Dyatt was lying or not, and if Olsson was the kind of man who hit his pregnant girlfriend, she wanted nothing to do with him. But maybe if she talked to him she could find out information to use against Chiba and Quenger if the need arose. "All right. Tell Olsson to come see me. But no promises."

"Okay. Thanks, ma'am." Dyatt pulled herself up, red-faced with exertion. She patted her stomach. "You won't tell anyone

I said it, right? That Maintenance isn't any good? Chief Chiba would get awfully mad."

"I won't tell anyone," Jodenny promised. "In return, I want you to come to me if anyone hits you again. We'll make sure they go up on charges."

Dyatt gave her a rueful look. "I told you. There isn't going to be a next time."

After Dyatt was gone, Jodenny checked on Olsson's duty assignment and saw that he was attached to the Repair Shop on the Rocks. The same one where Myell had been turned away before the theft of Castalia, which reminded her of an item on her to-do list. "Holland, did that report ever come in from Loss Accounting? The one about the missing dingo?"

"No, Lieutenant. Would you like for me to request it again?"

"No," Jodenny said. "I'll ask myself."

She went up to the Security Department in person and asked for Sergeant Rosegarten. "She's on leave, ma'am," said the apprentice mate on duty. "Can I get someone else for you?"

"How about Sergeant Polson?"

"Sure, he's here."

A moment later Polson came out of an inner office. He listened to her request and said, "No problem, Lieutenant, I can look that up for you. You want a hard copy or imail one?"

"Both," she said.

He printed out a six-page report bearing Senga's and Rosegarten's signatures. Jodenny was reading it at the counter when Al-Banna pinged her to say, "The captain's office needs someone to take a diplomatic pouch down to New Christchurch. You've been volunteered."

"But we're still taking on deliveries, sir, and Chief Nitta's on shore leave."

"You've got sergeants, don't you? Besides, you should be done with deliveries by this afternoon. The pouch has got to be there by seventeen hundred hours. Come back up in the morning or take an extra day off."

Jodenny didn't like it, but she knew she had no real choice. "Yes, sir."

She packed an overnight bag, picked up the pouch from the

bridge, and went to catch the next birdie down to the planet. Commander Rokutan was in the B-Deck hangar, signing off on a pilot's requisition. As he handed it back to the pilot he nearly dropped it.

"I thought you were going to call me and come visit someday," Rokutan said to Jodenny. "Those of us in Flight Support get lonely out here."

His smile was wide and disarming, his eyes quite lovely to look at. Jodenny said, "My fault. I've been remiss."

"Well, call when you get back," he said earnestly. "Enjoy your shore leave."

On the way down to the planet she mused a bit about Rokutan, then turned her attention to Rosegarten's report on the missing DNGO. Nothing in it surprised her. Myell's statement was clear enough, and Rosegarten had corroborated with RT Engel that the Repair Shop had closed two hours before launch. That was awfully early, but Engel said it was just for that day so the shop could conduct inventory. Chief Chiba had also been in the Repair Shop at the time and he corroborated Engel. Neither of them recalled seeing the DNGO during the drill, but they hadn't been looking for it, either. Rosegarten had attached a roster from the safety pod under T6's access ring to prove that Myell had checked in forty seconds after the General Quarters began. Strayborn had confirmed his arrival, and stated that Myell stayed put during the drill. In the report's conclusion Rosegarten said that it was likely someone had taken the opportunity of the General Quarters drill to steal the DNGO, but Myell was clearly not to blame.

The words on the page should have made Jodenny happy, but she was perplexed. Why had it taken so long for Senga to sign off on such a simple report, and why the delay in letting her see it? Did Rosegarten know about the ongoing animosity between Chiba and Myell, and would that have made a difference in her conclusion?

The birdie landed a short time later. New Christchurch was modern and antiseptic in design, a metropolis of cream-colored buildings, uninspired sculptures, and carefully maintained public parks. She took a cab to Team Space headquarters, delivered the pouch to the duty officer, and trammed back downtown, where Holland had booked her into a tourist hotel. She ran into Minnich and Erickson in the lobby.

Erickson said, "Join us for dinner, Lieutenant."

"Thanks, but I can't," Jodenny said. "Have a good time."

She knew officers who partied with their divisions, who went to strip joints on Sundowner or beachside bars on Kiwi. Not a good idea, but sometimes she envied them their ability to drop the barriers of rank and privilege. Jodenny went to her room and changed into civvies. "Holland," she said, "when's the first birdie in the morning?"

"Ten hundred hours, Lieutenant. There's another at seventeen hundred, but that's it for the day. Flights are severely limited on Sundays due to religious restrictions."

"I'll be on the first one." Jodenny stretched out on the oversized bed, grateful for the soft mattress. "Did I receive an imail from Sergeant Polson? The Loss Accounting report?"

"Yes, it's in your queue."

"Read it and tell me what you think."

Holland was quiet for a moment. "I see nothing illogical in Sergeant Rosegarten's conclusion. Sergeant Myell doesn't seem to be at fault."

"I agree. But something . . . I don't know."

Staring at the ceiling didn't help anything. Jodenny locked her gib, the empty pouch, and most of her money in the room safe and walked over to the colorful open-air marketplace near the public library. The sidewalks were busy with crowds enjoying the day. She window-shopped and had coffee in a bookstore café, watching occasional members of the *Aral Sea* pass in the street. A police officer in a spiffy green coat gave an apprentice mate a ticket for jaywalking, much to the amusement of his companions. Jodenny finished her coffee and was on her way back to the hotel when Quenger and Nitta emerged from a bar and headed off toward the warehouse district, sunglasses and hats shading them from the late-afternoon sun.

Jodenny hung back to watch them. The two of them wore civvies, not uniforms, which ruled out the probability they were off to conduct official business. Besides, the warehouse district was closing for the day, hundreds of workers streaming home on foot or by public transportation. She told herself that their business was not her concern and that she should go have a nice dinner somewhere. But Nitta was her chief, damn it, and if he was up to no good she needed to know about it.

Not much to see in this part of New Christchurch, just blocks of gray warehouses and emptying parking lots and mag-lev freight trains. The sun was below the buildings now, leaving the sky a rosy shade of gold. Quenger and Nitta cut across pedestrian traffic to a narrow side street. As Jodenny moved to follow a man stepped in front of her and held up a hand.

"New Christchurch Police, miss." He was young and clean-shaven and had an official air about him, but he wasn't wearing a uniform or hat. "May I see your ID?"

"What?" Jodenny asked. "Why?"

"ID, please. Do you have any?"

His expression was sharp, his eyes narrow. Jodenny felt chastised, although she'd done nothing wrong. She pulled out her Team Space identity card and handed it over. She expected him to run it through his scanner or a gib, but he simply examined it and handed it back.

"I'd like for you to accompany me and answer a few questions."

"Accompany you where? Questions about what?"

"This way, please." He touched her elbow and steered her toward a plain gray flit parked at the curb.

Fear flashed through her. New Christchurch Police were the most by-the-book cops in the Seven Sisters, and this man hadn't even flashed a badge. "I need to call my ship first."

His light touch turned into a firm grip. "This won't take long."

Jodenny hooked her foot around his and shifted her weight. It was a simple move, one she'd learned in self-defense class. Her would-be abductor fell in an untidy heap. The people around them said, "Hey!" and "Watch it!" but Jodenny's arm was free, and she deftly evaded his attempt to latch on to her ankle. She pushed her way through the crowd, hoping to lose him in the crush.

"Stop!" the man called out. "You're under arrest!"

Heads turned. Someone tried to grab her and nearly ripped off her sleeve. Jodenny began to push against people in her haste to get away. In just seconds a second unmarked flit descended from the sky and blocked the street up ahead. A handful of men emerged and sprinted her way. Breathless, Jodenny lunged for a door in the wall, found it locked, threw herself at the next one, and yanked it open. A security robot shaped like a floating red apple confronted her.

"Name and access card, please," it said politely.

Jodenny ducked underneath it and locked the deadbolts behind her. The building was dim and warm and smelled like machine oil. Not the most prosperous of businesses, judging by the dirty green carpet and cheap overhead lighting. She jogged toward a distant exit sign, calling out, "Hello? Is anyone here?"

"Please halt," the secbot said, following her. "You are not authorized to enter this area."

She ducked into a darkened kitchen and tried to activate a comm mounted on the wall. Only an annoying buzz greeted her ears. The company must have programmed it to turn off after normal working hours. Jodenny followed the hall farther, past a unisex head and a safety workstation. Though there was a perch for a medbot, it was empty and filled with someone's discarded soda bottle.

The secbot continued to follow her. Still in that polite tone, it said, "Please desist from any illegal activities. I am recording your image for identification and possible criminal prosecution."

Jodenny gave it a hard look. The camera lens mounted in its torso was cracked, and half of the grill on its speaker was bent. Whoever owned the place didn't invest much money into security. Then again, on Mary River, why bother? If the company was a Team Space contractor, they probably billed Fleet for phony equipment and pocketed the money.

"I'm not going to do anything illegal," she told the machine. Jodenny found a set of double doors and yanked hard, but they were electronically locked. She peered through a dirty glass window and saw a poorly lit warehouse filled with a dozen or more rows of equipment. "Can you tell if those men outside are really the police?"

"My external sensors are currently nonfunctional," it said. "You are requested to leave these premises with haste."

Jodenny scanned the hallway for anything she could use to jimmy open the door. "Call the police and verify that they have officers outside."

"My external communications are currently nonfunctional. You are beseeched to depart before criminal activity occurs."

She broke open a fire box, grabbed the ax inside, and swung the blade against the door locks.

"Stop!" the secbot screeched. "Violation! Violation!"

Two blows later, the damaged door plate gave way. The secbot extended grappling arms and reached for Jodenny. She buried the ax in its torso and threw herself aside as it spun and crashed to the floor. Poor thing. She had never killed a machine before, but regret and financial reparations would have to wait.

Once in the warehouse, Jodenny gazed at dozens of rows of construction equipment and machine parts. The heavily loaded shelves, some of them dangerously sagging, stretched at least thirty feet toward a corrugated roof. Dust and grime coated many of the crates. The whole company was probably on the verge of failure, or in some kind of serious financial trouble. She could safely assume there wouldn't be any more secbots coming her way, but voices in the hall indicated a different problem.

"In here," one said, and a door opened somewhere off to her right. "Cut off the exits. Get all the lights on."

Jodenny slipped into the nearest aisle and pressed herself close to the crates. The lights overhead flickered and came on full strength, but there were plenty of shadows and dark spaces left to hide in. If they had heat sensors or pocket scanners they'd track her down soon enough.

"Come on out, Lieutenant!" a second man shouted. "Save yourself trouble later on."

Jodenny hooked her hands on the shelf behind her and

hauled herself up. A bin of small gears nearly tipped, and in her haste to catch it she stirred up dust that nearly made her sneeze. She tried squeezing her way through but the bins and crates were packed so tightly that she had to climb up one more shelf in order to do it. She heard men moving around below her and coordinating their efforts on their radios.

"Not down here," the first man said. "You're sure she came this way?"

"Someone killed that secbot."

A third man spoke, answering a question she couldn't hear. "Not yet! Don't let them interfere. They're ours, no one else's."

"Lieutenant Scott!" It was the second man again. He sounded older and angrier than the others. "It's your duty to cooperate. All we want to do is ask some questions."

She still didn't think they were local law enforcement. Team Space security? Men from Fleet? Why try to cart her off so quickly and forcibly, and without a good reason? The law-abiding part of her wanted to show herself, clear up any mis-understandings. The cautious part warned her that going off with armed and deceitful strangers was never a good idea.

Footsteps came closer. "Lieutenant, you're just making things worse."

A radio squawked somewhere. The second man said, "They lost them, fuck them all—we've got to move!"

Running footsteps, a slamming door, and silence. Jodenny waited, listening hard, but they didn't return. After several minutes she dropped to the floor as quietly as possible. There, in the distance, a conveyer belt stretched toward thick rubber flaps. Cautiously, keeping in the shadows, she made her way to it. The warehouse remained quiet and calm. They really had just gone off and left her. She wriggled through the flaps to an empty parking lot and a sky tinged gold with sunset. The fresh air was as refreshing as a drink of cold water.

But she wasn't totally in the clear. A flit was parked at the front of the building and two men were sitting inside. Jodenny pulled back before they could see her. The fence at the back of the parking lot had a gap in it, and on the other side was a freight yard where a mag-lev train was beginning to roll away.

Jodenny squeezed through the fence, sprinted after the caboose, grabbed a handrail, and swung up to a small grated platform. "Not so difficult," she said, to cheer herself up, but when she rattled the caboose door it refused to open. Damn it. The entire train was probably automated, with no human crew onboard to assist her. Because she had no desire to end up on the other side of the planet she leaned over, but the dry hard ground was rushing by faster and faster. Leaping would certainly lead to injury or death.

"Fine," Jodenny grumbled, and eased herself to a sitting position on the platform. She tried to catch her breath and calm the hammering of her heart. She reached for her gib, hoping to enlist Holland's expertise, but her belt loop was empty. She'd left it in her room, along with the rest of her things.

Jodenny buried her face in her hands until the lights of New Christchurch were gone. The mag-lev raced parallel to the evening traffic on the Bethlehem Parkway, but probably no one could see her sitting on the platform. She was glad that it was a summer night, not the dead of winter, and though her gib was back in her room she at least had her ID and some money. When the train made its first stop or slowed down enough for her to jump safely, she would simply hire a flit and get back to civilization.

And do what? Make a report, she supposed. Face the real police, if they came asking about that secbot. Try to find out who the men were that had followed her into the warehouse, and why they didn't want her to follow Quenger and Nitta.

The caboose shielded her from the wind, but the train's speed had picked up and the ride wasn't as smooth as it might look from afar. The tracks hooked east across dark cornfields. Jodenny tried pinpointing the *Aral Sea* above but its orbit had taken it to the other side of the planet. She consulted her watch. Seventy-two hours until departure. If she didn't make it back before then she would be AWOL, and if she couldn't report to a Team Space office within thirty days she would be labeled a deserter.

"Don't be silly," she told herself.

Mary River's small gray moon rose above the horizon and

cast light onto a distant set of Spheres. The moon, like the Seven Sisters themselves, had been modeled on Earth and its satellite. It reminded her that there were forces and mysteries in the universe much greater than herself, and brought an odd sort of comfort. Some unknown race of beings had made those Spheres, built the Alcheringa, terraformed seven planets for human habitation, and made space travel viable for humans. She didn't believe they still existed, as some did. She didn't believe they were looking out for her or any other human. But she did like to think there was some kind of plan for her life, and that whatever she did, she couldn't mess it up beyond repair.

Jodenny leaned back and relaxed. A short time later the train slowed down at a crossing and she gathered enough courage to hop off. The distance to New Christchurch was too far to walk, but she had seen a farmhouse a few kilometers back and she used the stars to navigate her way. Again she was glad for the mild weather. The farmhouse was brightly lit and surrounded by a dozen or so flits. Noise and fiddle music spilled out of the windows, causing her to hesitate. A group of men had gathered to talk on a side porch, and their voices carried easily on the breeze.

"It's the extremists," someone was saying. "Giving us all a black eye. We're going to have to branch off, split into our own group."

Another man disagreed. "Can't split up now. Not now that everyone's realizing how serious the movement is."

"Serious is making an economic impact," a third man said. "Not blowing up a ship."

Startled, Jodenny crouched low behind a bush. They were members of the Colonial Freedom Project, or at least sympathetic to the cause. She fisted her hands and dug her fingernails into her palms. So many dead on the *Yangtze,* all because of terrorists who wanted to strike out against Team Space's monopoly on the Alcheringa. Their senseless violence had served to solidify public opinion against them, but it had come at too dear a cost as far as Jodenny was concerned.

The front door of the farmhouse opened. A small dog barreled out, circled three times to make a spot for urination, and then honed in on Jodenny with furious barks.

"Sparkplug!" a woman called out. "Stop that ruckus!"

Jodenny nearly panicked, wondering whether it would be better to flee or try to hide, but she decided to show herself. "Sorry, that's probably me he's all worried about. I hate to bother you, but I was on my way to New Christchurch and got stranded. I'm looking for a ride."

An elderly woman with silver braids stepped off the porch and smiled warmly at her. "Sure enough, you're a long way from everywhere. Come on in, child."

The woman pulled her inside the warm, cozy farmhouse, where adults were waltzing in a large living room that had been cleared of furniture. The shindig looked more like a birthday party or barn social than a clandestine meeting of the CFP. A buffet table filled with a lavish amount of food took up most of the hall, and children in suits and dresses kept darting by to poke their fingers into desserts and frosted cakes. In no short order Jodenny had been steered to a corner chair with a heaping plate of food balanced in her lap.

"My boyfriend and I had a fight—" she tried to explain, but Mrs. Jackson, her hostess, merely handed her a glass of wine.

"The Lord brought you here." Mrs. Jackson patted her hand. "There's no mistaking that. Now, you eat and drink, and I'll be back in a bit."

Jodenny drank the wine. Not so bad, really. The fiddlers in the living room stopped for a round of applause, then launched into a new song. A very pregnant woman in a blue dress shuffled by, both hands supporting her back, and Jodenny immediately offered up her chair.

"Thanks," the woman said, sitting in obvious relief. "You must be the stranger Mrs. Jackson's going on about. I'm Dottie."

Jodenny offered her hand. She had already decided using her real name wasn't a wise idea. "Kay."

"Got lost, did you?" Dottie asked.

"More than you can imagine."

Dottie leaned back. She had a pretty face, pink and glowing the way only pregnant women ever managed. "Well, the last bus went through hours ago. Tomorrow's the Sabbath and no devout believer will drive, but maybe my brother-in-law will take you where you need to go."

"I'd be very grateful."

"When my husband wanders through we'll grab him," Dottie said.

Dottie's husband Colby came by a few minutes later. He looked vaguely familiar to Jodenny, but she figured that after one more glass of wine everyone at the party would look like an old friend. "So how'd you get stranded out here anyway?" Colby asked, a glint in his eye. "Not like it's on the way to anywhere special."

"Bad luck," Jodenny said, "compounded with bad timing."

"Been there myself," Colby said.

Mrs. Jackson came by with more desserts. "Well, that sounds fine," she said, upon hearing the plan. "Tonight you can stay here with us, Kay. We'll be having services at sunrise, and it's great having guests."

Dottie started to lever herself upright. "Actually, we've asked Kay to stay with us. Always a spare sofa around, that's our motto."

Colby helped his wife up. "Is it? Good. Everyone needs a motto."

The flit ride to Colby and Dottie's place only took fifteen minutes or so. Jodenny sat in the rear, dead tired but as alert as she could make herself. She was grateful that neither of her hosts were pressing her about the circumstances that had brought her to the countryside, but worried that Colby was one of the men she'd overheard on the porch. It wouldn't do any good at all to deliver herself to the CFP, especially if they found out she was from Team Space. Colby and Dottie spoke softly in the front, their words too low for Jodenny to hear over the engines.

"I don't mean to be an imposition," Jodenny said. "I can go back to Mrs. Jackson's."

Dottie turned around and gave her a weary smile. "Don't

you worry. I wouldn't leave a pet with that woman, not unless I wanted it proselytized by morning."

Minutes later Colby was bringing the flit to a stop in front of a low farmhouse set on a hillside. Clouds had gathered overhead, hiding the moon and stars. A man stepped off the farmhouse's front porch as they approached, his features hidden in the dark.

"How'd everything go?" Colby asked, circling around the flit to help Dottie out.

"No structural damage," the other man said, and Jodenny immediately recognized the voice. Sergeant Myell stepped closer to the light of the flit dome. "They're finally asleep, and if you wake them I'll kill you both."

"Good," Colby said. "We brought home a guest, Terry. Hope you don't mind."

She'd never seen Myell out of uniform before. He was wearing jeans and a cream-colored sweater and was barefoot. He hadn't shaved in a few days, lending him a rough and roguish air, and he had his arms folded across his chest. When he saw her his face went slack with surprise.

Jodenny stepped out of the flit. "Hi, Terry. I'm Kay."

Myell's expression didn't change. "Hello . . . Kay."

Colby helped Dottie lumber inside. Jodenny followed, acutely aware of Myell staring at her. The living room was dark but for a small table lamp.

Dottie asked, "Would you like to take a shower, Kay?"

She glanced down at her grimy trousers. "That would be great. Thanks."

The water was luxuriously hot but she kept her shower short. Dottie had left clothes for her, including a nightgown covered with red roses and a pink bathrobe with lace collars. When Jodenny emerged from the bathroom, Colby was making up the living-room sofa and Myell was changing the sheets in the guest room. Jodenny stepped in behind him.

"Hello, Kay," Myell said, stuffing a pillow into a green linen pillowcase. "Tell me why you're not Lieutenant Scott?"

"It has nothing to do with you or your family. I promise."

He stopped what he was doing and gave her a penetrating

gaze. Jodenny tried not to squirm. Myell's eyes were deep brown in the honey light of the bedside lamp, and the beige sweater brought out flecks of gold in his irises. Jodenny wondered what it would be like to listen to the thump of his chest and feel his breath against her neck.

"They don't know about what happened," Myell said. "Wendy Ford and all that."

"I won't say anything."

He stared at her. Jodenny tried to read his mind. Was he as attracted to her as she was to him? If her life was a romance vid, they could share a night of illicit passion, give in to base impulses, break all the rules, and then break them again. But physical desire was a trap that could only lead to trouble, and she had no idea how he really felt about her. Assumptions had certainly gotten her into trouble before.

"I'll be on the sofa if you need anything," he said, and brushed past her on his way out.

Jodenny wanted to argue—it didn't seem fair for him to give up the guest room for her—but she didn't want to wake the children with an argument. Soon the whole house was dark. Rest came in fitful spurts, and in her dreams she returned to the speeding mag-lev. This time Myell was with her, his arms wrapped around her and his warm voice saying, "It's all right. We'll be fine." The train took them up into the sky and on a dreamy trip down the Alcheringa. She woke, then, the bedsheets cool against her legs, the window curtains stirring in the breeze. She imagined Myell standing in the doorway, waiting for her invitation.

"Terry?" she asked.

Silence except for the faint tick-tock of a clock somewhere. As Jodenny's eyes grew accustomed to the moonlight she saw the door was closed. Terry Myell had never been standing there with desire in his heart. Jodenny turned over, closed her eyes, and went back to her dreams.

CHAPTER **SEVENTEEN**

Colby's sofa was fine to sit on but hell for sleeping. Myell punched his pillow and tried to make himself comfortable on a frame that was just a few centimeters too short. He kicked off the blanket and sheets. To the accompaniment of the grandfather clock—had the damn thing always been so loud?—he pondered the presence of Jodenny Scott in the next room. Just when he'd begun to put Underway Stores out of his mind, she had to show up. Sure did look beautiful in Dottie's nightclothes, though. Or maybe it was the fact she wasn't wearing lieutenant bars that made him realize how attracted he was to her. And how much trouble that could cause. Sergeants were not supposed to lust so completely over their lieutenants.

He really should have gone AWOL back on Kookaburra.

Myell got up to use the bathroom and found himself standing outside the guest room. He wanted, more than anything, to open the door and see that she was sleeping okay. Of course she was. She was an adult, and she'd done a lot of sleeping in her life. All he needed to do to cement his sordid reputation was to be caught leering at her while she slept.

Back to the sofa he went. And punched his pillow some more, until sleep took him away. Somehow Colby and Dottie kept the kids quiet in the morning, because he didn't awaken until well after sunrise. Bleary-eyed and groggy, he padded barefoot toward the kitchen in search of coffee. The kids, Jodenny, and Dottie were in the backyard, playing softball with the basebot. He stepped out onto the back porch to watch them.

"Morning, sleepyhead," Dottie said.

Jodenny took her position at the plate. The basebot threw a pitch. She swung, but the ball sailed safely past her bat into Jake's glove.

"You swing like a girl," Jake said.

Myell choked on his coffee.

"Hold it higher," Jake said helpfully. "Swing from your hips."

Such attractive hips they were, too. Jodenny had borrowed pants and a short-sleeved shirt from Dottie. Her loose hair, freed from its customary braid, fell halfway down her back in dark, luscious curls. Jodenny's next swing sent the ball sailing into left field. Adryn sprinted to second base.

Jake pulled off his mask. "Come on, Uncle Terry! You're up!"

He stayed where he was. "I don't think so."

"We need another runner, and Mom won't do it," Adryn said.

"Yeah, come on," Jake wheedled.

Myell waited for Jodenny to join in the persuasive attempts, but she only smiled at something across the field. He ambled to home plate and hit the first pitch the basebot threw. The ball sailed high and landed somewhere near the barn. While the basebot hurried to retrieve it, Adryn, Jodenny, and Myell all crossed home plate.

"Apparently, you don't swing like a girl," Jodenny told him, smiling.

Erma fixed breakfast. Colby's came in from the pasture to partake of soy sausage and pancakes. Myell sat across the table from Jodenny and tried to keep the conversation focused on the kids' school projects, but Colby's and Dottie's curiosity wouldn't be denied.

"So what do you do, Kay?" Colby asked.

"Paperwork. Lots and lots of paperwork."

Jake speared his soy sausages with a fork. "When I grow up I'm going to join Team Space like Uncle Terry."

Dottie asked, "Have you ever been in space, Kay?"

Jodenny replied, "Yes. It's lovely. Adryn, what about you? What are you going to do when you grow up?"

Adryn chewed her food before answering. "A vet. I have a horse. Want to see?"

"After breakfast," Colby said.

"I've only been in space once," Dottie said. "Colby and I emigrated from Baiame."

Jodenny reached for her glass. "You didn't like it there?"

"More infrastructure and opportunities here," Colby said. "Inexpensive land, good programs for farmers. Baiame's a tough place to raise a family and keep a farm going."

"My grandparents had a farm there," Jake offered. "Everything went to seed after Grandma killed herself and Grandpa started to drink."

Myell shot Colby a frosty look. He had always figured Colby had told the kids about his childhood, but those particular details hadn't really been necessary. All they needed to know about their grandmother was that she had come from Australia as a little girl, had been pretty and smart, and that she had died. The Myell family story devolved quickly after that, and it was not one to be shared with children at bedtime or lieutenants at breakfast.

Dottie said, "I think both of you kids are done eating. Get to your chores."

"I'm going to clean off and go pack," Myell said to Jodenny. "After that we can be on our way back to New Christchurch."

He showered quickly, hoping Dottie wasn't explaining to Jodenny exactly what Jake had been talking about. She might be his division officer, but his family's history was none of her business. Myell rinsed off, threw on clean clothes, and went to pack his things. Dottie was in the guest room with his mother's teak jewelry box in hand.

"You should take this," she said.

Myell grabbed his rucksack. "You keep it."

"It's not—" Quite unexpectedly, she threw her arms around him and murmured, "I know it's hard. But she loved you."

He squeezed her tight. "Give it to Adryn. Honestly, what would I do with it on a starship? Someone would probably steal it, anyway."

Dottie didn't argue with him, but she didn't look happy, either. "I'll go make you some lunch to take with you."

He finished packing, made sure he had left nothing behind, and brought his rucksack outside. Colby had driven the flit up from the lane and was sitting on the hood, twisting a piece of straw between his fingers. Myell dropped his bag into the backseat.

Colby said, "Jake has a big mouth. But there's nothing wrong with talking about it."

"There's a time and a place," Myell said.

"Not with you," Colby replied. "There's never been a time or a place."

Myell didn't answer. The screen door on the porch swung open as Dottie, Jodenny, and the kids appeared. Jake and Adryn carried a large picnic basket to the flit and argued over where best to put it. Colby got to his feet and said, "We'll send pictures soon as the baby's born. Make sure you get back here before your namesake gets too old, right?"

"I will," Myell said. "You take care."

Jodenny again thanked Colby and Dottie for their hospitality and got into the flit. Myell gave Dottie and the kids hugs and shook Colby's hand.

"Promise you'll write," Dottie said, and he did.

Myell climbed behind the steering controls and started the flit down the lane. Jodenny said nothing in the seat beside him, and for that he was grateful. Both his gib and pocket server were at the bottom of his rucksack, far from any useful implementation.

When they reached the main road he asked, "Why didn't you want them to know who you were?"

"It was easier if they didn't know I was your boss."

Easier for her, maybe. Now that they had left the farm, he was incontrovertibly under her command again. That, if anything, was a reminder of why he wanted to leave Team Space. In truth, she had still been his superior officer when she was in that nightgown.

"How did you get stranded out of town?" he asked.

Jodenny rolled her window down. "It's not important."

One of the scenarios he'd envisioned during the long night kept gnawing at him. "Did someone just dump you in the middle of nowhere?" he asked.

"No, but that was the story I was going to tell anyone who asked too much." Her tone indicated that was all the answer he was going to get. "Once we get back to the ship, you shouldn't mention this to anyone. It wouldn't be in either of our best interests."

"Should I give you the car and walk back into town on my own, so people don't see us together?"

She sounded annoyed. "You know as well as I do what damage gossip does."

"I know what damage lying does," he answered.

She didn't answer. Myell gave up trying to pretend they were two normal people having a normal conversation. Kay, the woman who'd played baseball and admired a little girl's horse, had been left behind at the farm. If she had ever existed at all.

"What was said about my mother . . ." Myell kept his eyes on the road. "I'd appreciate it if that didn't get repeated."

Jodenny made a small surprised sound. "I wouldn't. Never."

He nodded. Another kilometer passed before Jodenny said, "I read the report from Loss Accounting about the missing dingo. Sergeant Rosegarten confirmed that it wasn't your fault."

"Good," Myell said.

"I heard Chief Chiba's been giving you trouble."

Myell turned south onto Bethlehem Parkway. The local Spheres appeared, solid and unyielding against the sky. "Nothing that you need to worry about, Lieutenant."

Jodenny made a small skeptical sound.

"Chiba just likes to show off," Myell insisted. "Has the power and likes to use it. Don't tell me there aren't officers who do the same thing, because we both know differently."

"There's a difference between showing off and bullying. That fight last week between the two divisions—someone could have gotten seriously hurt."

Myell hadn't forgotten about the clash. "I didn't ask anyone to get involved."

"If you knew someone in your division was being harassed, you wouldn't take the initiative to intervene?"

Damn her for making it sound so easy. Myell decided silence was his best strategy. Jodenny turned her head to the window and, after a moment, said, "Stop for a moment, will you?"

Warily Myell pulled the flit over.

"Do we have time to swing by those Spheres?" she asked.

He checked the clock. "If you want. The next birdie doesn't leave until late this afternoon."

Myell angled the flit across the fields and parked in a dirt lot. Jodenny said, "I'll be back in a few," and headed off with a water bottle in hand. He sat on the hood with his arms crossed, glad for the shade of the Father Sphere. Two eagles chased each other across the sky, but the grandeur of the site was ruined by overflowing trash bins and graffiti on the historic site marker. That was a shame. Like the pyramids of Earth, the Spheres deserved to be protected and preserved. But then again Spheres had never held archaeological treasure or dead pharaohs. They were as much a mystery as the Alcheringa itself, and such mysteries lost their allure as decades passed.

"Lieutenant?" he called out. "Anything in particular you're looking for?"

Jodenny emerged from the Mother Sphere. "No. Someone told me a theory, that's all. A stupid idea."

A low, mournful sound filled the air, like someone blowing an animal's horn. The noise stiffened the hairs on the back of Myell's neck. He slid off the hood and scanned the horizon, but it seemed to be coming from the interior of the Mother Sphere. Jodenny turned toward it.

"Careful, Lieutenant."

"It must be a trick of the wind," she said. "Spheres don't make noise."

The horn died away, leaving his ears ringing. When Jodenny started toward the arched entrance he said, "You sure that's a good idea?"

Jodenny gave him a considering glance and headed inside. He grabbed the torch from the flit and followed her under the arch inscribed with Wondjina runes. He had been inside Spheres before, of course. Sometimes, when Daris was in a particularly bad mood, he and Colby had taken refuge in the group a few kilometers from their farm. Once inside this one, it took a moment for Myell's eyes to adjust to the darkness. As he played the light over its interior he saw a large metal ring laying in the dirt. It was some kind of welded sculpture, at least three meters in diameter. The sight of it made him distinctly uneasy.

"This wasn't here a minute ago," Jodenny said.

"We should leave," he said.

Jodenny tilted her head at it, stepped back, then crouched down and put her hand on the ring. "It's an ouroboros. A snake eating its tail."

Myell wanted to backtrack to the flit, but he wasn't about to leave her alone. He bent low and thumbed the metal. It was roughly the width of his forearm and was faintly warm, as if it had been sitting in the sun and not inside a stone structure. He cocked his head, noting scales and wings, swirls and whorls.

"It's a Rainbow Serpent," he said.

"A what?"

Old childhood stories came to mind, along with the unsettling visions he'd had of the shaman. "Created the lands and rivers and all who live in it. Made the world itself."

"My mythology's a little rusty." Jodenny gingerly stepped inside the ring.

"Lieutenant," he warned. "I really think we should get out of here."

She probably thought this was one big adventure. Something to tell the wardroom about, or put in her performance evaluation. Supply lieutenant discovers ancient sculpture. But the weight of the Sphere pressed down on Myell and he could almost feel the shaman's glare on the back of his skull. "Lieutenant," he said again as she crouched down to the inside of the serpent.

"There are two symbols here. Like Wondjina runes."

Swallowing hard, he forced himself into the ring alongside her. The symbols were deeply etched into the metal, and spaced just a few centimeters apart.

Jodenny pointed at the first one. "At the risk of sounding caffeine-deprived, that looks like a cup of coffee."

Myell squinted. He supposed she could interpret it that way, though he wasn't so sure. The symbols weren't like any Wondjina runes he'd ever seen.

"And this one could be a slice of pie," Jodenny said, indicating the second symbol but being careful not to touch it.

The horn sounded again. This time it sounded like it was coming from the dome of the Mother Sphere itself, and the vibrations rattled the back of his teeth. "It's a warning," he said.

"Maybe just some kind of announcement."

"Or a General Quarters alarm—" Myell started, but then a wall of yellow light swept over them and cut off his words. The light shoved him hard through what felt like a brick wall. When his senses returned he was on both knees, dazed and coughing. The serpent ring was intact and the Mother Sphere unchanged around them.

"What was that?" he asked.

Jodenny grabbed his arm, barely able to stand. "Let's get out of here."

They mutually supported each other out of the Sphere and into the muted green sunlight of a tropical jungle. Humid air redolent of dirt and rot pressed in on Myell from all sides. He slid bonelessly to his knees, sweat already beading between his shoulder blades.

"Shit and spice," Jodenny said, staring into the distance.

The Mother Sphere they'd emerged from was just one of several Mothers trailing away like a line of old gray soldiers. Many of them were broken or crushed. Though the jungle was teeming with growth, the dirt and airspace around each Sphere was barren in all directions. Maybe it was radioactivity, maybe poison, but someone or something had tried to destroy these Spheres and left them so damaged that nothing alive grew near.

Myell didn't know what exactly had happened, he didn't know if he felt numb or dull with surprise, he didn't know what to make of any of it—but he knew one thing for sure.

They weren't on Mary River anymore.

* * *

Delayed reaction set in, making Jodenny vomit into the dirt. She heaved for a full minute, the acid of semidigested breakfast burning her throat. Afterward she wiped her mouth with her sleeve. Myell looked pale and shocky, almost as bad as she felt, but as she groped for the bottle hitched to her belt she was selfishly glad she wasn't alone. She took a sip of water, spat it out, took another, and swallowed. Her mouth tasted fuzzy.

"This isn't Mary River," Myell said when she passed him the bottle.

"No." Jodenny gazed at the row of Mother Spheres with a leaden feeling in her stomach. "It's nowhere in the Seven Sisters. We must have found some kind of Wondjina transportation device that's still working after all these years."

"Maybe it's simpler than that," Myell said. "We're hallucinating."

She toed the dirt beneath them. "Most vivid hallucination I ever had."

A few more moments passed before Jodenny was able to stand without feeling faint. She had spent time in the rain forests of Fortune and recognized kauri trees, several red cedars, and a mammoth cathedral fig. Daisies and bluebells, snails and bees—she didn't have to look far to confirm this was a world with a familiar ecosystem.

"You sure we're not in the Sisters?" Myell asked.

"If we are, it would have to be some remote corner of the tropics that no one has charted yet. No one ever reported this kind of formation of Spheres." Jodenny couldn't help but smile. "I think we've discovered another kind of Alcheringa."

Myell didn't answer. Already sweating from the heat, Jodenny turned in a circle to take in every detail she could. Green, green, green, as far as the eye could see. Birds of paradise sprouting amid giant tree roots. Mushrooms wider than the spread of her arms. She wrapped her arms across her chest and gave herself a gleeful hug. Jackie MacBride had discovered the Little Alcheringa, and others had discovered the river between the Seven Sisters, but she, Jodenny Scott, had discovered the secret of the Spheres.

"Maybe we're not supposed to be here," Myell said. "If the

Wondjina meant for us to use the Spheres, then people would have found snake rings a long time ago."

"Ouroboros," Jodenny said, because that sounded more scientific. "Let's explore some more."

"No," Myell said. "We should see if the ring will take us back."

"But the potential here—"

"Means nothing if we can't get home," he said, and pushed her back inside the Mother Sphere.

By the faint light that fell through the archway she saw the ouroboros was indeed still in place, with Myell's torch abandoned near one edge of it. Cautiously he leaned over and snagged it. He played the light over the walls around them, but they were as smooth and unmarked as any she'd ever seen before. He studied the symbols on the ring.

"Maybe one's for Mary River, the other for here," Jodenny said.

"Or maybe it's a warning," Myell said. "Stay away, don't use this. The thing is, Lieutenant, you can't really trust snakes."

He spoke as if the ouroboros had a mind of its own. Jodenny said, "We need to investigate those other Spheres. Get some plant samples, some—"

The horn sounded again, low and mournful. Myell stepped into the ring. "Come on."

"But we don't have any proof—"

"If we don't take our chance now, we might never get back."

"We can try—" Jodenny started, but Myell grabbed her by the arms and pulled her inside the ring just as the yellow light swept down out of nowhere.

Jodenny regained consciousness with Myell slumped in the driver's seat beside her. The Mary River sun had set, leaving the Father, Mother, and Child Spheres before her as silhouettes against the red and purple sky. She had only vague memories of Myell half carrying, half dragging her from the Mother Sphere to the flit.

"Sergeant." She touched his hand. Cool, but he had a strong

pulse. "Sergeant," she repeated, more loudly, and he shifted in his seat.

"Ouch," he complained.

"We're back."

Myell's head lolled. He opened his eyes. "Hell of a trip."

They sipped at their water bottles for several minutes. The sky faded to dark and the air grew cold. The Spheres were dark against the stars. "We have to tell someone," Jodenny said. "Otherwise the next person who walks in there will get a hell of a surprise."

"Tell who?" he asked.

"Fleet, for starters."

Myell snorted. "The organization that has a monopoly on all travel down the Alcheringa? If it is some kind of galactic transportation system, Team Space won't want anyone to know until they figure out how to control it and profit off it. That trip you and I just took might cost fifty thousand yuros, probably. Maybe a hundred thousand. They'd really have every colonist or traveler by the throat then."

Jodenny gazed in consternation at the Mother Sphere. "You'd rather tell the media? Who knows what might happen. People would come try it, and end up marooned or dead. We have a responsibility to our chain of command."

Myell sipped at his water and didn't answer.

She took that as acquiescence. "Do you have your gib? Mine's at my hotel. We need pictures, some kind of proof."

Myell reached into the backseat and rummaged around in his rucksack. He pulled out something small and wooden, a box of some kind.

"What's that?" Jodenny asked.

"Nothing." He sounded annoyed. He shoved it back into the sack, took out his gib, and stepped out of the car. "I'll get the pictures."

"Wait for me." Jodenny opened her own door, but her legs were still wobbly and threatened to give out if she took more than three steps. Myell eased her back to the seat.

"I'll be back soon, Kay," he said.

"Sergeant Myell," she said, making it a command. She

didn't want him to go alone. Myell ignored her and went back to the Mother Sphere. He returned a few minutes later.

"It's gone," he said.

Jodenny went to see for herself. The ouroboros had disappeared completely, without even an indentation on the ground to mark its prior existence.

"They're going to say we made it up," Myell said, and almost sounded relieved.

"But we didn't!"

He spread his hands in a not-my-fault gesture.

"If we wait long enough, it'll come back," Jodenny predicted. But several minutes passed, then a half hour, then an hour, and still the ring didn't return. They didn't even hear the horn. Jodenny was cold and had a headache and Myell, sitting in the archway with a torch in hand, didn't look much better. She took pictures of the dirt, hoping that perhaps a computer could pick out what human eyes couldn't see. Finally she said, "I suppose we should go."

The drive back to New Christchurch passed in silence. The Bethlehem Parkway was nearly deserted. Jodenny tuned the radio to the local news but heard nothing about her being wanted by the police or strange occurrences noted near Spheres. As Myell took the exit toward downtown she told him where her hotel was and said, "I think we should both keep quiet until we can figure out more about what happened."

"No problem." Myell stopped the flit around the corner from her hotel. "It's probably best you get out here."

Jodenny stepped out to the curb. Her leg ached and her eyes had a gritty, sandpapery feel to them. She wondered if she should order both of them to the hospital, to investigate any lingering medical effects of being pushed and shoved through space. "What about you? The birdie left hours ago."

His voice was neutral. "I'll check into the barracks."

She wished she knew what he was thinking. "I'll see you back on the ship, then."

Myell drove off without a backward glance. Jodenny walked around the corner to her hotel and decided that if she was arrested, she had to keep Myell and his family out of it.

The lobby was empty, however, and the clerk at the front desk ignored her. At the public kiosk in the lobby Jodenny put a call through to the ship. Vu's agent said she was busy but Strayborn answered on the first ping.

"Hey, Lieutenant," he said. "Enjoying your liberty?"

Strayborn might be under orders to lull her into a false sense of security, but she sensed nothing amiss about him. "It's been interesting. Anything going on up there?"

"Nothing we can't handle."

Still wary, she signed off and took the lift to her floor. Her thumbprint opened the door lock, and when she inched inside and flipped on the lights she saw that the room was as perfectly ordered as she had left it. Too perfect, perhaps. The bedspread was unwrinkled and tight, though she had been lying on it before she went out for dinner. The cleaning bot, she told herself. But she didn't rest easy until she opened the wall safe. Inside, untouched, were the diplomatic pouch, her gib, and her wallet.

"Holland," she said to the gib. "Are you there?"

"Good evening, Lieutenant. How may I be of assistance?"

She sat down on the edge of the bed. "Anything trigger your security alerts lately? Any inquiries or data trespassing?"

"No, ma'am."

Try as she might, Jodenny couldn't shake the feeling that someone had been in the room. Maybe it was silly, or maybe instinct. She packed up her things and went to check out. Down at the front desk, the clerk said, "Did you enjoy your stay, Lieutenant?"

Sure she did. She had enjoyed it so much she was thinking of recommending Mary River for anyone who enjoyed conspiracies, paranoia, and leaping onto mag-lev trains. Maybe they could package danger, sell it like a theme park. Throw in an unexpected journey to the other side of the universe with a handsome sergeant and they'd be sure to have a surge in customers.

Jodenny took a cab to the officers' barracks at Fleet and rented a room. She barely slept at all. In the morning she skipped the first birdie so she wouldn't see Myell and opted for the second flight instead. At the port she had a brief moment of panic when the security guard ran her ID through his machine and frowned.

"Something wrong?" Jodenny asked.

"Not quite." The guard's gib rang and he answered it with a distracted, "Johnson here."

She vowed to go quietly, no argument, let the lawyers figure it out. As long as they didn't handcuff her when they dragged her away, she figured she could live with the humiliation.

"Hey, Lieutenant!" someone called out cheerily. It was Erickson, standing with Minnich. "You're holding up the line!"

She held up a hand. A wave or a surrender, depending on what came next. The guard hung up his gib and whacked the scanner solidly with the palm of his hand.

"You're all clear, Lieutenant."

Until the very moment the birdie departed, she expected police to board and haul her away. While the ship arced toward the *Aral Sea,* she envisioned guards waiting for her in the docking bay. The skittishness made her angry. Why should she be so worried? Sure, she'd destroyed a secbot, but unknown men had been chasing her. Then a Wondjina transportation device had pulled her from Mary River to God-knew-where and back again. And she was fairly sure she was falling in love with Sergeant Terry Myell.

Unexpectedly she began to laugh.

"Lieutenant?" the RT beside her asked. "You okay?"

"Fine." Jodenny stifled a giggle. "No worries."

When the birdie landed she expected Commander Picariello to be waiting for her with his one blue eye and one brown eye, but there was only the normal security checkpoint. Jodenny went directly to her cabin. It was as clean and orderly as she had left it. She took a long hot shower and told herself to relax, but when she checked her imail there was a summons from Commander Al-Banna.

The message wasn't marked urgent, but she headed for the Flats anyway. One of the AMs from Flight Services was sitting behind the counter.

"Hi, Lieutenant," she said cheerfully. "Go right in."

The mate's easy manner was obviously a ploy. No doubt a dozen armed security techs were waiting in Commander Al-Banna's office. His hatch was open, though, and he was propping his prayer mat up in the corner. Muslims always knelt toward the bow while in space.

"Sir? You wanted to see me?"

"How was Mary River?"

She chose her words carefully. "It was interesting, sir."

"I don't see how. Mary River's probably the most boring patch of self-righteous prudishness in the galaxy. You going to stand there or do you need an invitation to sit?"

Jodenny sat.

Al-Banna took his own chair and leaned back in it. He squeezed a hand vise in his left hand, methodically working the muscles. "Kal Ysten has asked to be transferred out of Food Services to Flight Support."

Jealousy stabbed through her. Ysten didn't deserve Flight Support.

"Don't look so envious, Lieutenant. I told him he's going to you instead. Apparently he's desperate enough to get out of the galley that he accepted. If you can train the idiot properly, he'll make a fine assistant for you."

She was so alarmed that she lost her sense of tact. "Sir, I have enough idiots of my own."

Al-Banna grinned and squeezed the vise a few more times. "You don't have a choice. The minute we leave Mary River, he's yours. Take young Ysten and mold him into a fine officer. Either that or beat him until he bleeds. I have no preference."

"Yes, sir." She didn't know whether to be pleased or annoyed, honored or burdened. The aches of the trip through the Mother Sphere still lingered in her bones and muscles, and she had hopes of crawling into her bed for about twenty hours' sleep. She remembered the strength of Myell's hand in hers, and a row of broken Mother Spheres in the green-tinted sunlight.

"Lieutenant."

"Sir?"

Al-Banna put the vise down. "If Ysten gives you serious

trouble, you can come to me. I hope you know that's true about anything at all. You have questions, you have doubts, you tell me. Understood?"

She swallowed past a suddenly dry throat. "Yes, sir."

"Good. So what did you really think of Mary River?"

For a moment she was tempted to tell him everything.

"Just another day, another planet, sir," she said, and left it at that.

CHAPTER EIGHTEEN

Myell had spent a restless night in the open-bay enlisted barracks, listening to other men snore and fart and mumble. Intermittent sleep brought visions of Mother Spheres stretching off into the mist, their stones crumbled and covered with moss. Yellow light followed, sending him spiraling into darkness and sickness. "Choose," the shaman said, and the Rainbow Serpent hissed across the sky. By sunrise Myell was shaving bleary-eyed in a mirror, and at the spaceport he was first in line to board the birdie. Back on the *Aral Sea* he dumped his gear in his cabin. When he pulled out his mother's jewelry box, Koo climbed up on the rock in her aquarium and peered down at it.

"I told her I didn't want it," he muttered.

Myell rested his hand on the box for a moment, then stashed it unopened in his locker and stretched out on his bunk. He could still feel the enervating effects of the yellow light, the weakness that made his bones feel like water. For the first time he let himself dwell on what they had found. A secret transportation system. A whole new Alcheringa. But he didn't think it had been meant for mankind. Grabbing his gib, he started skimming Aboriginal mythology for references to the Rainbow Serpent. Some called it Almudj, others Ngalyod or Uluru, and many believed it was the bringer of rain, growth, and all fertility. The Great Creator.

Crazy, mitzi stuff.

But if he was nuts then Jodenny was, too. Myell remembered carrying her back to the flit, her body soft and warm in his arms. He had wanted to sweep her away for good, to someplace where regulations held no sway. But she wasn't Kay, wasn't someone he could hold and love, and it was hell to keep torturing himself.

Though he was dead tired, he pulled on his sneakers and headed for the gym. A few hard kilometers on the treadmill and maybe he'd forget what it was like to have had Jodenny in his arms and not be able to keep her.

Jodenny spent the day holed up in her cabin, inputting everything that had happened on Mary River into an encrypted log. She included the destruction of the warehouse robot and spending the night on Myell's farm, but didn't write down how Myell made her feel, or the way she'd wanted him to come to her door in the middle of the night. Of their remarkable trip she put in every detail she could remember: the feeling of the hard yellow light, the sickness it caused, the line of the broken Mother Spheres. Jesus Moon Christ, she might be sitting on the most amazing discovery since Jackie MacBride and the Little Alcheringa.

"Holland," she said, "has anyone ever found Wondjina Spheres in formations other than Father, Mother, and Child?"

"No, Lieutenant," Holland replied.

Jodenny sketched out the symbols that had been inscribed within the ouroboros. "Can you identify the symbols on my gib?"

"They don't match anything in the ship's databases."

She didn't know whether to be disappointed or even more excited. "Do they match any known instances of Wondjina runes?"

"No. Wondjina runes are usually straight lines, without any curves."

"Analyze the pictures I uploaded of the ground. Do you see anything other than dirt?"

Holland was quiet for a second or two. "Lieutenant, are you joking with me?"

"No."

Holland saw nothing that Jodenny didn't see. No ultraviolet images, no images invisible to the human eye. She had bagged and stowed her boots at the bottom of her locker for later analysis. Chances were that any mud, grass, or microbes she had picked up on that other planet weren't in any way unusual from those normally found in the Seven Sisters, and she couldn't think of any easy way to get samples tested. Supply lieutenants didn't have access to that kind of equipment or resources.

But ship's scientists did. Jodenny pinged Dr. Ng and waited for a callback, but her queue remained silent. Perhaps she'd scared him off too effectively.

The ship departed Mary River early that evening. Dinner in the wardroom was a busy affair, with everyone full of tales about how they'd spent their shore leave. "Didn't you get to go down at all, Jodenny?" Hultz asked, and Jodenny admitted yes, for a little while. Kal Ysten, she noted, didn't put in an appearance at all. She sent him a note saying she expected him to be in her office at oh-six-thirty the next morning. He sauntered in just a minute or so late, his hair still wet from the shower.

"I don't think Underway Stores is a good match for my abilities," he said.

Jodenny shut down the vid she'd been reading about Major Jackie MacBride. "For someone who got fired from Food Services, that's quite a bold statement."

"I didn't get fired." The tips of his ears turned red. "It was a mutual decision."

"I heard Lieutenant Commander Vu gave you your midterm counseling and you were failing in three categories."

"I don't think this is the best way to start working together, Lieutenant."

Jodenny stood up. "We don't work together. You work for me and you work for the people who serve under you. By tomorrow I want you to have memorized the names and faces of all division personnel. We're going to quarters now, so you'll get the chance to meet most of them anyway. For the rest of the day you'll be visiting their work spaces and doing safety inspections."

Ysten rolled his eyes. "Safety inspections? Is that the best use of my time?"

"Trust me." Jodenny headed for the hatch. "You don't want to know the other options I was considering."

Everyone had made it back from leave safely, although Nagarajan was sporting a pink hair streak and Nitta had an unsightly hickey on his neck. Jodenny tried not to stare at it, but wondered if maybe that was part of the business he and Quenger had been up to on Mary River. Myell, in the back row as usual, had dark circles under his eyes and wouldn't meet her gaze. Jodenny introduced Ysten and announced that he would be coming around to conduct the inspections. The division looked no more excited at the prospect than Ysten had.

In the lift afterward, Nitta asked, "You want company, Ensign? I can show you how everything works in Underway Stores."

Jodenny shuddered at the possible heights of irresponsibility the two of them might reach if she sent them off together. "He doesn't need company. You need to get those overdue COSALs into my queue."

Nitta gave Ysten a wink. "Lieutenant Scott's strict that way."

She ignored him. Back in her office she grew concerned about Mrs. Mullaly, who had left a message saying she was at the doctor's office and would be late to work. But when Mrs. Mullaly arrived midmorning she had a wide smile on her face. "Guess what, Lieutenant! I'm pregnant. Eight weeks along."

Caldicot gave her a hug. "That's wonderful!"

Jodenny patted Mrs. Mullaly's arm but held off on the hugging. The pregnancy had to have been assisted. Medical science still had a hard time extending a woman's ovulation past menopause. "I'm very happy for you," she told Mrs. Mullaly, though for herself she couldn't imagine midnight feedings or arranging child care or dealing with all the stresses of parent-hood. She was saved from further baby talk by a call from Master Chief DiSola.

"I've got good news, Lieutenant," he said.

"You're pregnant, too?" she asked.

DiSola gave her a quizzical look. "The ECP list was an-nounced. Strayborn made it, as did Kesnicki in Food Services. I already called them both. Officer indoctrination starts this afternoon and will last just over two weeks."

"This afternoon?" Jodenny tried not to sound too dismayed. The last thing she needed was to lose yet another member of the division. And once Strayborn was commissioned, there was no guarantee he would return to Underway Stores.

"There's going to be a party tonight to celebrate," DiSola said. "Hope to see you there."

Jodenny hung up. She reminded herself that personnel problems were small and inconsequential compared to the larger issues at hand. She told Caldicot and Mrs. Mullaly that she'd be out of the office for a short time, and headed off to find Dr. Ng.

The Space Sciences labs were on F-Deck. When Jodenny got off the lift she stopped, bothered by an odd uneasiness. She pushed the feeling aside, passed the officers' gym, and for several minutes wandered around a maze of workbenches, labs, and cubicles, passing geologists, astrophysicists, clima-tologists, and engineers, peeking into offices full of expensive equipment and colorful charts. She located Ng in a tiny corner warren that was scrupulously neat. Star vids covered all the walls—nebulae and comets and galaxies, blue and white and sparkling in the absence of overhead lights. A large tropical fish tank sat on one table, casting shimmering light through the room.

"Dr. Ng," Jodenny said from the hatchway.

Ng rolled back from his desk. "Whatever it is, I didn't do it."

"I need to talk to you." Jodenny moved inside and waited for the hatch to close. "I've done some checking. You have a doctorate in astronomy, specializing in the structure and de-struction of globular star clusters. You've published in very good journals on Fortune, and your research on galactic tides is widely lauded. But you're also an amateur archaeologist, and have participated in some unorthodox public discussions about the origins of Spheres. Some might call you a Wondjinologist."

Ng stood up, crossed to the aquarium, and lifted a small part of its lid. "The usual term is 'crackpot.'"

Jodenny sat down in a chair. The Large Magellanic Cloud spun lazily over her head. "You're on record as saying there's no way the Spheres could have been some kind of transportation devices."

Ng shook some fish food into his hand. A dozen gold and silver fish swam up in anticipation. "That's truly an unsupported theory. No one's ever found any kind of technology in the Spheres—not under them, not in their stone walls, nothing, nowhere. There's never been anything found at all except for the structures themselves and their runes."

"Isn't that odd?" Jodenny asked. "If they were sites of religious worship, you'd expect to find things like broken wine jugs or sacrificial offerings. If they were places where people actually lived, you'd dig up bowls or utensils. They're not tombs because there are no bodies, and they're not astronomical calendars because they don't line up with things like solstices."

Ng sprinkled the food into the fish tank. "Congratulations, Lieutenant. You just summed up the great mystery of our age. What are they, and who exactly built them?"

"I met someone who claimed to have traveled through a Sphere to another planet."

"I've met people who claim the Wondjina have kidnapped them and beamed them into spaceships for colonoscopies. It's not as rare as you would think."

Jodenny offered him a piece of paper. "How about these symbols? Ever seen them?"

Ng secured the aquarium lid and took the paper. Instantly he said, "They're not Wondjina runes. Where did you see them?"

"Someone found them in a Sphere."

"Did not."

Jodenny folded her arms. "Did so."

He stared at the symbols a moment longer. "I may have seen something similar. Give me some time to dig around."

"We have plenty of time," Jodenny said. They hadn't dropped into the Alcheringa yet, and it would be almost a month before the *Aral Sea* reached Warramala. "But just so you know, I still don't believe in your theories. Those symbols have nothing to do with what happened to my ship. I just figured you'd appreciate a good mystery."

Distracted, Ng sat at his desk and began typing on his deskgib. "I'll call you."

Maybe later, if he proved himself trustworthy, she would tell him about the ouroboros and ask him to get her boots analyzed. But for now Jodenny would settle for any information she could get, so that her report about the trip through the Mother Sphere would be complete.

One of the Class IIs had damaged herself in a collision on level thirty-six, and none of the other DNGOs were successful in extricating her. Come midmorning Myell climbed into an EV suit to do it himself, even though he was fuzzy-headed from staying up late reading. He'd had no idea how many tribes had constituted Aboriginal Australia, how many overlapping and divergent beliefs they held. He might actually have to seek out an expert to make sense of it all. Chaplain Mow led the ship's Gagudjun services and was the most obvious choice, but he was hesitant to call her. Once he started talking he might not be able to stop, and would confide in her the story of what he and Jodenny had found in the Mother Sphere.

"Everything's locked down," Hosaka said over the comm. "You're clear to go."

He powered down the shaft and entered the slots. Memories of his last trip were still sharp enough to keep him peering over his shoulder every now and then. He didn't see any suspicious movement, but his torch made odd shadows on the slot bulk-heads: a curved shape like a snake, a silhouette like the shaman's head. The Class II, Airmid, appeared up ahead with one of her grappling hooks stuck in a bin grating.

"Got it," he said, but that was premature. He spent nearly twenty minutes trying to pry the hook free. It was slow, labo-rious work, and he was starting to sweat inside the suit when a commotion came over his headset. Someone was cheering tri-umphantly in the command module, and someone else was clapping.

"What's going on?" Myell asked.

No one answered right away. Stuck in the dark, cold slots with only the dead DNGO for company, Myell tried again. "What happened?"

"Sergeant Strayborn made the ECP list," Hosaka said.

Strayborn sounded overjoyed. "That's soon-to-be *ensign* to you!"

"Congratulations," Myell said. "Good job, Gordon."

He was glad for Strayborn. The man had worked hard for his achievements. While Myell struggled to free Airmid, Nitta came by the command module with more congratulations. Maybe they didn't know the comm was open, or perhaps they didn't care, but when Strayborn joked, "Who's going to take over all my good work here?" Nitta's immediate response was, "VanAmsal."

Myell told himself that was no problem. He could work for VanAmsal well enough now that she no longer believed Ford's accusation. Once Airmid was free he tugged her into the shaft and took her to the command module. There was no way he could repair the damage to her arm and hook with his own tools. The DNGO would have to go to the Repair Shop, and he remembered all too clearly what had happened last time he ventured that way.

"You want me to go, Sergeant?" Hosaka asked.

"No," he said, hanging up the EV. "I'll do it."

Dread accompanied him all the way to the shop, his palms sweaty on the DNGO's leash. To his relief only RT Sorenson was at the counter. She wasn't the most cheerful sailor he had ever met, but as far as he knew she wasn't involved in Chiba's dirty work, either.

"How long have you been over here?" he asked as Sorenson logged Airmid into her gib.

"Just a few days," she said. "Pisses me off. I like working on Mainship better."

The rest of the day passed uneventfully. He skipped lunch in order to skim through a dry text about Aboriginal history and spent most of the afternoon trying to get Core to reboot three malfunctioning DNGOs. Around dinnertime Timrin pinged him to ask if he was going to the party for Strayborn at the No Holds Barred.

"Can't," Myell said. "I've got work to do."

Timrin made a sour face. "Don't be an idiot and sit there sulking."

"I'm not sulking." But of course he was. He dragged himself over to the bar, where at least forty people had gathered. Kevwitch hit a pool ball so hard that it smashed into a bulkhead and Sullivan was chatting up a young AT. Jodenny was there too, nursing a drink alongside Ensign Hultz.

"There you are." Timrin sidled up with two beers in hand. "Drink up and be merry."

Myell took a deep gulp. Over the rim of the glass he saw Commander Osherman approach and speak to Jodenny. She tilted her head, serious and intent on his words.

"Yeah," Myell said to no one in particular. "It's time for me to go."

"Drink up first," Timrin said, and so he did. But the beer didn't ease the raw feeling he got from watching Jodenny and Osherman together. Master Chief DiSola quieted the crowd in order for the division officers to commend their personnel, and Jodenny shook Strayborn's hand.

"Congratulations," she said. "You're going to make a fine officer."

Quenger was more boisterous. He thumped Sergeant Kesnicki on the back, mourned at how low Team Space standards had fallen, and then dumped a pitcher of beer over her head.

"Classy," Myell observed, but Timrin laughed loudly.

The music on the overvids began and several couples started dancing. The floor was sticky with spilled beer, the air hotter than usual. Myell loosened his collar. He felt like an outcast teenager at a school dance on Baiame. If he listened hard enough he could hear the prairie wind, the crackle of fields killed by drought, the creak of a corpse swinging from the kitchen rafters. Then the wind became the hissing of a Rainbow Serpent, and the overvids became the serpent's scales as it arched across the stars—

Myell's knees began to buckle. He flailed out, desperate for a handhold, and stumbled against some sailors behind him. Timrin's face loomed in his vision.

"Terry?" Timrin demanded. "You all right?"

"Just need some air," he choked out. He shrugged off Timrin's help and lurched out the back exit to a passageway. Myell was standing with his back against the wall and his hands on his knees when Jodenny approached.

"Terry?" She immediately corrected herself. "Sergeant?"

"I'm okay," he said.

She reached for his forehead to test for fever. Her fingers were cool and delicate. She said, "Maybe it's the aftereffects of our . . . trip."

He wasn't about to tell her about the shaman or Rainbow Serpent. "It's nothing," he insisted, straightening. "Have you told anyone about what happened?"

"No. You?"

He shook his head. They stood there quietly, the music from the bar muffled in the background.

"About Strayborn . . ." Jodenny said. "With him leaving and all, I need someone to run T6. I want you to do it."

Myell said, "I heard VanAmsal's going to T6."

A curious look crossed her face. "I get the say-so, last time I checked. I can't give you any help other than Hosaka and Ishikawa. Will that do?"

He knew there would be rumors, but didn't care anymore. "Sure. No problem."

Jodenny gave him one of her rare smiles. "Good. I'm glad."

Myell wanted to cup her head and kiss her until her toes curled, and wipe away any feelings she might have for another man, and keep that smile for himself forever. Because she would probably slap him or have him thrown in the brig, he nodded toward the party instead. "Better get back before they miss you. I'm going to head back to my quarters."

"You're sure you're okay?" Jodenny asked.

He nodded. With one last reluctant look Jodenny went back into the bar and left him alone. The air vent over his head sounded like the hiss of a snake, and every step back to his cabin was dogged by memories of Baiame.

CHAPTER **NINETEEN**

"I think it's a bad idea," Nitta said on the tram to T6.

Jodenny had a hangover from Strayborn's party, the tram was exceptionally crowded for such an early hour, and she was tired of discussing the topic. "We don't have a lot of choices, and he'll do fine."

Nitta grumbled under his breath. She hadn't expected him to do cartwheels over her choice of Myell to run T6, but she had no qualms or second doubts. She ignored Nitta's unhappy expression as they disembarked on the Rocks and crossed the access ring. When Jodenny saw Hosaka in the command module she sent Nitta down to the base of the hold and asked, "How did Ensign Ysten's inspection go yesterday?"

"Honestly, ma'am? I've had more thorough lookovers in a bar," Hosaka said.

"Didn't spend a lot of time?"

"Three minutes top to bottom. See that sprinkler over there? I've been trying to get it fixed for six months. Told the ensign, but he didn't care."

Jodenny called up Ysten's inspection on her gib. He hadn't noted it. She wasn't surprised. When Ysten crossed the access ring she pulled him aside and said, "Ensign Ysten, about your inspections. You weren't as thorough as I need you to be."

Ysten grimaced. "I did everything that was on the checklist."

"I'm going to reinspect this module. For every code violation you overlooked, you owe me a thousand-word essay on the importance of safety inspections."

He gazed at her disdainfully. "Essay?"

Hosaka covered her mouth with her hand.

Ysten said, "Reinspect all you want. I'll give you two thousand if you can find something I missed."

Jodenny had Ysten and Hosaka both wait outside. She noted the broken sprinkler. The exit sign was lit and clean. The medbot was fully charged. So was the fire suppression unit, but the replacement date had expired.

"Four thousand words," she said when she emerged. She handed Ysten the list. He immediately went inside to double-check her. Hosaka said, "Maybe I'll just go on down to quarters, Lieutenant," and was gone by the time Ysten came out.

"Two minor violations," Ysten fumed. "No big deal."

"Redo all your inspections, Ensign. Tomorrow I'll reinspect some of them at random. And tomorrow the penalty doubles— each violation is a four-thousand-word essay."

"Don't you think you're overreacting?" Ysten asked.

"Ensign Ysten, if you at all value your Team Space career, you will cease and desist with the attitude. Do I make myself clear?"

"You don't scare me."

Jodenny gave him her best full-wattage glare. "You should be scared. You're the lousiest officer on this ship. You're lazy, insolent, and bad with people. I don't know why you joined Team Space, but all you do is make people want to shove you out an airlock. So why don't you go get started on those inspections before I round up a volunteer party to do exactly that?"

Ysten stormed off with the air of injured dignity that only ensigns could manage.

Quarters went well. She announced Myell's new position and aside from Nitta, no one seemed to have a problem with it. VanAmsal even seemed pleased. By that afternoon news had spread to Chief DiSola, who stopped her on the Flats. "Heard you promoted Myell. You think that's wise?"

"Yes," Jodenny said. "I do."

She was still short on personnel, but with Myell in T6 and VanAmsal in LD-G things soon fell into a good routine. Jodenny found she actually had time to answer COSALs and data requests from Fleet. Dr. Ng left her notes saying he hadn't found anything yet, but hadn't given up. A week after they had left Mary River, Jodenny was still trying to hammer out a report that would describe what it had been like to feel the yellow light sweep her and Myell to a tropical rain forest that was nowhere in the Seven Sisters.

Rokutan pinged her. "Ready for that hangar tour?" he asked.

"Sure," she said, but before she could get there Commander Wildstein requested that she report to her office. "Come in," Wildstein said when Jodenny arrived, and led the way inside. It was bright but stark in there, not a single folder or file out of place. The air felt at least ten degrees colder than it had out in the passageway.

"We never had your welcome aboard interview," Wildstein said as they both sat down.

"No, ma'am," Jodenny said.

Wildstein gazed at her frankly. "Well, no point in doing it now. You've been aboard long enough to know how I work and what I expect. Meanwhile, there's been a complaint made against you and Sergeant Myell. That you were fraternizing together on Mary River and then you promoted him to be in charge of T6. What do you say to that?"

"So these dreams you've been having," Chaplain Mow said as she watered a spider plant. "Tell me more."

Myell gazed bleakly at the walls of her office, which were grammed a soothing shade of green. The ceiling simulated the sky and sun of a summer day on Fortune. From a discreet set of speakers came the sounds of songbirds and a babbling brook, and plants filled every shelf, niche, and cranny. He had called her that morning, after yet another sleepless night, and she had told him to come by on his lunch hour.

"They're just images, mostly," he replied. "A shaman with a staff that turns into a snake."

"If you're talking about an Aboriginal wise man, we prefer the term 'wirrinun.' And you know he's one because . . . ?"

Myell described him for her. He described the Rainbow Serpent as well.

"I've been doing a lot of reading," he added. "The Dreamtime, the Wondjina, songlines."

Chaplain Mow pinched dead leaves off a spider plant. Mildly she said, " 'Songlines' is a European term. When the Wondjina traipsed across the land and gave rise to everything, they made sacred paths you can still follow today."

"But you can't see them. There aren't any maps or markers. You have to . . . what? Follow your heart?"

Chaplain Mow poked her finger into the dirt of a ficus. "Are you from Aboriginal ancestry? I don't remember."

"I don't know. My mother was from Melbourne, but she never spoke about it." Myell supposed that there were colony records on Baiame that revealed where, exactly, his parents had emigrated from, but because of his light skin color, he'd never considered the possibility. "I don't look Aboriginal."

"No, you don't. But just because you don't come from a specific belief system doesn't mean you can't join it later." Chaplain Mow put her watering can aside and sat beside him, her gaze warm and inviting. "It's like family. There's the one you're born into, and the one you make for yourself."

Myell studied his left thumbnail and didn't answer.

"Is something else bothering you besides dreams of a naked Aboriginal?"

He didn't want to talk about it. Or did he? He had known she would see through him. Reluctantly he said, "I found out Daris is on Warramala. That he's been asking for me, that he wants to talk to me."

"Daris is the brother who abused you."

"If you call it that," he said.

"I remember we agreed to call it that a few months ago."

Myell longed for T6, where he didn't have to talk to anyone at all.

Chaplain Mow leaned forward in her chair, the watering can forgotten. "You don't have to speak with him, Terry. You don't have to listen to anything he says. Under normal circumstances, adults have the power to engage or disengage in dialogue with one another, and much more of an ability to protect themselves than children do."

"I don't want to reopen stuff that I left behind a long time ago."

She touched his arm. "You didn't leave it behind. You don't let it rule you, but you still carry it."

He didn't like to think that was true. Myell lifted his eyes toward the grammed ceiling, where clouds coasted by on an unseen wind. "Well, the good news is that I think I'm in love. The bad news is that she's completely unavailable."

"Really?" Chaplain Mow looked intrigued. "How completely?"

"One hundred and ten percent."

"Hmmm. Does she love you back?"

"I doubt it." Jodenny had followed him from the party. She had put her soft hand against his skin. But even if she did feel something, she had enough discipline to squash her feelings. He was the sappy fool who wanted to ignore the way the world worked.

Thinking of her made him restless, and he suddenly stood. "Sorry. I have to get back to work."

"We haven't finished talking about the Aboriginal you see in your dreams."

"I'll come back later," he said.

Chaplain Mow's skepticism shone through her expression.

"I will," Myell insisted.

Before she let him go, she supplied him with a list of resources to read about Aboriginals, advised him to get a medical checkup, and suggested he try relaxation techniques before bedtime. He was in the lift on the way to the tram when it stopped on E-Deck. Gallivan boarded, gym bag in hand. He was whistling cheerfully.

"Been looking for you, Gloom," Gallivan said.

Myell clenched his fists. "You can stop calling me that."

Gallivan only grinned. "Up for playing pool tonight? I need some extra money."

"Last time we played, I whipped your ass." Maybe that was true: he couldn't remember. It had been a long time since they had done anything together.

"I've been practicing. Besides, you've got very little time left to try and win my money."

Three weeks, more or less, before Gallivan's contract ended and he disembarked at Warramala. "All right," Myell said, and Gallivan got off the lift. Before the doors closed he wedged his foot between them.

"You know you can trust me, right?" Gallivan asked. "Chiba starts up again, anything like that, you let me know."

Myell had barely seen Chiba since returning from Mary River. "Why? Have you heard anything?"

"Haven't heard a peep," Gallivan said, and sounded sincere. "But it's when Chiba's the most quiet that you have to worry the most."

"Things are fine. I don't need any help."

"You always say that," Gallivan said, and the door started to slide closed. "Rarely is it true."

Sitting in Wildstein's office, goose bumps on her arms because it was so damned cold, Jodenny restrained from immediately defending herself. Nitta had probably made the complaint. It was exactly the kind of weasely thing he would do. Or maybe someone else in her own division. No one could have witnessed her at the Myell farm or at the Spheres, but it was possible they had been observed when Myell drove her back to New Christchurch.

"Is this a formal investigation, Commander?" she asked Wildstein.

"No. Commander Al-Banna doesn't know. Just you, me, and Master Chief DiSola. Does this allegation have any merit?"

"Absolutely not, ma'am."

Which was true. If Wildstein knew what Jodenny and Myell had been truly doing on Mary River, rumors of fraternization would be the last thing on her mind. But Jodenny wasn't ready yet to make that report. Not ready to be doubted, questioned, and put under more scrutiny.

"Commander Lueller in Admin has a need for a sergeant," Wildstein said. "He knew Myell on the *Okeechobee* and asked about him. What do you think about transferring Myell to put a stop to any rumors?"

Jodenny didn't hesitate. "I think it's a terrible idea. I'm already undermanned as it is. You take Myell and I'm going to have only one sergeant and one chief, which is about the same as having just one sergeant. I'll have to put an RT in charge of T6."

"What about if I rounded up a sergeant for you? A one-on-one swap."

"It wouldn't be the same for Myell, ma'am. Working in Admin, out of his rating, wouldn't look good for him on his next eval. He wouldn't have a chance of making chief."

Wildstein's frown deepened. "I heard he wasn't interested in a promotion."

"He needs to keep his options open."

"Ask him. If he's amenable, let's look into it."

Let's look into it. Jodenny mulled those four words as she left the Flats. Since when had Wildstein been so accommodating? That she hadn't pressed the issue of fraternization—that she was so willing to take Jodenny's denial at face value—was also strange. Her appetite gone, she decided to skip lunch and head for a Morale Committee meeting. Afterward she called Myell and had him meet her down on LD-G. They stayed in full sight of VanAmsal and let the noise of the mag belts cover their conversation.

"Who could have seen anything?" Myell asked after she told him about the complaint.

"It doesn't matter. Rumors don't need proof to fuel them."

Myell shook his head. "Commander Lueller didn't even like me on *Okeechobee*."

"He likes you now," Jodenny said, and resisted adding, *as do I*. A DNGO flew by them, a damaged crate in its claws. "I think you should consider it."

"You want me to leave?"

"I want you to do what's best for your career."

"You're assuming I have one left."

Jodenny hadn't heard self-pity like that from him before. His eyes were bloodshot, and he had left Strayborn's party after being dizzy. "Do you feel all right?"

"I wish people would stop asking me that," he said testily.

She gave him a level look.

"I'm not transferring," he said. "We could tell them what happened on Mary River, if that's what you want."

Jodenny shook her head. She watched VanAmsal inspect the damaged crate and slap a repair code on its side. "Not yet. When we get to Warramala, we should see if it happens again."

"Why would it? What happened was probably a fluke. If it was common, people would be reporting it all the time. Besides, if we're seen together there, it will just further the gossip. I don't like it that people think the only way I can get ahead is to sleep with you."

Didn't he want to sleep with her? Jodenny quashed an inappropriate mental image of him naked and warm in her bed. "I resent it, too. But you know we're not fraternizing, and I know it, so people will just have to find their fodder elsewhere."

"You think it's that easy?"

"No," Jodenny said. "But it shouldn't be that hard, either."

"If I were a lieutenant in some other division, would you—" Myell started to say, then clamped his mouth shut.

"Would I what?" Jodenny asked.

Myell shook his head.

Talking was getting them nowhere, and the noise from the mag-lev was giving her a headache. "Do you want that transfer to Admin?" she asked.

"No." Defiance in his tone. "I'm staying right here."

She couldn't say she disapproved. Better that he remain in her division, where she could keep a professional eye on him no matter how much he aggravated her. Wildstein didn't seem surprised or disappointed when Jodenny relayed Myell's preferences. Jodenny waited for Master Chief DiSola to raise the issue, but he said nothing. None of her fellow officers hinted that Jodenny had behaved improperly, although there was one wry remark the afternoon they painted the wardroom with the *Aral Sea*'s emblem.

"A fine reproduction if I do say so myself," Vu remarked as she wiped her hands clean.

Zarkesh, who'd been recruited to assist with the job, said, "It's all in the wrist."

Hultz said, "I think it looks great. I can't wait until we get the boys from Flight up here and whip their butts on Izim. Right, Jodenny?"

"Hmm?"

"Where are you?" Vu asked, a twinkle in her eye. "Daydreaming? You look like a woman falling in love."

Jodenny picked up a paintbrush and lied to everyone, including herself. "Trust me. I'm not falling anywhere."

CHAPTER **TWENTY**

The next day she took Rokutan up on his offer to tour the Flight Deck and hangar. The Flight Deck was on A-Deck, and it was from there that all the birdies, foxes, and other ship's craft launched and returned. A few dozen craft sat parked against the bulkheads, much as they'd been during the Hail and Farewell. The launch doors were closed, but during normal ops they would be open with a clearshield in place. The lifts, winches, and DNGOs that moved the ships around in the cavernous space were all quiet, and only one sergeant was on duty in the overhead booth normally manned by two dozen Flight crew.

"Everyone's off in meetings or training," the sergeant said when Rokutan brought Jodenny up.

Rokutan said, "Lieutenant Scott was interested in seeing how things worked up here."

"Sure thing, Commander," the sergeant said. He gave Jodenny a quick but thorough overview of the panels, vids, and sensors. "There's nothing going on while we're in the Alcheringa, but the minute we drop out at Warramala we'll launch the foxes, get the birdies out inspecting the towers, start receiving passengers and cargo, and start up training flights. Everything gets prepped, repaired, boarded, unloaded down in the hangar—the Flight Deck's only for launching and landing, and you don't want to be out there when the birdies fire up their engines anyway."

Jodenny nodded politely, well aware of most of that already.

"We do primary monitoring from this station here. There's always a Flight Duty Officer on watch, even when nothing's happening. In the event of an emergency that FDO can take remote control of any ship that carries our markers. There's a backup station on the bridge, and they can do the same. In a really big emergency, the bridge can actually ditch the clearshield by jettisoning the shield generators. We've got our own manual override—that control panel down there."

Jodenny could see the panel, which was marked with clear danger signs.

The sergeant snickered. "Course, you'd only do that if you're crazy, desperate, or bucking for a hero's medal."

He paused, his gaze flickered to the MacBride Cross on Jodenny's uniform. She pretended not to notice. Hastily the sergeant said, "Anyway, that's all that's exciting up here. The hangar's where the real action is."

"Thanks, Sergeant," Rokutan said.

A shielded evacuation ladder led from the Ops booth through the Flight Deck and into the hangar below. A dozen birdies were stripped open for maintenance, and at least thirty mechanics were busy running diagnostics or swapping out equipment. The Flight Support office was a tiny room with space enough for only three desks, some filing cabinets, and a few battered chairs. It smelled like machine oil and fried electronics circuits.

"Morning, sir," said Sergeant Gordon, a cheerful woman sitting at one of the desks. "Morning, ma'am. Like our office? Used to be a supply closet. The commander gets his own office in Ops. They like him up there."

Jodenny's gib pinged. "Excuse me," she said, and saw that it was Dr. Ng on her ID screen. "I forgot a meeting. Can I take a rain check?"

"Rain or shine, we're here," Rokutan said easily. "Come back anytime."

Jodenny hurried down to F-Deck. Ng wasn't in his office. She wandered around the science maze until she saw him standing in a small conference room, getting berated by another scientist.

"—that's not what you're funded for, Harry," the woman was saying. "Keep your eyes on your own work, and for god's sake give up these conspiracy theories."

Jodenny tiptoed away and waited a few minutes. When Ng did return to his office he had red cheeks and looked miserable. "Oh," he said, when he saw Jodenny. "Come in."

Ng had revidded his walls so that the Pleiades star cluster covered the overhead. *The Seven Sisters,* Jodenny noted. "Everything all right?" she asked.

"Yes. Fine." Ng's attention was solely on his deskgib. "I tried calling you. Those runes. They could be from the Wondjina."

"You said they weren't."

"They're not the kind of runes we're used to seeing inscribed on Sphere archways." Ng turned the deskgib screen so she could see it. His shoulders relaxed a bit as he warmed to the topic. "There are thirty-two distinct markings in that alphabet, most of them simple vertical and diagonal hash marks. Symbols that would have been easy to carve into trees and stone to convey short messages—things like 'This way to the village.' Pre-medieval Vikings on Earth had a similar system. Of course, we don't have any kind of Rosetta stone, so no one knows what they mean. We do believe that beings we call the Wondjina built the Spheres, and maybe made the Little and Big Alcheringas, so they would have needed another alphabet to communicate complex messages—engineering logs, scientific research, things like that. The Vikings had another alphabet, too."

"No one's ever found another Wondjina alphabet."

"True. Except for the Spheres, all traces of their civilization have vanished. But about forty years ago an old woman named Mary Dory told the police that she walked into a Mother Sphere near Arborway on Fortune and walked out of a Mother Sphere on some other planet. This was back when people still hoped that Spheres might hold treasure, or dead pharaohs, or all the secrets of the universe. She was as drunk as a skunk when she talked to the police, though, and no one else who visited the Sphere found anything amiss, so it got filed as a piece of urban legend. Twenty years later it was documented in a thesis by a graduate student specializing in modern folklore." Ng tapped on his deskgib, indicating the pie-shaped symbol. "The student found this same symbol in Mary Dory's diaries."

Jodenny stared at the symbol. She and Myell hadn't been the first to travel through a Sphere, but they'd been damn close.

"Where exactly did Mary Dory see it?"

"The diary didn't say. And by the time the graduate student went looking, the old lady had disappeared. No one knows what happened to her."

"Can I access the thesis and diaries?" Jodenny asked.

Ng shook his head. "No, just abstracts and some sample pages. I doubt the diaries were ever archived in their entirety, and if so they wouldn't be included in the standard Team Space databases. But when we get to Warramala I can check in some civilian libraries there."

Jodenny stared at the pie-shaped symbol. An old woman, a bottle of booze, a mysterious trip. "Can I get you to test some soil samples? From the bottom of some boots."

Ng stared at her. "Whose boots? Soil from where?"

"Don't ask. I just want to see if there's anything unusual. Any unidentified plants or minerals."

"You won't even tell me who saw these symbols, and when, and where—don't you understand? If you can step through a Sphere and wind up somewhere else, maybe that has something to do with what happened to the *Yangtze*."

"How could it?" Jodenny demanded.

Ng waved his hands in irritation. "I don't know. I can't know, until I get more facts. And you're the one who's got data she won't share. Do I think the Spheres can magically transport anyone? No. Not based on what we know right now about them."

"But you think they could make a starship explode," Jodenny said.

They stared at each other for a moment.

Jodenny broke the silence. "Please test the boots. If there's nothing unusual on them, there's nothing to talk about. When we get to Warramala we can check the libraries, and go from there."

Ng didn't look happy about it, but he didn't fight her, either. Jodenny left the Space Sciences labs with images of runes in her head. On the Flats she saw Olsson waiting for a lift. He stabbed the call button when he saw her, a guilty expression on his face.

"AT Olsson," she said. "I've been trying to reach you."

"Yes, ma'am," he said, and darted a nervous look around.

"You haven't answered my imail." Jodenny had only sent the imail because AM Dyatt had begged her to, and his failure to respond was annoying.

"Sorry, ma'am." The lift doors opened, and Olsson hurried inside. "I can't talk. I'm late to watch."

He was probably lying, but she let him go anyway. She turned away from the lift and saw RT Bartis gazing at her from the corner of the Supply Officer's suite. He blinked at her and turned away, and she went back to her office thinking only of Ng and Wondjina runes.

* * *

Chang wanted off that night's midwatch and offered seventy yuros for anyone to take it. Myell swapped for free. Walking cold decks during the wee hours was preferable to being chased by Daris through nightmares. At midnight he reported to the watch office, where thirty other men and women were donning belts and other gear.

"Remind me why robots can't do this shit," AT Hull said from behind him.

"Because Team Space needs to keep you busy somehow, bucky," someone else replied.

Myell turned around. "Because robots can tell when a sensor is triggered, but they can't tell from a sailor's expression if he's up to no good."

Hull shrugged. "I guess."

Interesting duty was patrolling the Rocks, where there was plenty of opportunity to meet women. Shitty duty was the underdeck crew bars, off-limits to civilians, where off-duty sailors drank and brawled. Myell and Hull pulled rotation on E- and F-Decks, which would be mostly quiet. Hull hated working in Ops and wouldn't stop complaining about it.

"Twice last week Chief came to work pissed," Hull said. "Lieutenant saw it but didn't do anything. Why don't we all throw back a dozen pints before coming to work? What's the point if no one cares? Might as well sit around all day cruising message boards rather than actually try to get anything done."

They got off the lift at F-Deck and started down the passage. The officers' gym was open twenty-four hours a day, but no one was inside.

"—so then she told him she'd sleep with him if he changed the roster, and he did, then he finds out she gave him herpes—"

The hydroponics lab was shut down and the door lock said it was secure. Myell double-checked by turning the knob and scanned the lock with his gib.

"—he would have gotten kicked out too, but the Sweet test came back borderline and they gave him a third chance—"

The ship's training library was used for night classes conducted by live instructors. Locked. The post office handled packages, handmail, and imail. Locked. While Hull droned on about his division, Myell went through the entire checklist and stopped only when he saw a light on in Space Sciences.

"Everything okay, Dr. Ng?" he asked the scientist sitting in his office.

Ng shielded his deskgib as if protecting some highly classified secret. "Yes, Sergeant. Thank you."

Myell and Hull went upladder to E-Deck. The AT started another long sob story and Myell interrupted him to ask, "If you're so miserable, why don't you ask for a transfer?"

Hull grimaced. "One department's the same as the other, right? Hey, let's get some coffee."

"Your job is checking hatches and keeping an eye out, not getting coffee."

"I'll get coffee, you check the hatches." Hull headed for the nearest vending machines.

Myell tried one of the back doors to the E-Deck gym. Unlocked. The passage led to maintenance rooms for the swimming pool, saunas, and steam rooms. A few meters down the passage he found a door clumsily propped open with a towel. He eased into the men's locker room. White tiles gleamed underneath his boots, and the smell of soap hung heavy in the warm, moist air.

He heard something odd—a squeak, then a thud. He stopped, afraid that the Rainbow Serpent and the Wirrinun were about to put in a special waking appearance. But the next thud sounded too prosaic to be of supernatural origin. He rounded the corner to where Engel had Olsson pinned against a row of lockers. Spallone stood a meter or so away, vicious glee on his face. Olsson was naked and wet, blood staining the corner of his mouth.

"Let him go," Myell ordered.

Spallone barely glanced at him. "Fuck you, Myell. Turn and walk away."

"Don't leave!" Olsson pleaded, and Engel shook him.

"Shut the fuck up," Engel said.

Myell put a hand on his radio. "Back off now, the two of you, or we can talk about it with the duty officer."

Engel glanced over his shoulder at Spallone. Myell kept his expression stony. He predicted Spallone rushing him a second before Spallone tried it. He caught him by the arm, twisted the arm behind his back, and shoved him up against the wall. Spallone cursed and spat, but Myell leveraged his arm until it was close to breaking.

"You want more, swipe?" Myell asked.

Spallone didn't stop struggling. "You and me, Myell. You and me."

"Anytime, shithead."

Hull piped up from the doorway, where he was observing them all. "Coffee, anyone? Scalding hot, poured over your head? Who wants it?"

Myell said, "Engel, let him go."

Engel reluctantly backed off from Olsson, who slid to the floor with a thump and sat there with his hand pressed against his jaw. Spallone grumbled and swore some more but finally calmed down enough that Myell released him.

"Are we reporting this, Sergeant?" Hull asked.

"No, you're not," Spallone said.

Hull grimaced. "Not the sergeant I meant. Sergeant Myell?"

From the floor, Olsson said, "I won't testify."

"None of us will." Spallone's eyes were on Myell only. "Leave it alone or pay the consequences. It'll be our word against yours, and you know how that always goes."

Myell did know. "Your word means shit. Get the fuck out of here."

Spallone smirked. "Keep your eyes at the back of your head," he said, and he and Engel walked away and out the back door.

Olsson pulled himself up to the bench. "Shit."

"You all right?" Myell asked.

"Yeah." Olsson grabbed a towel and wrapped it around his hips, but didn't seem inclined to say more.

Hull was watching the door worriedly. "We're really not reporting this? Just let them get away with it?"

"Give us a minute," Myell said to Hull. When they were alone Myell said, "You're going to tell Security what happened. You've got two witnesses to back you up."

Olsson's tone was tight. "Leave it, Myell, before someone gets hurt in a bad way."

"That'll be you, next time they get you alone in a corner." Myell didn't like Olsson, but he wasn't going to be responsible for anything happening to him. "If you care for Dyatt, if that kid's yours, you need to take care of things before you get yourself hurt or killed."

Olsson put his hands over his face. "No one can help with this."

"Is it about the dingo that was stolen?"

Silence.

"I know something's going on," Myell said. "You don't have to go along with them. You could ask for a transfer—"

"Myell, leave it alone." Olsson stood and started pulling his clothes from a locker. "You're the last fucking person I'm going to talk to."

Myell said, "Then at least talk to Chaplain Mow."

"What the hell can a chaplain do?"

"Get you reassigned, like Dyatt. Maybe more, depending. We can go right now. She won't mind."

Olsson shut the locker door and leaned his head against it. For a moment all he did was breathe noisily through his mouth. Then he said, "I'll go on my own."

"Trust me," Myell said. "Walking around alone isn't what you want to be doing right now."

Sanchez had qualified, Gunther was close to taking his oral exams, Hultz had passed her written tests, and Ysten was almost done with his qualifications. Jodenny scheduled herself for a bridge training watch and made sure that it was during a shift when Osherman would be off duty. The Officer of the Day was Lieutenant Hamied, a severe-looking woman with tight, worn features. Once Hamied took turnover and made sure they were sailing smoothly along the Alcheringa, she asked,

"What's the normal output range of the power plants while in port?"

"Two hundred fifty to three-fifty Hawkings," Jodenny said.

"Under what conditions can the Officer of the Day authorize a search warrant?"

"Only if the CO and XO are incapacitated and all legal requirements as outlined in TSINST 5367 are met."

Hamied asked, "When do you notify the captain of an injury or illness among the crew?"

"Good question," said Chief Roush, the Assistant Officer of the Watch. He draped himself over the nearest railing. "Who can say, these days?"

"Was there a problem?" Jodenny asked.

Hamied allowed, "A little one."

Roush stroked his jaw. "There was an accident back on Kookaburra and the duty officer didn't tell him right away. Hell to pay for that, you can be sure."

"Lieutenant Commander Greiger?" Jodenny asked. "That accident?"

Roush said, "I hear it took the local police a while to find him, and they didn't know he was Team Space right away. Even after it was reported, Lieutenant Anzo didn't say boo to the captain until the morning."

Hamied reached for Jodenny's gib. "Let's see your qualification list, see what we can sign off."

They went through two dozen questions, easy stuff mostly. Then Jodenny took her place on the podium and settled in to watch the evening's proceedings. From the bridge, the city was a metropolis that included power grids, telecommunications, water treatment plants, air scrubbers, traffic jams, law enforcement problems, and medical emergencies. On any given night, the crew of five thousand sailors and a civilian population twice that size could get into considerable trouble, but for the first hour Hamied's only concerns were a brief power outage on D-Deck and a report of a stolen gib on G-Deck.

Two hours into the watch, a Security report came in of two do-wops fighting on the Rocks over a Sweet deal gone bad. The senior Security officer on duty had them arrested and

taken to the civvie jail in T1, where they would face a magis-
trate in the morning. Shortly thereafter someone suffered a
cardiac emergency in T14, the prison colony. They had their
own doctors and security guards to respond to that. Around
midnight a radiation alarm went off in T3; the manifest
showed there was some radioactive materials stored on level
fourteen, and a team of rad techs responded.

"False alarm," came the report, twenty minutes later.

The rest of the watch was routine. Around oh-four-hundred
Jodenny found herself yawning uncontrollably. She walked
around, drank a large cup of coffee, and leaned backward,
stretching her spine. At the crest of the bridge dome was a
wooden carving of a gum tree. Every Team Space ship had
some kind of totem like that, in honor of Jackie MacBride and
her crew. This tree, with its maze of spindly branches and
green leaves, had a snake entwined around its trunk. A snake
that wound around and around, and bit its own tail.

"Something interesting up there, Lieutenant?" Chief Roush
asked.

Jodenny rubbed her arms against a sudden chill. "Not so
much."

They turned the watch over at oh-six-hundred and Jodenny
was back in her cabin twenty minutes later. She splashed her
face with cold water and changed uniforms. After quarters she
would check in at the office and return for some much-needed
sleep. On impulse she had Holland call up the logs and reports
about Greiger's accident. A flit, a country road, neither alcohol nor drugs believed to be contributing factors—maybe
Greiger was just a lousy driver.

"Was there ever a follow-up report from Kookaburra about
Lieutenant Commander Greiger's medical status?" she asked.

Holland replied, "Not that I can see, Lieutenant."

Maybe he had died of his injuries. More likely he was off
enjoying medical leave at the beach while she cleaned up his
damned division.

Her eyes returned to the deskgib. Lieutenant Jennifer Anzo,
the officer who had failed to report Greiger's accident right
away, had graduated from Officer Candidate School in the

same class as David Quenger. Quenger, in turn, had been slated to take over Greiger's job until Jodenny arrived. She queried Anzo's duty assignment and saw that she was attached to the Data Department, working for Osherman. There was a pattern there, a network of connections she couldn't quite see, but she was too tired to think it through.

With only fifteen minutes until morning quarters she swung by the mess decks and found Francesco in a corner booth, looking hungover and nursing a cup of coffee.

"Do you know Lieutenant Anzo in Data?" she asked.

"Not by name. Why?"

Jodenny slid into his booth. "Heard she got into trouble with the captain when she didn't report Greiger's accident."

Francesco reached for the imitation sugar. "You can get in trouble for a lot less. You don't want to be making too many inquiries about Data, anyway."

"Why not?"

He dumped the sugar into his cup. "Close-knit bunch. Keep to themselves. Something dirty happens, they sweep it under the rug and don't want you peeking."

"Did something dirty happen?"

He wagged a finger at her. "Precisely my point. Don't ask, don't get lied to."

Jodenny checked her watch. She was perilously close to being late to quarters. "Something dirty about Greiger? It's no secret he wasn't doing a good job in Underway Stores. But why would Anzo delay reporting his accident?"

"I don't know what you're rambling on about."

"But you suspect."

Francesco reached for more sugar. "I suspect a lot of things. Why did Commander Matsuda keep Greiger and Chiba in Underway Stores, when everyone knew they were trouble? Was he part of whatever they're up to? Where did Matsuda disappear to, anyway? And remember that dingo your division lost when we were leaving Kookaburra? Bigger stuff than that's gone missing. People hush it up, investigations get quashed. You can guess who did it, but they've always got alibis on the other side of the ship when shit happens."

Jodenny had to go immediately or set a bad example for her sailors. "Thanks for the info. You all right, or just up too late?"

Francesco poured himself more coffee. "A gentleman never tells."

Jodenny was almost late to quarters. Myell watched her rush in just a moment before Nitta called the ranks to order. Her face was haggard, as if she'd been up all night. After quarters she asked Myell to take on Ensign Ysten for the day, training him in tower operations.

"Yet another in a long line of skills I'll never need to know," Ysten said as he and Myell rode the lift to the command module.

Myell wasn't thrilled with the idea of Ysten hanging around all day. He, Hosaka, and Ishikawa were finishing up the June inventory and the DNGOs were acting up again. Thera had a three-minute gap in her memory and Andromeda failed to acknowledge a retrieval order from Core. Myell had both robots report to the bottom of the hold.

"I'll go take a look at them, Sergeant," Hosaka said.

"No, I will," he said, enjoying the power of delegation. If one of them had to be stuck with Ysten, it might as well be her. "I'll be back soon."

Hosaka mouthed a mild obscenity at him as he left. Myell only grinned. He took Andromeda to his workbench and stripped out her transceiver. It tested fine when he ran a diagnostic, but just to be sure he swapped it out for a standby unit. While he was wrestling it in he spied a tiny silver chip. He might have ignored it completely if he hadn't seen ones just like it back when he served on the *Kashmir*. He extracted the master chip and held it up to the light.

"Well, hello," he said. "What are you doing here?"

Master chips were only in use on Class IV and Class V DNGOs. Andromeda was a Class III, and the chip appeared fairly new. He had it running through the diagnostic unit when Hosaka pinged and said, "Circe won't respond."

"Have Core reboot her."

"I tried, Sarge."

Ensign Ysten cut onto the line. "Sergeant, really, you need to handle this yourself."

Myell knew Ysten didn't like Hosaka, and hadn't since she had complained to Jodenny about his safety inspection. "I'll be right up," he said, and sealed Andromeda up again. He almost left the master chip out on the bench, but reconsidered. He reached far into the top drawer and pressed up with his fingers until a small compartment fell open. Chief Mustav had kept a liquor flask in there, all the better for warming oneself up on cold mornings in the hold. The chip easily fit inside.

Up in the command module, he tried recalling Circe. She ignored all requests.

Ysten said, "You'll have to get her."

He could have sent Ishikawa or Hosaka, but it would be more expedient to do it himself. As a favor to Hosaka he took Ysten up to the observation module, where Ishikawa had already hauled out an EV suit and gear.

"Would you like to come into the slots with me, sir?" Myell asked.

Ysten's lips thinned. "I'll stay right here on terra firma."

Over the comm, Hosaka announced she was locking down the tower. Five minutes later the DNGOs were stilled and Myell was gazing at the drop from the safety of the ledge. That first step never got any better. He maneuvered down the rungs a short distance to level forty-eight and peered into the slot. His headlamp picked out bins, grates, and navigation markers.

"How long does this normally take?" Ysten asked over his headset.

"Depends on how badly she's stuck, sir," Myell replied.

He moved slowly through the zero-g, trying hard to keep from imagining monsters lurking in the shadows. Why did Andromeda have a master chip inside her? For the same reasons other DNGOs did. Someone outside of Core was radioing her instructions. Such a person would have needed access to the DNGOs to make the modifications. Someone who worked in Repair. What had Dyatt said the night he took her to

Chaplain Mow? That Olsson and the others were at the shop in the middle of the night—

The General Quarters alarm tore through his headset, making him jerk in surprise.

"Damn it," Hosaka said. "Goddamned GQ!"

Up in the observation module, Ishikawa asked, "What do we do?"

Myell ordered, "Go to your stations. I'll follow as soon as I can."

"You know we can't," Hosaka said. "We can't leave anyone in the shaft unattended."

Their delay would drag down the department's response rate but it was the captain's fault for having a drill at such an inopportune time anyway. The obnoxiously loud siren made Myell's ears ache and he dialed down his comm. He headed back toward the shaft.

Ysten asked, peevishly, "Where are you, Sergeant?"

"Still at D—"

Something bright and fast-moving flashed in the corner of his eye.

"Shit!" Myell tried to jerk away, but the DNGO slammed into him and sent him reeling against the nearest bin. The lamp in his helmet flickered and went out. For a moment he felt no injuries. What fortune. Direct impact with a flying hunk of metal and he wasn't even hurt. Then red sparkles filled his vision and a bone-deep pain seared through his right side, hip, and knee as surely as if he'd been set on fire.

"Terry!" Hosaka's voice was sharp in his ear.

"Report, Sergeant!" Ysten ordered.

"Dingo—" he started, and coughed up blood. Some of it splattered against his helmet but most of it clogged his throat or hung in the zero-g. The DNGO that had hit him hovered just a few feet away, having automatically gone into standby mode.

"Sarge, where are you?" Ishikawa asked.

Darkness and his own blood obscured the bin markers. Myell's suit temperature must have dropped thirty degrees, because his lungs were freezing up in his chest. Fire and ice battled through him. Although he could wrap his hands around the thruster controls, he didn't have the strength to squeeze the handles or steer himself in any given direction. Even if he did move, he feared ramming himself against the DNGO or into bins. More blood clogged his throat and his efforts to clear it produced an odd choking screech. The voices on his headset faded in and out, accompanied by the GQ alarm.

"Which dingo hit him?" Hosaka asked.

Ishikawa sounded near tears. "Circe."

"What does it matter?" Ysten demanded.

"If we can kick her out of standby, she can tow him out to the shaft." Hosaka's voice turned stern. "Terry! Do you see Circe? Can you get to her?"

The DNGO's blue lights blurred at the edges. Every breath sent red-hot spears into Myell's side, and for one clear moment he imagined his injuries—crushed ribs, maybe a punctured lung, some other fractures. He tried to get closer to the robot and saw that something was wrong. The hull markings, the scratches . . .

"Terry, listen to me," Hosaka said. "Hold on!"

He remembered his mother, dead too early by her own hand. And surely he was dying too, because he could almost see her image reflected on the DNGO's hull, and wasn't that how things worked? That the dead came to escort you to the other side? She would have been more useful if she'd come on those cold winter mornings to protect him from Daris, but anger served no purpose and he was glad of the company. She looked like Colby, her skin smooth and dewy, her hair short and golden. The last present she had given him was a gram of herself on a beach, and then she had hanged herself.

"Terry," someone said—maybe his mother, maybe Hosaka, maybe even the sour Ensign Ysten. It didn't matter. Blood was in his throat again, and this time he couldn't cough it out no matter how hard he tried.

His heart stuttered and all sensation faded away.

CHAPTER TWENTY-ONE

J odenny was sitting at her desk after quarters, fighting fatigue for just a little while longer. On her deskgib was the sketch of the glyphs she and Myell had seen on Mary River. Wondjina runes, or so Ng believed. On her desk itself was Sergeant Rosegarten's report on the missing DNGO. *You can guess who did it, but they've always got alibis on the other side of the ship,* Francesco had said.

"Holland, can you access the lifepod rosters during the last GQ? Tell me where Chief Chiba and RT Engel went."

"Chief Chiba reported to lifepod H-23. RT Engel went to lifepod I-26."

"Show me their response times," Jodenny said.

There it was, on the screen. Chiba's alibi. And the numbers didn't work at all. He'd checked into H-23 ninety seconds after the first alarm, but he couldn't have gotten there from the Repair Shop in that short amount of time. Not with the trams between Mainship and the Rocks locked down. Likewise Engel could have never made it to I-26. Jodenny called up the supervisors of both pods and wasn't at all surprised to see Nitta's and Quenger's names.

"Holland, call Commander Picariello for me," she said, just as the General Quarters alarm started to blare. For a moment Jodenny was perplexed—was she just imagining the alarm, based on her reading?—but the intensity of it jerked her to her feet and to the front office. Caldicot had a morning watch to stand and Mrs. Mullaly was all alone.

"Where do we go?" Mrs. Mullaly asked.

For a moment Jodenny couldn't remember. *You got through this before,* she told herself. *You can do this again.* Overhead the comm announced, "This is a drill. This is only a drill. All crew and passengers to lifepods. Power Plants retain full power."

A knot of tension eased in Jodenny's chest. "Do you know where your lifepod is?"

Mrs. Mullaly's voice shook. "Back in our tower, but I'll never make it."

"You go to C-Deck," Jodenny said, because there was an auxiliary pod there for civilians with day jobs on Mainship. She'd learned that much from going over watch qualifications with the junior officers. "Do you know how to get there?"

Mrs. Mullaly wrapped her arms over her stomach. "I don't want to climb any ladders. Can't I just stay here?"

"No." Jodenny tugged her out into the passage, which was busy with sailors dashing to their stations. She urged Mrs. Mullaly up the nearest ladder and tried to shelter her against jostling while staying focused on the present day. *Aral Sea,* not *Yangtze.* A drill, not a tragedy. She fought off memories of an AT sheared in two, of burning hair and melting plastasteel. On C-Deck, they moved aft toward the lifepods. Beneath the wail of the siren she heard a ping on her gib. Who the hell would call her during a GQ?

"In there," Jodenny said, getting Mrs. Mullaly to her station. Chief Roush checked her in. Jodenny whirled to head off to her own lifepod, but her gib distracted her again. She accepted the call and glared at Ysten's face.

"We're in the middle of a drill, Ensign!"

"There's been an accident. A dingo hit Myell—"

Jodenny ducked into an alcove. She didn't think she had heard him correctly. "What? Where are you?"

"He was in the slots—"

"Patch me through your board."

"I don't know how—"

"Holland, patch me through," Jodenny ordered. The audio channel filled with an odd, strangled sound that she first supposed was a DNGO malfunctioning. But no, it was someone choking. Myell, choking to death.

"Hosaka, report!" Jodenny ordered.

"He's on level forty-eight, D-block, but I can't get any of the dingoes to pull him out. Core won't release them under a General Quarters lockdown."

Ishikawa's voice joined the line. "I can do it, Lieutenant. I can climb down and get him."

Hosaka said, "There's no time for you to get into an EV suit—"

"I don't need one." Ishikawa sounded afraid, but also confident. "All I need is oxygen—"

Jodenny lost the rest of Ishikawa's words as she rushed down the nearest ladder. She landed with both feet on D-Deck and sprinted for the tram station. Myell's choking grew worse, became strangled, fell silent. Shit, shit, shit, she thought as she reached the station. The platform was empty, with one car locked in place and powered down. Jodenny peered down the tracks. She could run the distance, but it would still take too long to cover the kilometer that separated her from the Rocks.

"He's not responding," Hosaka said. "I can't raise him!"

"Ensign Ysten, get into an EV suit and go get him," Jodenny ordered.

"Me?" Ysten squeaked out. "I haven't been in a suit since the academy."

Hosaka cut in. "I've got Emergency Services on the line, Lieutenant. They'll be here in three minutes."

Emergency Services had their own tram system for getting around the ship, with private cars running on separate lines. The team responding would most likely be coming from Mainship, but neither she nor Myell had time for her to flag them down to hitch a ride. Cursing, she jabbed her gib and said, "Captain Umbundo, this is Lieutenant Scott. This is an actual emergency, this is *not* a drill, please respond."

A few seconds passed before she got a response. "Commander Larrean here. What's your emergency, Lieutenant?"

"I have a critically injured crewman in T6," she said. "I'm on D-Deck, platform two. Car 731's right in front of me. Can you activate it?"

"Standby," Larrean said. Several more precious seconds passed. Jodenny spliced into the command module cameras and saw Ishikawa climbing down the railings of the shaft with only an oxygen mask strapped over her face.

Umbundo's voice came over her channel. "This is the captain. You're authorized for voice command on car 731."

The tram doors slid open and Jodenny jumped onboard.

"Full speed to T6," she ordered, and nearly lost her balance as the car lurched forward and sped up to its top velocity. Jodenny hung tight to a pole and stared at her gib while Ishikawa disappeared into the slots on level forty-eight. She spliced into the stream from his EV suit and saw that he didn't have a pulse.

Thirty seconds. One minute. Ishikawa didn't have thrusters to move through the slots. Every meter had to be navigated using handholds. The General Quarters alarm abruptly silenced, leaving Jodenny with a ache in her ears.

Hosaka said, "Lieutenant, Emergency Services is here."

Ishikawa emerged from level forty-eight, towing Myell behind her. The inside of his helmet was bloody and his limbs were lax. The zero-gravity allowed Ishikawa to make quick progress, but even if Myell was still alive, brain-death might already be setting in. The man who woke up—if he woke up—might not be the man she knew at all.

Ishikawa reached the command module just as Jodenny's tram slid into the first station. The Rocks were deserted, all the stores left open. Secbots patrolled overhead to prevent looting. Jodenny ran for the access ring, her right leg twinging in pain. Myell wasn't brain-dead, damn it, not with that family who loved him so dearly back on Mary River, not at the age of twenty-eight, not while working in the stupid slots. When she reached the module he was flat on the deck, with two medics working on him and a medbot hovering overhead. The medics had inserted an airway and were pumping oxygen into him.

"Pulse is coming back," one said.

"He's got internal bleeding," said the other.

Beneath the blood, Myell was shockingly pale. His fingers were curled up and his lips tinged blue. Ishikawa sat nearby, shivering violently. Hosaka was on the comm with Mainship and Ysten was staring at everyone, utterly useless.

"Yes, Master Chief," Hosaka said. "Lieutenant Scott's here now."

The medics quickly stabilized Myell, then loaded him onto a stretcher. Jodenny remembered him playing baseball on his brother's farm, running the bases with his head down and fists loose. She hadn't realized how grim he usually looked, how clenched and unhappy, until she'd seen him surrounded by people who loved him.

Hosaka said, "Lieutenant. The SUPPO wants to talk to you."

"Get Ishikawa a blanket," Jodenny said to Ysten. She forced herself to the comm. While she briefed Al-Banna on what little she knew, Hosaka showed Ysten where the thermal blankets were kept. They shook one out and wrapped it around Ishikawa. When the lift came back up it was full of representatives from Security and Safety.

Chief Bishop from Security said, "Who can tell me what happened?"

"I can," Hosaka said. "One of the dingoes stopped responding in the slots. Sergeant Myell went down to retrieve it. The GQ went off, and a minute later Circe smacked right into him. AT Ishikawa pulled him out."

"Anyone would have done it," Ishikawa said, rather shyly.

Ysten hadn't done it. Jodenny said, "You saved his life. You were extremely brave."

Ishikawa's cheeks turned pink. "Sergeant Myell's a good guy."

Was that a note of admiration she heard in the AT's voice? A hint of infatuation? The idea almost made Jodenny smile, but the blood on the deck made her guts churn. She said, "I'm going to Sick Berth."

She didn't remember much of the trip over. Gallivan and Timrin were already in the waiting room when she arrived.

"He's in surgery," Gallivan said.

"How does a dingo run into someone?" Timrin demanded. "Wasn't the tower locked down?"

"We don't know exactly what happened." No longer sure she could stand straight, Jodenny sank down in the nearest chair. Gallivan pressed his cup of coffee into her hands.

"You probably need this more than I do," he said.

What she needed was some way to erase the image of Myell lying white-faced and bleeding on the deck. Timrin sat down across from her and bowed his head. Gallivan came and went, preferring to pace outside. The wallvids provided background noise with ship's news and announcements. After several loops of the same information Timrin got up and shut it off. Master Chief DiSola came by to check, as did LCDR Zarkesh, Chief Roush, Ensign Hultz, and Sergeant VanAmsal. More representatives from Security and Safety showed up, all to take statements. Hosaka arrived, having changed out of her bloodstained jumpsuit.

"The level was locked, Lieutenant," she said. "I swear it."

Jodenny squeezed Hosaka's arm. "It's not your fault."

Lunch had long come and gone before Wildstein arrived with Commander Picariello at her side. They took Jodenny into a small side lounge where no one else could overhear. "How did this happen?" Wildstein asked.

"He's still in surgery," Jodenny said, not caring how peevish she sounded. "Thank you for your concern, ma'am."

Wildstein grimaced. "I know he's still in surgery, Lieutenant. I've been listening to the reports. What happened?"

Jodenny went through the story again. She expected Wildstein to reprimand her for calling Larrean and circumventing the chain of command, but instead Wildstein turned to Picariello and asked, "Commander?"

"Lieutenant Scott, do you think this was an accident?" he asked.

She blinked in surprise. "Could it be anything else?"

"Sergeant Myell stood a security watch the night before last, and he and his partner broke up a fight between some sailors in the E-Deck gym. Sergeant Spallone, RT Engel, and AT Olsson were involved."

Chiba's men. Jodenny said, "Sergeant Myell didn't mention a fight to me. But I don't see how this kind of accident could have been engineered."

"I understand there's some long-standing animosity between Myell and Spallone," Picariello said. "If Myell dies, if this wasn't an accident—it could be murder."

Wildstein and Picariello stayed for a short time, but departed when it became apparent Myell wasn't coming out of surgery anytime soon. Jodenny blinked at the clock, her eyesight so bleary that she could barely make out the digits. She'd been awake well over twenty-four hours. Just as she was thinking of finding more coffee, Dr. Lee emerged in surgical scrubs.

Dr. Lee asked, "Are you Sergeant Myell's division officer?"

"Yes." Jodenny indicated Timrin. "This is his roommate. How is he?"

"He had a dislocated shoulder, two broken ribs, a punctured lung, and a sprained hip. I've already started healing the fractures and they'll be fine. He was without oxygen for a period of time, but I don't see any indication of severe brain damage."

"*Severe?*" Timrin asked.

"He might evidence the usual symptoms of a concussion—confusion, irritation, mood swings. He doesn't remember anything since breakfast, so there's retrograde amnesia as well."

Jodenny knew too much about amnesia. Sometimes the disaster on the *Yangtze* seemed like it was just inches away, able to be grasped if she simply reached out. At others it was a blank white wall, featureless and smooth. She asked, "What's the good news?"

"That is the good news." Lee rubbed the side of her head and stifled a yawn. "He's alive and should be back to limited duty in a week or so. He can have visitors now. One at a time."

Timrin went in to see Myell first. Jodenny went to the head and washed her face with cold water. She didn't imagine the incident would fade away even though Myell was expected to recover. The safety investigation would take days if not weeks to complete. Someone or something would need to be blamed. Ishikawa deserved an award. When Myell returned to duty he would need to do something a little less strenuous than being run over by DNGOs, and someone would have to take care of the jobs he'd been performing.

She had no intention of letting anyone in the slots until Circe's erratic and potentially fatal behavior could be explained, accident or not.

Vu came looking for her. "I heard the good news. Come on, I'll buy you dinner."

"It's not dinnertime," Jodenny said.

"It's almost eighteen hundred hours."

Anger made her fists clench. Most of Underway Stores had been off work for at least an hour. None of them felt any responsibility to at least drop by Sick Berth on their way to more important activities? Even Nitta hadn't bothered to put in an appearance.

"I'm not hungry," she said.

Vu wasn't persuaded. "Sure you are. You just don't know it."

Timrin came out of the recovery room. "Terry would like to see you, ma'am."

Jodenny went inside. Myell didn't look half bad. Still pale and groggy, but not bleeding. His hair stuck up in all directions. A sheet demurely covered him to the neck, and she could see the outline of healing casts underneath it.

"Kay," Myell murmured.

No use correcting him when he was obviously under the influence of drugs. "Sergeant. You gave us a scare."

The fingers of his right hand twitched. She hesitated, then slid her hand into his grasp. His skin was cool and dry. She told herself she would have held Ishikawa's hand if it had been the young AT on the bed. Strayborn, too. Even Nitta.

"Sorry," he said.

"Everything's fine," she assured him. "Rest up. You've earned it."

Myell murmured something she didn't quite catch. His eyes slid closed. For a moment she thought he'd up and died on her, but a quick look at the monitors dissipated that particular fear. Jodenny studied his face, watching tension ease away into drugged sleep. She bent and kissed his cool lips and yes, there it was, she was doomed for her feelings. She pulled her hand from his lax grip and backed away to the waiting room.

"Let's go get dinner," she said to Vu, but the food was tasteless and all she could think about was Terry.

CHAPTER TWENTY-TWO

He didn't remember much about the accident itself—
pain, yes, but only an echo of the agony; voices that
hadn't made much sense; the feeling of falling, though certainly the shaft had never initialized gravity. Afterward there
had been only a great red desert under a burnt-toast sky, and
the Wirrinun dragging out designs in the dirt with the tip of
his spear.

"Your path will fork," the Wirrinun said. "Uluru is your future."

"Uluru?" In this dream he was as naked as the Wirrinun,
but he felt curiously unembarrassed. Myell craned his neck,
trying to make sense of the Wirrinun's designs, but the lines
wavered and shimmered and refused to hold still. The landscape around them both was without distinctive features of
any kind. "Am I dead? Is that what you're trying to tell me?"

"You will have to choose." The Wirrinun slammed his staff
against the ground and the Rainbow Serpent spiraled out of
the dirt, carrying Myell up toward the sky. "Choose, choose,
choose," the snake echoed, its voice oily and coy, and Myell
slipped from its neck and fell toward a long line of shattered
Mother Spheres. Just as he hit the broken stonework of the
nearest one, it transformed into the soft mattress of a hospital
bed. A dark silhouette moved above him, a woman with perfume that almost smelled like strawberries.

"Kay?" he asked.

"No, it's Chaplain Mow." She touched his forehead with
warm, soft fingers. "There was an accident yesterday. Do you
remember?"

"I was dreaming," he said, groggy from sleep and sedatives.
"A snake. The Spheres."

Chaplain Mow moved to the bedside table. "Here. Drink
this."

A straw in his mouth, blessed coolness: never before had
water tasted so good. After a moment the chaplain took the

glass away and he grasped her arm. "Did you tell them about our trip?" he asked, sure she was Jodenny. "Do they know about the other planets?"

"I don't think they know," she replied. "But if you'd like, you could tell me."

The General Quarters that nearly killed Myell also resulted, indirectly, in the destruction of Lieutenant Francesco's career.

Jodenny didn't hear about the scandal until the day after the accident. She had gone to bed and slept ten hours straight, without a single dream to disturb her. The morning had been spent going through logs and procedures with the Safety Department representatives. She was sure that Myell hadn't done anything wrong during his trip to the slots, and the data sensors confirmed it. His EV suit had been properly operating, the DNGOs had all been locked down, and every safety code had been strictly adhered to. But Circe, who'd been located and removed by a special team, showed no record of colliding with Myell. As far as the robot was concerned, there hadn't even been an accident.

"Something must be wrong with her programming," Jodenny said.

Al-Banna, who had sat in for part of the meeting, took her aside afterward. "You're sure your people did nothing wrong? Sergeant Myell didn't bring this on himself in some way?"

The implication made her temper rise. "No, sir. In no possible way did he bring this on himself."

"Sometimes people do," Al-Banna said, but he didn't press her on it.

Later that afternoon she was in her office when Holland asked, "Lieutenant, would you care to be informed of a development in the officers' wardroom?"

"What development?" Jodenny asked.

"Lieutenant Francesco has been relieved of duty pending an official investigation into charges of fraternization with Chief Vostic."

Hultz had all the gossip, and was glad to share it over the

gib. "When the GQ went off one of their RTs walked in on them—it wasn't pretty, from what I heard."

Jodenny didn't know which was worse—Francesco falling for his own chief, or them fooling around in his office. She remembered kissing Myell in Sick Berth, and chided herself for her hypocrisy.

"She's still at work but he's been relieved," Hultz said. "Quenger's taking over for A. J. for the time being. Poor guy."

Jodenny called Francesco but he didn't answer. She decided a visit to Sick Berth could wait. She continued to be upset with her division, though. She snapped at Amador for daring to ask who would take Myell's place. She caught Mauro leaving his issue room fifteen minutes early for lunch and put him on report. When she found Lange in IR3 watching the East Enfield vs. Suffolk game on his gib, she snatched it from his hands.

"Where did you get that?" Jodenny demanded.

"It's mine, Lieutenant!"

"Yours is in Chief Nitta's desk. This must be stolen."

"Chief Nitta gave it back to me," Lange said sourly. "You were supposed to have Strayborn sit down with me but you never did. Chief said I'd been punished long enough."

Jodenny had in fact forgotten about her promise. Jaunting through the universe via the Mother Sphere and Myell's near-death had left her slightly preoccupied. She let Lange keep the gib but issued him five demerits for watching soccer on duty and then went back to her office, intent on berating Nitta for going behind her back.

"No one's here but me, ma'am," Dicensu said when she stormed in. "Mrs. Mullaly has a doctor's appointment. Chief and RT Caldicot went for coffee. Oh, and Commander Picariello's in your office."

Picariello was sitting in front of her desk, his long legs stretched in front of him. "What do you know about the animosity between Chief Chiba and Sergeant Myell?"

Jodenny closed the hatch. "You think Chiba tried to kill him?"

"It's worth a look-see. Wasn't there an incident between them on the mess deck not long ago?"

"The day before we dropped into Mary River's system."

"And then, a fight between Underway Stores and Maintenance."

Jodenny sat down. "Chief Chiba used to be in Underway Stores. He didn't like Myell then. Then there was the rape allegation, which you know about."

"Yes. And I know about what happened while Myell was in custody."

She remembered Strayborn saying he'd been put in the brig. "What was that, sir?"

Picariello hesitated. "You didn't hear? Some of the men who worked for Chiba got into Myell's cell."

Jodenny leaned forward. "He was in Security's custody and he got assaulted?"

Picariello's blue and brown eyes hardened. "There were no injuries. Sergeant Myell wouldn't press charges."

"Was Lieutenant Commander Senga involved, sir?" Jodenny asked. "He seemed a bit hostile toward Myell when I first talked to him."

"You let me worry about Senga. My concern is making sure nothing like what happened in T6 happens again, and I don't care who I have to incarcerate to make sure of it."

"There's more." Jodenny told him about what she'd discovered regarding the missing DNGO and Chiba being logged into a lifepod he couldn't possibly have reached in the allotted time span. Picariello listened with a grave expression and went off vowing to look into it. Jodenny checked the time, wondering if it was a wise idea to go visit Myell in Sick Berth in light of what had happened to Francesco.

Dicensu was still minding the front office. He asked, "How's Sergeant Myell, ma'am?"

Jodenny picked up a pile of handmail that had come in. "If you're so interested, why don't you damn well go and ask him?"

Dicensu cowered. "Because Chief said not to."

"Chief Nitta said what?"

"When Terry got hurt we wanted to go to Sick Berth," Dicensu said. "A lot of people did. The chief ordered us to stay away and not bother him."

Ysten came in, looking as unhappy with the world as ever.

Jodenny knew she should move the conversation with Dicensu to somewhere more private, but her temper overrode her judgment. "What else did the chief say?"

Dicensu's face furrowed. "That it's Myell's own damn fault for getting hurt."

He did a good Nitta impersonation, but Jodenny had a sudden suspicion. "He said all of that to you?"

"Some of it." Dicensu hung his head. "Some he was telling Barivee and I kinda overheard."

Ysten unexpectedly spoke up. "I've heard that talk, too. Chief Nitta's been saying it was Myell and Hosaka who screwed up, otherwise nothing would have happened."

Jodenny retreated to her office with Ysten on her heels. "I've imailed you my essay," he said. "Four thousand words. Plus another two for good measure. You were right."

She sorted through the handmail. Reports, leave requests, a flyer from the Morale Committee. "Right about what?"

Ysten locked his gaze on the bulkhead. "About what you said. I'm not a good officer. I'm lazy. I don't take initiative. I could have gone into the shaft to save Myell, but instead a nineteen-year-old AT showed me up as a coward."

Jodenny put down the mail and gave him her full attention. "Go on."

"I thought you were exaggerating, so I went back and asked Lieutenant Commander Vu to tell me again her opinion of me. Then I asked Master Chief DiSola."

"And?"

Ysten took a deep breath. "Lieutenant Commander Vu told me if it were up to her, I'd have to turn in my commission tomorrow. Master Chief DiSola said he pitied anyone under my command." His face colored. "I never wanted to be that kind of officer. It wasn't my intention."

"So what are you going to do about it, Ensign?"

"I'm going to improve. I'm going to work for you until I earn your approval."

"You'll have a lot of work to do," she said. "I'm firing Chief Nitta."

Jodenny couldn't kick Nitta off the ship. Only the captain

could do that, after months of documentation and progressive disciplinary action. But she had decided that she could no longer afford to have him in her division. She went to Master Chief DiSola and said, "Chief Nitta doesn't work for me any longer."

DiSola leaned back in his chair. "He doesn't?"

"He works somewhere else. I don't care where else. I don't care who I have to take to square it."

"I don't know if it's going to fly," DiSola said cautiously.

"Let me tell you what's going to happen if you don't transfer Nitta. I'm going to give him Myell's old job. He'll sit in T6 every single day for the rest of this deployment. No chiefs' lunches. No late mornings or early knock-offs. He'll be complaining so incessantly that you'll have a constant earache and a headache to match. Am I painting a pretty picture?"

"Pretty enough. What if I say no?"

"Then I'll go above your head."

DiSola's voice was calm, though his cheeks had spots of red. "That strategy isn't always going to work for you, Lieutenant."

"But it'll work for me today," Jodenny said.

Later that day Nitta was called to Master Chief DiSola's office. When he emerged an hour later, he returned to Underway Stores, threw his plaques into a box, and left without a single word. Two days later Jodenny introduced Chief Faddig to the division. Faddig had been working in the ship's Public Relations office, writing press releases about *Aral Sea* and her crew. He knew absolutely nothing about supply requisitions, balance sheets, or DNGOs. His primary qualification, and the only one Jodenny cared about, was that he was not Nitta. Nitta was now in Ship's Services, where Vu assigned him to work in the laundry with a dismayed Ensign Hultz.

Mrs. Mullaly, badly rattled by the General Quarters and fearful for her unborn child, decided to quit. She knew the ship would have more drills, but at least she'd be in the Towers with all the other wives when they occurred.

"Sorry about the short notice," she said. "Will you have trouble filling the position?"

"We'll be fine," Jodenny assured her.

If she wanted a new civvie, the position would have to go to Outsourcing for recruitment. Al-Banna said, "Move Myell into it. He's going to have to ride a desk for a while anyway."

Wildstein suggested, "Maybe we could put him somewhere else."

"Why?" Al-Banna asked. "Underway Stores is short on personnel as it is, or so Lieutenant Scott here likes to tell me every week."

Jodenny said, "I'll ask him, sir," and went to Sick Berth with Faddig in tow. It had been almost three days since she had seen Myell. He was sitting up in bed.

Myell's expression brightened. "Lieutenant."

"You're looking better, Sergeant." She would keep this thoroughly professional, as she would with any member of her division. "This is Chief Faddig. He's taking over for Chief Nitta."

Myell shook Faddig's hand. "Welcome to the division."

"I hear it's an exciting place to be," Faddig said.

Jodenny said, "Mrs. Mullaly's leaving and we need someone to fill in her job. Do you want the position?"

He gazed squarely at her. "I'm not sure I'm the admin type, Lieutenant."

"You need light duty and the schedule will be easy."

Myell frowned. Jodenny suffered an attack of self-consciousness. Maybe he blamed her for the accident in some way. Maybe he knew she'd kissed him after surgery and was uncomfortable because her affection was not reciprocated. She said, "I can ask the SUPPO to transfer you elsewhere."

"No." Myell fiddled with the edge of his sheet. "I'll do it."

"Good," she said briskly. "We'll leave you to rest, then."

"Actually, Lieutenant," Myell said, and there was no mistaking the hope in his voice. "Can I have a word with you in private?"

She didn't trust herself. The accident was still too recent, her feelings for him too raw. "I'm sorry, but I'm due for a meeting."

Myell imailed her later that day, asking her to stop by. Jodenny told Holland to delete it unanswered. Rude, she knew, but given what had happened to Francesco, it was the only reasonable action she could take.

Gallivan and Timrin visited every day Myell was in Sick Berth. VanAmsal dropped by with some books. Kevwitch came round and asked Myell if he wanted Chiba hurt and hurt bad.

"It was an accident," Myell insisted. "Leave it be."

But Security seemed to think it was more than just a random collision. Two chiefs came down to ask him about the fight he'd broken up in the locker room between Spallone, Engel, and Olsson. They also wanted to know about the incident between Myell and Chiba on the mess decks, and the fight that had occurred between Underway Stores and Maintenance. Myell downplayed it all, because he really couldn't see a connection between all that and the fact Circe had malfunctioned during a General Quarters. He'd seen DNGOs do worse.

"It was just bad luck," he told Timrin.

Timrin shrugged. "If it is, then they won't find any evidence of wrongdoing, will they?"

Chaplain Mow called to see how he was doing. Myell remembered a hazy visit from her after his surgery and thanked her for it. Commander Wildstein and Master Chief DiSola stopped by for brief chats, which startled him—after the Ford incident, they'd both been cold as ice. Dyatt came by, so large and close to giving birth that Myell wondered if she just shouldn't grab a bed in the next cubicle over and spread her legs.

"Look what Joe gave me!" She waved her hand so that he could see Olsson's engagement ring on her finger. "They reassigned him to Engineering. We're getting married just as soon as the baby's born and we know it's his."

"That's great," he said, and thought back to Olsson in the locker room, Spallone's threats. A vague memory nagged at him, something about the Repair Shop and DNGOs. He rubbed his forehead, trying to remember.

Dyatt's smile faded. "He's been told not to talk to you, but he wants you to know he didn't have anything to do with what happened. I believe him, Sarge. He's made some bad choices, and so have I, but we're both trying to do right."

Timrin dropped by with the news that Nitta had been transferred. "Lieutenant Scott's getting some wash-up to take his place. As good as pissing in the wind, if you ask me."

Jodenny brought Faddig around but wouldn't stay. She wouldn't return Myell's calls. He brooded on that, telling himself not to be unreasonable. Gallivan had told him how she'd spent most of the day in the waiting room, waiting to see if he emerged from surgery alive, but she would have done that for anyone. She was just that kind of officer. By the time Dr. Lee released him he had resigned himself to unrequited love. He was looking for his boots when Chaplain Mow came by.

"You look much better," she said.

"Thanks. At least my insides don't feel like they're still broken."

"Your ribs or your heart?"

He opened the closet doors. "I don't know what you mean."

Chaplain Mow sat in the visitor's chair. "Did you hear about Lieutenant Francesco and Chief Vostic?"

"Got caught, I hear." Timrin had told him. "Stupid of them."

"Do you think the fraternization rules are fair?" Chaplain Mow asked.

The boots were under a spare blanket on the bottom shelf. Bending carefully, one arm pressed against his ribs, Myell fished them out. He told himself that as soon as he got back to his cabin he was going to slide into bed, pull a sheet over his head, and sleep for another week. "It doesn't matter what I think. I was wrong about how she feels."

"Perhaps. But that doesn't change how *you* feel." Chaplain Mow leaned forward. "What about the trip through the Mother Spheres the two of you took?"

He was almost too flummoxed to reply. "She told you?"

"No. You did. You weren't exactly clearheaded at the time."

Myell got one boot on with ease, but his right side lit up

with fire as he reached for the other. "You shouldn't have listened. It was nonsense from the drugs."

Chaplain Mow gazed at him steadily.

"It was," Myell insisted. If he breathed slowly and shallowly, the pain was just about manageable. "People visit Spheres all the time. Nothing ever happens to them. And we couldn't make it happen again."

"But you made it happen once," Chaplain Mow insisted. "It's the greatest discovery since Jackie MacBride found the Little Alcheringa, and it brings us all closer to the Wondjina. Don't you see? You told me that the Rainbow Serpent said you would have to make a choice. Secrecy versus the truth, Terry. The path where you continue to hide your knowledge, or the road where you follow the spirit path that's been laid for you in your visions."

Spirit path. Road to ruin, more likely. "You don't know that for sure."

"No one knows anything for sure," she replied. "Do you feel up for a walk? There's someone you should meet. Someone who might be able to help."

Chaplain Mow seemed so earnest, so sincere, that something hard inside him softened just a little. Bed would have to wait. "All right. But unless you want me to go barefoot, I need your help with this damned boot."

CHAPTER **TWENTY-THREE**

T9 held a new colony bound for Warramala. Chaplain Mow took Myell to the eleventh deck and a hatch emblazoned with an official-looking seal.

"Who are we going to see?" he asked.

"A very wise man," she replied.

The doors slid open. The suite beyond had been furnished in standard Team Space decor, with none of the opulence he expected in a diplomatic suite. A large map of Warramala hung on one bulkhead, flanked by a map of Old Australia. "Sit," Chaplain Mow said, indicating one of the grain-colored sofas, but he remained standing while she went into a side room. The Australia map was marked up with tribes' names, some of which he'd come across in his reading: Nyamal, Wakaya, Gowa. Where had his mother come from? Had she been of Aboriginal descent, or had her ancestors been those who'd invaded the country and tried to destroy the native culture and people? He was following the landscape from rain forest to desert when Chaplain Mow returned in the company of a dark-skinned man with startling familiar features.

"Sergeant Myell." The man offered his hand. "William Ganambarr."

"Governor of this colony," Chaplain Mow added.

"Call me Terry, sir," he managed to say. Ganambarr was the Wirrinun. Or perhaps the Wirrinun's twin. They had the same small eyes and high forehead, and skin that had been weathered by time and wind, and wiry gray-black hair. But this man wore a business suit and fine shoes, and no markings had been drawn on his skin. He was graceful and lithe as he sat in an armchair and motioned Myell to one of the sofas. Chaplain Mow got Myell a glass of water.

"Kath tells me you have made a great discovery," Ganambarr said. "If it's true, people can traverse from planet to planet without the necessity of costly transport—a most amazing thing."

"Yes, sir, it would be." Myell was still trying to wrap his mind around the governor's resemblance to the Wirrinun. He lifted the water glass and took a sip.

Ganambarr steepled his hands together. "Did Kath tell you our colony consists entirely of Aborigines from Earth?"

"No, sir."

"Never before has such an endeavor been attempted. After the Little Alcheringa between Earth and Fortune was discovered, the people allowed to go forth and colonize were those survivors of the Debasement who had money, influence, or the proper skin color. Left behind all these decades to deal with the aftermath of ecological disaster were the poor and the dark and the illiterate." Ganambarr's tone was even, though his eyes had turned hard. "It's taken my people twenty years of dedicated effort to fund this colony's transport from what's left of Earth. Even then, Team Space only wanted us to go to Baiame. It took ten years of lawsuits to be allowed to emigrate to Warramala instead."

"I understand what you're saying, sir," Myell said. "If it was possible to move to another planet without Team Space's approval or assistance, it would change everything."

"Everything." Ganambarr repeated the word. "Endangered societies would have the same chance at resettlement as those groups that have been traditionally entitled. The Unigar, the Shan, the Han—all on the verge of extinction, forced to eke out an existence on the planet our collective ancestors debased and defiled. The knowledge you have is priceless beyond measure."

Myell spread his hands. "I don't have any proof. I don't know how to make it happen again or why it happened in the first place. Please don't put the burden of saving the universe on my shoulders."

Chaplain Mow said, "We're not trying to, Terry," but Ganambarr nodded gravely.

"It is an awesome responsibility," Ganambarr said, "and one which would not have been placed on you were you not able to bear it. Your fate is far different than you ever imagined it would be, Sergeant. You are walking the path of the Eternal Dreamtime."

"I'm not Aboriginal," he protested. "I don't even know what I believe in."

Ganambarr smiled suddenly. "The spirits will guide you. They do that to those among my people who are of high degree and clever minds. You are uninitiated, but your rite of passage is just beginning."

The mystical talk bothered him more than he wanted them to know. Myell started to stand. "I have to get back to my quarters."

"Wait," Ganambarr said, and touched Myell's knee.

The cabin lurched around him. Myell groped for something

to balance against as the entire room vanished into a vast plain. White sunlight blistered the sky. On the horizon, dark thunderheads rolled up against each other in preparation for a terrible storm. He could see a large monolith of rock in the distance—*Uluru,* a voice whispered inside his head—and when he gazed down at himself, he saw that he was dark-skinned and dusty, painted with white markings, clad only in a loincloth with a long stick in his hand.

Something hissed on the ground nearby. The Rainbow Serpent coiled toward him, its mouth opening wide, wider than Myell himself, wider than the world—

Ganambarr's cabin reappeared. Myell's knees gave way and he landed on the sofa with a solid thump.

"Terry? Are you all right?" Chaplain Mow asked.

"Uluru," he gasped.

"One of the greatest of all spirit places." Ganambarr leaned forward. "Did you see it?"

"No," Myell lied. Chaplain Mow pressed the glass of water into his hands and he gulped it down. The unnerving vision of himself as some kind of ancient Aboriginal made his voice shake. "I didn't see anything."

Ganambarr scrutinized him carefully, then rose and disappeared into the next room. When he returned, he had a small cloth bag in his hand. "This is a dilly bag. In it, you keep your most sacred objects. Will you take it and carry it?"

"I don't have any sacred objects," Myell said.

Ganambarr's tone was polite. "Perhaps you will acquire some."

He took the bag and put down the water glass. "I really have to go. My lieutenant will be looking for me."

Ganambarr walked him and Chaplain Mow to the door. "Think of us, Sergeant. Come back to us if you find yourself in need."

Myell nodded, but didn't trust himself to speak aloud.

"Take this." Ganambarr pressed something small and hard into his palm. "Everyone has a totem ancestor. Until you determine your own, perhaps you will make do with this one."

Myell didn't look in his hand until he and Chaplain Mow were in the lift.

In it was a stone carved in the shape of a gecko.

Myell returned to work the next day with two vows in mind. One, he would refuse to think about the Rainbow Serpent or Wirrinun when he was on duty. He had a job to do, even if it was just sitting in an office doing paperwork, and spiritual mumbo-jumbo, no matter how compelling, was just going to distract him. Two, his relationship with Jodenny would be based entirely on professional respect. He would not think about what it would be like to hold her in his arms, or run his fingers through her hair and down her back, or feel her legs entwined with his. At quarters, when she welcomed him back and everyone gave him an embarrassing round of applause, he offered her only a brief nod. At the office he said, "Lieutenant. Tell me where to start."

"RT Caldicot will show you," Jodenny replied.

Myell went to Mrs. Mullaly's former desk. Faddig helped him adjust his chair to a more comfortable height. Dicensu got him coffee and offered to get him snacks. VanAmsal dropped by to see if he needed anything.

"I'm fine," he protested. "Everyone can stop fussing."

Because of the ongoing investigation, Jodenny had sent Amador to run T6 and reassigned Hosaka to LD-G under VanAmsal's supervision. Later that morning Myell asked Faddig, "Did Amador clear out my workbench?"

"I don't know," Faddig said.

Jodenny, who happened to be nearby, asked, "Is there stuff you want to keep?"

"Maybe. I'll go over at lunch and see."

On the tram to T6 he ran into Minnich, who was on his way to help Amador and Ishikawa finalize the June inventory.

"You nervous about going back there?" Minnich asked.

"No," he said, but the moment he stepped off the tram he broke into a sweat that had nothing to do with the ship's climate.

Don't be silly, he told himself. T6 held nothing to be afraid of. He had no memories of the accident. He knew that he had flat-lined and was alive only because Ishikawa had pulled him out. Yet the whole experience seemed to belong to someone else, and the only thing they had in common was prescription painkillers and a medical chit that kept him off watch until further notice.

Minnich went to the command module. Myell headed for the base of the hold. Above him the DNGOs glided and soared as they performed their duties. He'd asked Hosaka about Circe's fate, and had been told she was in Security's custody until the investigation was complete. He felt bad for her, sitting on a bench somewhere, powered down and inert.

He tried to remember what he had been working on the morning of the accident, but the hours between breakfast and waking up in Sick Berth were a long stretch of white nothingness, like a wheat field during Baiame's winter. He had told himself that remembering those hours wasn't important, but they belonged to him, were part of his life, and he wanted them up in his head along with all his other memories, good and bad.

"Everything okay, Sarge?" Ishikawa asked, from a respectable distance away.

"Hmm?" Myell rubbed his forehead. "Oh. Yes, it's okay."

She drew nearer. "You still don't remember it, huh?"

"I know I was trying to get Circe out of the slots. Everything else is a blank."

"You had a dingo in pieces down here. Andromeda. I couldn't find anything wrong with her, so I put her back together and sent her into service."

"I really don't remember," he said.

Ishikawa studied him for a moment longer, then abruptly smiled. "Okay. Want anything from the vends? I'm starving."

"No, thanks."

Myell sorted through the workbench drawers, hoping to find something that would jog his memory or at least some souvenir of all his months spent in T6. In the end he had only a small log he'd kept about DNGO quirks and the gram of his mother on the beach in Australia. She was probably the same age as he was now, with a happy smile on her face and laugh lines around her eyes.

"They had my favorite halvah," Ishikawa said as she returned. "Chocolate chip. Want some?"

Myell put the gram in his pocket. "No. I'm heading back to Mainship."

"I'll walk with you. I need some requisition codes from Caldicot."

Back at his new desk, he set the gram out in plain sight and checked his queue. Jodenny had gone off to a department head meeting. Faddig was trying to figure out how to format a COSAL.

"How are you with DLRs?" Caldicot asked. "I'm routing you over last month's. They need to be spot-checked and archived. Lieutenant's annoyed because I keep procrastinating on them."

"Why do you keep procrastinating?"

Caldicot smirked. "Because it annoys her."

Myell started on the DLRs. He hadn't exchanged more than a dozen words with Caldicot in the months since she'd joined the division, and now they were expected to work side by side.

"What else annoys her?" he asked.

"Be just two minutes late in the morning. Don't do anything right away. Don't ever proofread your work."

He was troubleshooting the second batch of DLRs when he grew aware of Jodenny and Faddig standing in front of his desk. He hadn't even heard her return.

"Aren't you supposed to be off the clock?" Jodenny asked. "You're under orders to only work half days."

"Staring up at the overhead gets pretty boring, Lieutenant." She of all people should know that.

Jodenny didn't even blink. "You could study for the chief's exam."

Myell saw her scheme now. The entire reason he'd been reassigned to the admin office was so that she could make him study. Resigned, he said, "Yes, ma'am," and shut down the reports.

"I'm walking that way," Faddig said. "Let's go."

Back in his cabin Myell dictated an imail to Colby and Dottie but didn't mention the accident. They wouldn't get it for several months, and by then it wouldn't matter. He tried reading more Aboriginal mythology, but the words wandered all over the page and he nearly fell asleep. He went down to the lounge, which was remarkably clean and quiet with everyone still at work. Myell slouched down on a sofa and turned on the vid. It had been so long since he played Izim that he lost his first life five minutes into the game.

In his next incarnation he followed a dragon moth down into a labyrinth of caves. The twists and turns reminded him of the slots. He closed his eyes and tried to focus on level thirty-eight, where Hosaka had said the accident took place. What had he been doing? Attempting to retrieve Circe. The level had been locked down. Nothing should have been moving—

Blankness. Dr. Moody had warned him he might not get his memory back. His brain hadn't had time to properly store all the data before it was whacked against the inside of his skull. Other memories might return to him in bits and pieces. Myell returned to the game but lost the rest of his lives in quick succession. The sofa was so comfortable he drifted off to sleep. When he woke, Gallivan, Hosaka, and Kevwitch were playing Snipe around him.

"Must be nice, lazing around all day," Gallivan said. "Wish I had that life."

A few minutes later they decided to go eat and dragged him along. On the mess decks, Gallivan carried his tray for him and Hosaka got him an extra serving of sashimi. Spallone was standing near the buffet but Kevwitch glared at him and Spallone immediately left.

"Spill it," Myell said when they were all sitting in a booth. "Who put you up to this?"

Gallivan asked, "Put us up to what?"

"Eat up." Hosaka pushed his plate closer. "No worries."

Timrin had a watch that evening. Myell waited up for him

to return. "All right," he said, with Koo climbing down his arm. "Who organized the carrier escort duty?"

"You think you're that important, bucko?"

Koo paused on Myell's forearm. He had placed the stone gecko Ganambarr had given him on his pillow, and she obviously couldn't decide what to make of the odd intruder. Her tail flicked as she edged closer.

"Three people walked me to dinner and made sure I got back here safe and sound." Myell still didn't know whether to be touched or irritated. "Everywhere I've gone today, someone's been with me. I don't need babysitters. What happened in the slots was an accident."

Timrin peered into a mirror and picked at his teeth. "We'll see. Until then, expect more mates to walk you around the ship."

"Mates?" Myell asked.

"Teammates, at least," Timrin said. "What more could you ask for?"

CHAPTER TWENTY-FOUR

As Jodenny made her way down the aisle of the H-Deck amphitheater, wondering just how many hundreds of hours of her career had been lost to boring meetings, David Quenger grabbed her arm.

He demanded, "What's this bullshit about you blaming Chiba for Myell's accident? If you can't run your division right, if you can't prevent a simple accident, then you should resign your position right now."

Jodenny kept her voice low and calm, though her instinct was to outshout him. "Chiba has a history of threatening Myell."

"Fuck that."

"You want to defend him, you talk to Security," she said,

and pushed past him. Danyen Cartik waved her toward an empty seat and she sat blindly, blood rushing past her ears.

"What's wrong?" he asked. "You look like you could kill someone."

She rubbed the spot on her arm where Quenger had touched her. "It's nothing."

"So you say. How's your sergeant? The one that almost got flattened?"

"He's back to work." He was also unfailingly polite and professional, as if they'd never taken a trip among the stars together, as if they were nothing more than lieutenant and sergeant. In most ways his attitude relieved her. In others—well, she had gotten what she wanted, no use crying over it.

Senga took the podium. "Warramala's a lot more diverse than our last stop. The wild woolly frontier, or so they like to think of themselves. Big believers in life, liberty, and the pursuit of fortune. We'll have shuttles running to two ports: Katherine Bay and Waipata. Katherine Bay's a big resort on the east coast of the southern continent—"

Jodenny scanned her queue as Senga talked. She remembered Katherine Bay fondly from her last stop. Excellent scuba diving there. Good opportunities for shopping. And a set of Spheres just a short flight away, where maybe she could jaunt to strange new worlds. But as she went through her imail she saw her leave chit had come back marked "Disapproved."

"See me," said Al-Banna's attached note.

Jodenny had already approved her own division's chits, but as she combed through the records she saw that Myell's had also been bounced back.

Senga said, "The biggest problem you're going to run into in Katherine Bay is sunburn. Waipata's got a lot more redlight districts, and with the Warramala World Cup game starting a few days after we arrive, you can imagine the possibilities for trouble."

"Go East Enfield!" someone shouted, followed by a ripple of laughter.

"We're also going to be arriving in the middle of Gagudjun Corroboree. They're expecting thousands of people for that.

Add in thousands more of drunk soccer fans—" Senga made a sour face. "It doesn't get more exciting than that."

On the way out of the meeting Jodenny caught sight of a familiar face and cornered Francesco. "A. J.! I've been trying to reach you."

"I know." The strain of the scandal showed on his face. "Sorry."

"You don't return my calls, you moved over to transient berthing—"

"I know," he returned, more forcefully, and Jodenny realized they were standing in the middle of the passage, the most public of places.

"Let me buy you some coffee," she said.

"I can't." Francesco made a show of checking his watch. "I'm working temporarily over in Safety and I need to get back."

"Then let me take you to dinner tonight."

"I'll call you," Francesco promised.

"A. J.—"

"What?"

Jodenny's question stalled in her throat. Francesco grimaced and said, "Yes, I did it. Yes, I'd do it again. She's worth it."

"Make sure you call me," was all Jodenny could say.

Jodenny trudged over to the Flats to find Al-Banna, but he was stuck in his own meeting. Wildstein said, "He disapproved your leave because Rokutan and Zarkesh already put in for time off and Vu's going to be tied up with her annual inspection. Someone's got to stick around."

"What about Sergeant Myell's chit, ma'am?"

"He's not cleared medically."

"I believe he is," Jodenny said, but she didn't press the issue. If Myell was stuck on the ship, there was no chance he'd go traipsing off to a Mother Sphere to investigate without her. And there was less chance Chiba could, say, run him off a mountain.

Master Chief DiSola caught her in the passageway. "I talked to your AT Lund the other day. He says you're mother-henning him."

"AT Lund is terribly sick," Jodenny said. "I want him to rest."

"I don't suppose his sudden interest in returning to work has anything to do with the broken entertainment system in his cabin? And his malfunctioning gib?"

"Are they both not working?"

"Stopped right after we left Mary River," DiSola said.

"How unfortunate," she said. "I'm sure he's called in a service request. Lieutenant Commander Zarkesh will no doubt make sure it's properly addressed."

The corner of DiSola's mouth turned up. "No doubt."

Jodenny trammed over to T6's loading dock and took Ysten into the bowels. The Direct Conveyance System that moved inventory over to Mainship was able to pinpoint every smartcrate's location at any given moment in its journey, but it required maintenance and quarterly inspections. More equipment provided umbilical services to the Towers—power, atmosphere circulation, heat, and water—and the same services to the shops and restaurants on the Rocks. The air stank of grease and the rumble of machinery made casual conversation difficult.

"What exactly are we looking for?" Ysten asked, wiping sweat from his forehead.

"Any obvious safety hazards." Jodenny flashed her torch over the equipment as they followed the narrow passage. "Check the fire suppression equipment, the sprinklers, the medbots."

"Where do those other belts go?"

"The other towers." Jodenny took a long sip of water from the bottle on her hip. "If you needed to move inventory from Underway Stores to, say, T4, you'd have Core redirect the system."

"Why would we want to give stuff to other towers?"

"Temporary storage, or if one of the civilian colonies purchased supplies from us." Jodenny's gib vibrated and she read a text message. "Oh, crap. I don't have time for this."

"What's the matter?"

"Sweet test. My number came up."

"Go ahead. I'll carry on down here."

Jodenny hesitated.

Ysten gave her a stubborn look. "I told you I was going to do better."

"I know. Just be careful—it's easy to get turned around down here, and even easier to slip or hurt yourself."

"Yes, ma'am," he said, but without rancor, and maybe there might be hope for him yet.

She climbed back up to the ring and trammed back to Mainship. The drug tests were run out of a small office near the Security Department. Several dozen sailors were already waiting in line, but officers and chiefs were sent to the front. Jodenny stepped up to the desk, verified her identity with a retinal scan, and let a young tech swab the back of her hand. She verified her identity again, per procedure.

"Thank you, Lieutenant," the tech said. "You're all set."

While she was in the neighborhood she decided to stop by Commander Picariello's office. He didn't look happy to see her, but he said, "Here's a hard copy of the final report on Sergeant Myell's accident. The Safety Department's report is attached."

Jodenny flipped through the pages. "This says it was an accident. There's nothing about Chiba or the fight in the gym."

"They're not pertinent to what happened in T6," he said. "The Safety Department concluded that the dingo's programming was corrupt. You can see it right there."

"But, sir—" Jodenny said.

"An accident, Lieutenant. That's all there is," he said, and she knew that tone. It was an official, bureaucratic, listen-to-no-common-sense tone, dictated by someone higher than him or by the needs of Team Space; it was a parasteel wall, and she had run into it before with Commodore Campos. She didn't know enough about Picariello personally to appeal to his human nature, and the differences in their rank meant she couldn't appeal to him as a peer.

"Yes, sir," she said.

She read the reports in the passageways as she walked back to her office. Twice she nearly walked into people or into a bulkhead. There was no blame for Myell or any of her sailors, which she supposed was good news. But Picariello's abrupt disinterest in exploring other explanations, on the heels of what had seemed like genuine enthusiasm, left her cold.

"Everything okay, Sergeant?" Caldicot asked. "You're awfully quiet."

"I'm reading." Myell scanned the reconciliations that Amador had forwarded. The June inventory had come out at a ninety percent accuracy rate, lower than April and May, but Jodenny was going to have to live with it. Circe was missing a chunk of data and another DNGO, Athena, had gotten herself stuck and couldn't be retrieved until the Safety Department authorized the resumption of operations in T6. In the subreport he saw five hundred records had been reconciled by hand. He tried pulling up the individual records, but he didn't have the necessary clearance in his new position.

He visited Faddig later that morning and said, casually, "If you want me to compile the reconciliations, I'll need to access your agent."

Faddig still had not grasped the jargon of his new job. "Do I want you to do that, or is it something I should do?"

"You could do it, Chief. I'll show you. The whole thing shouldn't take more than a day or two."

Faddig blinked. "My agent's name is Dooley. He'll be expecting your call."

Back at his gib, Myell enlisted Dooley's help to scan the records that Hosaka and others had adjusted by hand. The principal perpetrators of faulty data were all Class III DNGOs built back on Fortune. Still using Faddig's agent, he traced Circe's upsynchs for the previous six months. Until the deployment, her accuracy rate had been nearly dead perfect. Only after leaving Fortune did she begin to have all those crazy errors. He checked the maintenance logs. There, just after leaving Fortune, he had sent her to Repair for routine maintenance.

He checked Hera as well and saw her ~~problem had started~~

earlier, during the last deployment. She had gone in for routine maintenance a few days before her first faulty upsynch.

"New batch of F-789s just came in," Caldicot said. "Do you want them, or should I do them?"

"I'll do them." He shunted a copy of the DNGO reports to his pocket server. Reconciliation reports were no longer his problem, really, so why couldn't he stop poking at the puzzle? Because Circe had nearly killed him in a bizarre accident? Anybody else might consider that a strong incentive to mind his own business.

Just before lunch, Jodenny returned from taking a random Sweet test. She went into her office and called him inside a few minutes later.

"These are the final reports on your accident," she said, handing over a file. "Circe's programming was a mess when they opened her up. She never acknowledged the lockdown order from Core."

He skimmed the pages. "Core should have caught that and sent a warning."

"The Data Department is investigating why that didn't happen."

Myell's gaze caught on his own name. It was odd to see himself described as taking part in events he didn't remember. "So there were two technical glitches? Circe didn't respond to the lockdown, and Core didn't notice the lack of a response?"

"Three, actually. She still doesn't show any record of hitting you." Jodenny focused on him. "Everyone's concluded your accident really was an accident."

He wasn't going to comment further until he had studied the whole thing. "Can I have a copy of this?"

Jodenny glanced toward the clock. "I'll have Caldicot make you one. Time for you to log out and go rest. Dr. Lee was pretty explicit on your medical chit."

"I still have another half hour. And today's a big day. I get to go to the pool."

She frowned. "It's not too soon?"

"I'm only going to swim a few laps." Myell tried not to think of Jodenny in a bathing suit, water beading off her shapely legs. "By the way, have you seen my leave chit?"

She cleared her throat. "Commander Al-Banna doesn't think you're medically cleared."

"But I am. The medical chit says I can go."

"Maybe going down to the planet alone isn't such a good idea."

Myell leaned against the hatch. "Alone?"

"I have to stay onboard."

"So?"

"So it's not a good idea for you to go where you're thinking of going."

Myell said, "You don't know where I'm thinking of going."

"I know where I would go," Jodenny said. "To see if it would happen again."

"That's you, Lieutenant," he said, and ignored the small weight of the dilly bag in his pocket.

Caldicot pinged to tell Jodenny that Lieutenant Commander Rokutan had arrived. "I'll be right out," Jodenny said. She switched off the comm and gave Myell a pointed look. "We'll talk about it later, Sergeant."

Rokutan was in the outer office, bending over a stack of files he'd knocked to the floor. Myell knew him in passing, had heard of his sports reputation at the academy, and was well aware of how many young sailors had a crush on the handsome officer. Rokutan peered up at Jodenny and offered her a crooked grin. "I hoped that you might want to do lunch before the Garden Committee meeting."

Jodenny returned Rokutan's smile in a way that made Myell inwardly cringe. She said, "Sure. RT Caldicot, I'll be back later."

After they were gone Caldicot asked, "See how she looks at him? I think they're dating."

Officer courtship rituals. Meetings, coffee, secret late night rendezvous in officer berthing. Myell stood up, certain that he wasn't going to wait around for someone to walk him to the pool. "I'm leaving. See you tomorrow."

On his way to the lift he found Dr. Ng from Space Sciences

wandering around in puzzlement. Myell remembered him
only vaguely from the night he'd broken up the attack on Olsson. "Can I help you?" Myell asked.

"Is Lieutenant Scott's office this way?" Dr. Ng asked.

"She's not in. Is there something you need?"

Ng held up a sealed envelope. "Could you just give her
this? It's for her eyes only."

"Sure," he said.

He spent a moment wondering why Jodenny would need
any kind of paperwork from Space Sciences. No good reason
came to mind. None that related to Underway Stores, at least.
As her aide, wasn't he required to screen out crank mail or irrelevant material? With no sense of guilt whatsoever, he broke
the seal. The two-page report inside was the results of an
analysis on a pair of standard-issue boots that would have no
trouble matching Jodenny's foot size. The soles had contained
samples of mud, silica, mold, spores, and trace minerals, none
of which was flagged as unusual.

Myell hurried down the passage, one hand pressed against
his aching ribs. "Dr. Ng?" he called out, and was relieved that
Ng was still waiting for the lift.

Ng scowled at the open envelope. "That wasn't for you to
read, Sergeant."

"Sorry. It's just—well, the lieutenant hasn't dragged you
into her nutty theories, has she?"

Ng's expression became guarded. "Which theories are
those?"

Bold with suspicion, he dropped his voice. "Interplanetary
travel. Being magically transported from planet to planet. She
acts like it's a big secret, a conspiracy. We're all worried about
her."

The lift doors opened. Ng boarded stiffly. "Thank you,
Sergeant."

Myell stuffed the report in his pocket. The throbbing in his
ribs made him contemplate skipping the gym, but he went
anyway. He changed into swimming trunks, hung the dilly
bag in his locker, and eased into the large, mostly empty pool.
Getting a soil analysis of her boots was a good idea, but

Jodenny should have told him. Myell was pondering what to do about it when the swimmer in the next lane, a woman with short hair and a pert nose, splashed him.

"Sorry," she said.

"No problem."

She flashed him a grin and took off down the lane with a powerful backstroke. Myell bobbed up and down, admiring her strength. She made the return trip and hung off the edge of the pool. "I'm Eva," she said.

"Terry."

Again that bright smile. "Myell, right? I saw you on the news. You nearly got killed."

If she watched the news or listened to gossip, she had probably heard about Ford as well. Myell braced himself, but Eva's gaze was clear and untroubled.

"How long have you been onboard?" he asked.

"Not long enough to eat at Minutiae," she said. "Ever try it?"

Minutiae was one of the nicer restaurants on the Rocks. "Never," he said.

"Are you free tonight?"

He was, in fact, completely free that evening.

"Good," she said, and climbed up the ladder. Eva was as lithe as Jodenny, her hips a little smaller, her neck long and delicate. "Nineteen hundred okay? I'll see you there."

The pool seemed colder and less therapeutic after she was gone. Myell stuck it out for another fifteen minutes and moved over to the spa, where hot water made his muscles much more relaxed. When he returned to the locker room, Chiba was waiting for him.

"I'm not here for trouble," Chiba said.

Myell's pocket server and gib were both far away in his locker, and he felt terribly vulnerable in only a bathing suit and rubber sandals. "Then what are you here for?"

Chiba folded his beefy arms. "There's a lot of nasty rumors going on, so let's get this straight: I had nothing to do with what happened to you in the tower. It was an accident."

"Maybe I don't believe you."

"You know my style, Myell. Think it through."

Myell did know Chiba's style. But he also knew that DN-GOs that had been to Maintenance and Repair were consistently showing glitches, and Chiba was the boss of all the people who could have messed with their insides.

"What do you care what I think?"

Chiba snorted. "I don't care what you think. I care what the captain thinks. There's too much attention focused on this department. You let everything get nice and quiet and we won't have any more problems."

Myell considered the request and promised reward. "I'll think about it."

"Do more than think," Chiba said. "There's still a lot more time left on this deployment, and things could get much, much worse."

Chiba sauntered off. Myell made sure he was gone before he sat on the nearest bench and tried to towel off goose bumps that had nothing to do with being cold.

CHAPTER TWENTY-FIVE

Lieutenant Commander Wildstein showed up for dinner in the wardroom that night. Startled, Jodenny said, "Good evening, ma'am. Can I get you a drink?"

"Beer would be fine." Wildstein eyed the decorated bulkheads and rearranged furniture. "I like what you've done to the place."

"It's all Jodenny's doing, ma'am," Zeni said as AT Ashmont brought out another chair.

Wildstein took a mug. "I'm not surprised."

Dinner was a delicious-smelling caponata made with zucchini, tomato, eggplant, and garlic. They were shaking out their napkins when the comm came on. "Attention all crew and passengers. Warramala transition commencing. Five, four, three, two, one."

Conversation, which had been stiff in Wildstein's presence, turned to upcoming shore leave and things to do.

Vu added, "There's great shopping."

"The best thing about Warramala is the rain forest," Wildstein said. "Solitude for kilometers."

"I like the mountains." Rokutan motioned for Ashmont to refill his wineglass. He had come to dinner at Jodenny's request, and now gave her a smile. "Good hiking."

Maybe one day they would go into the wilderness together. Backpacks, boots, a tent for two. Myell would be nicer to curl up beside, their sleeping bags zippered together, their legs entwined. She reached for her wine. Tony, she thought. Tony not Terry.

"I'm an ocean girl myself," Hultz said. "Surfing, skiing, scuba—all good things."

"I'd like to try scuba." Rokutan's gaze caught Jodenny's. Another thing they could try together, perhaps. She smiled. After dinner Rokutan invited her to his cabin, as they both knew he would. She accepted, as they both knew she would. Within minutes she was sitting on his bed as he kissed her cheek, the corner of her mouth, her throat. He smelled like wine.

"What are you thinking?" he asked.

She was thinking there was no such thing as easy sex, no matter what people said. Not on a spaceship and not when the person was someone you worked with.

"I'm thinking this is just what the doctor ordered," she lied.

Rokutan eased her back and began unbuttoning her blouse. "Is that all I am to you? A prescription?"

Jodenny touched his jaw. "A panacea."

"A substitute for the real thing?"

"That's a placebo," she said.

Without a hint as to whether he'd been joking, Rokutan bent his mouth to the cleft between her breasts. Jodenny felt dizzy, as if she'd had too much to drink. She ran her fingers through his short hair and closed her eyes and damn it, it wasn't enough, he wasn't the one she wanted.

"Terry," she said.

He lifted his head. "What?"

"What?" Jodenny asked.

Rokutan's eyes narrowed. Jodenny fingered the fringes of hair at his temple. He dipped his head to kiss her right nipple and yes, that felt nice, and there he was planting hot kisses above her belly button. She needed escape. She needed unconditional touching. She needed to get out of her own mind, to slide along in frictionless darkness just as the *Aral Sea* slid along in the Alcheringa.

But to escape at the expense of someone else wasn't her style.

Jodenny put her hands on the side of Rokutan's head and lifted him gently. "Maybe this isn't such a good idea."

"It's good enough for the here and now."

She slid her feet to the floor and sat up. Her fingers shook slightly as she rebuttoned her blouse. "I'm sorry. This isn't fair to you."

"I hate when women say that," Rokutan said with a sigh. He put his hands on her shoulders and turned her toward him. "Look, Jodenny, whatever's going through your head, this isn't about true love, right? We're friends and colleagues. Friends and colleagues who both need a little unwinding and relaxing. Nothing more and nothing less."

Jodenny's fingers stilled.

"Whoever you're pining for, he's a lucky guy," Rokutan said. "But he's not here, and I am. We both are. So, you know, take advantage of what you have in front of you, not what's behind or ahead of you. Live in this moment, not some other one. They only come one at a time."

He kissed the corner of her mouth, and she let him. *Terry* . . .

Berthing was quiet at such a late hour. Jodenny was almost back to her cabin when Chief Nitta stepped into the passage. His uniform was disheveled and he had a mean look in his eyes, as if he'd been off kicking puppies and kittens.

"Chief," she said. "What are you doing here?"

"Bitch," he said.

Jodenny put her hands on her hips, using the gesture to activate the emergency button on her gib. "Go back to your quarters, Chief."

"I'd go back to work, but you kicked me out." Spit appeared at the corner of his mouth as he took an unsteady, menacing step forward. "You think you can ruin my career? Since day one you've been breaking my balls, trying to get me in trouble. Where's the inventory, Chief? Where's the fucking COSALs? I've got people giving me all sorts of shit because you can't keep your whiny mouth shut—"

"How much have you had to drink, Chief?"

He gave her a lopsided smile. "You think you're special, but you're not. We can hurt you when you least expect it—"

Jodenny calculated the distance back to the lift. She could physically defend herself if necessary, but he was heavier and stronger than she was, and unpredictable. Retreat might be the better part of valor.

"—and you'll never know. You'll be facedown dead and never know."

He coughed harshly. Blood appeared on his lips. "Chief?" she asked, alarmed, and he managed a flash of surprise before he crashed to the floor.

Jodenny palmed her gib. "Holland, I need help. Medics and Security, right away."

"Security's already on its way," Holland said. "Are you hurt, Lieutenant?"

"Not me," Jodenny said as Nitta began convulsing. Hultz and Zeni both appeared at the doors of their cabins, woken by the commotion or by their own agents.

"What the hell?" Zeni asked as Nitta gasped and bucked on the floor.

"What's he doing in officers' country?" Hultz asked.

Quenger came out of his cabin rubbing sleep from his eyes. "Jesus shit," he said, and kept his distance.

"Medbot, activate," Jodenny ordered, but the unit could do little. Froth was coming out of Nitta's mouth by the time the medics carted him off. Jodenny would have followed but two Security techs asked her to come make a statement. She went with them, acutely aware of Zeni, Hultz, and Quenger watching her as she went. While she was waiting in Picariello's office a tech brought her tasteless coffee and told her Chief Nitta had died in Sick Berth. Jodenny made him repeat the information twice.

"Died of what?" she asked.

"I'm sure they'll do an autopsy, ma'am," the tech said.

Senga poked his head in once but didn't ask her questions. Picariello, when he arrived, asked why she'd been out in the passage so late at night.

"That's personal, sir," she said.

Picariello raised an eyebrow. Jodenny kept her face as blank as she could. Her personal life was her own, damn it, and had nothing to do with Nitta being somewhere he didn't belong.

"Do you think Chief Nitta wanted revenge for being transferred out of Underway Stores?" Picariello asked.

She had already considered the idea. "He might have been mad about it, but he wasn't dumb."

Al-Banna arrived, grumpy at being roused from sleep. Jodenny repeated the story for the umpteenth time. His expression turned thunderous as she described what happened.

"Goddamn Sweet," he said.

Picariello said, "We won't know for sure until the autopsy."

Jodenny looked at both men in bewilderment. "He was using Sweet?" she asked. Impossible. She would have noticed. Then again, hadn't he displayed all the classic signs? Mood swings. Unexplained absences from work. As a division officer she was supposed to notice such things, and to refer sailors to appropriate counseling or treatment programs.

"There have been rumors." Picariello checked the clock. "In any case, it's late. Go get some rest, Lieutenant."

"Take tomorrow off," Al-Banna added.

"No, sir." Jodenny stood, her legs like rubber. "I'll be fine."

Picariello motioned for a guard. "Escort Lieutenant Scott back to her cabin."

She went, and all the way back she saw only Nitta's wide, unseeing eyes, like so many of the dead on the *Yangtze*.

* * *

That same night, over at Minutiae, Myell and Eva ate steamers culled from the ship's artificial seabeds and mushrooms drizzled with tofu cheese. Eva had a glass of wine. Myell kept a clear head. Small talk consisted of comments about their work, shipmates, berthing, and hobbies. Eva didn't like her job much and disliked her roommate, who brought strange men home unexpectedly. Myell allowed that he wasn't sure about his new job but had a great roommate.

Eva squeezed his hand. "You're lucky."

The conversation stayed casual. Myell wasn't brave enough to attempt anything that would require more than pleasant nods or exclamations of agreement—topics such as How I Adore My Division Officer, or How the Last Girl I Dated Cried Rape. When the bill came, they split it fifty-fifty and strolled down the Rocks to an ice cream shop. She ordered chocolate chip on a sugar cone. He opted for butter pecan in a cup. If she noticed that they were being surreptitiously trailed by Gallivan, she didn't mention it. A full moon had been grammed onto the dome above, and as they drew closer to the main gazebo they heard snazzy tunes from a swing band. Couples spun and dipped in the plaza.

"Do you dance?" she asked.

"No."

"Will you try?"

He would try, even though dancing reminded him of the school dances back on Baiame. The pretty girls had always flocked to Colby, the weak ones to Daris. Eva tugged him into the crowd, arranged his arm around her waist, and placed her hand on his shoulder.

"Move forward, back, side. Forward, back, side. You've got it, Terry."

Her breasts pressed against his chest. Myell tried to relax but he suspected that he looked as awkward as he felt. Gallivan was probably laughing his ass off.

"Maybe we should get more ice cream," he said.

Eva kissed his cheek. "Not now. I've got you exactly where I want you."

He tried to let the music carry him, but was entirely too aware of her warmth and closeness. Myell tried thinking about Jodenny and her betrayal of their pact by talking to Ng, but the clamminess in his hands and tightness in his chest kept him firmly rooted in the off-balance present. If Eva noticed his anxiety, she chose not to comment on it. Her smile stayed wide, and when his steps faltered her guidance kept them going.

"My ribs are starting to hurt," he said. "Let me take you home."

He walked her back to Admin berthing, where the lights had been turned down in the lounge and couples snuggled on the sofas. Eva put her hand on Myell's arm. "My roommate's on duty. Want to come in?"

"Never on a first date."

"Don't you believe in seizing the moment?"

"I believe the best things are worth waiting for," he said, and kissed her on the cheek.

Gallivan caught up to him in the lift. "Why didn't you take her to bed?"

Myell cuffed him. "Two words. Wendy Ford."

"You don't think—" Gallivan didn't finish his words. "You did think."

That Chiba might have sent Eva to find out what he knew or suspected? Of course he had. "And I made sure no false accusations could be made," he added, holding up the pocket server.

"You recorded everything?" Gallivan asked. At Myell's nod he said, "Smart bucko."

They returned to Supply berthing. The minute they stepped off the lift Myell sensed something wrong. Far too many people were clustered in the lounge and passageway, their faces showing shock or satisfaction.

"It's Nitta," VanAmsal said grimly. "He's dead."

"Lieutenant Scott found him," Amador said.

Lange snickered. "Maybe they were together. Maybe she was fucking him."

Myell punched him in the face. Lange went sailing backward over the sofa. Gallivan and Amador dragged Myell to his and Timrin's cabin and sat on him until some semblance of reason returned.

"Got your Irish up, did he?" Gallivan asked.

Timrin pulled a bottle of whiskey from his locker. "Give him a belt of this."

Myell threw back a shot. "What did he die of?"

"Looks like Sweet," Timrin said. "Message boards say he tested positive this morning, but you know how reliable they are. I never figured him for it."

Myell drank some more of the whiskey. He'd heard occasional rumors about Nitta, but nothing worth paying attention to. His gaze fell on Koo's terrarium. The rocks were bare, and her favorite corner was empty. He lifted the lid and peered inside, dread mixing with the alcohol to make his stomach churn.

"Where is she?" he demanded.

"Where's who?" Gallivan asked, bewildered.

Myell moved around the rocks and plants. "Koo. Where did she go?"

He lifted blankets, shook out boots, and even searched through desk drawers, but Koo was nowhere to be found. Timrin and Gallivan both tried to assure him she'd turn up, but he imagined her somehow tangled up in the morning laundry and gone down the chute. Or maybe Chiba had broken in and caused her harm—

"Wherever she is, she's fine," Timrin said.

In the morning Lange muttered an apology, but Myell barely acknowledged it. The mood at quarters was grim and Jodenny was pale as she addressed the division.

"As you know, Chief Nitta passed away during the night," she said. "His death is a great loss to the department and to the ship. There will be a memorial service this afternoon in Hangar Bay 3. Uniform is service dress with medals. I expect you all to be there. Underway Stores, dismissed."

Myell and Caldicot trammed over to the office, but Jodenny didn't. Caldicot was off running errands when she finally returned. Myell brought her a large cup of coffee.

"Thank you," she said, standing by the wallvid and looking at the inky blackness of the Alcheringa.

"Did you get any sleep at all?"

"It doesn't matter. You've seen one dying sailor, you've seen them all, right?"

Myell closed the hatch. Jodenny covered her face with both hands and said, through tears, "Damn it, I didn't even like him."

"No one did," Myell said.

Her shoulders shook. He couldn't stand by and do nothing. Myell put his arms around her and rubbed a small circle of comfort on her back as she cried against his shoulder. He asked, "Should I call someone? Commander Vu?"

"No," Jodenny sniffed. She pulled away. "I'm fine."

"Jodenny," he said, and it was the first time he'd ever used her given name.

She reached for a tissue. "I just need to be alone for a few minutes. Off with you before Caldicot starts wondering."

Myell went, leaving her alone, cursing himself as a coward for doing so.

The memorial service was held in the ship's auditorium. The chiefs' mess made an impressive turnout, with rank after rank at parade rest for the entire ceremony. Underway Stores showed up, more or less, and most of Maintenance. Even Osherman was there.

"Sit with me, Lieutenant," he said.

"No."

"Stop being a stubborn pain in the ass and just sit," he said.

Though Jodenny hated to admit it, there was some comfort in having him by her side. She shifted in her chair, sensing accusing stares leveled at the back of her head. But what had she done? Nitta had been the one trespassing in officers' country. Nitta had been the one who threatened her.

Master Chief DiSola began the eulogy. "I first met Hiroji back in Supply School . . ."

Jodenny told herself she wasn't going to cry. She already regretted breaking down on Myell's shoulder. What kind of leadership was that? Nitta's death was hitting her so hard only because of the *Yangtze,* she decided. At the reception afterward, people expressed their condolences to Jodenny as though she'd lost someone important, and she resented them for it. Half the people offering sympathy about Nitta hadn't even liked him. The *Aral Sea* was a ship full of hypocrites, and she herself was probably the biggest of them all.

Quenger and Chiba were at the reception, of course, as was Myell. Jodenny watched them circle the room but never approach each other.

Later that night Holland told her, "Sick Berth has released the autopsy report on Chief Nitta, Lieutenant. He officially died of an overdose of Sweet."

Jodenny blamed herself for not seeing the symptoms. But if he had been cruising on a Sweet high when she saw him, maybe the nonsense about enemies and hurting her had been just that, nonsense. After all, Picariello and Al-Banna had both told her that it was nothing but the ravings of chemicals and hallucinations.

A comforting thought.

She didn't believe it for a moment.

CHAPTER TWENTY-SIX

"You've got a crush on Lieutenant Scott," Gallivan said to Myell at breakfast, half an hour before quarters, as they sat in a corner booth on the mess decks. On the overvids, Hal and Sal showed excerpts from Chief Nitta's memorial service. His autopsy results were already the subject of rumor and gossip on the ship's message boards.

Myell stared at his gib. "You're wrong."

Gallivan snatched one of Myell's pieces of toast. "Punching Lange in front of a dozen witnesses cemented the rumors."

"What rumors?"

"What do you think, that we're all daft? Saw her sitting with Commander Osherman during the memorial service, though. Heard they were an item on the *Yangtze*."

Myell peered over the top of the gib. "Do you want me to punch *you*?"

"Certainly not," Gallivan said. "I'm just saying nothing good can come of it."

"Shut up, Mike."

Gallivan managed to stay quiet for only a moment. "Did you find your lizard yet?"

"No." Myell knew it was absurd to grieve over a missing gecko, but he felt sick just the same. "Tell me, what part of 'shut up' don't you understand?"

"You going to eat those hash browns?"

"Have them." Myell pushed his plate away. He'd lost his appetite.

For the first time since taking over Underway Stores, Jodenny rushed through quarters. All she wanted to do was get back to her office, turn off her gib, and shut off all the lights. Otherwise, just one more sympathetic comment or imail about Nitta's death would make her start screaming. She hurried out of T6 as soon as possible, made it back to the office before Myell or Caldicot, and was settling into her plan for total retreat when the comm pinged. She only answered it because Ng's caller identification flashed on the screen.

He said, "I'm sorry about your chief, but still angry with you for wasting my time."

"Wasting your time? What do you mean?"

Ng told her about his conversation with Myell, and how he'd left the soil analysis from her boots—nothing surprising in it at all—with him. Once Myell and Caldicot were back from T6 and working at their desks, Jodenny emerged from her office with a stack of folders. Myell was on a call that sounded personal.

"I'll talk to you later," he murmured. A pause. "Okay, lunch." He hung up.

Jodenny handed the folders to Caldicot. "Take these to Lieutenant Commander Vu. Right now, please."

When they were alone, Jodenny asked, "Is there something you forgot to give me, Sergeant?"

Myell went to a filing cabinet and began sorting through paperwork. "Such as?"

"Something from Dr. Ng?"

"The same Dr. Ng you confided in? About that thing we agreed to keep quiet?"

Jodenny wanted to grab the papers out of his hands and throw them into the air. "I only told him what I had to."

"Did you tell Commander Osherman, too?"

Jodenny glared at him. "What? Why would I?"

"I saw you with him at the memorial service. You two have a history."

"My history, Sergeant, is none of your concern. Do I ask you who you're going to lunch with? Who you're whispering with on the comm?"

As Myell opened his mouth to retort Faddig emerged from his office wearing a baffled expression. "These F-189s—" he started to say, but stopped. "Everything all right here?"

"The lieutenant and I are having a disagreement," Myell said.

Faddig perked up. "About what?"

"Inventory," Jodenny snapped. "Step into my office, Sergeant."

Behind closed doors Jodenny said, "I don't have to ask you—" and at the same time Myell said, "You don't get to decide—" and a part of her observed how close they were to each other, how dangerously close. She could even smell the faint trace of soap on his skin. The comm pinged.

Jodenny hit the speaker button. "What is it?"

"Watch your tone, Lieutenant," Al-Banna said.

She was immensely glad they were on audio only. "Sorry, sir."

"Just so you know, the glitches in Core have been repaired. You're authorized to start sending people into the slots again."

"They fixed all the errors?" Jodenny asked.

"You don't trust the Data Department?"

"We're talking about people's lives, sir."

"I know what we're talking about." Al-Banna terminated the call.

Jodenny sat at her desk. As much as she wanted to throttle him for talking to Ng, fighting with Myell made her feel sick. By excluding him from Ng's theories she was treating him as poorly as Nitta and the others had. But she wasn't quite ready to admit it.

"Call Amador," she said, "and tell him I'll be over there at fourteen hundred to pull Athena out."

A little too sharply Myell asked, "You?"

"Yes, me." Jodenny's anger began to rise again. "I won't send anyone in until I'm confident the problems are cleared up."

"I'll go in. I've got the most experience."

"No one's going into the slots until I do, and that's an order."

Myell threw up his hands. "Do you know how stubborn you are?"

"Not half as stubborn as you!"

They didn't speak to each other for the rest of the morning.

Myell waited until Jodenny was off to a meeting and Caldicot at lunch before he used Faddig's agent to read the Data Department's report on the glitches in Core. Then he got Dicensu to cover the office and went up to C-Deck to track down Ensign Cartik, who was listed as one of the report's authors. Cartik, who worked in one of a dozen small cubicles, was surprised to meet him.

"Not everyone who gets flattened by a dingo lives to tell the tale," he said, clearing a chair for Myell.

"How many people get flattened by dingoes, sir?"

"You're the only one on this ship. There was an accident on the *Oceania* a year or so ago, though."

Myell hadn't researched the problem on other ships. "Same glitches?"

Cartik squinted at him. "What's your interest in it all?"

"Purely personal, sir. Lieutenant Scott said I should follow up on anything that I didn't understand."

Well, maybe she hadn't said it in so many words. But the mention of Jodenny's name seemed to assure Cartik. He tapped on his deskgib. "The Class III on the *Oceania* did ignore a lockdown order, but it was corrupt all the way through its registry. The *Oceania* pulled all their Class IIIs and inspected them. No other unit had the same problem."

"But we didn't pull all of ours, did we?"

"No." Cartik looked uncomfortable. "They decided not to."

"Who decided not to, sir?"

Cartik shut down his screen. "I don't have that information."

"One more question, sir. I noticed Circe had no record of the collision with me. Are we sure she was the one who did it?"

"I don't know what you mean," Cartik said.

"How do we know it wasn't another dingo on that level?"

Cartik's gaze went over Myell's shoulder. "Sergeant," Commander Osherman said. Myell wondered how long he'd been standing there. Osherman continued. "Good to see you've recovered from your accident."

Myell stood. "Yes, sir. Thank you."

"The sergeant was just on his way back to Underway Stores," Cartik said.

Actually, Myell was on his way to T6. If he timed it right, he could be in the slots before Jodenny arrived. He would try again to talk her out of it. But when he reached the tower, Jodenny was already up in the observation module getting into the EV suit. Amador was manning the command module.

"She won't listen to me," Amador told Myell. "Stubborn as hell."

Ysten arrived. "She's really going in?" he asked incredulously.

"Yes, sir," Myell said.

Ysten edged out Myell for one of the command chairs. "Where is she?"

"About to come down," Amador said. A few moments later, Jodenny powered by the command module windows. She gave them all a brief wave. Myell's stomach knotted. He tracked her progress on the overvid.

"I'm entering level twelve now," Jodenny said.

Although he would have traded places with her, Myell was suddenly glad not to be in those dark, narrow confines. He double-checked that the level was locked down and verified all traffic had stopped.

"Athena should be halfway between Mike and November blocks," Amador said. "Should take you about ten minutes to get there."

"I know." Jodenny sounded amused. "I've been in the slots before."

"Yes, ma'am," Amador said.

"One of the ensigns on my last ship got lost in them once," she offered. "Blew his headlamp and got turned all around. It would have been kind of funny if he hadn't been so petrified."

Myell wondered if she ever said the *Yangtze*'s name.

Jodenny continued. "It didn't help that the chief kept telling him about the Legend of the Lost AT. Had him half convinced a ghost was going to creep up and grab him by the back of the neck."

Did she know she was rambling nervously?

"I never heard that one," Ysten said, and Myell realized he was wrong. She wasn't telling the story to quell the anxiousness of being in the slots. She was telling it to keep Amador and Ysten occupied.

Her headvid showed her passing B-block. "Way back when, on one of the first Team Space freighters, an AT went into the slots to pull out something that had been requisitioned—this is in the days when you had to pull the small items by hand—and something went wrong. He reported being lost. Then he lost his headlamp, so he couldn't see where he was. Core couldn't track the marker on his suit or pinpoint where he was. His comm stayed open, though, and you could hear him trying to hold everything together. They sent in a chief to pull him out but he couldn't find him—every time it seemed like they were getting close, the chief would turn down a block and find no one there."

"How long did this go on?" Ysten asked.

"By the time they sent a second team in, it had been almost twelve hours. By the time they sent the third team in, the AT's suit was almost out of power."

Myell kept his eyes on Jodenny's EV display. The Legend of the Lost AT was a fairy tale told to impressionable young sailors or ensigns. Jodenny continued. "He was delirious near the end. Kept telling his lieutenant that he could see tigers and lions and other animals. They figured he was out of it from dehydration."

"They found him, though, right?" Ysten asked.

"No," Jodenny said. "Never. Even when they reached Fortune and combed through every centimeter of the tower, they never found the body."

Ysten drew himself up in his chair. "I don't believe that."

"Would I lie?" Jodenny asked. "Oh, here, look. Here's Athena."

Telling the story had made her trip go quickly. Athena now caught the focus of Jodenny's headlamp, and it only took a once-over to see the bin gate had closed while the DNGO was retrieving a crate. Jodenny's light caught the address on the bin overhead.

"She got herself stuck," Jodenny reported. "Did you say Mike block?"

"Yes, ma'am," Amador said. "She'd just finished making a pickup."

Jodenny opened the gate, braced herself, and tugged Athena and her cargo free. The DNGO had automatically powered down to conserve energy, but Jodenny fitted her with a restraining bolt anyway.

"Careful, Lieutenant," Myell's voice said in her ear. He sounded very tense. "Who knows what's in her cache?"

"I hear you." Jodenny unhooked the gib from her belt and

swiped it over the smartcrate Athena had been clutching. The crate's coded information instantly downloaded for her. "What does Core say Athena was retrieving?"

"Cleaning supplies," Amador replied.

The smartcrate listed its contents as plumbing equipment. She wanted to open it up, but she didn't have the crate's authorization codes and hadn't brought any kind of crowbar. Jodenny shoved it back into the bin, closed the gate, and leashed Athena to her belt. "We're on our way out."

Fifteen minutes later she dropped Athena off at the command module and let Myell and Ysten help her out of the EV suit. "Let me know what Repair Services says."

Amador went to take the DNGO over. Ysten excused himself to go stand a training watch. Myell said, "Lieutenant, if you want to know what's wrong with Athena, the Repair Shop isn't where you should send her."

Jodenny reached down to tighten her boots. "It's not?"

"It might be better to run a diagnostic here."

"Sergeant—"

"At least check her out before you send her over. Once they take her apart, you'll only have their word for it."

Myell sounded painfully earnest. Jodenny sighed and pinged Amador. "Bring Athena down to Sergeant Myell's old workbench."

Jodenny and Myell went down to the bench. Amador showed up a few minutes later with Athena bobbing behind him. Once he was gone, Myell plugged Athena into the board and powered her up. The DNGO's lights blinked as she raised and spun her head. "There's my girl," he murmured, one hand on her hull. He connected her to his gib and data filled the screen.

Jodenny said, "At least her memory looks intact."

Myell studied the information silently for a moment. "I meant to tell you about Ng, but then Chief Nitta died and you were already upset."

She supposed she could concede a little as well. "Maybe I overreacted. I did promise not to tell anyone."

He shrugged. "I might have told someone, too."

"Might have?" Her voice came out with a squeak.

"It slipped out while I was in Sick Berth. Chaplain Mow."

The lift arrived. Perhaps alerted by Amador, Ishikawa approached timidly and asked, "Anything I can help with, Lieutenant?"

"No," Jodenny said. "Thanks anyway."

Ishikawa lingered.

"You're dismissed, AT Ishikawa."

When they were alone, Jodenny asked, "What exactly did you tell Chaplain Mow?"

"Everything, it turns out." Myell pried Athena's registration plate off and peered inside. He changed the subject. "This is a Class III made by a company called Fortunate Robotics. The dingoes that have had problems in the last few months all come from there. Maybe there's a design or factory flaw they all share—or maybe something else is going on with them."

While Myell poked around the DNGO's innards, Jodenny told him about Dr. Ng's theories and about the Wondjina travel reported by Mary Dory forty years earlier. Myell said, "She doesn't sound like a very reliable witness," and pulled out something small and silver.

"What's that?" Jodenny asked.

He studied it in the light. "A master chip. I haven't seen one in a long time. When I first got into Team Space, Class I and II dingoes worked on a distributive system. They gave each other storage and retrieval commands. But they were too easy to manipulate. There was a lot of fraud and theft, because you could install one of these and make a dingo do something that wouldn't be logged into its records . . ."

His voice trailed off.

"Sergeant?"

"The morning of the accident," he said. "Andromeda."

Jodenny didn't like the increasing chalkiness in his face. "Do you remember something?"

"I found—" Myell tore open one of the workbench drawers and reached inside it. "Jesus, I found one, how could I forget that?"

"You found one what?"

He pulled another master chip from the drawer. "In Andromeda. The morning of the accident."

Jodenny gazed up the shaft. "So there's more than one."

"There could be dozens. Any of the units I sent over to Repair—it's Chiba's people. They stick these things in our dingoes and then we wonder why they're glitched."

"By controlling the dingoes they can steal whatever they want," Jodenny said. "But the annual physical inventory will show the items are missing."

Myell dropped onto his stool as if all the energy had suddenly drained out of him. "Not if they change the records in Core."

Jodenny hooked her own gib into the board. "Core thought Athena had finished making a delivery in Mike block when she shut down. I found her at Lima block, retrieving a crate. Let's see what she was taking."

The container ID spilled on to the screen.

"Invalid number," Myell said. "That container doesn't exist."

"Then they're not just stealing things. They're smuggling cargo as well. Guns, Sweet, stolen property—it could be anything." Jodenny gazed upward again. "We've got to find out what's in that container."

"That's not necessary, Lieutenant Scott. We'll take it from here."

Standing at the base of the nearest ladder, holding up Inspector General badges, were AT Ishikawa and Commander Osherman.

CHAPTER TWENTY-SEVEN

Jodenny stared at the young woman she'd known as AT Ishikawa. "*Agent* Ishikawa? But you're only eighteen years old."

Ishikawa grinned. "Twenty-four, Lieutenant. I only look eighteen."

The four of them had moved up to the command module. Myell had taken a seat but Jodenny was standing by the windows, beyond which DNGOs arced and flew through the shaft. Osherman said, "The two of you have gotten yourself tangled up in a fleet-wide investigation that's included year-long operations on several ships, including the *Yangtze* and *Aral Sea*. Your initiative is appreciated, but you're jeopardizing a case much larger than you can imagine."

Only he could mix praise and recrimination so deftly. Jodenny didn't care if he was unhappy with her. If someone had actually taken the time to clue her into the smugglers operating in her own department, she wouldn't have stumbled into it like a woman in a darkened room full of furniture. The idea of Osherman working for the Inspector General left her cold. He was a spy—a legal spy, a spy out for the greater good of Team Space, but a spy nonetheless.

"They're reprogramming the dingoes, aren't they?" Myell asked. "Using master chips to give them off-the-book commands."

Osherman said, "Obviously I can't confirm anything. I have a duty to protect the integrity of this investigation."

"What about a duty to protect Sergeant Myell's life?" Jodenny remembered him limp on the floor of the observation module. "Circe nearly killed him because she had one of those damned chips in her."

"It wasn't Circe," Myell said.

Jodenny gave him an inquisitive look but he was focused inward, on something only he could see. "The hull markings were wrong," he said. "I remember that now. It was Castalia, the unit stolen back at Kookaburra."

Osherman's expression gave away nothing. "It doesn't matter. The people who've subverted the dingoes—well, let's just say they didn't realize they had glitched the command routines that kick in during a General Quarters. In my opinion it was truly an accident."

"The people who've subverted the dingoes," Jodenny repeated the phrase. She focused on the tower shaft, where the DNGO lights were entrancing, almost hypnotic. "Chief

Chiba, because nothing could go on in Repair that he didn't have a hand in. Lieutenant Quenger, who went to the academy with Lieutenant Anzo—the same lieutenant who delayed reporting Lieutenant Commander Greiger's accident to the captain and who covered for Chiba and Engel when they stole that dingo during the GQ. She works in Data, so it was easy to falsify the lifepod entries to give them alibis. But she made a mistake and made the report times unrealistic. More people who work for Chiba. Chief Nitta? Was his overdose an accident, or was someone trying to shut him up? What about Commander Matsuda's disappearance back on Kiwi?"

Osherman stayed silent. Jodenny turned around to stare at him. "Why? What are they smuggling or stealing? Weapons? Explosives?"

"Leave it alone, Lieutenant," Osherman said. "You did enough harm with your curiosity back in the warehouse district on Mary River. By following Quenger and Nitta like some amateur detective, you almost wrecked our entire operation."

"Those were your people who tried to detain me?" Jodenny had never told Myell about the events that had brought her to his brother's farm and could see the curiosity on his face.

"I can't—" Osherman started.

Ishikawa said, "It doesn't hurt for her to know that, sir, and she's earned it. Yes, Lieutenant. It was a joint effort between Team Space and the local authorities. We couldn't afford to let you make Lieutenant Quenger suspicious. If you'd come with us, we could have explained things there and then. But you ran, which increased suspicion that you were somehow involved or trying to get involved."

Outside the shaft, a DNGO hovered and spun in place, its lights blinking. Jodenny had the uncomfortable feeling it was eavesdropping. "What did I ever do to warrant suspicion?"

Osherman grimaced. "You called in an admiral's favor at Fleet to get reassigned to this ship ahead of any other eligible lieutenant. Then you got yourself put in charge of Underway Stores, the very center of our investigation. No one knew what your motives or plans were."

"My motives . . ." Jodenny shook her head. "My only motive was to do the job I'm supposed to do."

Ishikawa was eyeing the DNGO outside the window. Her hand moved across the controls, and it flew off. "On Mary River, you evaded our people and disappeared. We didn't realize you'd gotten out of town until our people saw you return with Sergeant Myell. There was a great discussion then about whether or not to remove you from the equation, but Commander Osherman believed it would be best to keep you. He's always been your advocate."

"Have you?" Jodenny asked.

Osherman's gaze was level. "You doubt it?"

She couldn't say, one way or the other. The only comfort was that if Ishikawa was telling the truth, then they probably didn't know about her and Myell's trip through the Mother Sphere. "Did you make that complaint about fraternization?"

"There was no complaint," Osherman admitted. "Lieutenant Commander Wildstein was asked to convince you to transfer Sergeant Myell. We've been worried about his curiosity as much as yours."

But Wildstein had done a piss-poor job, and that had probably been deliberate. Certainly she could have come down harder on Jodenny, made the fraternization issue a bigger leverage point.

"I didn't ask for Underway Stores. Why wasn't Quenger put in charge?" Jodenny asked. "You might have had more opportunity to find out how their operations work."

"Captain Umbundo had his own ideas," Osherman said tightly. Jodenny tried to put herself in the same position as the captain—knowing there were thieves on his ship, but unable to properly chase them down because of an outside investigation. Realizing how poor leadership was contributing to the problem, but prevented from shifting or punishing personnel while the investigation continued. Jodenny had simply been a wild card thrown into the mix.

Myell spoke up from where he'd been watching the conversation. "What about the dingoes? If some of them are operating independent of Core, what's to prevent another accident?"

Ishikawa responded. "We don't know how many have been compromised, Sergeant, and we can't do a full inspection without scaring the people we're trying to catch."

"I'm not sending any of my people into the slots knowing they could be killed," Jodenny said.

Osherman said, "Once we get to Warramala this will all be over. We've asked the captain not to conduct any more drills. He's not happy, but he understands."

Myell didn't look happy, either. "What if there's a real emergency?"

"Then this ship will have bigger problems than a bunch of rogue dingoes," Osherman said. "Lieutenant Scott, it's vitally important that you and Sergeant Myell understand how delicate this operation is. You can't discuss it once we leave this room. I'll tell you right now that there are several places being monitored—"

"You're listening in on my division?" Jodenny asked.

"—as are several communications channels, gibs, imail, and personal imail."

"Personal accounts are protected," Myell said.

"Not if there's a court order." Osherman cocked his head in consideration. "Is there something you'd like to tell us, Sergeant?"

"Don't be ridiculous," Jodenny said. "He nearly died."

"We don't know everyone who's involved, and so everyone's a suspect. Is everyone here clear? No talking about this. No confiding in anyone. Word gets out, more lives might be lost."

"More?" Jodenny asked sharply. "Who?"

"I can't say." Osherman turned to Myell. "Do we have your cooperation, Sergeant?"

"Yes, sir," he said, without enthusiasm.

"Lieutenant Scott?"

"I don't like it," she said. Beyond the window, another DNGO descended from the shaft and blinked at them, its hull shiny and reflective.

"You don't have to." Osherman stood abruptly. "As far as anyone knows—and if anyone should ask you—Athena glitched doing exactly what Core was telling her to do. Agent Ishikawa will take care of the log entries. Please leave your gibs with me, and I'll make sure they're returned to you in the morning."

Jodenny and Myell caught an empty tram back to Mainship and sat in seats across from each other. Myell kept his gaze on the advertisements blinking overhead. Jodenny wondered who else in the Supply Department could possibly be working undercover. Surely not just Ishikawa, an able technician without access to the wardroom or chiefs' mess. Maybe an officer like Weaver, who always had a sharp question or two. Ysten? Surely not. The truth was she didn't know who she could really trust. Meanwhile she had to sit back, keep silent, and watch the entire Supply Department be compromised.

Forgetting that Osherman had confiscated her gib, she reached for it and grasped only empty air. Myell eyed her speculatively. "You did good work today," she told him.

He didn't need her to tell him that. He was self-sufficient beyond her measure, able to make his own decisions without outside influence. Maybe he had learned that in the hold, but Jodenny suspected the skill could be traced back to a failed farm on Baiame.

"Didn't get us anywhere, did it?" Myell asked, but she had no answer.

The next morning Jodenny sent Faddig to conduct quarters and holed up in her office, unable to face the fact that Osherman's investigation and the unmasked smuggling ring were going to stain Underway Stores, the Supply Department, and the *Aral Sea* as a whole. The scandal would blight Team Space itself. Any hopes she'd had for a good tour were gone. Commodore Campos had been right. Someone else should have taken the job.

"Hey, Lieutenant." Gallivan knocked at her hatch. "Tonight's your last chance to hear me play over on the Rocks. My going-away party."

"Oh," she said. "Sure. What time?"

"Starts right after dinner. Bring your dancing shoes."

Left alone again, Jodenny pulled up the only vid she had of her, Jem, and Dyanne, taken in the wardroom of the *Yangtze*. Try as she might, she couldn't imagine what advice Jem would give her in a time like this. The vid was still on display when Myell returned from quarters.

"Anything exciting going on?" she asked as she signed off on COSALs.

"No, ma'am."

He sounded as glum as she felt. Jodenny glanced up and saw him staring at the vid.

"Lieutenant Commander Ross and Lieutenant Owens," she said.

"Friends of yours?"

"Taught me everything I know."

"What would they say about this?"

Jodenny bristled. "They would tell me to follow orders, and that's exactly what you and I are going to do."

"You don't know that Commander Osherman is telling the truth," Myell said. "He could be just as much a part of it as anyone else."

Jodenny pressed the palms of her hands against her eyes. "Do you know something I don't, Sergeant? Do you have proof he's lying? Because otherwise he's an official investigator appointed by Team Space and operating with the authority of the admiralty, and anything you or I do could be construed as obstructing justice. You may not value your career, but I don't intend to be a lieutenant all my life. Is that clear?"

"Yes, ma'am," Myell said tightly.

He was gone by the time she uncovered her eyes.

Later that morning she was on her way to the Flats when she bumped into Chang. He handed her a gib. "I was told you needed this, Lieutenant."

Not her own gib, which Osherman still had; Jodenny opened it up and saw the serial chip had been dug out.

Chang gave her a wink. "See you later."

Jodenny palmed the hot gib off into her pocket, where it burned against her thigh for the entire DIVO meeting.

"Lieutenant," Al-Banna said at the end of it, "I hear dinner in the wardroom has become exceptionally popular. When were you planning on inviting me?"

"You're welcome anytime, sir."

"I'll be there tonight," Al-Banna said.

After the meeting Jodenny locked herself in her cabin. The hot gib linked directly to a personal pocket server. Myell had charted DNGO glitches over the previous six months. The graph showed an increase whenever the *Aral Sea* took on supplies, which didn't surprise her. The DNGOs were at their busiest then. But every month there were also increases in DNGO glitches in the hours just *before* planetfall, when the towers slotted for that destination were released into orbit.

"Need to check Bowels," Myell wrote several minutes later. "Don't trust Osherman."

The man just never gave up. But Jodenny understood what he was trying to say. If the DNGOs were rerouting Team Space property into the towers for smuggling purposes then the DCS system was compromised. A visual inspection of the conveyance belts would confirm or deny it. She checked her watch. The towers destined for Warramala would start to be released at oh-five-hundred.

"No," she wrote back. "Not your concern. Do not, repeat, do not, go to Bowels."

She'd go herself, and keep Myell out of it. Because when all was said and done, Jodenny didn't know if she trusted Osherman either.

CHAPTER TWENTY-EIGHT

"Hurry up," Timrin said. "We don't want them to run out of beer before we get there."

Myell reached into his locker for the gift he'd gotten Gallivan. It wasn't much, just something to help him kick off his new career as a civilian musician. His knuckles brushed something unfamiliar and he pulled out the jewelry box Dottie had slipped into his rucksack. He hadn't forgotten about it, but he hadn't taken it out since Mary River.

"Give me a minute," Myell said. "I'll meet you in the lounge."

Timrin went ahead, grumbling about prima-donna roommates. Myell set the box down next to Koo's empty terrarium and lifted the carved lid. The contents had been jumbled over the years, mixing earrings with necklaces and broken watches. Nothing triggered any memories. He fingered a blue-white stone pendant and a turquoise bracelet. Cheap stuff, nothing he'd want to give to anyone, especially maddening lieutenants. Her order to him not to investigate the Bowels still rankled. Couldn't she see how much trouble they could get in by *not* taking a look? A stone pendant drew his attention. He held it up to the light, sure that his eyes were playing tricks on him, but there was no mistaking the design.

A snake eating its own tail.

An ouroboros.

He dug out the carved stone Ganambarr had given him. The color was the same blue-black, and the type of rock was similar if not identical. He didn't know enough to tell if both had been carved by the same hand, but they each had a small gouge on the bottom, as if the maker had left a mark.

The comm pinged. "Hurry up in there!" Timrin said from the lounge.

Myell put the jewelry box back and added his mother's ouroboros pendant to his dilly bag. Finding it was probably only a coincidence, but maybe it was a message. "You will have to choose," the Wirrinun had said. And so he would. He would disobey Jodenny and go to the Bowels. But not before he said good-bye to Gallivan.

True to his word, Al-Banna came to dinner in the wardroom and brought his wife. Sayura Al-Banna was a tall, statuesque woman with jet-black hair and a warm laugh. Al-Banna nodded in approval at the wardroom's improved decor and atmosphere. "It's about time someone took charge and cleaned up this place," he said as Ashmont served soup.

"It was Jodenny, sir," Hultz said helpfully.

"It was all of us," Jodenny replied. She had been slightly uneasy about Rokutan coming, but he was on watch. Francesco hadn't dined in the wardroom since the scandal broke, and she missed him terribly. But it was Quenger's absence that worried her most. He wouldn't miss a chance to rub arms with the SUPPO unless for a very good reason.

"You keep looking at the clock," Hultz said, after dinner had broken up.

"Do I?" Jodenny asked.

"Come on, Lieutenant, play euchre with us," Al-Banna said from a corner chair.

She partnered with Vu for one game only, then stood up apologetically. "You'll have to excuse me, sir. RT Gallivan's having a going-away party and I promised I'd show up."

"Why don't we all go?" Vu suggested.

Jodenny couldn't think of a worse suggestion, actually, but within minutes almost all of them were traipsing over to the Rocks, dinner uniforms and all, to the bar where Gallivan's rock 'n' roll band was belting out standard classics. The place was large and crowded, with two levels stretching away into dark corners and a dance floor already jammed with military and civilians alike. Gallivan waved from the stage and Timrin came over to buy Jodenny a beer.

"Have you seen Sergeant Myell?" she asked him. "I have to ask him something about a COSAL."

Timrin waved to a dark corner. "Back there somewhere. Having a good time for a change."

Jodenny sat at the bar and sipped at her beer. She resisted Zeni's entreaties to dance and instead watched couples grope and shimmy to the beat. She didn't see any sign of Myell at all. After an hour she made her way to the head and slid out a side exit. The air on the Rocks was cooler than it had been inside, but the crowds watching the final quarter of Talofofo vs. Lake Eerie were just as lively. Jodenny made her way through the throngs to T6's access ring and went down to the loading dock, where all was blessedly quiet. She dug through a supply locker until she found a spare jumpsuit and boots and changed into them, grateful to be out of her skirt and heels. Armed with a flashlight and her gib she climbed downladder and almost immediately stepped on Myell's shoulders.

"What are you doing here?" he asked, and got out of her way. He too was wearing a jumpsuit but had obviously dressed in a hurry, with the zipper stuck halfway. She caught a glimpse of his bare chest and tore her gaze away.

"Me?" Jodenny demanded. "Why do you insist on ignoring my orders?"

"Why do you give me orders you know I won't obey?"

She glared at him. He was entirely unperturbed. "Fine," she said, and flashed her light down the passageway. The mag-lev belt ran along the starboard bulkhead, protected by a clearshield. Smartcrates delivered by the DNGOs were humming along toward Mainship. They followed the crates to where the mag-lev met the Rocks and settled down to see if any diverted off to any of the branch lines. Tram noise from overhead, coupled with water, power, and sewer sounds, made casual conversation difficult.

"How long should we wait?" Myell asked.

Jodenny shrugged. "Give it an hour or two."

The air was dripping with humidity and smelled like machine oil. There wasn't much room to sit on the deck but they wedged themselves between air-conditioning units. Jodenny decided she was crazy to be sitting alone with Myell. Her leg inadvertently pressed against his, his bulk solid against her right hip. If she were a good lieutenant she'd put a halt to their amateur investigation and go back up to the light and crowds. As it was, they could do just about anything they wanted to down here and no one would be the wiser. Jodenny glanced at Myell. His cheeks were flushed.

"You all right?" she asked.

"Fine," he said. "Hot down here."

Ninety minutes later their watch paid off. A set of pushing gear came alive and knocked aside three crates so that they were no longer destined for Mainship but instead for some other tower. Jodenny and Myell tried to follow, but the mag-lev was faster than they were and soon the crates were out of sight.

"It doesn't matter," Jodenny said. "The only towers to be released are T14, T16, and T19, and these belts run to even-numbered towers. T14 is the prison colony. What's in T16?"

"Trains and bridges, I think."

She wiped sweat off her forehead with her sleeve and wished she'd had the foresight to bring water. Myell took the lead and had to bend over to pass beneath jutting ducts. He helped her over a patch of something dark and foul on the floor. The noise from the tram system receded, and the air got a little cooler.

"More legends," he said. "People who hitchhike on ships and live under the Rocks."

Jodenny had heard that one. "They ride the circuit for years and years, living so long in the dark that they go blind."

The belt abruptly descended down through the deck. They climbed downladder into a passage that was narrower, dirtier, and darker than the one they left behind. Jodenny could almost feel the grime sinking into her pores and blood. "Here comes another one," Myell said as a smartcrate overtook them. "Greedy bastards, aren't they?"

They were getting close to T16 when lights flickered in the passageway and voices echoed against the bulkheads. A maintenance crew from Tower Operations, she told herself, but she stopped walking and shut off her torch. Myell stood beside her, so close she could feel his body heat.

"I hear Chiba," he whispered.

Silver-white light scorched across Jodenny's line of vision. The mazer charge threw Myell back against the bulkhead. The next charge stabbed through Jodenny's side to her spine and sent a skewering pain up to the base of her skull. She'd never been mazered before, although once at the academy she'd been punched so hard in a boxing ring that she saw stars. She saw them again now, bright lacy pinpoints falling like snowflakes, and as all her limbs went numb she pitched forward helplessly, unable to brace herself as the deck slammed up under her face.

A moment or two of blackness, not much at all. She came to her senses prone on the deck, her right arm pinned beneath her, drool down the side of her face. With blurred, doubled vision she saw Quenger and Chiba looking down on her with contempt.

"Now, Jo, Jo, Jo," Quenger said. "Look what you've done to yourself this time."

He crouched beside her and ran his fingers across her cheek. Jodenny wanted to recoil, but her body felt distant and unreal, as if it belonged to someone else. In a deceptively mild tone Quenger said, "Couldn't mind your own business. Couldn't keep your hands off everything. Stealing the division officer job wasn't enough, is that it?"

Chiba said, "Oh, fuck her and Myell. Let's be done with this."

Quenger's expression brightened, as if he truly was considering peeling away Jodenny's clothes and raping her on the deck. She wouldn't be able to stop him. Chiba and Quenger both could do whatever they wanted. Then a third person drew near, and Jodenny's pulse soared with recognition. The lying, double-crossing son of a bitch—

"We don't have much time," Osherman said. He gazed down at Jodenny dispassionately. "Leave them here. We're never coming back, anyway. By the time anyone finds them we'll be long gone."

"Leave them alive?" Chiba lifted his mazer again and aimed it at Jodenny's head. "No. No witnesses."

So this was it. They were going to die in the filthy, rotten Bowels and it was Jodenny's fault for not discouraging Myell from his speculations. So stupid. She'd been so stupid.

Quenger stood up. "So do it already. We've only got a few hours."

Chiba scowled. The mazer lowered a few centimeters. "Why don't you get your hands dirty on this one? You never do the hard work."

"I could do it," Quenger blustered. "You don't think I can?"

"Wait. What's this?" Osherman crouched down to the deck. He picked up a small cylindrical object, some kind of computer equipment. "Looks like a pocket server."

Chiba said, "They've been fucking recording us—"

The mazer struck again. Jodenny knew nothing.

* * *

The sound of a hatch slamming shut brought Myell around. At first he thought he was back in Sick Berth after the accident in T6, but that couldn't be right unless the staff had turned out the lights and lowered the thermostat by several degrees. He strained to make out his surroundings but saw only a blurred red glow moving a few meters away. It took several moments for him to realize that the light was an exit sign and that he was the one who was moving about.

He tried to drag himself upright, but there was no upright to be found. The gravity had disappeared while he was unconscious. He twisted in midair and grasped for any available handhold. His fingers scraped the soft, fine strands of a woman's hair.

"Jodenny," he croaked out, but she didn't answer. Myell pulled himself closer. He touched a shoulder, a possible breast, another breast, and there, the belt of her jumpsuit.

With one hand firmly around her belt he tried again for a handhold on the deck or bulkheads. He attempted to drift toward the red light, but he had no real maneuvering ability. When his icy fingers touched a flat surface he twisted around to get his feet against it. He pushed off toward the emergency light and the hatch beneath it.

Myell slapped the exit control but nothing happened. His chest began aching as he considered the possibilities of where they might be. "Medbot, activate," he mumbled. He repeated it again, louder. A green light lit up on the opposite bulkhead as the unit flew toward the sound of his voice.

"Environmental conditions unsound," the medbot said. "Initiating emergency protocols."

An air vent hissed. Myell turned toward the stream of cold oxygen and gulped in deep breaths. The backup atmospherics would last only about ten minutes, depending on consumption. By the light of the medbot's headlamp he could see he was floating near the ceiling of T16's command module. The control panels were all powered down. Beyond the plastiglass windows, the tower shaft was pitch-black. The scant heat and air that had come in when their attackers had shoved them inside were already dissipating.

"Jodenny, wake up." He pulled her limp body close to his. Her face was shockingly pale, but her lips weren't blue. Yet.

"Contacting Emergency Services," the medbot said.

Myell wrapped his legs around her to anchor her. Still clinging to the emergency light, he used his free hand to slap her cheeks. Her hair, loose from its braid, rippled like seaweed.

"Unable to make contact," the medbot announced.

Of course not. T16 was unmanned and disconnected. In just a few hours it was going to be let loose into Warramala's orbit and picked up by escort tugs.

"Jodenny." Myell resisted the impulse to therapeutically kiss her and force some air past those pretty lips. She was unconscious but breathing. The medbot had reached its own diagnosis.

"No external injuries noted and vital statistics within range. What caused this condition?"

"I don't know." The last thing he remembered was walking in the Bowels with Jodenny. He checked his and Jodenny's suits. Their gibs were gone, as was his pocket server, but he still had his dilly bag. Myell used Jodenny's belt to tether the two of them together and wrapped one hand around the medbot. "Services no longer needed. Return to your roost."

The medbot immediately swooped back to its perch, taking the two of them with it. Not as fast or agile as a Class III, but it served its purpose. Myell was within kicking distance of the storage closet. His fingers ached with cold as he pulled it open and fished for an EV suit.

"Couldn't shut up," he chided himself as he pulled the suit on. "Couldn't stay home and mind your own goddamned business."

Once the EV suit was sealed he turned on the controls, and the first blast of heat made him groan in relief. The air smelled better and cleaner than the backup atmospherics. He was able to maneuver now too, and it was easy to retrieve Jodenny. Harder to get her into the suit, but finally she was sealed inside.

They now had ten hours each of air, with two additional canisters in the closet and more probably stored in the observation module on level fifty.

Myell pulled Jodenny to the chair and hooked her into it. He tried all the buttons on the control panel but nothing worked. He tried the hatch again, but it had been sealed on the other side. The only way out was into the shaft, down to the loading dock, and maybe out through the mag-lev belts.

"Terry?"

"Hey." Myell went to her and tried to smile reassuringly. "How do you feel?"

"They zapped us," she said thickly.

"Who?"

"Quenger. Chiba. Osherman. I thought they were going to kill us." Jodenny paused. "Osherman, that goddamned son of a bitch. Something happened—it's all fuzzy now. They found something? I don't remember."

"Maybe my server," he said.

"Your what?"

"I was carrying a pocket server set to record upon voice activation. Even if they took it, the data's backed up in my personal account. Timrin could get into it."

"What else have you recorded?"

Myell said, "Nothing that would embarrass us."

"Oh."

She lapsed into silence. He listened to the sounds of his own breathing and ignored a growing queasiness in his gut. He counted to thirty. He wondered if maybe she had lapsed back into unconsciousness, but then Jodenny shifted and asked, "Where are we?"

"T16."

"Our gibs?"

"Gone. The hatch is sealed, there's no power except for our suit batteries, the medbot can't contact Mainship and we have"—he checked the suit chronometer—"six hours until we're let loose into orbit."

"Plenty of time." Jodenny freed herself. "What's exactly in this tower?"

He tried to remember the ship's manifest. "Some suspension bridges, a few trains, railroad equipment. Maybe some power stations. And anything that's been smuggled in since we left Fortune."

"We might be able to get out through the loading dock."

Myell bit back the taste of bile. Space sickness would have to wait. "Let's try it."

They used their EV thrusters to direct themselves out of the command module, through the eerily dark shaft, and down to the loading dock. The tower was so large around them that Myell felt like a tiny fish swimming in a black sea. If it wasn't for the hiss of Jodenny's comm on the open channel, he would have very easily scared himself into thinking he was all alone.

"When we miss morning quarters, they'll start looking for us," Jodenny said.

"They won't think to look here," he replied.

The loading dock looked ghostly in the torchlight. The tower's DNGOs were stacked in large racks, each of them silent and useless. The mag-lev belt of the DCS was disconnected from the hull, and a thick plate covered the hatch. Myell put his gloved hand against a rivet the size of his fist.

"There's no possible way they're shuffling supplies into this tower," Jodenny said. She gasped suddenly. "Christ! Did you see something move?"

Myell had not seen anything. He didn't want to see anything. He wondered if the heat in his suit was working, because his skin was cold from head to toe.

"I saw something," Jodenny whispered.

Neither of them moved to investigate. Being in Team Space had never demanded much bravery, Myell knew. It required endurance of petty annoyances and mammoth wastes of time, and the discipline of listening to superiors talk of nonsense and trivia, and the ability to think one way but act another, for days and months and years at a time. He had been truly scared only a few times in his military career—once while doing firefighting training in boot camp, another when Chiba's men had entered his Security cell during the Ford affair—but all in all, he could safely say he had never been asked to chase something down in the icy darkness, something his lieutenant only thought she saw.

"There's nothing there," he said.

She either didn't believe him or had to prove it to herself. Jodenny used her thrusters to skirt around the dark silhouette of a forklift and swept the area with her light. This time it was Myell who caught the glint of motion.

"There!" he said, and Jodenny turned her beam. An unsecured wrench floated in midair, no doubt disturbed by their EV thrusters.

"So much for that." Jodenny tilted her head upward, or downward, or sideways—it was hard to say, and his stomach was churning again. "They can't take the bridges out of here through the DCS. How do they remove the ends of the tower?"

"They release a hundred sealing bolts, each of them twice as large as we are." Myell tried to remain calm and objective. "The important thing is that it will be opened, sooner or later. All we have to do is hold on until then."

"Could be a week."

"Could be today. Or maybe we can figure out some way to make them open it early. I'll go get the other oxygen tanks from the observation module so at least we'll be able to breathe."

"I'll keep looking for a way off this loading dock."

He hated to be separated from her, but the sooner he had those tanks in hand the better he'd feel about their chances of avoiding suffocation. Myell steered himself along the shaft with his headlamp as a guide. The open maws of the slots were particularly ominous, given their circumstances, and he forced himself not to look at them.

"Terry?" Jodenny asked over the comm. "Did you say we were in T16? This wall marker says T18."

Myell continued to sail upward in the shaft. "That's good. At least we won't be released into orbit."

"Not for two months, anyway."

He stopped to think about that. "So I guess you could say our situation hasn't improved."

"Not yet, no."

The observation module appeared above him. The hatch had no power but the manual override worked and he hauled himself in. He saw the control panel, two chairs, the EV closet, and a free-floating, perfectly preserved corpse.

"Jodenny?"

"What's wrong?"

"We're not alone. There's a body up here."

"I'll be right up," Jodenny said.

Myell moved into the module. The gray-white hand of the dead man slapped against his visor as if in jovial greeting and he powered back in alarm. His headlamp illuminated more of the corpse, which was long and stiff and wore an officer's jumpsuit. The face had bloated in the weightlessness before freezing solid, but was still recognizable.

"It's Commander Matsuda," he said when she drew near.

"The old SUPPO?"

"Now we know where he disappeared to."

She stared at the body for a full minute. "He must have been dead or unconscious when they put him in here. He didn't get into an EV suit."

"At least he didn't starve to death."

"Neither will we, Sergeant."

Moments earlier, she had called him Terry. If they were going to die, he would prefer they do it on a first-name basis. Together they inspected Matsuda's corpse. His gib was gone and there were no obvious wounds, no readily apparent cause of death. In his pocket were his identification card and twenty yuros.

Jodenny asked, "Should we just leave him here?"

The prospect of tugging the corpse around like freight made Myell's stomach churn. "You want to take him with us?"

"Not really."

"He's been here for months already. Nothing's going to happen to the body."

They left Matsuda and took six extra air tanks from the closet. Myell had hoped he'd feel better once they reached the command module, but the bulkheads spun lazily in his vision, and he fought the urge to take off his helmet and gulp at non-existent air.

"Can we wake up the dingoes?" Jodenny asked.

"We have no way of controlling them. They'd just sit there like lumps."

"Can we use their batteries to power up the control panel?"

Myell turned so she wouldn't see him close his eyes. "Different systems. We'd need a dozen electricians to make it work. Same with the medbots."

"Look at me, Terry."

He blinked open his eyes and saw her visor pressed against his.

She said, "You're green."

"Spacesick," he admitted, just as his teeth started to chatter. "It'll pass."

"I'm going to turn up the heat in your suit and see what the medbot has in stock."

Myell only nodded. He didn't trust himself to open his mouth and not vomit. Jodenny returned in a few minutes with a skin patch. She slid open his visor and pressed it to the side of his neck. The visor slid shut again with a click.

"Stay here," she said. "I'm going to poke around the loading dock some more."

The patch helped but made him drowsy. Loosely moored to the bulkhead, he ignored the drifting feeling and tried to figure out a way to escape. Not the loading dock. Not the command module. They couldn't blow the bolts on the ends of the tower and there were no escape pods. Myell tried to remember more about T18's inventory, but he hadn't memorized the list.

"Terry?"

He must have dozed off, because she said it several times. "I'm here," he said. He checked his watch and saw that it was almost oh-four-hundred.

"I'm going to start nosing around in the slots, see what I can find."

"I'll come along."

"You stay put."

"I feel better." He did, in fact. Once in the shaft, he saw Jodenny's lamps glittering some distance below his feet. "What are we looking for?"

"Anything that might be useful. Or edible."

He assumed she didn't mean Commander Matsuda.

J odenny didn't want to admit it, but she was extraordinarily glad of Myell's company. The tower was creepy enough as it was with Matsuda's body floating around. She imagined more horrendous discoveries in the slots, where the darkness seemed thicker and more ominous than it did in the shaft.

With hydraulic crowbars they started cracking open random smartcrates on level one and discovered electrical parts. On level two, bin after bin of cement mixes, instant rebar, and steel supports. Level three was a plumber's delight: pipes, fittings, valves, and pumps. Myell held up a glove full of screws and bolts.

"Too bad we can't fry them for dinner." He sounded better than he had up in the command module and some of the color had come back to his cheeks.

"I prefer baked, not fried," Jodenny said. "Ever been to Minutiae?"

"It's not as good as they say. Have you tried Cairo Delight?"

"Food's too spicy." Rokutan had taken her there. At least she'd gotten a meal before she let him take her to bed in his clean, shipshape cabin. She wondered if Myell's cabin was messy, if his sheets smelled like he did, where he would put his hands and mouth while making love.

"You didn't order the right things."

"How about we keep looking and forget about food?"

Myell hefted the pipe in his hand. "Too bad we couldn't just bang out an S.O.S."

"No one would hear it."

"The bridge doesn't monitor sealed towers in any way?"

"There are remote fire sensors," Jodenny admitted. "Nothing here's going to burn without oxygen. And then there's the . . ."

Myell gave her a moment. "The what?"

"Radiation sensors," she said.

They split up and started searching for smartcrates with yellow and black warning labels. There was a good chance they would find nothing, Jodenny knew. But searching was at least action, and even a little hope was better than none at all.

At oh-seven-hundred she called a break. "Let's rest for a bit."

Myell met her in the shaft and they floated in the zero-g, the lights of their EV suits tiny in the encompassing darkness. She hooked a tether line to him to conserve thruster use and checked their oxygen. Unlike everywhere else on the *Aral Sea*, T18 was a great hallowed hall of silence, devoid of comm announcements, gib pings, passing conversations, or death roars of Izim moths.

"How long have you been carrying around a pocket server?" she asked, trying to sound conversational about it.

"Since Kookaburra. What happened with Ford—that was her word against mine. I didn't want to get into that situation again. And I wanted to get evidence against Chiba."

Jodenny couldn't help herself. "What happened with Ford?"

"Do you want the truth, or do you want the rumors instead?"

Bitterness in his voice, which she should have expected. She pressed close to him so that she could read every nuance on his face. "I know you didn't do it."

Myell gazed at her steadily. "We'd been seeing each other on the side for a few weeks. Just a few minutes here or there. Whenever people weren't looking. She was afraid of Chiba, wanted to break up with him, didn't know how. One night we met in one of the hydroponics labs and—well, you know. Security happened to go by. She was afraid of what Chiba would do, so she claimed rape. That's what I think. They wouldn't let me even talk to her, afterward. It's possible that the whole thing was a setup from the start, because Chiba wanted me out of Underway Stores. It backfired when he got transferred instead."

"How did you stand it for so long?" she asked. "The gossip, the harassment—you shouldn't have had to."

Myell turned his head. "It goes on every day, if not in our division, then in others."

Jodenny wished she could dissolve their EV suits and wrap her arms around him.

"The day we met," he said. "I was thinking of not coming back to the ship. Then you came up to me and said my boots needed to be polished. Who could resist? I fell in love with you right then and there."

Jodenny couldn't find anything to say.

"Sorry." Myell sounded crestfallen. "I guess that's out of line."

"No," she replied. "It's been so long since anyone said that to me . . . do you want to know when I fell in love with you?"

"Do you love me?" Myell asked.

"Yes." And saying it lifted a great weight off her heart, a weight the size of the *Yangtze*. "We'll both probably be court-martialed, and it's the most reckless thing I've done in years, but yes. I do love you."

He smiled. "Then tell me."

"When we were in your brother's guest room and you couldn't understand why I was there, but you trusted me anyway. You were wearing a beige sweater."

"And you were wearing a nightgown with red roses on it."

"I thought you might knock on my door that night."

"You wouldn't have let me in."

She grinned. "Probably not."

They resumed their search, working steadily from different ends of the shaft. At one point fatigue overtook Jodenny and she checked her watch. Morning quarters had come and gone. Her stomach rumbled with hunger and her throat ached. Three days to die of thirst, was that it? The silence of the tower struck her as cruel, and she clicked on her comm switch.

"Terry? Where are you?"

"Forty-two," he said. "More rebar. You?"

"Level eighteen. Plastics." Jodenny worked her way past more bins. "How's your oxygen?"

"About a half hour left."

"Mine, too. Let's get back to the command module."

Back in the module, they waited for the tanks to run down and swapped the old units for new ones. The thought of returning to the dark slots made Jodenny weak in the knees, and Myell seemed in no hurry to return either, but they had to keep looking. Sometime around lunchtime, just as Jodenny was beginning to believe she'd never eat again, her comm clicked.

Myell said, "I've got something here. Some kind of medical imaging equipment."

"It's a start. Where are you?"

He didn't answer.

"Terry, this is no time for heroics. Tell me where you are, and that's a direct order."

"Sorry." He didn't sound at all contrite. "Write me up when we get out of here."

Jodenny understood his reasoning but she wasn't going to stand for it. His last report had put him somewhere on thirty-eight. She sailed up the shaft, picked level thirty-seven at random, and moved down it with a few choice, muttered curses.

"You should go up to the command module, Jodenny. Safer that way."

"Not for you."

"No," he said quietly. "Not for me."

Standard EV suits didn't come equipped with Geiger counters. He would have no way of determining how many roentgens he'd been exposed to or when to stop. She imagined his hair and teeth falling out, the sperm dying off in his testes, and the lesions that would sear his skin.

"It'll go faster if we work together," she heard herself say. "If they come fast enough, the radvaxes will take care of everything."

"I've got five crates open," he said. "Get out of here before you expose yourself."

A trail of red alarm lights lit up above her head. Jodenny squinted at their brightness and followed them toward Myell. Even if the bridge sensors were immediately noticed, what priority would it rate, a radiation leak in an unmanned tower, and how long would it take to send a team out to investigate?

She hoped to hell the duty officer was paying attention. When she reached Golf block she saw Myell floating listlessly.

She pushed her face plate close to his. "Terry?"

His expression was resigned. "I wanted you to stay safe."

"Safe is when I'm with you," she told him. "Come on. Let's get out of here."

They took refuge in the command module and reminisced about Mary River.

"I almost went with Colby and Dottie to that dance," he said. "They wanted me to come and socialize. I don't know what I would have done if I'd walked in and seen you there."

"Same thing you did when you saw me drive up with him. Kept quiet until you knew what was going on." Jodenny cocked her head. "That's your way, isn't it? You keep quiet until you know the whole story."

He shrugged inside his suit. "Sometimes I just keep quiet."

Strapped into the chairs, they turned off their lights to conserve power and sat in the red glow of the emergency exit light. The shaft before them was so dark and fathomless Jodenny imagined it was like the Alcheringa itself.

"Jodenny," he said, as if trying the name out for size. "Kay. Where did you get the name Kay from, anyway?"

"Jodenny Katherine Scott. Katherine comes from my mother."

"Is she still alive?" Myell asked.

"No. Both my parents died when I was an infant."

"I'm sorry."

She had never known them. Had never had anyone like that to love and lose. But his mother had killed herself when he was just a child, and his father had drank himself to death afterward.

"We're going to get out of here," she told Myell. "There's not going to be any death today."

"I know," he said, but there was little conviction to his voice. She checked her watch. An hour had passed since he'd started opening crates. If the bridge hadn't noticed by now, they might not notice at all. How long did it take radiation sickness to kick in?

"Terry, I never thanked you for being on my side from day one."

"All part of the job, ma'am." He reached out and patted her gloved hand clumsily.

Her eyelids grated like sandpaper. She needed rest in a desperate way, but feared running out of oxygen while asleep.

"Hear that?" Myell asked drowsily some time later. "Drums."

She heard nothing. "Talk to me. What was it like, growing up on Baiame?"

"Like hell," he said. "Can't you hear them? I'm not delirious, I swear it."

The hatch opened, spilling light into the module. Help had finally come.

CHAPTER **TWENTY-NINE**

The first rad tech who saw Jodenny yelped in alarm. "Jesus! What the hell—"

"I'm Lieutenant Scott," she said. "This is Sergeant Myell. We were trapped and left to die here by Commander Osherman, Lieutenant Quenger, and Chief Chiba. Notify Security and the officer of the day. The source of the radiation leak is some opened crates on level thirty-eight. And there's a dead body up in the observation module." Jodenny powered past the techs with Myell in tow. "We'll be in the access ring."

Gravity pulled her to her knees the minute she tried to step past the hatch. Myell wasn't much stronger but they managed to sit upright and started stripping off their helmets and EV suits. They slumped to the deck when they were done.

"You would think they'd put sofas out here." Myell rubbed the sides of his head with both fists. His hair stuck up in spikes, and he smelled as rank as she did.

"How do you feel?" she asked him.

"Happy to be alive. You?"

"Happy," she agreed.

They were alone, the rad techs still in the tower, no one else yet arrived. The loss of heat from the suit made Jodenny cold all over. Myell must have been cold too, but instead of looking for a blanket he leaned in close. His eyes were dark and wide.

"Kay," he said.

She would have replied but his mouth was on hers now in a clumsy, fumbling kiss, and though his lips were cold they were also soft, and faintly salty, and for about ten blessed seconds she forgot about everything. So many weeks of waiting. So much longing, pent-up, on both their parts. She hadn't known how hungry she'd been for him. Myell was a strong kisser, not shy at all, but when she tried to pull him down to the deck he groaned and broke away.

"Not in public," he said.

"I'll resign," she said.

"No." Myell brushed her hair back from her face and let his hand fall away as two medics from Emergency Services appeared. Within moments the medics were scanning them for radiation exposure.

"Christ," one said, which didn't sound encouraging at all.

"We've got to get you both to Decon, Lieutenant," the other medic said.

Jodenny replied, "Not until the OOD shows up. You could go, Sergeant."

"No thanks, Lieutenant. I'll wait with you."

The Officer of the Day was Lieutenant Hasonovic from Drive. By the time he arrived, Jodenny and Myell were sitting on the medical litters with thermal blankets around their shoulders. Myell's face had started to turn red and Jodenny felt so tired she could barely stay awake, but they'd both taken their first doses of radvax.

"Record my statement on your gib." Jodenny waited for Hasonovic to turn it on. "Sergeant Myell and I were inspecting the DCS when we were assaulted by Commander Osherman, Lieutenant Quenger, and Sergeant Chiba. We discovered the corpse of Commander Matsuda in the observation module and with no other way of establishing a link to the *Aral Sea,* triggered a radiation leak to alert the bridge of our presence."

Jodenny paused. "Anything else, Sergeant?"

Myell blinked owlishly. "That sounds like everything."

"Okay. End of statement." Jodenny turned to the ES techs. "We're ready to go."

"Wait!" Hasonovic followed them down the passage. "Did you say corpse?"

The nearest decontamination station was at the civilian hospital in T11. Jodenny lost track of Myell there, although she was sure he wasn't far. A female nurse with blunt black hair helped her shower and dress in Sick Berth pajamas. A second dose of radvax followed, and then she was put to bed in a small room. The doctor who came to talk to her was a tall, gangly woman with a wide face.

"I'm Dr. Genslar, and you're extraordinarily lucky." She ran a fast-tissue repairer over Jodenny's cheek, which was covered with a large bruise from hitting the deck when she was mazered. "Without those radvaxes, you'd be vomiting up your intestines right about now."

"That's nice." Jodenny closed her eyes. "How's Sergeant Myell?"

"He'll live a fine, productive life." Dr. Genslar studied her gib. "You've got visitors out there, but I told them to come back in about eight hours."

Jodenny closed her eyes. "Make it ten."

Sometime later a nurse woke her up for a third dose of radvax. Still half asleep, Jodenny inspected the pillow to see if any of her hair had fallen out. She probed her teeth with her tongue. None seemed loose. Maybe it was too soon, or maybe it wouldn't happen at all. She went back to sleep and dreamed of floating in the darkness, listening to Myell over the comm as he said he was opening up more smartcrates. When she woke the next time, voices were arguing nearby.

"How long is she going to be out?" Al-Banna asked.

Dr. Genslar answered, "As long as it takes, Commander.

Those two took in mighty high doses. Any further exposure and those radvaxes wouldn't have done shit."

The voices retreated.

Although sleep was still an inviting option, Jodenny forced herself to focus on the medical equipment around her. She disengaged the dermal packs delivering saline to her body. The head was a few inviting feet away, and she considered it a good sign when the room stayed steady while she used it. The deck was cold beneath her feet, but she found a robe hanging in the closet and wrapped it over her pajamas before going in search of Myell.

A few meters past her room there was a nurse's station. The nurse on duty had her back to Jodenny as she answered a ping. Jodenny shuffled to the next room, which was empty, and to the one after that, in which Myell lay sleeping. She touched his face, kissed him to make sure he was still breathing, and returned to her own bed in hopes of catching a few more hours of rest.

The next time she woke, she had a headache but was definitely in the mood for breakfast. Dr. Genslar came before the food did and asked, "Ready to return to full duty?"

"Not really."

"Good. You're not Superwoman. You're going to be dragging your feet for the next few days."

"Am I released?"

Dr. Genslar consulted her gib. "If you can eat and keep it down, I'll consider it. Do you have your story straight?"

"Which story?"

"The story about how you and that handsome sergeant wound up in the tower together. I've heard a few theories already, none of them flattering."

Jodenny's cheeks heated up. "I told the OOD what happened."

"And you've got burns on your skin that look like mazer marks," Dr. Genslar said agreeably. "Doesn't stop people from gossiping anyway. So who do you want to talk to first? The list keeps growing. Commander Larrean, Commander Al-Banna,

Commander Picariello, Lieutenant Commander Vu, Chaplain Mow, Dr. Ng—"

"Sergeant Myell."

Myell shuffled in while she was eating breakfast, and from the slightly wary look on his face she guessed Genslar had mentioned the gossip to him, too. Or perhaps in the unforgiving hospital light he saw the obstacles in front of them more clearly. Maybe the ordeal in the tower had driven him to a place he hadn't intended to go, and here was where he corrected his path.

"Hi," she said, her throat dry.

"Hi." He came closer to the bed but didn't reach for her hand. "You look better."

Jodenny studied his eyes. "So do you."

"You look—" Myell glanced around. "Gorgeous in those pajamas."

Jodenny couldn't help but smile. Myell pushed aside her breakfast tray and kissed her. She felt the tiny shock again, the thrill of the forbidden mixed with his solid, undeniable presence. His hair was scruffy between her fingers, his hands firm on her shoulders.

When they broke apart, Myell sat on the edge of Jodenny's bed and said, "Dr. Genslar says people are talking about our romantic tryst gone wrong."

"People are idiots."

"I think we should deny everything."

"Me, too." Jodenny squeezed his hand. "But whatever you hear, whatever the next few days bring, remember that we have a date. Minutiae."

"Cairo Delight," he said. "What about your career?"

She didn't have an answer for that. It seemed foolish to risk everything she had and everything she'd worked for just for the sake of romance. Yet for the first time in her career she understood why people did, in fact, break the rules that kept them apart.

"One day at a time," she said. "Can you forward the data you recorded on your server to Security so they'll have the proof that Chiba and Quenger attacked us?"

"I already did."

He leaned forward for another kiss but a nurse appeared at the door and said, "Lieutenant Commander Vu's here to see you, Lieutenant. You ready for visitors?"

Myell mouthed, "No."

Jodenny squeezed his hand again. "Yes. Send her in."

"I'll be back in my cold, lonely bed," Myell said, and rose.

"Wait." Jodenny kissed him before he left. She intended to use that kiss—and the one before, and their first one on the deck of the access ring—to fortify herself for the trials to come. In fact, she intended to store up a warehouse full of those kisses for future emergencies.

Vu came in, her face a tight mask of worry. She wrapped Jodenny in a hug and said, "You scared everyone half to death! Are you all right? You didn't show up for quarters, and neither did Myell. You didn't answer your pings . . . people were speculating. The message boards are going wild."

"I bet. What are the rumors now?"

"You two somehow got trapped in T18 and discovered Matsuda's body. Jesus, to think of him there all this time—I mean, I didn't like him so much, but still. What happened?"

Jodenny repeated what she'd told the duty officer. Vu didn't look convinced.

"And so you were down there, the two of you together, nothing else going on, and someone attacked you?"

"I saw them. Osherman, Quenger, and Chiba." And the minute she got her hands on Osherman, she was going to strip the skin from his body with a rusty knife. Then she'd really hurt him.

"Jesus," Vu said.

Jodenny's next visitor was Picariello. He did not hug her. He pinned her with his blue-and-brown gaze and said, "This is a mess."

She had combed her hair and moved to a chair. Dr. Genslar had been right—fatigue drained her energy all the way to her bones. "Did you get the data Sergeant Myell sent?"

"We got it," Picariello said. "Voices of the men who attacked you and maybe killed Commander Matsuda, though that's a big question mark. Data analysis should confirm their identities. What happened after you were attacked?"

"First tell me where Osherman, Ishikawa, Quenger, and Chiba are."

Picariello grimaced. "Ishikawa's onboard, according to Core, but no one's been able to physically locate her. The others left the ship on the first shuttle yesterday morning."

"They escaped? No one stopped them?"

"Stopped them for what? When you and Myell missed morning quarters your ensign notified us, but no one suspected foul play."

Jodenny wanted to hit him. "How can you say that? You know Chiba's animosity toward Myell. The minute we disappeared, you should have been questioning him."

"Don't presume to tell me my job, Lieutenant," he warned.

That official tone was back, the one she so despised. She needed time to think. "I don't feel so good—" she said, and staggered from the chair into the head. With the door half closed she stuck her finger down her throat. Breakfast blueberries stained the toilet bowl.

"Do you need help?" Picariello asked from outside the door.

"I think—" Jodenny interrupted the words to retch again. "Maybe."

Picariello left. When the nurse came to check on her Jodenny allowed herself to be put back to bed and asked for all her visitors to be turned away. When she was alone, she pinged Myell and updated him. She asked, "Did you happen to record the night when Osherman and Ishikawa told us they worked for the IG?"

"You bet."

"Good. I'm going to get a lawyer down here to help us. Now might be a strategic time to throw up, faint, do something dramatic. Delay until we can figure out how to proceed."

"No problem at all," he said.

CHAPTER THIRTY

"Lieutenant! It's nice to hear from you again."

"Thank you, Holland," Jodenny said to the borrowed gib in her lap. "Can you get me Chaplain Mow?"

Chaplain Mow was delighted that she was awake and worried when asked to name the best lawyer in the Legal Services office. A few minutes later Jodenny reached Lieutenant Commander Cheddie. Notoriety helped: he had seen the missing persons alert and agreed to drop what he was doing to come over to the hospital. He appeared fifteen minutes later, a thin man with freckles and a sad excuse for a mustache.

He asked, "Am I going to be working with you or Sergeant Myell?"

"Both of us."

"Then let's start with your side of the story first."

Jodenny began with Myell's accident and moved on to their inspection of the slots, the discovery of the master chip, Osherman and Ishikawa's revelations, and most of the ordeal in T18. Cheddie made only occasional notes in his gib. When she told him about Myell's recorded data, his eyes brightened considerably. She finished and waited for his response.

"Why do you think you're going to need legal counsel?" he asked.

"Because Osherman said he was working for the Inspector General, but he participated in the attack on us. Ishikawa supposedly works for the IG too, and she even saved Myell's life a few weeks ago, but no one can find her." Jodenny fingered the edge of her bedsheet. "If they're not who they said they were, I don't want to be blamed for believing them. There are also too many rumors going on about me and Myell, and I want those stopped. And if anyone wants to make trouble out of the fact we opened those radioactive containers, it was my decision."

"I don't think anyone will object to that," Cheddie said. "What about Matsuda?"

"What about him?"

"Maybe you killed him."

"He's been dead since before I checked onboard."

"Maybe Myell killed him."

"He had nothing to do with it!"

"You only say that because you're lovers."

Jodenny glared at him. "Sergeant Myell and I have not been involved in a sexual relationship."

"You were using the cargo holds for your romantic rendezvous. A lieutenant and her sergeant. People will eat it up."

"You can leave now," Jodenny said.

"I'm simply preparing you for what people are saying." Cheddie made another note on his gib. "I have a friend who works in the forensics lab. Are you aware that Sergeant Myell's fingerprints are on the identification card that Commander Matsuda was carrying?"

"Of course they're on it," Jodenny said. "He pulled it out of Matsuda's pocket when we were inspecting the corpse."

"You're sure? I thought you were wearing EV suits."

"Have you ever seen the gloves on an EV suit? Too bulky for fine work. He took one glove off." At least, she thought he had. He must have.

"I'm just saying," Cheddie said. "They want, they could make an argument that his prints are on it because he helped kill Matsuda. There might be some way to date them, but still, it could be tricky."

"As sure as I am sitting here, I'm telling you Myell had nothing to do with Matsuda's death. If you can't believe that, you shouldn't defend us."

"Belief has nothing to do with defense, Lieutenant. I'll go talk to him, see what he says."

"Do you really think we have anything to worry about?"

"Right now? No. You're the heroic victims of a vicious assault. You also discovered a murder victim and uncovered a smuggling ring. You didn't report anything, but you believed Lieutenant Commander Osherman, who may or may not be an IG agent."

"How could he work for the IG and leave us to die?"

"Maybe he intended to tip someone off to your location and wasn't able to," Cheddie said. "Maybe he did get the word out, but it was ignored or overlooked. Unfortunately, heroism aside, you're also the bringer of bad news, which is going to work against you. Data should have caught the dingo problems, and Core is going to come under as much scrutiny as Supply. Some unhappy people will try to discredit you by alluding to your relationship with Sergeant Myell, your professional capabilities, and your conduct since you came onboard."

The nausea suddenly rolling in her gut had nothing to do with radiation sickness. "That's what I thought."

"Of course, you have me, so it'll all work out just fine."

"Oh." Jodenny almost but not quite laughed. She had more than Cheddie, if she could just hang on.

Cheddie went to talk to Myell. For a while she dozed, lulled to sleep by the sound of the air vent over her bed. She awoke when Cheddie returned with Myell in tow. Jodenny was careful not to leap into Myell's arms or do anything else Cheddie might misinterpret.

"I didn't kill Commander Matsuda," Myell said.

"Of course you didn't," Jodenny replied. She thought he looked pale, and cleared a space on the foot of the bed for him to sit.

"Here's what we'll do," Cheddie said. "I'll arrange a meeting with the SUPPO and the Security Officer, maybe the XO. Lieutenant Scott, you tell them what you told me, all the same details, nothing left out. Sergeant Myell, you'll corroborate. The thing to stress is that you believed you were following Osherman's orders. I'd like to set it up for right after lunch."

"Excuse me." Myell lurched off toward the head. Cheddie grimaced at the sounds that emerged.

"Only if you're well," he said.

"We'll be fine," she assured him.

Cheddie was gone when Myell came out. Jodenny said, "You didn't have to do that for his benefit."

"I didn't."

"Oh. All right, back to bed you go."

Myell gazed meaningfully at her mattress.

"No, your own," Jodenny said, nevertheless pleased. She walked him back to his room and made sure he was tucked under the blankets with some appropriately affectionate gestures. Dr. Genslar came in seconds after she smoothed the sheets.

"Am I interrupting anything?" the doctor asked archly.

Myell said, wearily, "Dr. Genslar thinks the rumors about us are true."

Jodenny eyed the physician. "Fraternization is against regulations."

"Yes, I know. And while I was a lieutenant, I was a firm believer in regulations. The nurses tell me there's been some emesis. Is that true?"

"Guilty as charged," Myell said.

Dr. Genslar ran a scanner over Myell's abdomen. "You might need another radvax. Lieutenant Scott, you can return to your bed. I'll take care of this."

At the hatch Jodenny asked, "Why aren't you a lieutenant anymore?"

"I resigned so I could marry my chief," Genslar replied. "Gave up a very promising career in the Medical Corps."

From under his blankets Myell said, "Good for you."

Genslar replied, "We divorced five years later."

By the time the meeting rolled around, Myell was still vomiting and Genslar vetoed his attendance. Jodenny fidgeted in her chair in the physician's conference room, wishing she could be by Myell's side. Wrapped in a thin bathrobe, tapping her slippers against the deck, she stood up when Al-Banna and Picariello entered. Captain Umbundo was with them, which startled her.

"Sir!" she said.

"At ease," Umbundo said.

Jodenny felt foolish addressing them as she was, but she explained what had happened as clearly as she could and omitted only the personal aspects of her and Myell's ordeal in the tower. Cheddie took notes. Picariello stared at the bulkhead. Captain Umbundo's face was impossible to read, but Al-Banna leaned forward and seemed interested in every word.

When she was done Umbundo said, "You've been one busy lieutenant."

"Yes, sir." Jodenny took a steadying breath. "Was Lieutenant Commander Osherman lying about being an Inspector General agent?"

Picariello said, "It's best if we don't discuss that, sir."

Cheddie said, "Captain, the lieutenant and Sergeant Myell were nearly killed. They deserve to know who to trust, and if their lives are still in danger."

Picariello said, "It's not wise—"

Umbundo held up a silencing hand. "You did stumble across something, Lieutenant. You weren't the first. I can't jeopardize any ongoing investigations by telling you more, but rest assured that you're in no danger as long as you follow orders. Until this affair is concluded—and I'm assured that will be very soon—you and Sergeant Myell will be in protective custody on Mainship. There are too many people who would benefit if your voices fell silent."

Jodenny knew how Myell would feel about protective custody. "Surely there's another way, sir."

"Follow your orders, Lieutenant," Umbundo said.

He stood, nodded at Picariello and Al-Banna, and departed without any further word. Jodenny watched him, agape. That was all he had to say?

"A few days of relaxing in a VIP suite won't harm you, Lieutenant," Picariello said. "Sergeant Myell can stay in transient berthing."

"No, sir," Jodenny said stubbornly. "Both of us go to VIP quarters or both of us go to transient."

Picariello shared a look with Al-Banna, who said, "You might reconsider allying yourself with Sergeant Myell."

"I've heard about the fingerprints, sir. They're perfectly explainable. I don't believe for a single instant that he's somehow tied to Commander Matsuda's death."

"Frankly, neither do I," Al-Banna said. "However, some irregularities have come to light regarding your April inventory. It looks like Sergeant Myell and Ensign Strayborn wrote off three hundred transactions to make your score better than it actually was."

Jodenny had expected some kind of divide-and-conquer, but not so soon. "That can't be true."

He handed her a gib. "It's all in the raw data."

She scanned the information. "Holland would have caught it. I have her check for discrepancies and run standard fraud tests on every inventory."

"Your agent was impaired," Picariello said. "The subroutines were compromised so that she wouldn't alert you. If you'd done a manual check you would have seen the changes."

Her cheeks heated up. "Why would Myell and Strayborn do such a thing?"

"You tell me," Picariello said. "And then you tell me why any of us should trust anything Sergeant Myell has to say."

"Here he is," Timrin said.

"You, bucko, are as green as an avocado," Gallivan said as he and Timrin appeared at Myell's bedside. Gallivan was as cheerful as ever. Timrin had a few more worry lines than Myell remembered.

"Shut up," Myell said, and reached for a bucket.

Gallivan handed him a glass of water after he was done retching. "At least you showed up in time to bid me a tearful farewell."

"You're leaving today?"

"On the fifteen-hundred-hours birdie. Otherwise I'd stick around to see how this mess turns out. Three days left in damned Team Space and I'm free forever."

"Lucky you." Another wave of nausea swept through him but quickly passed. Maybe Dr. Genslar's last radvax was taking hold. Myell said, "Can you see if they're still in the conference room?"

Timrin asked, "Who?"

"Lieutenant Scott, Al-Banna, some others."

Timrin poked his head around the corner. "Looks like it. What are they talking about?"

"Fraternization. Murder. Motives." Myell put the bucket aside and swung his legs off the bed. He should be there, protesting his innocence. Timrin's hand kept him seated.

"There's a few things you should know," Timrin said. "Security's been down in Underway Stores since yesterday, turning things top to bottom. They found Lange's porn collection and the cat VanAmsal's been keeping over at LD-G. Caldicot's saying you and the lieutenant have been carrying on since we left Kookaburra, which is rubbish. And they called Strayborn in for questioning, something about you and him gundecking the April inventory."

"Did you do it, Terry?" Gallivan asked.

Myell gaped at them. "Strayborn squared it away."

"Not, apparently, to the right people," Timrin said.

Gallivan added, "Before you do drop your shorts in the lovely lieutenant's company, you should know that she and Lieutenant Commander Rokutan have been consorting in a most familiar way."

"Says who?"

"Rokutan himself. Told Zarkesh, who mentioned it to Zeni, who made a joke in front of Ashmont—"

"Enough." Myell's stomach threatened to revolt. Somewhere down the passageway a comm was buzzing in a most annoying way. "It's just gossip."

"I'm only telling you as a friend. Apparently she has a birthmark right about—"

"Shut up," Timrin said. "The point is, if you're not careful, Terry, they're going to blame as much as possible on you."

No one was answering the damn comm. Myell said, "Lieutenant Scott won't let them."

"Looks like their chat group is breaking up," Gallivan said. "Large group of officers heading this way."

A moment later Jodenny appeared in the doorway with Cheddie behind her. Myell didn't like the pinched expression on her face, the utter lack of anything remotely resembling affection. He expected her to wear a mask of professionalism in front of others but this woman was a stranger, unsympathetic and harsh.

"Good morning, Lieutenant," Gallivan said, but she ignored him completely.

"Did you fake the April inventory?" she asked Myell. "Write off three hundred transactions?"

A cold fist wrapped around his heart. "That's not what happened."

"You did. You and Strayborn."

"Lieutenant—" he started.

Jodenny turned to Cheddie. "Tell them I'm ready to go back to Mainship. I'll take the VIP quarters. Sergeant Myell can stay in transient."

He needed to make her understand. "Kay—"

Her voice was as cold as her gaze. "That's *Lieutenant* to you," she said, and walked away.

"Ouch," Gallivan said.

Cheddie eyed Gallivan and Timrin. "Sergeant Myell, once you're feeling better, you'll be going into protective custody while we settle this whole thing."

"Yes, sir," Myell said woodenly. He should have expected it. Love never lasted; friends always betrayed. He'd been stupid enough to forget the lessons of Baiame and the whole Ford affair, but now they came back like buckets of ice water dumped over his head.

"But the last time—" Timrin started.

"It doesn't matter, Mick," Myell interrupted. "Leave it alone."

Cheddie nodded and followed Jodenny.

"You can't let them do that," Timrin said.

Myell squeezed the bridge of his nose. Protective custody. Not again. Then again, why not. His reputation was ruined. If he wasn't blamed for Matsuda's murder, he'd still get demoted for the trick with the inventory. Jodenny despised him. And somewhere just beyond the horizon, Chiba was mocking him with laughter. Nothing meant anything if Chiba walked away free.

"Jesus, what's that?" Gallivan demanded, recoiling from a dark splotch on Myell's pillow.

"Koo!" Myell said.

Timrin chuckled. "Scared of a little gecko, are you?"

"Shut up," Gallivan said.

Myell picked Koo up. For a lizard on the lam, she appeared pretty healthy. She peered up at him, circled in his palm, and poised with her head held high. His eyes watered. It was silly to be so emotional, but he'd thought her dead for sure. "Where did you come from?"

"She must have been in my jacket pocket," Timrin said.

Koo flicked her tail and curled up in the palm of Myell's hand. "That's a good girl," he murmured. Surely her reappearance wasn't a coincidence. He stared into her beady eyes and waited for inspiration.

"So what are you going to do?" Timrin asked. "Let these officers push you around?"

Koo's tongue darted out in search of an imaginary fly. In that instant he caught a glimpse of a barren landscape, the sun boiling like gold on the horizon, the uncurling of a vast snake. Whatever the future held, it wasn't to be found in the confines of protective custody.

"No." Myell tested his footing. "Are there any clothes in that closet?"

Gallivan opened the door. "Just some pants and a scrub shirt. Why?"

"I need a uniform. I need the two of you to help me get out of here. Then I need to be on that birdie at fifteen hundred hours."

"You're going down there?" Timrin asked. "You can barely stay on your feet."

Gallivan folded his arms. "And just how do you propose to get on that birdie? You don't have a flight pass."

"No," he admitted, "but you do."

"It'll never work," Timrin said. "Your face has been plastered over the news for almost two days. Security will recognize you in a heartbeat."

Myell reached into the bedside table for his dilly bag. "Then I'll go with Plan B."

"Which is?" Timrin asked.

Where could he find haven in the middle of a starship? Who would shelter him and assist him in getting down to the planet?

"Take me to the governor," he said.

CHAPTER **THIRTY-ONE**

Everything was arranged in short order.

"My launch will take you down to Waipata," Ganambarr said. "I was expected to travel on it, but I'll go down with the rest of the colony in the tower. This diplomatic visa will allow you to bypass Customs and Immigration, and then you'll be free to begin your search."

"Are you sure you're up to it, Terry?" Chaplain Mow asked, having been summoned to Ganambarr's suite as soon as Myell showed up, sweating and shaking, on the doorstep.

"No problem." Myell was sitting on the sofa because his legs felt rubbery after the walk over, and he wasn't sure they could support him much longer. He fumbled for the ouroboros pendant that had been in his mother's jewelry box. "Can I ask you one last thing? Have you ever seen this before?"

Ganambarr examined it carefully. "The craftsmanship is very good. I don't know who made it, or who it belonged to." He gazed at the map of Old Australia. "We've lost so much, you know. From the time the Europeans first sent their convicts, through the systematic trampling of rights under so-called modern law, to the Debasement. The sons and daughters of the land left it, sometimes against their will, sometimes by choice. What is a land without its children, Sergeant? What is a land with no one left to respect it?"

Myell didn't know how to respond. Chaplain Mow cleared her throat. Ganambarr shook himself from a reverie and said, "The launch is waiting. You should hurry." He gave the pendant back. "Hold it tight, and perhaps you'll find your answer someday."

"Yes, sir. Thank you for all of your assistance."

Myell had asked Gallivan and Timrin to stay out in the passage to keep them from being implicated in his crimes. They were still waiting for him, heads bowed low in conversation, when he emerged from Ganambarr's quarters.

"Don't ask," Myell said. "If you don't know, you can't be charged with anything."

"Fuck them," Gallivan said. "What can they do? Keep me in Team Space against my will?"

"They could," Myell said. "It's called administrative hold. And you, Mick, could jeopardize your pension. Thanks for your help. I'll take it from here."

Timrin scratched his jaw. "I don't like it."

Myell squeezed his shoulder. "I know." To Gallivan he said, "Take care of yourself."

Gallivan said, "The same to you. And good luck with your lieutenant."

His lieutenant. No, not his anymore. In Ganambarr's launch Myell curled up in a seat, pulled his civilian jacket tighter, and watched the *Aral Sea* recede in the vidscreen. The radiation sickness was still with him, making his bones watery and his muscles ache, but the worst was past. He fell asleep and woke when they touched down. Koo, nestled inside his shirt pocket, poked her head out in interest.

"The governor asked me to give you this," the pilot said, and handed over a package full of paperwork and yuros. "Said you'd be needing it."

As promised, the visa got him past all the counters and clerks without even having to log his DNA. The Waipata terminal, a sprawling complex that linked air, sea, space, and rail transportation, was so busy that he began to feel dizzy under the onslaught of voices, music, advertisements, and announcements. The Corroboree and the World Cup had brought an influx of extra visitors, many of whom were headed for the Wondjina Spheres to the north. He stood, momentarily overwhelmed, wondering how he was possibly going to find Chiba and the others while avoiding the Shore Patrol, who would surely be searching for him soon.

He knew one way. It was a beginning point where he had none, a resource that Chiba and Quenger didn't have. To use it he only had to put aside a lifetime of humiliation and trust Colby, who was so many light-years away. He had to recognize the person he'd once been, and keep that person from coming into existence again.

The alternative was letting Chiba and Quenger get away with it all, in which case he might as well have remained on the *Aral Sea* and endured Jodenny's scorn.

Didn't mean he had to like it. Didn't mean he could quell the butterflies in his stomach, or maybe that was just the radiation sickness again.

Myell checked the map kiosk, took an escalator down two levels, and rode a people-mover for several minutes. When he was far from the space gates he located a public comm and asked for city information. The address he wanted was unlisted. He ran another query, rode the people-mover to yet another terminal, located an employee entrance for the port workers, and went inside. A shift manager took his request and told him to wait.

He waited with his hands in his pockets and Koo resting her little weight against his heart. After a few minutes a thin man in faded overalls approached. He was older than Myell expected, his complexion weathered by hard living and the strength of Warramala's sun, but his features hadn't changed at all over the course of a decade. What did surprise him was his brother's height. Ever since leaving Baiame he'd remembered him as a giant, but now he seemed only a centimeter or two taller than Myell.

"Terry," the man said.

"Daris."

"I didn't think—" A mixture of regret and guilt crossed Daris's face. "I didn't think you'd want to ever see me again."

"I didn't come so you could make amends." Myell made sure every word was hard and tight. "I don't want to hear anything you have to say about the past. All I want is to find some people. Can you help, or should I leave?"

Daris's cheeks reddened and he ducked his head. "I'll try."

"I'm looking for Chief Petty Officer Massimo Chiba, Lieutenant David Quenger, and Lieutenant Commander Samuel Osherman, all from the *Aral Sea.* They would have arrived here on the first shuttle yesterday. I need to know where they went or where they are now."

Daris nodded. "Sit down in the lounge there. It may take a bit."

Anger surged through him—he sure as hell didn't take orders from Daris—but just as quickly the hot spark faded, and Myell sat down on a lumpy red sofa. He rubbed his face with his hands and ignored the fear that the Shore Patrol was closing in on him as he waited. He helped himself to a cup of bland-tasting coffee as a few minutes turned into a half hour. Koo wriggled in his pocket and he took her outside into the thick Waipata afternoon.

"I think this is where you and I part company." He put her down at the base of a shrub. "Things might get hairy from here on in."

She gazed at him, flicked her tail, and darted off.

"You don't have to be so sentimental," Myell called after her.

Back in the lounge, a half hour turned into an hour and then ninety minutes. He went outside a few times but Koo didn't return. Myell tried some snacks from the machine, but they tasted oily and his stomach threatened another revolt. Employees came and went, bitching about their jobs and coworkers. Myell was thinking about leaving when Daris returned and said, "Two of them bought tickets to Port Douglas and flew up last night. Nothing up there but the Corroboree. The other one, Osherman, I don't know, is probably still in the city. He didn't leave this terminal under his own name, at any rate."

Myell rose. "That's all I needed to know."

Daris caught his arm. Myell jerked free and almost swung out, but Daris backed away.

"Sorry." Daris held up both hands. "But don't leave. While

I was pulling the info up, your name flashed across the security list. The Shore Patrol, terminal guards, and Waipata City
Police are all looking for you. They'll catch you if you're on
the streets. Stay the night and I'll try to get you some creden-
tials."

Myell eyed him warily. "Stay where?"

"I have an apartment."

No. He wouldn't put himself in that kind of position. Just
being in the same room as Daris made him feel jittery, like a
small electric shock was being run through him from scalp to
toes.

"I have a friend," Daris said. "He does good work, fast.
You'll need ID."

Myell stared past Daris to a bulletin board full of handwrit-
ten announcements. Transportation for sale. Someone looking
for a roommate. Common sense warred with ingrained fear.
Yet he was no longer a child, unable to fend for himself.

"I can help," Daris said, more softly. He looked broken,
suddenly, and so much like their father that Myell nearly
shuddered.

"All right," Myell said. "Let's go."

Daris lived twenty minutes from the terminal. They took a
P-train three stops and walked the rest of the way in the thick,
swampy air of sunset. Brightly colored parrots flitted from
roof to roof above them in a neighborhood that was prefab and
bland. At a convenience store they stopped to pick up food
and supplies. Daris's apartment was on the second floor of a
corner complex. Just three rooms, neat but impersonal, with
stacks of paperbacks piled up in corners and on shelves.

"People leave them," Daris said. "At the terminal. The
cleaners throw them away."

The sofa was long and hard, but it would do. Daris disappeared into the bathroom and Myell was left only with the
hum of the climate control, a little too cold for his taste. He
wished he was at Colby's house instead of this drab apartment. He wished he was anywhere else, in fact.

Daris returned. "You want some dinner?"

"No. Why don't you have a vid?"

"There's never anything interesting to watch."

To fill the silence Daris tuned the radio to evening news. Myell leaned back with absolutely no intention of dozing off, but the next thing he knew, Daris was sitting in the side chair, reading a flattened book while tearing at the crusts of a tomato sandwich. The quirk was as familiar to Myell as his own hands.

"Want a sandwich?" Daris asked.

"No," Myell said. "Are you going to ask why the Shore Patrol is after me?"

"No."

"You're not curious?"

"I'm curious," Daris said, not meeting his gaze. "But it's none of my business."

Damn straight. The old Daris would have demanded every detail, voiced unsolicited and wrongheaded suggestions, and insulted him for getting into such a predicament.

"My friend Lem will be by in an hour or so," Daris said. "He'll want at least a thousand yuros. If you don't have the money, I could get it on credit."

"Why would you do that?"

"Because," Daris replied, with a shrug.

Myell tried half a sandwich, but the tomatoes tasted metallic. He forced down some soy milk instead. Had to keep his strength up, at least until he found Chiba. In the bathroom he pulled out the coloring kit he'd bought at the store and dyed his hair blond. He had just finished when Lem, a stooped man with corkscrew black curls, dropped by as promised with a bag full of equipment. He set his gear up on the coffee table.

"Just for you?" Lem asked.

Myell thought hard. "Can you make one up for a woman I know?"

"You got her picture?"

He didn't, but he knew there were public vids of her from the *Yangtze* disaster.

"Easy enough." Lem pulled down Jodenny's picture in seconds. "Same last name, how's that? You just got married."

The two IDs cost him much of Ganambarr's money, but the job was done within minutes. Lem took off into the night. Daris pulled some sheets and a blanket from the closet and said, "I usually turn in early. You take the bedroom, and I'll take the sofa."

"Why?"

"So you can lock the door," Daris said.

"Your front door doesn't lock?" Myell asked, perplexed. Then he caught on. "Oh. Do I need to?"

Daris locked gazes with him.

"No. I'll never raise my hand to you again, Terry. If I do, God or you or anyone can strike me dead."

Myell heard the conviction in that promise, understood that this was the closest Daris was going to get to an apology, and knew that Chaplain Mow would urge him to accept, forgive, and move forward.

"Fine," Myell said. "I'll take the bedroom."

He did, in fact, lock the door. Just because he could. Myell didn't like the idea of sleeping on Daris's bed and so he spread the blankets on the floor and stared at the dark ceiling. He heard nothing from the other apartments, no music or conversation or arguments. He curled up on his side, the blankets tight around his shoulders, the fake identity cards heavy in his pocket. In the morning he would go back to the terminal, find a flight up to Port Douglas, somehow find Chiba, resolve everything.

Not everything, perhaps. Not his relationship with Daris, sound asleep in the other room. That was a knot too twisted to be worked out in one night. Still awake at midnight, he went out to the living room. Daris was sitting by a light with a book, but he didn't look as if he'd been reading it.

"Say you're sorry," Myell said, "and mean it."

"I'm sorry."

"What for?"

Daris didn't flinch. "For hitting you. For belittling and humiliating you. For being an asshole of a brother, day in and day out. For ruining everything. For not being a man when Mom died and Dad started drinking."

Myell replied, "You were only fifteen when she died. That wasn't your fault."

"The rest of it was."

In the dark apartment, with only the whisper of the climate control vents to fill the air, Myell felt something soothe over the raw, scraped feeling he'd been carrying with him for so long.

"Can you forgive me?" Daris asked.

"I'll think about it," Myell replied.

CHAPTER **THIRTY-TWO**

Jodenny paced the VIP cabin, stir-crazy with boredom and angry with herself. She should have given Myell more of an opportunity to explain. Whatever had happened with that inventory, he had still saved her life in T18. When she remembered how she had treated him in front of Gallivan and Timrin, she felt sick. Cheddie visited at dinnertime and brought news that only made her feel worse.

"Myell's AWOL. He probably got off the ship somehow. My guess is he's down on Waipata chasing Chiba."

"Jesus," she said, and rocked back in her chair.

"Still think you should have joint counsel? He's not exactly proving your innocence, here."

"What I need is a gib. There's not even a desk unit here!"

Cheddie said, "Commander Picariello considers it in everyone's best interest if you don't have one right now."

"He can't refuse me."

"Sure he can," Cheddie said. "Gibs aren't guaranteed. I think you proved that in your own division."

Jodenny fumed. "I want to see the captain."

"I'll put in a request, but don't expect any quick response."

"Is this protective custody or house arrest?"

"Don't worry. I'm guarding your rights. They can't take any statements from you without my presence. There are no bugs or electronic surveillance devices in these quarters, or so I've been told. Be patient. Things will settle down in a few days."

"A few days might be too late." Myell was barely well enough to be out of bed—how could he go traipsing around Warramala? If he ran up against Chiba, he'd be in no condition to defend himself.

"Can you ask Ensign Strayborn to stop by?" she said. "Assuming I can have visitors."

Strayborn came by after dinner wearing a wary expression. "Glad to see you're up and around, Lieutenant. They treating you okay?"

"Well enough. What happened with the April inventory?"

"I've been advised by my lawyer not to say anything. I don't want them to take my commission away, Lieutenant."

"Tell me what happened. If it's not too awful, maybe I can help."

Strayborn shook his head.

"I need to know, Ensign," she said. "I need to know if I can trust Myell."

"Why is it so important to trust Myell?"

Jodenny dropped her gaze. "Because I'm in love with him."

"Christ." Strayborn sat and rubbed his hands over his face. Glumly he continued. "You'll find out anyway. We only wanted to get the reconciliation done. It was late, you'd called in an inspection for the morning, we knew the dingoes had been acting up—Terry didn't want to. The rest of us persuaded him. I told him I'd square it with you and the chief but honestly, I didn't think it would make much of a difference. It's not the first time I've seen large-scale glitches happen, and you never questioned us about it."

"Who else was involved?"

"Ishikawa, Hosaka, Su, and Lange. But I was the one in charge."

"Will the others back your account up?"

"They don't have to. Myell recorded the whole thing, the bastard. I don't know if he thought there would be a problem later, or if he was nervous about being in the observation module with Ishikawa by himself, but Security uncovered it this morning when they were going through the tower logs."

Jodenny fought a sigh of relief. Myell's name would be cleared, mostly, in that regard. But Strayborn's career was in jeopardy.

"I'll do what I can," she said. "Maybe they'll settle for a letter of reprimand."

After Strayborn left, Jodenny was left with only her grim imagination and the idea of Myell down on Warramala getting into god knew what trouble. She spent a sleepless night envisioning the worst and heard nothing until Cheddie brought more bad news.

"Fleet has ordered you down to headquarters," Cheddie said. "Admiral Nilsen wants to see you. Commander Senga will take you down."

"What does the admiral want?" Jodenny asked.

"I don't know. But she's got appointments all day and then a box seat for the quarterfinals tonight, so you have to hurry."

Jodenny had time to grab a fresh uniform but nothing else. Fifteen minutes later she was strapping herself into the CO's launch across the aisle from Senga, who poured himself a drink and grabbed some peanuts. The pilot popped his head in to say they were being bumped up the priority line for departure.

Jodenny asked, "Are we coming back up tonight?"

Senga smirked. "I am. You're not. Didn't they tell you? You're being reassigned to Fleet until this is all straightened out."

"Reassigned?" Jodenny squeaked. Fucking Cheddie, he was her lawyer, he should have told her. But what if no one had told him?

"I thought you knew." Senga didn't sound apologetic at all. "The Master-at-Arms will pack up your cabin and send your stuff down."

The birdie launched. Jodenny turned to the vid so Senga couldn't see her eyes. Goddamn them all. The *Aral Sea*'s mammoth shape began to fall away, the sun glinting off the hull, shifting and changing its silhouette like a living thing. She didn't expect she'd miss the ship itself but already the loss of her people and her fellow officers was a hollow place in her chest. The descent into Warramala's atmosphere went smoothly as the launch, with no delays in orbit. Waipata, the capital, had been built on the southern continent along the Motuponui River. The port was a mammoth series of transportation domes glittering green in the sunlight. Jodenny and Senga were ushered through a private Customs lounge and their cards scanned in by a polite young woman who tried to give them strings of Corroboree beads.

"Maybe later," Senga said.

Jodenny took some beads and twirled them between her fingers. She had been to the Warramala Corroboree before, she and Jem and Dyanne, all of them caught up in the riot of dance, drink, and song. When she followed Senga outside, Warramala's humid air slapped her in the face like a hot, wet towel. She didn't need a mirror to see her hair spring into curls. They quickly located the admiral's flit and slid inside to cold air and tinted windows.

"Beer?" Senga asked, leaning forward to the small refrigerator. "Compliments of Fleet."

"No." Jodenny stared out past the green and brown landscape toward the Team Space buildings in the distance. They'd stick her in some shit job again, something no one else wanted to do, and it was so much like being on Kookaburra that she didn't know how she was going to stand it. When something crashed against the nose of the flit it took her a few seconds to turn that way. The tourist who had lost control of his luggage cart began to argue with the Team Space chauffeur.

"Christ," Senga said. "Stupid dill."

The argument grew more heated. Senga stepped out to intervene. Jodenny squeezed the bridge of her nose, imagining the upcoming months of boredom, scandal, and innuendo. Meanwhile Myell was out there somewhere, maybe still ill from the radiation, maybe needing her help, and what was she doing? Sitting on her ass while others determined the course of her destiny.

Screw that, she decided, and slid out the side door.

She threw herself into the crowds and circled back into the terminal. Somehow she had to get some yuros, find out where Quenger and Ishikawa had gone, and stop whatever plans they had. No worries. She had barely gone five steps when she heard someone call, "Kay!" and Myell grasped her arm. He was dressed like a tourist and had dyed his hair blond.

"What are you doing here?" he asked.

"Looking for Osherman and Chiba." Jodenny peered at him earnestly. "Hoping to find you."

Myell didn't immediately reply. She saw that he didn't know whether or not to trust her. Well, she'd certainly given him ample cause for doubt. She wanted to throw her arms around him and beg for forgiveness.

"Terry—"

"Come this way." Myell hustled her down a concourse of tourist stalls and fast-food restaurants. Jodenny looked up for overhead cameras, sure they could be tracked by security forces, but Warramala was one of the least monitored places in the Seven Sisters: they valued privacy and liberty here more than anywhere else.

"Give me your gib," Myell said, and when she did he tossed it into a trash can.

"Hey—" Jodenny protested.

"Fleet can track it."

He hustled her into a rent-a-room, told her to stay there while he got her something to wear, and returned five minutes later with a yellow sundress, a wide-brimmed hat, and a pair of sandals. She changed quickly while he waited outside. When she emerged she said, "I know that fixing the inventory was Strayborn's idea."

Myell's expression gave her nothing to work with. "We can talk later. We've got a boat to catch."

"What boat? To where?"

With one hand holding a duffel bag and another on her arm, Myell walked her along the people-movers. "Port Douglas. It's where Quenger and Chiba went."

"Why don't we fly up there?" Jodenny asked.

"Security there is too tight. The gates probably already have your picture."

"Don't we need ID for the boat?" she asked as he stopped by a ticket kiosk.

"It's taken care of." Myell punched in data and waited for plastic tickets to spit out. "I'm Alan Foster and you're my wife, Noreen."

So they had gotten married. Too bad Jodenny didn't remember the details. She followed Myell down a ramp to the waiting passenger ferry. Four decks high and a hundred meters long, it was the largest ship at the piers. Rust and tan-colored Corroboree banners hung from several railings, and a throng of pilgrims stood at the stern receiving blessings from the river. Do-wops danced and sang on the open deck above them.

The purser who took the tickets from Myell asked, "You and the missus going all the way to Port Douglas?"

"Yes," Myell said, with a fairly good Kiwi accent. "How long until we get there?"

"We'll be there Friday, sir. Just in time for the solstice and World Cup."

After walking through a weapons scan they crossed the gangway. The ferry was old but clean, and Jodenny smelled fresh paint as Myell led her through a crowded lounge filled with passengers. Their cabin was small but decently furnished in various shades of blue. No deskgib, though, and no vids. A tiny balcony offered an obstructed view of the river.

"Lie down," Myell said. "You don't look so good."

"I'm fine," Jodenny said, but her knees had gone weak and she sat in the armchair near the balcony. She grabbed a pillow to hide her shaking hands. Maybe she hadn't fully recovered from the radiation yet. Maybe the sheer audacity of what she had done, gone AWOL, was catching up to her.

"I'll have some lunch sent down once the galley opens," he said.

"Where are you going?"

"Casino. We need more money."

He left. Jodenny rubbed her eyes and watched the landscape glide past the window. The mighty Motuponui was the largest river on the continent, a wide torrent of freshwater that drained from mammoth lakes in the mountainous north. The river then crossed thousands of kilometers of dense rain forest. The ferry would carry them along the last leg of the river's journey through a set of timeworn hills, but for now the countryside was flat, the riverbanks in full, heavy bloom.

A steward sent by Myell brought her lunch a few minutes later. After devouring soup and sandwiches she went to examine herself in the mirror. If her picture wasn't all over the news yet, it soon would be. She rang the porter and borrowed a pair of scissors. *Good-bye, hair,* she thought as the locks fell into the washbasin. After sunset she ventured up to the lounge deck. A group of do-wops had started an impromptu concert with their guitars and drums while soccer fans clustered around the vids for the semifinals. The casino was already crowded, players jammed around tables and playing slot machines that shouted encouragement to bet even larger sums of money. Myell was slouched at a card table with a depressingly small pile of chips.

"Hi, honey." Jodenny gave him a warm peck on the cheek. "Are you winning big?"

Myell blinked at her, his gaze fixing on her short hair. "About to, darling."

"Your husband's a lousy player," the man to Myell's left said.

"My husband is a great player." Jodenny peeked at his cards and saw he was going to lose the hand. "Sweetie, I'm all out. Lend me some?"

Myell pushed her some yuros. Jodenny gave him another kiss and a squeeze of the thigh for good measure. At a crazy-seven table she took a stool between two immensely large women wearing Kookaburra T-shirts. Jodenny's cards totaled eighteen. She held and won fifty yuros. She bet half of it again, lost it when the dealer flashed a lightning card, doubled the second half on a wild hand, doubled it again by trumping the player next to her. At a farca table across the room she got into a game with more tourists and a man too casual to be anything other than a card shark plying his trade up and down the river. She let him win the first hand but came back to phase him in the second. Myell had lost most of his money and was morosely feeding the last of it to a slot machine.

"Come on," she said. "I've got enough for us."

Myell gave her a sideways look. "I want to finish."

Jodenny went down to the shops. Although she cringed at the prices, she bought herself sturdier travel clothes and a pair of shoes. At a public gib she checked the headline news from Waipata and saw nothing about her or Myell. She returned to their cabin and indulged in a hot shower. Myell showed up after midnight with beer on his breath.

Jodenny said, "You can take the bed. I'll sleep on the floor."

"No, ma'am." Myell kicked off his shoes but didn't undress any further. He stood in the darkness, swaying a little. "That wouldn't be right. Floor's fine."

He dropped a pillow on the floor and disappeared into the bathroom. Jodenny pulled the blanket from the bed and added it to his nest. After a moment's deliberation she scooped up both pillow and blanket and put them back in place.

He scowled when he came out. "I told you I'll take the floor."

"You can take that side of the bed."

Myell went to his side and sat with his back to her. She held off from touching his shoulders. His stomach growled in the quiet cabin.

"Did you eat?" she asked.

"I'm not hungry." Myell lay down, resolutely facing away from her.

Jodenny curled up on her side. Let him sulk. He still had some apologizing to do for that fudged inventory, and leaving the ship without telling her, and making her worry so badly. She stared at his back in the darkness and made the magnanimous decision to apologize first.

"I'm sorry for doubting you," she said.

His shoulder hitched up fractionally. For a moment she hoped they might discuss it, but he apparently wasn't in a conversational mood. "Good night, Lieutenant."

"Good night, Sergeant," she said.

CHAPTER THIRTY-THREE

Myell woke with sunlight on his face. When he cracked his eyes open he saw Jodenny sitting in the armchair with her knees drawn up. Her short hair still startled him. It made her look older in a way that reminded him she was not a green ensign, nor a seasoned commander, but someone caught on a merciless learning curve somewhere in between.

The smell of garlic woke him further, and he eyed the tray on the table.

"Breakfast," Jodenny said. "Yours. I already ate."

He tried not to drool like a starving wolf as he tore into the mofongo and gulped down mango batida. The riverbanks, lush and green, slid by the balcony windows as the boat churned along.

"Thanks," he said.

She gave him an appraising look. "Tell me what happened with the April numbers."

Her and that damned inventory. Myell supposed, after sulking over it for most of a day and night, that she had a right to be angry. He rubbed his hand through his hair and recounted as best he could how they'd come to write off three hundred transactions. He didn't blame Strayborn any more than he blamed himself.

"So you did it because you wanted to get ready for inspection?" Jodenny asked.

"We did it because we were lazy. Because it probably was the battery, and the glitches didn't seem like a big deal."

He couldn't bear to look at her anymore, not when she wore that piercing expression. Myell went to wash his face and hands. When he came out of the bathroom he saw that she had made the bed, put the tray into the hall, and tidied up the cabin. His domestic lieutenant. He wanted her so badly that he felt like he had a low-grade fever. Better to get out of the cabin before he embarrassed himself.

"I'll just—"

"No." Jodenny faced him. "I was wrong. I took the first chance I had to distrust you because I was afraid. Of us and for us. Of what it would all mean."

"There's no *us*," he protested. "It's not worth the damage to your career."

"There's been an *us* since the first day I met you. I want there to keep being an *us*." Jodenny pressed herself against him and covered his lips with her own. In the kiss he sensed her sincere apology, her hunger for him, her eagerness to put things right. She pulled away first and gazed into his eyes.

"What do you want?" she asked.

Myell picked her up and carried her to the bed.

"We should probably go slow," she said as she stretched out beneath his straddled knees and reached for his waist.

"I agree." Myell kissed her forehead and the base of her throat, drinking in the scent of her skin, soaking in the heat that sparked between them. "Start back from square one."

Jodenny slid his trousers down from his hips and worked her hand beneath his boxer shorts. "We'll get to know each other slowly. Be methodical."

Clothes were a nuisance. Why had they ever been invented? Groaning, Myell pulled Jodenny's sundress over her head and unfastened her bra. Her warm, deft fingers made him grind down against her, his breath fast, his nerves on fire. "Are you sure?" Myell asked.

"Absolutely."

She arched up to kiss him, and the hunger of her lips shot through him. His heartbeat sped up as he shifted, stiffened, moaned. He couldn't touch enough of her, couldn't help the need to inhale the smell of her hair. The fingernails of her free hand dragged trails of fire down his back and ass. If she stopped now he would throw himself in the river.

"Jo," he murmured as her tongue flicked against his left nipple. "Are you sure, sure?"

"Less talking, more kissing," she instructed, her breath moist and sweet. "And don't call me Jo."

It had been too long since Wendy. Since any woman had touched him. He tried to slow down by thinking about DNGOs and COSALs but it was no use. Within moments Myell was climaxing helplessly in her hand. Everything fell away— worry, fear, doubt. The cabin blurred, or maybe that was just his watery vision.

He slumped beside her, trying to catch his breath. "I'm sorry."

Jodenny kept kissing his chest. "Don't be. You needed that."

He ran his fingers through the short strands of her hair. "What do you need?"

"Well," she drawled with a wicked smile. "I'm glad you asked, sailor."

They spent most of the morning exploring each other's bodies, and Myell did in fact learn a thing or two about pleasing supply lieutenants. After fortifying themselves with lunch from room service they went back to mapping erogenous zones and comparing notes. They dozed in the afternoon, the river sliding by outside, the sky a cloudless blue. For dinner they decided to dine out, but lost a half hour to washing each other in the small, cramped shower unit beneath a stream of hot water.

"Maybe we should eat in," Jodenny said, her lips against the hollow of his throat.

"We need money," he said.

They ate dinner in a dark, wood-paneled restaurant with wide views of the river. Myell couldn't stop touching her under the table. In return she slipped her right foot out of a sandal and rubbed it along the inside of his thigh. His fists tightened on the silverware. By the time they reached the casino it was already flush with high rollers. Jodenny's luck had turned, and she lost two hundred yuros to a trader from Los Niños. Myell began a steady losing streak and was sure he'd be broke before midnight, but a chance bet at roulette brought back most of what he'd lost.

"We're no better off than we started," Jodenny said.

Myell thought, *We're a lot better off than we started,* but that was gooey and sentimental, and he was wary of another change of her heart. Twenty minutes later he doubled their winnings at roulette. Back in the cabin, beneath those river-washed sheets, he celebrated by worshiping the curve of her belly and her firm thighs. She urged him to go fast and hard, then made him lay perfectly still while she moved her lips and hands over every inch of him in exquisite torture.

"You're trying to kill me," he complained.

"Yes," she said, her voice husky. "That's exactly my plan."

Later they lay spooned together, his arm hooked over her waist, her head tucked neatly under his. "Jodenny," he murmured. "What will we do when we get back?"

"Maybe we won't go back. We'll live in the jungle, in a treehouse for two. You can fish and I'll weave baskets." Jodenny pressed her hand on his bare hip, a warm and comforting reassurance. "Or we could finish this, go back, clear our names, and fight any disciplinary action they try to impose."

"Work in separate divisions, deny our relationship to everyone, sneak off for a quickie now and then in the slots?"

"The treehouse sounded better, didn't it?"

She sounded both wistful and sad, no doubt contemplating the end of everything she'd worked for over the years.

"You love what you do," he said, nuzzling behind her ear.

"Not always. And not if it means losing you."

They resolved nothing, promised nothing. Myell listened to the river slap against the ferry's hull. He refused to think of the Wirrinun, or the Rainbow Serpent, or anything beyond their cabin. At dawn he sensed a shift in the ferry's engines. He wriggled out of the bed and slipped into his pants. From the balcony he saw the looming shore of Port Douglas. The sky was brightening but overcast.

From the bed Jodenny asked, "Are we there?"

"Nearly."

"You don't sound happy about it."

He pulled on his shoes. "Fleet's had plenty of time to try and track us. I expect to see police."

They dressed and packed up their meager belongings. Breakfast was a buffet in the main dining room, and they ate as much as any of their sleepy, bleary-eyed neighbors. On deck, protected from the light drizzle by an awning, they watched the ferry's captain ease the ship toward a dock.

"There's trouble," Jodenny said.

Myell followed her gaze and spied three Warramala police officers in the crowd that had gathered to greet friends or family.

Jodenny scanned their fellow passengers. "What we need is a diversion."

A group of do-wops were clustered on deck, exhausted from their revelry. Crumpled streamers hung out of their pockets, and their clothes were stained and wrinkled. While Myell watched, Jodenny went and spoke to their leader. The doubt left his face when she handed him several money cards.

"We just bought ourselves a celebration," Jodenny said when she returned.

For a few minutes Myell was concerned that she had been duped, but as the gangway was hoisted into place the do-wops suddenly regained all their energy. They picked up their instruments and began singing and clapping. They sounded small and somewhat ridiculous against Port Douglas's sober grayness, but as they went down the gangplank a beam of sunlight broke through the clouds and set a more cheerful backdrop.

"Now?" Myell asked.

"Wait."

On the dock, two do-wops stumbled against each other. Loud words were exchanged. Someone swung a fist. As the police officers moved to break up the disturbance, Jodenny and Myell slipped behind the ferry buildings.

"Where now?" Jodenny asked.

Myell replied, "I'm not sure. They came this way, but then where? Up to the Corroboree?"

"It would be a good place to get lost in the crowd."

Port Douglas had a main street of shops, small hotels, and offbeat restaurants. The townsfolk had decorated for the holiday and every shop window was filled with T-shirts, dreamcatchers, boomerangs, incense, drug paraphernalia, and velvet artwork. It was a kitschy patchwork of symbols and clichés

that angered Myell. *So much we've lost,* Ganambarr had said.
They bought bus tickets and boarded an old electric bus with
worn seats and marginal air-conditioning. The other seats
filled with do-wops, backpackers, a handful of budget travelers, and an old man wearing a bush hat. The bus rattled its
way out of town and up a winding road.

"Honeymooners?" the old man asked Jodenny. "You've got
that look."

"Absolutely," Jodenny said.

Myell watched the road for signs of pursuit but no Team
Space cars appeared. Two hours after leaving Port Douglas
the bus pulled to a stop in a dusty parking lot in the middle of
the jungle. A dozen other buses had arrived before them and
were discharging passengers. He saw tourist kiosks set up to
sell food, drink, and other necessities, but the Spheres themselves remained unseen. The humid air made him break out
into an immediate sweat and Jodenny pressed a water bottle
into his hand.

"It's going to get worse," the old man said. "Sun wipes out
a lot of people."

As they followed the other travelers up a footpath to the
crest of a hill the jungle gave way to a rocky plateau and cliffs
that fell off to the sea. The Mother, Father, and Child stood in
their usual regal alignment, but unlike the ones back on Mary
River these were surrounded by at least a thousand sincere
pilgrims kneeling in noontime prayer, two thousand tourists
snapping vids, and three thousand do-wops dancing and
singing to popularized, historically suspect Australian gods.
The air was filled with conversation, drumbeats, and didgeri-
doos. Myell smelled roasting food, fragrant tobacco, melting
chocolate. An open-air concert was going on in a shaded
pavilion while newsvans and security guards kept their cameras trained on the crowds. Beyond the cliffs, the blue sea glit-
tered like a carpet of diamonds.

"Needle in a haystack," Jodenny said.

They chose the tourist campground just north of the Spheres,
where do-wop tents and state-of-the-art recreational vehicles
stood side by side. Everything there was relatively quiet, with

no sign of Chiba or Quenger. They tried the pilgrim grounds, but a brown-robed friar refused them entrance. Jodenny's shoulders began to turn pink and Myell was sweating through his shirt. They returned to the Spheres and stopped at different carts to buy water, sunblock, and some nutrition bars. At a shady spot near the cliff's edge they took a break and relaxed in each other's arms.

"It's an aberration, you know," Myell said, nuzzling the top of Jodenny's head.

"What is?" she asked.

"Corroboree. The original Aboriginal word was *Carribae*. None of this can be authentic if it doesn't even have the correct name." It was one of the many things he had read during his research on the Rainbow Serpent. He should have asked Daris where in Australia their mother had come from, if she ever spoke of it to him, if they had Aboriginal ancestry. He considered telling Jodenny about the Rainbow Serpent and the Wirrinun, but couldn't make himself say anything. How could he explain them to her, when he didn't even understand them himself?

When the afternoon began to wane they brushed dried dirt and grass from their legs, put their shoes on, and went back to the Spheres, which had turned golden pink in the slant of the sun. The first stars of the evening began to shine even brighter, and the rangers gave permission for the lighting of several bonfires. Jodenny and Myell circulated, still looking for Chiba and Quenger, but many in the crowd had donned cheap tribal masks covered with paint and glitter.

"If we split up, we'll cover more ground," Jodenny said.

"No. We'll never find each other again."

"We'll always find each other," she replied, which made him smile.

Night had darkened the sky, but the floodlights illuminating the Spheres gave off enough light to keep her from tripping over reclining bodies. Jodenny searched the crowd and did her best to keep from looking up at the stars, where the *Aral Sea* might be the largest one of them all. Near the Child, she thought she saw Ishikawa.

"AT—" she said, touching her shoulder, but the woman wasn't Ishikawa.

"Hi." The woman smiled. "Love partner?"

"Have one, thanks."

Jodenny started to turn away, but a pilgrim in a dark brown robe and hood grabbed her arm.

"Don't scream," Osherman said. "Don't make a sound, or you'll just end up getting your boyfriend killed. Understand me?"

CHAPTER **THIRTY-FOUR**

"Come on." Osherman pulled her toward an airvan. "We've got some talking to do."

Jodenny resisted ineffectively. Had he always been so physically strong, or had all the strength in her body evaporated? "Let me go."

"Do you want to help Quenger and Chiba get away?"

She stomped on his insole and wrenched free. Al-Banna blocked her path. Like Osherman he was dressed in pilgrim robes.

"Lieutenant!" he snapped. "Stop causing a scene and do as you're goddamned told."

Ingrained obedience made Jodenny falter. The two men escorted her into the van and to a bucket seat. Banks of surveillance equipment had been mounted on racks. Vids displayed feeds from dozens of cameras, all of them pointed at the Spheres and crowd. Two armed techs she didn't recognize worked the controls.

"You, too?" she asked Al-Banna. "You're working for the Inspector General?"

"Someone had to step in when Matsuda disappeared," he said. He reached for a thermos wedged between the consoles. "Coffee?"

Osherman asked, "Jodenny, where's Myell?"

She folded her arms.

"We've picked up Quenger on camera two, sir," one of the techs said. "He's heading for the Mother Sphere. No sign of the others."

Osherman sat at the console and slid a headset over his ears. "Lieutenant Scott, when this entire operation falls into ruin, I'm going to blame it all on you."

"You left us to die," she retorted.

"No. I saved your life. Chiba and Quenger were ready to shoot you like dogs. But I convinced them to leave you in the tower, like they'd done with Matsuda. Disappearing crew don't cause as much trouble as dead ones do. I told Ishikawa to notify Commander Al-Banna or the bridge where you were once I was off the ship."

"She never did," Al-Banna said. He poured himself the coffee, his expression dark. "We don't know where she is, or what became of her."

"You could have told me, back on the ship," Jodenny said. "When we were meeting with the captain."

"Captain Umbundo didn't even know. Not then." Al-Banna lifted his cup. "There are more secrets on the damn ship than there are dingoes, and you can quote me on that."

Osherman spun in his seat toward her. "If you had stayed out of this, you wouldn't have been in danger in the first place. Now tell us where Myell is before he ruins what's left of this operation, and that's a goddamned order."

Jodenny kept silent.

"Sir," Osherman said to Al-Banna.

"We both know Lieutenant Scott has no good reason to trust us," Al-Banna said. "But if I were you, Lieutenant, I'd say we're your best chance for getting out of this with your career and life both reasonably safe. The commander understands the importance, now, of leveling with you."

"Does he?" Jodenny asked.

A muscle clenched in Osherman's cheek. "What do you want to know that you don't know already? Our office has been investigating black-market smuggling throughout the fleet for the last eighteen months. I was spearheading the investigation on the *Yangtze*. After the disaster, I transferred to the *Aral Sea*. The smuggling ring involves Supply, Flight Ops, and Data. We convinced Matsuda to turn on his partners, but they found out. Greiger turned coat next, but they scared him with that car accident on Kookaburra and he clammed up. We got AT Olsson, finally, no thanks to your and Myell's interference."

Jodenny took her time digesting all that. "Why are Chiba and Quenger here? Why are you?"

"They think they're meeting with someone from the Colonial Freedom Project to sell off several thousand assault mazers and grenade launchers stolen from the *Aral Sea*," Osherman said. "What they don't know is that it's a sting. If they see Myell, the whole operation might fall apart."

A comm beeped. Osherman snatched up a receiver and listened. "Camera five," he ordered, and the vids focused on a line queued up outside the Mother Sphere. Myell was just a few meters behind Chiba and obviously following him. "Fuck it! Try to grab him without anyone noticing. I'll be right there."

"I'm coming," Jodenny said.

"No. You're staying here." Osherman patted the weapon under his jacket and turned to one of the techs. "Under no circumstances is Lieutenant Scott to leave this van or go anywhere near the Spheres."

"You can't—" Jodenny said, but Osherman was already out the door. When she tried to follow the tech blocked her path.

"Sorry, ma'am," he said, his hand on his weapon. "You heard the commander."

Jodenny turned a pleading eye toward Al-Banna. "Sir?"

Al-Banna poured more coffee. "What do you think you could possibly do, Lieutenant?"

"I don't know. Help in some way."

He shook his head. "Or interfere some more. I can't take that chance. Here, drink some coffee."

She took the cup and let it slip between her fingers. The hot liquid splashed over all of them, causing a yelp or two. Jodenny slid right past the tech and out of the van. She immediately lost herself in the crowd and made her way toward the

Mother Sphere. She had broken yet another order, but Myell might need her. That was all that mattered.

Myell had started to despair of ever finding anyone. This endeavor, like so many others, would be marked by failure. Then, over the sea of heads, he saw the ugly face that had defined many of his days and nights on the *Aral Sea*. Chiba stood in profile, one hand to his ear, listening to a commset. When Chiba started to walk toward the Mother Sphere, Myell followed without any hesitation at all. Perhaps fate had always decreed that things would end this way—just the two of them in the dark hollow of a Sphere, finishing business that had been long neglected.

Just before he entered the Mother Sphere, Myell heard a commotion off toward his right. Two men in tourist clothes were headed his way, and their intent expressions told him they were either cops or employed by Team Space. But a group of drunk do-wops fighting over a girl slowed their progress, and he was able to duck under the archway into the Mother. The inside was anything but dark. Temporary lights had been strung up on poles, and a sizable crowd was leaving offerings to a makeshift shrine of flowers and candles. Two park rangers manned a post, their stances lazy. Myell scanned for Chiba but found Lieutenant Quenger instead. Out of uniform, Quenger looked like any other casual tourist. A man wearing a gray-feathered mask approached and gave him a slight bow. Quenger didn't bow back, but he didn't turn away, either.

He realized he was on the verge of interrupting some kind of rendezvous. Myell tried edging closer to eavesdrop while still evading the men with the serious expressions, both of whom had made their way inside and were scanning the crowd for him. When he glanced back at the arch he saw Osherman arrive, followed seconds later by Jodenny. She saw him and mouthed words he didn't understand—a warning, he thought, his guess confirmed when something small and hard jabbed him in the back.

"If you want to get shot, scream for help," Chiba said in his ear. "If you want me to shoot your pretty Lieutenant Scott, try to escape. This whole deal is a trap, isn't it?"

Myell kept his voice level. "I don't know what you mean."

"Always the fucking do-gooder, aren't you? Or are you recording this, too?" Chiba's breath was hot and foul. "I told Quenger this was a setup, but did he listen? Ten million fucking yuros, he said. But they're going to have to go through you to get to me. I'm not spending the next twenty years in the brig."

This was a bad place for a showdown and surely Chiba knew it. Myell considered the chances of cheating death twice in the same week. But he couldn't let Chiba injure Jodenny or any bystanders, either.

"You're such a fucking chicken," Myell said. "Full of piss but never able to deliver. That's why Ford came to me, not you. She was tired of a chief who couldn't even get it up."

"Shut the fuck up. You think you can distract me? You think I'm that stupid?"

"You don't know how stupid I think you are," Myell said.

"I'm going to enjoy—" Chiba started, but the mournful call of a horn cut off his words.

Myell knew that sound. He'd heard it on Mary River and in almost every dream since. The tourists turned their heads, looking for the source, and a baby began to cry. The air inside the Sphere turned dry and tingly, as if a lightning bolt was about to strike down at any second.

Osherman must have known what was going to happen. "Out, out, everyone out!" he shouted. Slowly at first, then with mounting urgency, the crowd started squeezing out through the arch. Quenger's accomplice fled in the confusion but Quenger himself hesitated too long. A pilgrim threw back his hood, grabbed the lieutenant, and handcuffed him.

"Fuck this—" Chiba said.

Myell elbowed Chiba as hard as he could. Chiba doubled over but then threw his body weight forward. They fell to the ground, grappling and punching, as the horn returned with a deafening blast. Chiba gouged his face and went for his eyes.

Myell kneed him in the groin and locked his hands around Chiba's throat. Out of the corner of his eye he saw a snake ring appear around them, and felt Jodenny and Osherman trying to pull them apart.

"Terry!" Jodenny yelled. "We've got to get out!"

Osherman shook his head. "It's too late—"

With a slam of yellow light, Warramala fell away.

Jodenny pulled herself to her knees, unsure of everything except the cold sweat soaking her underarms and the slam of her heart against the walls of her chest. The new place was so musty that she sneezed, and the sneezing made her head hurt even worse.

"Fuck," Chiba groaned from behind her.

Like her, he probably couldn't see anything in the darkness. Jodenny groped blindly in front of her until she found a body. Osherman or Myell? The body shifted and someone whispered, "Kay?" and she knew.

"Chief Chiba." Osherman sounded more clearheaded than Jodenny felt. "I'm right behind you. If you move, I'll shoot."

Chiba didn't sound impressed. "Where the fuck are we?"

That was an excellent question, but Jodenny was too busy resting her head on Myell's chest to consider it. His hands touched her hair. She could have stayed there forever, bent awkwardly over him, the rush of relief making everything bearable.

"Are you hurt?" she whispered.

He caught and kissed her hand. "No. You? Your hands are freezing."

"I've got a light," Osherman said. White illumination flared and settled. When Jodenny's eyes adjusted she saw that the four of them were enclosed within the same kind of ouroboros that she and Myell had encountered on Mary River. Beyond the ring were the smooth walls and high ceiling of a Mother Sphere. Myell didn't appear injured from the fight, but Chiba had a bloody lip.

"Jodenny, give me your belt," Osherman said. "Hold this while I tie his hands."

"What the fuck for?" Chiba asked.

Osherman said, "You're under arrest."

Chiba started to swing at him. Jodenny fired without hesitation, and the mazer charge sent him spasming to the ground.

"I was hoping he'd do that." Osherman started securing Chiba's hands.

Myell sat up, one hand steadying himself against the ground. "Where are we?"

Osherman tied off the belt with an extra tug. "Not on Warramala."

"Not on Warramala," Jodenny repeated. She scooted as close as she could to Myell and let him rub her cold hands. "Could you be a little more specific?"

"Look at the symbols," Myell murmured.

Instead of just two symbols, the inner ring of this ouroboros contained at least a hundred, maybe two hundred. None of them matched the ones they'd seen on Mary River. Her assessment of the situation must have shown on her face, because when she lifted her eyes Osherman gave her an accusing look.

"You know," he said. "You've used the system before, haven't you?"

"Have you?" Jodenny countered.

Myell intervened. "By accident, Commander. On Mary River. It took us someplace else and then back again. We don't know anything more about it than that. But you seem to."

"If you'd told me," Osherman said, lips thin, "we might have avoided this. You triggered the call, Sergeant. Once you entered the Mother Sphere on Warramala, the transport system was activated. Who knows how many people saw us disappear. It's going to be hell covering it up."

Jodenny stared at him. "What does the Inspector General office have to do with ancient alien transporters?"

"Nothing." Osherman leaned back, looking suddenly weary. "I was debriefed about the WTS—that's Wondjina Transport System—for reasons that have nothing to do with smugglers. Be thankful at least one of us knows how it works. This ring is fully automated. It's programmed to travel along a predesignated route of stations. The station symbols are inscribed on the inside. We just keep going until it brings us back to Warramala."

Jodenny gazed with dismay at the dozens and dozens of glyphs. "Do we have to go to every station? Can we just skip some, or go backward?"

Osherman said, "No. It only goes in one direction, like the Alcheringa. The symbol shaped like a crescent moon represents Warramala."

Jodenny shivered. Not only did Team Space know about the ouroboroses, but they'd figured out how the system worked. She imagined a vast network of uncharted worlds, the possibilities for travel and colonization, a Team Space monopoly. Step into an ouroboros on one world and step out on another. Too bad you felt like shit afterward. The walls of the Mother Sphere seemed to press in on her, tightening the air in her chest.

"I'm going outside to take a look," Osherman said. "The odds aren't good, but maybe we've landed somewhere in the Seven Sisters. The only way to know is if the Spheres are in a normal triad formation. You'll hear a horn a few seconds before the ring tries to take you to the next station. If I'm not back when it blows, step out of it and wait for me."

Osherman left them the flashlight and headed for the far patch of daylight that marked the archway. Jodenny watched him go and rested her head on Myell's shoulder.

"We'll be home soon enough." He kissed her softly. "At least this time we're not going to start vomiting and losing our hair."

The call of the horn made them jump. Osherman jogged back in and stepped over the ouroboros. He said, "Four Fathers outside. We're nowhere near home."

Hard yellow light came and took them away.

At the next stop Jodenny was too groggy to even open her eyes. If Myell hadn't been holding her in his arms, the weight of her body would have carried her down through the bedrock and into oblivion.

"Anything?" she heard Myell ask.

"Two Fathers, three Mothers," Osherman said. She heard him shuffling around. "I count one hundred and fifty-seven glyphs on this ring. That's one hundred and fifty-seven stations. The interval between stations seems to be about seven minutes."

Jesus Christ. They'd only gone through two, and she felt worse than she had after the radvaxes.

Myell said, "One hundred and fifty-seven multiplied by seven-minute intervals means it will take us eighteen or nineteen hours of travel to go all the way around. Can we survive that?"

"We might not have to pass through every one," Osherman said. "One of the glyphs might land us in the Sisters."

He didn't sound optimistic, and he hadn't answered Myell's question. Jodenny tried not to think about what eighteen hours of travel would do to them. At the next station she must have lost consciousness, because when she opened her eyes it was to morning sunlight filtering through alpine ash trees. She was lying wrapped in Chiba's pilgrim robe on cold ground near a small campfire. A glowering Chiba was tied to a tree several meters away, and on the other side of the campfire Osherman was napping with his head cradled on his knees.

"Fucking untie me, Lieutenant," Chiba called out to Jodenny. "This is inhumane."

Jodenny sat up. The inside of her mouth tasted gummy. Behind her stood a Mother Sphere and behind that, half hidden in the trees, two Children.

"Sam," she said, and Osherman lifted his head. "Where's Terry?"

"Looking for food," he said.

"I'll look for food." Chiba pulled on his bound arms. "I'm starving here."

Jodenny went searching for Myell. The forest was full of pine and oak, and the bite in the air indicated winter wasn't far off. Distant peaks, glimpsed through the trees, were already covered with snow. A small brown deer darted through the brush just as Myell came over a small rise. He'd pouched his shirt up to hold a dozen small, unimpressive-looking apples.

"Find some flour and we can make apple pie," he said.

Jodenny ran her hands up and down the hard muscles of his arms. "You're freezing."

"You could warm me up." He tugged her close, and there certainly wasn't anything cold about his mouth against hers.

"Good idea," Jodenny murmured. "Medical necessity and all."

After some very nice groping and fondling, Myell showed Jodenny the small stream he'd discovered. It ran icy cold but she endured it long enough to swallow several times and scrub her face. Myell had a water bottle from Warramala with him, and he filled it to the brim before they returned to the encampment.

"Thanks," Osherman said as Myell shared the water and divvied up the fruit.

"What about me?" Chiba called out from his remote spot.

Osherman replied, "If you behave and keep quiet, I'll let you have some."

Jodenny noticed that Myell kept his distance from Chiba. She didn't think he was afraid of him, but rather that he didn't consider Chiba worth noticing anymore. She sat against Myell, his arms around her waist, and she saw Osherman's disapproving expression. That really wasn't worth noticing, either. She held her hands out toward their small campfire.

"What's the plan?" she asked.

Osherman said, "The minute any of us step into a Sphere, it'll send a ring our way. Like hailing a cab whether you want one or not."

"Any Sphere?" Myell asked. "We could try one of the others?"

"They'd just take us farther and farther into the network," Osherman said. "Without any kind of map, we'd get more lost. Better to stick to the sure thing."

Transiting a hundred and fifty-four more stations wouldn't be pretty, but the idea of stumbling blindly from planet to planet was much worse.

"Team Space has known about this for a long time," Jodenny said. "Why aren't there outposts or new colonies? The system should be rife with explorers."

Osherman poked at the fire. "There have been attempts. They haven't ended well. Explorers have disappeared. One entire colony disappeared without a trace. Team Space hasn't been too eager to send people to their deaths until more is known about the network, and what's really out there."

The three of them were silent for a moment.

"You said any of us could trigger a ring," Myell said. "Why us? Why not Commander Al-Banna, or Captain Umbundo, or any stranger who happened to walk by?"

Osherman's tone was casual. "It only works for certain people."

Jodenny asked, "Certain people like who?"

"I'm going to get more firewood." Osherman rose to his feet. "Keep an eye on the chief over there. I think he's been trying to free himself."

Jodenny planted herself squarely in front of him. "Sam. Tell me."

Myell rose to stand with Jodenny. Osherman gazed over both their shoulders and into the trees. A muscle pulled in his cheek. Finally he said, "You know that yellow light that flashes when the ring activates? It registers your DNA or something like it if you're in near proximity to it. Afterward you can never step into a Sphere again without triggering the system. You get access to the whole network."

Jodenny said, "But neither of us had ever seen anything like that before Mary River."

Osherman sighed. "Sergeant Myell, no. But you were exposed on the *Yangtze*."

A shiver ran down her spine. "That's ridiculous."

"Let's talk about it later, Jo. In private."

Myell tensed behind her. She insisted, "Tell me now."

Osherman turned back to the fire. "The ring on the *Yangtze* was disassembled. It was being taken from Kookaburra to Fortune to be studied. As we drew nearer to the Alcheringa it somehow triggered an energy transfer from the planet surface. You were there. You saw the ring, you saw the yellow light, you saw it all."

Cold all the way to the center of her bones, Jodenny said, "I would remember something like that."

Osherman shook his head. "While you were in surgery getting your leg repaired, Team Space gave you a memory block."

"You're lying," Myell said. "No one can give you a block without your permission. It's illegal."

"Why would I lie?" Osherman asked, annoyed. "Besides, the known side effects of memory blocks include depression, mood swings, and suicide attempts. Does any of that ring a bell, Jodenny?"

CHAPTER THIRTY-FIVE

"I don't believe you," Jodenny said.

Osherman tossed broken twigs onto the fire. "For years scientists all over the Sisters had been trying to capture a ring from a Sphere so it could be studied. A trio of engineers on Kookaburra finally succeeded. Because of my Inspector General clearance, I was debriefed about the WTS and ordered to get it aboard the *Yangtze* without anyone finding out about it. A team of scientists came with us, as did the lead agent for that project. None of them thought it would be dangerous. No one thought it would try to activate."

Jodenny searched her memory high and low, forced her mind back, back, back to the morning of the explosion. She had signed off on the duty log and turned her responsibilities over to Lieutenant Odell. Then she had gone to the mess decks and was enjoying a nice cup of horchata when the first alarms started to blare . . .

Hadn't she?

Jodenny Scott, Assistant Division Officer for Underway Stores, glanced at the nearest clock on the *Yangtze*'s bridge and stifled a yawn. The overnight watch had been long and dull, and not even the prospect of the upcoming Alcheringa drop could fill her with excitement. Between now and then the only exciting thing worth contemplating was an icy cup of horchata with extra sugar. She had both hands wrapped around it when her relief showed up early.

"Couldn't wait to start the day?" she asked Lieutenant Odell.

"It was either come in early or stay home and listen to the baby cry," Odell said, rubbing her eyes. "When the hell is someone going to find a cure for colic?"

Jodenny signed out at oh-six-hundred, sixty minutes before the ship transitioned into the Alcheringa. She swung by her cabin, picked up her gym bag, and headed back to F-Deck. A long treadmill run soon had her feeling more alert. She showered, put on a fresh uniform, and was heading toward the lift when the comm clicked to life.

"Alcheringa drop commencing in twenty seconds," she heard. "Fifteen . . . ten . . ."

The blast of a horn drowned out the rest of the announcement. It sounded low and mournful, as if calling faraway warriors to a battle already lost, and made the hairs on Jodenny's neck stand at attention. An emergency sensor lit up over the hatch to Science Lab B, and the General Quarters klaxon began to shriek.

"Emergency in Tower 6," the bridge announced. "Emergency Services responding. Hull breach in Mainship, Deck F. All crew and passengers to lifepods."

For a moment Jodenny stood rooted to the deck. T6 belonged to Jem and the Underway Stores Division. Maybe someone had collided with a DNGO, or a hazardous material smartcrate had broken open. But a hull breach, here, on Deck F? Impossible—

"Lieutenant," her agent said, "you should evacuate to your lifepod."

"I will, Katherine," Jodenny said, just as the hatch to Lab B burst inward. A civilian scientist stumbled out of the room and grabbed her by the arms.

"It's not supposed to work!" he gasped. "We didn't mean for it to—"

Jodenny pushed into the lab to see if anyone needed her help. Sucking wind dragged at her, and she clutched at a fixed table in order to keep from being dragged toward a large hole in the stern bulkhead. An enormous chunk of parasteel had somehow evaporated. The lab was located in the ship's interior, but the bulkheads beyond it also appeared breached, and the emergency clearshields weren't holding well. Severed conduits and vents hissed smoke and sparks, and a live power line had two men trapped on the other side of the room. Between Jodenny and the trapped men were pieces of a metal sculpture that had been arranged on the deck. Hanging high over the pieces was a shimmering, yellow-white hologram in the shape of an ouroboros.

"Jodenny!" a voice shouted, and for the first time she realized one of the trapped men was Sam Osherman. She hadn't seen him since they'd broken up a month earlier, though she'd cursed his name daily. He yelled, "Jo, get out!"

The call of a horn filled the room again.

"It pierced the ship," said the scientist. "Jesus Christ, it sliced right through the hull—"

"Jo, leave now!" Osherman said. He dragged the scientist forward so that they were standing in the middle of the ring. The ouroboros over their head glowed brightly. "Get out!"

Jodenny retreated a step or two but she couldn't just leave him there, the bastard. "I'll get help!" she yelled, just as a flare of yellow light blinded her. She tumbled backward, trying to shield her eyes, but the world was full of light, bright light, hot light boiling away her skin, and when she opened her eyes Osherman and the scientist were gone. The disaster had already begun, and the *Yangtze* was doomed.

She pulled herself clear of Myell's arms and took several unsteady steps away from both men. "What happened after that? Did I really rescue anyone? Earn that goddamned MacBride Cross?"

"Of course!" Osherman looked appalled that she doubted it. "You got out of the lab and started for your lifepod. Everything that happened after that, the people you saved and the injuries you sustained, is true. The block was just a little part of your treatment afterward. It's supposed to be an improved version, with not so many side effects. But it didn't take too well with you."

Jodenny didn't believe him. He had been her lover, once, but then had stood aside and let them tamper with her memory to the point where she picked up pieces of broken glass and pressed them to her veins. The treachery of it all, from Osherman to her doctors to the admirals of Team Space, made her feel brittle inside, ready to snap into pieces. She couldn't bear to look at Myell, a man whose mother had killed herself. Her suicide attempt was the one thing she had never wanted him to know about.

"You used the ring to escape," Myell said to Osherman. "You left the ship."

"Yes," Osherman said. "It was only six stops until the Point Elliot Spheres. A picnic, compared to this trip."

She couldn't bear to listen anymore. Jodenny walked away blindly, the trees blurred in her vision, her movements jerky and stiff. When tears ran down her face she wiped them off with her sleeve and kept going.

"Jodenny! Kay!"

Myell caught up to her but she shrugged off his hand and said, "I'm fine."

"You're not fine," he said. "Who could be?"

He pulled her into his embrace. Jodenny fought with a few thumps of fists against his chest but the punches were perfunctory, and he didn't let go. Her knees gave way. They both sank to the ground as sobs tore out of her.

"I'm sorry," she said when she could speak.

"Sorry for what? None of this is your fault."

"What I did to myself . . . what your mother did." Her face was hot with shame. "I didn't want you to know."

Myell's expression was fierce. "What happened to you and

what happened to my mother are two entirely different things. Never compare them. Never blame yourself."

His lips found hers in a hard, determined kiss. Jodenny let him cradle her to the ground, where he nuzzled against her cheek and whispered in her ear and told her everything would end well. But her fear wasn't so easily assuaged. She cupped his strong, stubbled face and said, "What if they try to block this from us? What if we get back and they do it again?"

"They won't," Myell promised, and pressed his weight against her until the forest and trees and sky disappeared, and the only real things were their two bodies. "We'll die before we let them do that to us."

Yellow light. Pushing, pushing, pushing them onward. Jodenny made it through the next few stops without too many ill effects but Chiba and Myell both started to suffer terribly. Twelve stations after leaving Warramala they landed in a Sphere with a broken dome, and in the cast of sunlight Chiba went into convulsions. Myell's eyes were only half open, his skin cold and clammy to Jodenny's touch.

"We have to stop," Jodenny told Osherman.

The station consisted of three Mother Spheres and a Child set in a thick rain forest. Jodenny fought ferns, vines, and slippery moss until she got Myell to a small clearing under the auspices of an enormous red cedar tree. Birds flitted overhead. Parrots and cockatoos and pigeons, mainly, with some exotic species as well, all the colors of the rainbow. The temperature was mild enough but the ground was damp with recent rain and it took Jodenny several minutes to get a campfire going. She settled Myell close to the flames. He was unresponsive to her cajoling, but that didn't stop her from talking to him.

"Remember," she said into his ear. "We have a dinner date. I already know what I'm going to wear, and you can bet it's not a uniform. What about you? That sweater you wore at your brother's house—that was nice. Do you still have it?"

It was ridiculous discussing wardrobe choices when their clothes were millions of light-years away, but she didn't have much to say about the weather and gossip about Underway Stores was in short supply. She would have happily traded all her current problems for the challenge of keeping Lange from playing Izim.

"If we get back to Mary River," she said, "we can go visit Colby and Dottie, and they'll put us up in that nice guest room. All night long I waited for you, but did you come visit? No."

His trembling eased, and he might have slept. When Osherman joined them several minutes later he had an armful of mushrooms, macadamia nuts, and mangoes. "Some of these look harmless enough," he said. "Not so sure about the mushrooms. I suspect a lot of things around here are poisonous."

Jodenny said, "Sam, we can't do one hundred and forty-something more stations."

"We don't have a choice." Osherman put down the food. "Unless you intend to make your home here for the rest of your days and wait for a rescue that might never come."

Jodenny tightened her hold on Myell. "How's Chiba?"

"Conscious and swearing up a storm. I left him tied up back there, near a waterfall. Give me the water bottle, and I'll get some for all of us." Osherman glanced at Myell's bone-white face. "Jodenny, I know how you feel. What about your career?"

"If it's Terry or my career, there's no contest."

"There are other men in Team Space."

She replied, "There are other jobs."

Myell wasn't sure where he was. The last thing he clearly remembered was the sound of Jodenny's voice and a glimpse of bamboo trees by firelight. The landscape around him was now flat and parched, cracked open by drought, and the only sound was the whistle of the wind. The western horizon was gold with sunset, the rest of the sky purple. He thought that if he glanced down at himself he might see dark skin and dusty feet. An overwhelming sense of isolation swept through him.

He was alone in this ancient land, abandoned by all, consigned to a future bereft of friends or hope or even the tiniest drops of moisture. He would shrivel to nothing more than salt and bone and be scattered like the dust, unremembered, unmourned.

A woman's voice floated across the landscape, sweet like water.

"And that's how the emu and the kangaroo changed skins," she said.

"Tell me another, Mom," said a young boy.

Myell turned around to see the farmhouse where he had grown up. The windows were gaping squares of rust-colored light, the timbers splintered by age. He could see shapes moving inside, indistinct, fluid. Himself and his mother in one room. His father, swaying drunkenly down the hall, saying, "Don't tell him that crap, Adeline." Silence, now. The creaking of a rope, as a heavy weight swayed from a rafter. Myell knew if he went to the door it would fall away beneath his hand and deliver him into the land of memory, where pain lived and thrived.

"No," he said to whoever was listening. "I won't go."

"You don't have to," his mother said. She was standing right beside him now, her sun-colored hair pulled back from her fresh, dewy face. This was his mother not as she had died, worn and wasted and gray. This was his mother as she had stood on an Australian beach, a smile on her lips. She was not so tangible that he could reach over and touch her, but that didn't stop him from trying.

"Terry," she said. *"Jungali."*

That was a name he hadn't heard since her death. Jungali, she would say, and kiss his nose. My little Jungali, she would sing, as she poured water over his head in the tub. His special name, she said. His father never used it. His mother never mentioned it in front of Colby or Daris. Perhaps they had their own names, or perhaps he was the only one so favored. Before he could ask, his mother dissolved like dust in a storm. All the gray particles of her being reassembled into the shape of the Wirrinun.

"Choose," he said, and slammed his staff into the ground. The Rainbow Serpent burst from the ground and swallowed the Wirrinun whole. It swayed before Myell's eyes, lifted its alligator head to the height of Myell's head, and repeated, "Choose."

"I don't understand," Myell said. "What am I choosing between? Are you the Wondjina? Where are we?"

"Older than the Wondjina," the snake insisted. "Wiser."

Lightning sheeted across the sky, followed by bellows of thunder. Myell had never conversed with a snake before and preferred to see his mother again, but he felt strangely calm in this place. He decided he was not dreaming in the normal fashion, nor was he anywhere that could be pinpointed by a map or star chart. He was in the great elsewhere older than Time itself.

The snake's eyes widened as if it were pleased. "In the Dreamtime, yes. But will you stay?"

The sky split open. Rain flooded through him and carried him away to a land of rain forests and desert and seashore, and the dark-skinned natives who walked across its width and length with songs on their tongues, and the winged, furred, and scaly creatures who climbed out of the ground or descended from the trees to take part in the cycle of rain and drought that extended back to the eternal time of the Dreaming. Among the people and animals and trees he saw a dozen wirrinun, or maybe a hundred dozen, or a thousand dozen, all of them leading their people single file across the landscape. Each of them wore Myell's own face. Each was named *Jungali*.

"No," he said, and the land fell away to the flat landscape outside his parents' farmhouse, which was nothing more than stone and shadow.

"The world you know as your own is itself but a shadow," the Rainbow Serpent said, coiling its tail as if holding up a finger to test the wind. "Surrender it and embrace the Dreaming. You will be well rewarded."

Myell wanted to. His bones already felt like the rocks of the world, his blood like its rivers. It would be easy to surrender— to *choose*—the ancient power of the Dreamtime. To embrace what was his birthright. But then he thought of Jodenny. Of Colby and his family, of friends like Timrin and Gallivan and Chaplain Mow.

"No," he said. "I choose Terry, not Jungali."

"As you wish." The snake twirled its way up toward the sky. Impossibly high it rose, a sinewy ribbon climbing toward heaven. "Touch my skin."

Another choice. Trust it, distrust it. Myell took one last glance around the dark landscape. He reached out and laid his hand flat against the shining colors.

"Jodenny," he whispered, right before the snake took him up into the sky and down the Alcheringa, the great river between the stars.

J odenny meant to stay awake. The hunger pains in her stomach should have helped, but it had been a long day of keeping vigil over Myell. Once or twice he had murmured words she didn't catch, but he had never woken. She tried rubbing her knuckles over his breastbone, but he remained stubbornly unconscious.

"He'll be all right," Osherman had said, which angered her. He couldn't know that. Couldn't promise it.

When Jodenny finally fell asleep she dreamed of snakes and birds and vines closing in, choking her with their growth. She awoke in the middle of the night to the sound of insects and the rustlings of animals in the brush. The air was heavy and wet. Osherman had predicted rain before sunrise.

"Sam?" she asked. He was nowhere to be seen. Jodenny shook Myell's shoulder, but he wouldn't wake. She searched for the mazer and flashlight, but they too were gone. She lifted a burning branch from the fire and stepped past the choking ferns toward the waterfall where Osherman had left Chiba. The rain forest stirred all around her, palm fronds bowing in the breeze, lianas tugging at her trousers. A few drops of rain pelted her face and she heard a steady pattering, but the canopy overhead caught and collected most of it. She hoped the rain stayed off them. Myell would probably catch pneumonia if he got drenched. *We don't need any more bad luck,* she thought grumpily, and then a mazer shot zipped by her face so close that her nose began to tingle.

The bolt hit a massive cathedral fig tree instead, searing a hole right through it. The mazer was set to kill, then. Jodenny threw her makeshift torch to the side and dived to the ground, where she rolled behind a bush.

"Come on out, Lieutenant," Chiba said, a snarl to his voice. He stood a few meters away with Osherman's flashlight in hand, an easy target if only she had a mazer as well. "Let's talk."

Jodenny found a good-sized rock in the dirt and hurled it at him. A solid thump and Chiba's yelp of pain let her know she'd hit her target. He dropped the light. Jodenny scrambled to her feet and tried to flee behind the fig tree, but faster than she could have imagined Chiba tackled her and drove her to the ground. She landed hard, his weight and strength nearly crushing her. Jodenny scratched and kicked and screamed, everything she'd ever learned in self-defense classes vanishing in near-panic.

"Always a bitch." Chiba pinned her arms. "Not so high and mighty now—"

Jodenny squirmed one hand free and hooked her fingers into Chiba's eyeballs. He yelped and fell away. She started to crawl again, but his hand clamped down on her ankle. Jodenny grabbed the nearest plant at hand, a stem with heart-shaped leaves. She ripped it out of the ground and whipped it around into Chiba's face. He recoiled with a gasp.

"Fuck, what's that?" he demanded.

Jodenny's hand began to burn. She crawled away from Chiba anyway, putting as much distance between them as possible. He was still saying, "Fuck, fuck, fuck," and now he was wheezing for air. Maybe he was allergic to whatever was in the plant. Cradling her hand, Jodenny picked up the flashlight and went in search of first the mazer and then Osherman. The mazer had rolled under some bushes. Osherman was curled up on the ground ten meters away, just beginning to wake up.

He'd scraped open his scalp when he fell, and blood matted his head.

"Chiba," he said when he could form a coherent word.

"He's not going anywhere," Jodenny said.

He insisted that they check. Chiba wasn't where Jodenny had left him. They stumbled through the brush, trying to follow a trail of broken branches, and then the clear mournful call of an ouroboros cut through the air.

"Fuck," Osherman said.

By the time they reached the Spheres, Chiba was gone. "He won't get far," Osherman said, which sounded a lot like wishful thinking. Jodenny thought he might plunge into a chase after him, but common sense ruled and they went back to where they had left Myell.

He was still asleep, his face wan in the firelight. Jodenny used a piece of cloth and some of their water supply to wash and bandage Osherman's head with her left hand.

"What's wrong with your right hand?" he asked.

"Nothing," she said, though it was swollen and red. She poured water over it, but the stinging didn't ease.

Osherman shifted clumsily from his position and settled beside her. He was taller than Myell and had a different smell to him—blood, unfortunately, but also something spicy and strong, something that reminded her of the *Yangtze.*

"Go to sleep," he said. "I'll keep watch."

Her fingers were hot, but she otherwise felt cold. "You've got a head injury. Better we both stay up."

He poked at the fire. "You know, back on the *Yangtze*—I don't know if I told you this. My job was one thing. What happened with us—well, I shouldn't have let it. I could have put you in grave danger."

"Or maybe you just slept with me to find out if I knew anything about the smugglers?" None of it mattered, really. The *Yangtze, Aral Sea*, all of Team Space, were millions of miles away. Chiba was gone and Myell was perhaps dying and what was her honor, really? Why should she care?

"No," Osherman said. "I didn't just use you that way."

"It would have been a logical tactic."

"Jo, no," he repeated, and touched her arm. "I didn't want you involved."

"I don't believe you."

"What if I told you that I was afraid Lieutenant Commander Ross's influence would subvert you?"

She stared at him, all injuries and fatigue forgotten. "Jem had nothing to do with smuggling."

Osherman's expression was shuttered. "This isn't the place to talk about it."

"No," Jodenny said. "You'll never convince me."

"Jo . . ."

Jodenny turned her back to him. Her hand still ached like a son of a bitch and fury kept her wide awake. To insinuate that Jem condoned or participated in criminal activities was a new low for Osherman. She closed her eyes against angry tears and when she opened them again, hours had passed. The fire was cold, Osherman sound asleep, and sunrise had started to lighten the edge of the sky with dark gold. Myell was standing nearby and staring at her with an odd expression on his face.

"Terry?" she asked.

He walked into the forest. Jodenny pulled herself up. Her hand was red in the sunlight, swollen, but it didn't hurt as much as it had the night before. "Terry—" she called, but he moved so quickly that she lost track of him for several seconds. Then she saw him enter the Child Sphere and followed him into the gloom. Though she'd heard no horn, an ouroboros was waiting for them.

She touched Myell's shoulder. "Terry?"

"I know where to go." Myell bent down next to the ouroboros. "Two stops on this line, transfer over to a Father for one stop, transfer back, and we'll be back on Warramala."

Jodenny rubbed his shoulders. "Come on back to the fire. Let's see if we can scrounge up some breakfast."

"Do you believe me?" His gaze was earnest. "We're four stops away. The Rainbow Serpent told me."

Jodenny kept her opinion of talking snakes to herself. Myell was quiet on the walk back. She started the fire again, had him sit close to it, checked on Osherman, and went in search of water and food. For several minutes she soaked her stinging hand in a pool of water, and that seemed to help. When she returned Myell and Osherman were arguing.

"A dream means nothing, Sergeant. We're staying with the Mother Sphere we know."

"We'll never make it." Myell sounded entirely sure of himself. "Humans were never meant to travel this way, Commander. It's the Wondjina's network, not ours."

Osherman retorted, "I'd think twice about counting on the word of a talking snake."

Jodenny stepped out of the trees. With forced cheer she said, "Some mangoes here. Anyone hungry?"

Osherman asked, "Did the sergeant tell you about his dream?"

Jodenny met Myell's serene gaze. "Yes."

"And your opinion?"

She shrugged, still angry with him over the previous night's conversation about Jem. "Four stops sounds much more manageable."

"What's wrong with your hand?" Myell asked, noticing the way she was holding it.

"Some kind of plant. I grabbed it the wrong way."

Myell made a careful examination of her palm and fingers. "Probably a stinging tree. Sometimes comes as a shrub. You'll need a doctor to fix it properly."

Osherman smothered the fire. "Then we'd better get moving again. Chiba's got several hours on us, but he'll be sick, maybe injured. He won't be still traveling. We can catch him."

Jodenny looked at Myell.

"Chiba doesn't matter," Myell said. "The snake will take care of him."

"Sam, at least look at the ring in the Child Sphere," Jodenny said. "See if any of the glyphs match ones we've already passed through."

"It's probably gone already," Osherman said. But when they got there, the ouroboros hadn't moved on. After a moment's inspection he said, "No. I don't recognize any of these."

"You don't have to," Myell said.

Osherman brushed dirt from his knees. "Jodenny, it's crazy. You detour off here, and god only knows what corner of the galaxy you'll wind up in."

"I know the way home," Myell said. In the glow of the flashlight she recognized the set of his jaw. "Do you trust me, Kay?"

Jodenny didn't hesitate. "Yes. I just don't trust your snake."

Osherman spread his hands. "Jodenny, choose. Come with me and we'll get home for sure. Go with him and you could be lost forever."

Decide between the two of them, between crazy and safe, between the proven path and the way of Myell's Dreaming. Jodenny knew Osherman to be a methodical, intelligent man not prone to flights of fantasy, even if he was horribly wrong about Jem. She knew Myell was stubborn, reliable, and practical. She remembered that Osherman had more knowledge about the Wondjina network. She remembered the way Myell had sacrificed himself for her in T18.

"Jodenny," Osherman said. "You'll never get home if you go with him."

"Maybe not." Jodenny reached out and took Myell's hand anyway.

After Osherman was gone, Jodenny buried herself in Myell's arms and asked, "Are you sure about this?"

"Yes," Myell said.

At the first stop she vomited. At the second stop they lurched outside to a dimly lit world blanketed with sleet. A half-frozen creek barred their way to the Father Sphere a hundred meters away. They stomped across it, Jodenny's feet aching with cold. Wind whipped at their thin clothes. When they reached the Father, they had to dig at ice-crusted snow with their bare hands to get under the arch. Jodenny's hands and feet were numb by the time they reached the inside, which was also freezing cold.

"We're almost there," Myell said, his teeth chattering.

A mistake. They had both made a mistake. She lay against him in the icy darkness, willing the end to come mercifully. She said, "Terry—"

"Don't give up now," he insisted.

The next stop was filled with warm sunlight from a jagged, charred breach in the Sphere's side. Bones lay nearby, some of them burned and charred. They staggered back to a Child Sphere where the ground was covered with ash. Myell collapsed inside the ouroboros, his lips blue. Jodenny hammered at his chest.

"Goddamn it!" she yelled. "Wake up!"

He wasn't breathing. She did it for him, sweat rolling down her back, her arms and shoulders aching from the strain of doing compressions. Four minutes. Five—

Yellow light.

She thought she heard the hiss of a snake, but it was simply Myell as he gasped for air. Jodenny began to cry.

"They're back," a man's voice said, and a light nearly blinded her. "Lieutenant Scott, Sergeant Myell, you're both under arrest."

CHAPTER **THIRTY-SIX**

Jodenny didn't see Myell for the next five days. Every day she asked about him and every day her handlers said, "He's fine, Lieutenant." She suspected he was being held at the same secluded facility she was, but had no evidence and no way of finding out. Her room had a bed, a desk, and an adjoining head, but no deskgib, comm units, or media access. The wallvids showed her a picture of a deep, tranquil forest at the height of summer, with simulated sunrises and sunsets. The door locked and unlocked only when guards came to escort her to medical appointments or debriefings. Not interrogations, her handlers told her. *Debriefings*.

"Please draw for us all the glyphs you saw on the ouroboros," they asked, and she managed to sketch out a dozen or so. They showed her others, but she couldn't say for sure whether or not she'd seen them. Jodenny was also interviewed, extensively, about the worlds she had visited, and their formation of Spheres. More than once she was asked to recount the exact events that had taken her, Chiba, Myell, and Osherman on their journey.

"Tell us again why you decided to split up," said one of her interrogators. None of them wore insignia or uniforms, and Jodenny wasn't sure if they were Team Space or some kind of ultrasecret civilian intelligence agency.

Jodenny said, "He wanted to keep going through the Sphere we'd been traveling through. Sergeant Myell and I didn't think we'd survive it."

The interrogator consulted his gib. "Sergeant Myell had another idea. Based on information he received from a snake."

The interrogator's voice was mild, his expression blank. Jodenny said, "If you bring him in here, you can ask him yourself."

The interrogator didn't answer. He was about fifty years old, with short black hair and bright green eyes. He was physically fit, with the ramrod-straight posture of a military man. He said his name was Wolf, which seemed unlikely. He was in charge of the others—the woman with a heart-shaped face, the younger man with a scar on his cheek. She wondered if he had ever gone traveling through a Sphere, or if he knew what it was like to set foot on an utterly new world.

Wolf and his friends didn't seem seemed particularly interested in Chiba's fate, though they asked repeatedly about Osherman. Late at night, unable to sleep, she pictured him lost in the network, lurching from one Sphere to the next. She wondered what fate was waiting for her and Myell. Would they ever be allowed to leave this place, wherever it was? Would Team Space try to suppress their memories as they had after the *Yangtze*?

"I would like to see my lawyer," she told Wolf on the third day.

"What is it you think you've done wrong?" he asked.

"I don't think I've done anything wrong. But I'm being kept here incommunicado against my consent, and I haven't been charged with anything. That violates the Seven Sisters Constitution."

Wolf only said, "I see," and went back to showing her pictures of different glyphs, asking if she recognized any from her travels.

Her hand had mostly healed up from the stinging shrub injury, though sometimes her fingers still tingled. The doctor who treated her was sure that the residual effects would fade.

"And the memory block?" Jodenny asked, letting her bitterness bleed through. "What about the effects from that?"

The doctor raised an eyebrow. "Your retrograde amnesia has been attributed to head injuries you received on the *Yangtze*. There's no record of a memory block."

"I'm not surprised," Jodenny said. "It was put in without my permission."

"Hmm," the doctor replied, but said no more.

On the fifth day Jodenny woke early, did sit-ups and push-ups, showered under a welcome spray of hot water, and dressed in the civilian clothes they had given her. Breakfast was delivered on a tray by a young woman. Afterward two guards escorted her down several flights of stairs to a long hallway of closed doors. The building itself, decorated in soothing shades of dark gray and blue, was quiet all around her. She was shown into a conference room where Myell was sitting with Wolf.

He looked well enough, though there were dark circles under his eyes. He stood up immediately, saying, "Lieutenant Scott," and in his voice she heard her own emotions: enormous relief, along with apprehension about their current situation.

She sat next to him, but not so close as to actually press her leg against his. Wolf, his expression as carefully blank as ever, said, "Lieutenant, Sergeant, this morning marks the end of your debriefing. We're satisfied that that you're not holding back information about your experience. We're grateful for your full cooperation to date, and would like to extend an invitation for you to join our project."

Looking perplexed, Myell asked, "Which project is that, sir?"

"You need to ask?" Wolf replied.

"Exploring the Wondjina Transportation System," Jodenny said. "Finding out more about it."

Myell said, "But it makes people sick. It wasn't made for human use."

Wolf steepled his hands together on the tabletop. "Your security clearances have been updated and backdated to the day you left Kookaburra. You'll be signing your agreement to them shortly. What happened to you, and any information you've gained from that experience, is strictly classified. If you were to speak of it to others, the entire project would be jeopardized. If you stay here, with us, you'd be able to explore the matter more fully with like-minded researchers and explorers. It's a rare and precious opportunity."

Jodenny sat back in her chair. The walls and overhead were smooth, but she imagined somewhere a camera was recording this session.

"Commander Osherman said we were somehow encoded," she said. "All we have to do is step into a Sphere from now on and the system will activate."

Wolf's expression gave nothing away. "Not exactly, but it's accurate enough that you should never attempt it. We'll be watching to make sure you don't."

"You're not listening," Myell said, to both of them. "It wasn't made for us to use. Who knows what might happen if you keep sending people through—not just to them, but to all of us."

"So you believe," Wolf replied, leading Jodenny to wonder what exactly had transpired during Myell's debriefings. Wolf continued. "If you join us, Sergeant, you'll be able to see first-hand what accomplishments we've made and how the system could benefit everyone in the Seven Sisters. If you choose not to participate, you'll be unable to tell anyone about your experience upon pain of court-martial or worse."

Jodenny already knew what Myell's answer would be. As for herself, she was sorely tempted to say yes. Traveling among the stars, setting forth on new planets, maybe meeting the Wondjina themselves—she could happily sign up for a project such as that. But then she remembered Myell's heart stopping at the end, and his body lax in her arms.

"I want to return to regular duty," she said. "I'm sure the *Aral Sea*'s departed by now, but perhaps the *Alaska* has an open billet."

"Two open billets," Myell insisted.

"You'll never get another chance like this one," Wolf warned.

Jodenny reached under the table and squeezed Myell's hand, surveillance cameras be damned. "We know that."

"Let's hope you don't regret it," Wolf said, rising to his feet.

"What happens now?" Myell asked.

"Once you sign your new clearances we'll notify Fleet that you're ready for active duty. I'll convey your request to return to ship duty, but nothing's guaranteed."

Jodenny asked, "You're not going to erase our memories?"

Wolf's gaze narrowed. "I'm not sure why Commander Osherman told you that story, Lieutenant. As far as our doctors can tell, nothing of the sort was done to you by Team Space. Or, if it was, the chemical markers are no longer detectable."

Jodenny pushed down a shiver. "Who else would want to block my memory of an ouroboros? And why?"

"I don't know. If your memory had been intact, we would have simply debriefed you, offered you the same deal we're offering you now, or sworn you to secrecy."

Wolf left the conference room. The woman with the heart-shaped face came in with flatgibs for them to review and sign. Jodenny read through document after document that outlined her new security clearance and the penalties she faced if she violated its terms, including court-martial and life imprisonment. She would be bound to it for the rest of her life, even if she left Team Space and became a civilian. After she and Myell were done affixing their signatures, a guard took them down more stairs to a small self-service café and said, "If you'll wait here, someone will be with you shortly."

The guard took up position at the door. Jodenny grabbed a cup of horchata and slid into a booth. Myell's coffee went untouched as he sat across from her and leaned forward intently.

"You're all right?" he asked. "Your hand?"

Jodenny wanted to laugh. "It's fine. You're the one who stopped breathing."

"I don't remember much. Snow and ice, but nothing after that."

"You're okay now?" she asked, and it wasn't so much a question as a reassurance. They were both alive and well, and would soon return to their professional lives. Though she was ridiculously happy just sitting with him, Jodenny had no idea what to do next about their relationship. She could resign her commission. He could leave Team Space at the end of his contract. Or they could both continue on active duty, and willingly violate fraternization rules.

"Things are going to work out," Myell said, as if reading her mind. "A few months, and I'm free of Team Space."

Jodenny clutched her cup. "You shouldn't have to give up your career. You deserve to be a chief, and Team Space needs people like you."

Myell glanced toward the guard, who didn't appear to be listening to them. "I never figured myself for a career sailor. Whatever happens, for the next few months you're just another lieutenant and I'm just another sergeant. Easy, right?"

He smiled, but she could see that the effort was for her sake. Three or four months was manageable, she supposed, though it sounded like a lifetime. She was still mulling it over when another guard came to take them to their rooms, where fresh uniforms in correct sizes and with proper insignia had already been laid out. Twenty minutes later Jodenny was escorted to an underground parking facility, where Myell was standing outside a limousine-flit with tinted windows. He looked as uncomfortable in his uniform as she felt in hers.

"Our ride, apparently." Myell held open the passenger door. "After you, Lieutenant."

Jodenny slid into the cool, dark interior and was startled to find a three-star admiral sitting inside.

"Ma'am!" Jodenny said.

"So you're the infamous Lieutenant Scott," Admiral Nilsen said flatly, and waited until Myell was seated beside Jodenny. "The equally infamous Sergeant Myell. How exciting for me to meet you both."

"Thank you, Admiral," Myell said, a little tentatively.

The car began moving. The windows made it impossible for Jodenny to see where, but her attention was in any case focused solely on the woman across from her.

"I'll be brief," Nilsen said. "The *Aral Sea* hasn't left orbit. Her departure was delayed. Captain Umbundo is adamantly opposed to your returning onboard. The legal investigation into the smuggling ring is still ongoing, there have been several internal reassignments, no one has been able to locate Agent Ishikawa, and he has enough on his hands without you two adding to the mixture. Several of my staff have suggested I simply stick the two of you in the dullest, drabbest jobs possible, somewhere where you can't possibly cause any more trouble than you have already."

"Yes, ma'am," Jodenny said, her stomach churning.

Nilsen continued. "At the same time, it'll be less of a hassle for my office if you're far away from curious journalists. We've squelched most of the reports of you two disappearing in the middle of a Mother Sphere, but interest isn't going to die anytime soon."

Myell spoke up. "The media can't reach us if we're on the *Aral Sea,* ma'am."

"My point, exactly." Nilsen tapped something on her gib. The flit sped up. "Truth be told, I have my doubts about you, Lieutenant Scott. You received excellent evaluations on the *Yangtze,* your actions during that disaster deservedly earned the MacBride Cross, and I'm told that aside from disobeying Commander Osherman's orders, you were performing well on the *Aral Sea.* But the rumors of fraternization are discouraging, you sometimes let your emotions overrule your head, and you have a tendency to jump the chain of command when things don't go your way."

Myell protested, "It's not like that at all—"

"No." Jodenny felt herself blush, but she held the admiral's gaze. "It's all right. It's true."

Nilsen lifted her chin. "On the other hand, my nephew speaks quite highly of you, and by all accounts you've treated him better than any other division leader he's ever had."

"Your nephew?" Myell asked.

The corner of Nilsen's mouth quirked. "Peter Dicensu's not the brightest sailor ever to join Team Space, but he means well. He speaks well of you too, Sergeant Myell. Commander Al-Banna says that your recent evaluations are not representative of your true performance. He also believes you were unfairly accused in the matter of AT Ford and have been cleared in regard to certain inventory irregularities. He thinks you might have a promising career, if you don't derail it with hasty choices."

Myell said, "Choosing to get off a train isn't the same as derailing myself, ma'am."

"I'm not much for transportation metaphors," Nilsen said. "I also didn't get to the position I have because I followed every rule and regulation that came my way. Neither one of you should take that as advice. Merely consider it a point of information."

The flit slid to a stop. The passenger door opened on its own, revealing a busy curb at the Waipata spaceport. Nilsen said, "Better hurry if you want to make that last birdie."

"Thank you, ma'am," Jodenny said, and Myell echoed.

They raced through the terminal and boarded the last shuttle to the *Aral Sea* with only moments to spare. "I forgot Dicensu had an aunt," Myell said, once they were safely in their seats.

Jodenny leaned back and let her eyes close. "Thank goodness for nepotism."

Their first stop back on the ship was the Supply Flats. Al-Banna had stayed behind on Warramala to fulfill his Inspector General duties, and Captain Umbundo had elevated Lieutenant Commander Wildstein to Supply Officer for the duration of their cruise. Wildstein didn't seem either pleased or displeased to see them, and she asked no questions about what had happened on Warramala. To Jodenny she said, "You. Flight Support. Commander Rokutan needs an Assistant Division Officer."

Myell didn't like the idea of Jodenny working for Rokutan, even though whoever she slept with prior to their relationship was really none of his business. Jodenny didn't look excited, either, but off she went without a farewell glance.

"You," Wildstein said to Myell, "are staying right here. Bartis is in the brig for aiding and abetting Chiba and someone's got to clean up this place."

Myell gazed unhappily at the piles of work on Bartis's desk. "Yes, ma'am."

Underway Stores was being run by Ensign Ysten, who most people believed was in over his head. The Maintenance division had been reorganized, with Lieutenant Commander Zarkesh moved over to Tower Ops because of his failure to properly supervise Quenger and Chiba. Lieutenant Anzo and several members of the Data Department had been relieved of their duties pending indictment as part of the smuggling ring, as had Commander Senga from Security.

"Always knew he was a rotten one," Timrin said that night, at Myell's welcome-back dinner. VanAmsal was there, as well as Chang, Minnich, Kevwitch, Amador, and several others. No matter how much they asked, Myell refused to discuss what had happened while trapped in the tower with Jodenny or anything that had occurred on Warramala.

It didn't take him long to discover that Chaplain Mow was no longer onboard. As with Dr. Ng, she had been hastily transferred to Fleet on Warramala, no explanation given. Governor Ganambarr and the Aboriginal colonists in T9 had all departed, leaving him with no one he could confide in or consult. Neither the snake nor the Wirrinun had appeared since his trip among the stars, and he wasn't sure he would ever see them again. He felt an unexpected loss at that, but relief as well.

Four days after leaving Warramala the ship dropped into the Alcheringa and started downriver to Baiame. After a while people stopped asking Myell about Chiba and the smugglers. Eva sent a few imails that he refused to answer. Slipping back into normal routine wasn't as hard as he feared it would be, except that as the days and weeks dragged on he saw precious little of Jodenny. She never came to the Flats, no longer frequented the E-Deck gym, and rarely went over to the Rocks. Apparently she spent all of her time either at work, on watch, or in the Supply wardroom.

VanAmsal said, "I heard Rokutan's keeping her at arm's length. That's a boys' club over there, you know?"

"Any rumors about . . ." Myell tried to sound nonchalant. "Them being together?"

VanAmsal rolled her eyes. "Is that what you think of her?"

No. He didn't. But he certainly wished he were working for Jodenny again. Wildstein was relentless. She came in early, worked through lunch, and went home late. She had rigid paperwork requirements, and took great satisfaction in reprimanding Myell about something new every day.

"These evaluations should be filed by MOC code, Sergeant, not alphabetically," she would say. Or, "Why haven't you finished the DLRs I gave you an hour ago?" A few days before they reached Baiame she asked, "Why is it, Sergeant, that you can never remember to put incoming requisitions in my middle tray, not the top one?"

He was tempted to tell her exactly where she could put those requisitions. But then Wildstein's gaze focused on the clock and she asked, "Shouldn't you be at the chief's exam?"

"No, ma'am," Myell said. "I'm getting out of Team Space when my contract expires."

"That's a plan." Wildstein took the requisitions from him. "Then again, plans change. Go take that exam, Sergeant. The results won't be announced until we get to Fortune. If you pass, you might stay in. And if you get out, at least you'll have it on your record for future employers to see."

He supposed she had a point, but he was woefully unprepared. Weeks had passed since he'd practiced any questions. Nevertheless he got RT Sorenson to cover the office and hurried up to the auditorium. Several officers were stationed at the registration desks, Jodenny among them. She looked rested and healthy, and in no way pining for him.

"Sergeant Myell." Ensign Hultz had him sign in. "I heard you weren't taking the exam."

Myell took a tablet gib. "Figured I'd give it a shot."

He sat near VanAmsal, who was already hard at work. Myell concentrated on the questions and ignored Jodenny. In the second hour the exam changed to essay format, and in the third he was faced with a harder series of fill-in blanks. The auditorium was quiet but for breathing and the tap-tap-tap of gibs.

Just after noon, with his stomach growling and vision beginning to blur, Myell finished up, turned his gib in, and headed for the mess decks. As the lift doors were closing he heard Hultz call, "Hold up!" and she boarded, along with Jodenny and some officers he didn't know from the Navigation Department.

"I'm just saying," a lieutenant said. "It wasn't my idea in the first place."

"You can't wriggle out that easily," one of his friends said.

Jodenny didn't participate in the conversation. She stood with her gaze on the deck indicator, expression inscrutable. As the decks continued to slide by she didn't look his way once, not even a tiny bit. The lift stopped at the mess deck to let everyone out. Myell abruptly changed his mind and headed upladder for the vending machines on the Flats.

"So how was the test, Sergeant?" Wildstein asked when he returned to the office.

"I think I passed," he said. It was Jodenny who had failed, and he was determined to tell her so.

"Lieutenant Scott, I relieve you," said Lieutenant Hamied.

"I stand relieved," Jodenny said, and suppressed a yawn. She had qualified to stand Command Duty Officer shortly after they left Warramala, and this was the third night watch she'd pulled in a week. Someone in Scheduling obviously held a grudge. Jodenny didn't mind. The alternative was lying alone in her lonely bed, thinking about Myell, and that only led to frustration and sadness. Funny how just one month of separation could feel like ten years. In some ways it was better to stay completely away from him, to pretend he was on some other ship or planet, than to catch fleeting glimpses in the passageways. Two days earlier they'd boarded the same lift, and his nearby presence had been enough to send her spiraling back to the too-short time they'd had together on Warramala, the memory of his body pressed against hers. Not being able to reach out and touch him was a worse punishment than anything Team Space could have dreamed up.

But not for much longer, she told herself. The *Aral Sea* was soon due to slide out of the Alcheringa and arrive at Baiame. Flight operations would begin almost immediately, with tower releases commencing three days hence. In a week they'd depart the last of the Seven Sisters and begin the long trek toward Fortune. Jodenny could keep her feelings at bay until then. No problem at all.

The bridge was beginning to liven up with the arrival of the morning shift. Jodenny took a three-hour nap in her cabin, then went up to the officers' gym for a few kilometers on the treadmill. A hot shower and extra sugar in her horchata made the world more manageable. She made it to Flight Support a half hour before the Alcheringa drop. Rokutan was up in Ops, going over final fuel schedules.

"Hey, Lieutenant," said Sergeant Gordon, who was busy on the deskgib she and Jodenny shared. "How was your midwatch?"

"No problems." Jodenny cleared off a corner chair. She'd thought the Flight Support office was small when she first saw it, but now she knew it was absolutely minuscule. She glanced out the open hatch to the row of shuttles lined up on the hangar deck. Beyond them, the Fox fighters were queued up for launch. A group of pilots were debriefing in the center of the hangar, and a sudden burst of laughter rose above the sounds of machinery.

Gordon glanced upward. "The commander left that handmail for you. And he wants to know how you're doing on the safety manual."

Jodenny picked up the pile. Rokutan had welcomed her to

the division warmly enough, but all she'd done for a month was sort mail, take attendance at morning quarters, and update the division safety manuals. "You've got to work up to it," he'd said when she expressed a desire to do more. Because he seemed to be happily dating a lieutenant from Admin, she didn't think he was holding their casual encounter against her. "He's defending his turf," Vu had said, which was silly. She didn't expect to make Division Officer again for a long time, whether it be on the *Aral Sea* or *Alaska* or any other freighter. She was no threat to his career.

Just after noon, the ship dropped out of the Alcheringa. The Flight Deck above them began launching robot recons to inspect the towers, soon to be followed by the foxes. Jodenny was more interested in the datastreams coming in from Baiame—local news and entertainment, along with any imail left for them by the last freighter to pass through. The news feeds seemed unusually skimpy, however.

"Maybe not so much has happened lately," Gordon said.

Someone knocked. "Sergeant Gordon," a voice said, and Jodenny snapped her head up to see Myell standing in the hatchway. Myell continued. "Could you excuse us for a moment? The lieutenant and I need to talk."

Gordon blinked. "Sure thing."

When she was gone Myell deliberately closed the hatch, leaving just the two of them alone.

"Are you crazy?" Jodenny asked.

Myell gazed at her steadily. "Nowhere in ship's regulations does it say that a lieutenant and a sergeant can't have a private conversation behind closed doors."

She rose. "You don't think people are watching us?"

He advanced on her, his eyes dark and mouth grim. "We said we would keep this professional for three months. That doesn't mean ignoring me in public. It doesn't mean not even saying 'Good morning, Sergeant,' or 'How are you, Sergeant?' in a lift."

Jodenny flushed. "Ensign Hultz spoke to you."

Myell took her by the arms, and the nearness of him nearly made her dizzy. "Ensign Hultz isn't the woman I love."

She would have answered but his mouth covered hers, and suddenly everything that she thought mattered fell away under his demanding kiss. Jodenny arched up against him, wanting him to touch her everywhere, eager to guide his hands under her uniform and around her hips. He groaned a little, and nuzzled the side of her neck.

"I'm sorry," Jodenny whispered. "I shouldn't have ignored you."

"You never will again," he vowed, and tightened his hold.

Which was exactly when the General Quarters began to shriek.

For a moment all Jodenny could think was, *Another goddamn drill.* Of all the inopportune timing . . . but then something made an enormous whump on the deck above them, and fire alarms began to shriek along with the General Quarters. She froze in Myell's arms.

"What the hell was that?" Myell asked, gazing at the overhead.

Holland spoke up. "Lieutenant, a General Quarters alarm has been triggered by Flight Operations. There has been a subsequent explosion in the hangar outside your position. I highly advise against evacuating at this time."

Myell moved Jodenny aside and started tapping on the deskgib. She felt ice-cold without him to ground her, and the comm announcement did nothing to assuage her fears.

"Fire and Security crews to A and B Decks. This is a Level One alert."

"Level One," Jodenny murmured.

"Someone's trying to board the ship," Myell said. He didn't elaborate on who that might be, but there were only a few possibilities. An unknown alien species might have popped out of nowhere, bent on the conquest of Team Space. The colonists of Baiame themselves had perhaps decided to revolt against the Seven Sisters. Or the Colonial Freedom Project had launched another terrorist attack.

Myell thumped the deskgib in disgust. "Vids are out. We can't see what's out there."

Jodenny didn't think she could move. Not when just outside the hatch was a hellish inferno of smoke and flame, and maybe burning bodies melting onto the deck, and who knew what kind of destruction set off by whoever was trying to invade the *Aral Sea*. But somehow her rubbery legs supported her all the way to the hatch, where she pressed her hand against the metal and found it warm, but not searing hot.

Myell was examining the small office. Jodenny already knew there was no second exit, no convenient, man-sized air duct to make good an escape. They were sealed up in a corner of B-Deck, and by the time fire crews reached them they'd either be baked alive or suffocated by the fumes. Already the air was warm and acrid, oily in her mouth.

"Any EV suits?" Myell asked.

Jodenny shook her head.

The lights flickered, then dimmed to half power. Jodenny couldn't hear anything from the hangar but she could imagine screams and moans, and the whoosh as the vacuum of space emptied compartments of air.

Myell wasn't giving up. "Is there any firefighting equipment?"

"No." Jodenny squeezed the word out. They didn't even have an old-fashioned extinguisher full of foam or water.

He grimaced. "We're going to have to go out the front door, then."

Jodenny found that she could in fact move, especially when it came to grabbing his arm. "You heard Holland."

"I heard," he agreed, and though he didn't say it, she could hear it in his voice: he trusted his own judgment over that of a computer program. Myell freed the belt from around his waist and quickly looped it between the two of them. "We'll have to crawl out. Where's the closest exit?"

"I don't know." Panic tinged her voice, and she didn't bother to hide it.

Myell took her by the shoulders. "Jodenny, listen to me.

We're going to get out of this, and get out together. But you have to *think*. Where's the nearest exit?"

Jodenny swallowed hard, her throat tight. Diagrams of the hangar flashed before her eyes, fuzzy in some areas, crystal clear in others. "About twenty meters to our right. There's an escape tube with upladders and downladders, and maybe some EV suits."

They tied parts of their shirts over their mouths to protect their airways, then crouched low and got the hatch open. It was a dark, smoky mess out there, impossible to see far. Suppression foam drizzled down from the overhead, sticky and warm. Intense heat washed over Jodenny as she tried to make sense of shouts and muffled calls, and the blast of the General Quarters, and what might have been the high whine of mazer fire. Though he couldn't possibly see where they were going, Myell began to crawl along the bulkhead toward the promised escape hatch. She followed on hands and knees, shaking so badly she thought she was maybe having a seizure.

"It's not far!" Myell called back to her. How foolish he was. Twenty meters under these circumstances was easily equal to a half million kilometers. Doggedly she kept at his heels, choking on smoke, the deck hot beneath her unprotected hands. An explosion rattled her bones. A fuel tank on one of the birdies must have blown. Something clutched Jodenny's ankle and she let out a yelp of fear.

"Terry!" she yelled. "Stop!"

But he couldn't hear her over the klaxons and whoosh of flames. Jodenny reached for her ankle and touched someone's raw, burned hand. Blindly she tugged three times on the belt that connected her to Myell and reached for the limp form of a sailor. He was too heavy for her to lift in any way, but she dragged him a few inches, paused to choke on smoke, then tugged him some more. Her lungs were searing in her chest, and she could feel blisters forming on her face and eyelids. *Burned alive* was how they would be found. No MacBride Cross could protect against the element of fire. Without warning Myell's hands fumbled next to hers, and suddenly he was pulling on the sailor and pushing Jodenny forward. As the bulkhead bumped up against her back she realized she was now in the lead. If she didn't find the damned escape tube within seconds, all three of them were doomed.

Jodenny crawled, dragging her trembling, aching body forward and forward and even more forward, careful to keep the bulkhead at her right shoulder. She feared they would pass right by the airlock, but then the tiles under her pained hands changed texture. She rose against the bulkhead and jammed her finger against the ID plate. Fresh air lapped at her, cold as a winter breeze. She grabbed Myell's shoulders and yanked with all her strength. He in turn brought the injured sailor with them, so that all three of them sprawled onto the small deck of the EV space and against the ladder that led up and down.

Jodenny was choking too hard to lift herself up. Through watering eyes she saw Myell's dim outline as he rose on his knees and slapped the controls. Powerful fans whooshed to life, sucking the smoke out of the lock and replacing it with fresh atmosphere, but the damn klaxons continued to bang against her skull. Myell collapsed against Jodenny and they clung to each other. The sailor between them groaned, alive but seriously injured.

"Medbot activate!" Jodenny shouted, and the little robot swooped down to start administering emergency aid.

"We're safe." Myell kissed her forehead. "We're alive."

Something wet soaked into her sleeve. Not foam from Myell's uniform, but instead blood that was flowing down the side of his face. Jodenny discovered a chunk of metal embedded in his forehead just over his right eye. The eye was swollen shut.

Alarmed, she tried to stanch the bleeding. "Terry—"

He caught her hand and squeezed it. "It's okay."

It wasn't okay. Myell's eyes slid closed and he slumped against her, his body lax and heavy. Jodenny maneuvered him to the deck in a panic, barely aware of the stern voice now bellowing over her gib.

"Lieutenant Scott!" It was Captain Umbundo. "Respond if you can hear me."

Jodenny blearily wondered what she had done wrong this

time. "Sir?" she croaked out. "Sir, we need medical assistance. I have two injured men here—"

"You need to go upladder to the Flight Deck," Umbundo said. "We can't get the clearshield to drop and the fire suppression equipment is damaged. There's an emergency release near the hangar doors. Do you understand what I'm saying? *You have to vent the Flight Deck.*"

Jodenny squeezed her eyes shut. It would be so much easier to just go to sleep, all her cares and worries forgotten, Myell's blood on her hands along with that of so many others.

"Everyone will die," she pointed out, in what she thought was a reasonable tone of voice.

"Put out those fires!" Umbundo commanded. He must have assumed all of the Flight Deck crew were already dead, or so far gone it didn't matter. "Do you understand me, Lieutenant? The entire ship is in peril."

Jodenny staggered upright. Myell was unconscious, his breathing fast and labored. The injured sailor, his face bright red, was equally insensate. The medbot was doing its best for both of them and would have already transmitted their location back to Core. Jodenny groped for the EV suit hanging in its closet, got herself into it, and turned on the headset. Someone must have patched her into the bridge, because over the klaxons she could now hear Umbundo and other bridge officers, and behind them, fire and repair reports.

"Lieutenant, do you understand what you have to do?" Umbundo asked. Under his words she could hear his unvoiced question: *Do you understand you won't be coming back?*

"Yes, sir." And so for the sake of ship and duty she began her long climb upward, the last trip Lieutenant Jodenny Scott would ever make.

EPILOGUE

If Terry Myell spent one more day on the planet Baiame he might just end up hijacking a ship of his own and sailing off down the Alcheringa, regulations be damned. Of course, he wasn't as stupid as to say the word "hijack" aloud. Since the attempted takeover of the *Aral Sea,* everyone took that prospect way too seriously. That was despite the fact that the CFP rebels who had boarded the *Aral Sea* had never gotten farther than A-Deck. Security had held back their advances, and Jodenny's jettison of the clearshield generators had taken care of the rest. Myell still resented Umbundo for ordering her into the inferno, but the tactic had worked well enough.

Still, here they were, a month later, the ship stuck in orbit around Baiame until the *Alaska* arrived. The CFP, emboldened by the destruction of the *Yangtze,* had toppled Baiame's weak colonial governor and seized Team Space assets shortly before the *Aral Sea*'s arrival. Now most of the rebels had fled to the hills, pursued by military and civilian security forces. Myell had been deployed planetside to help reorganize the supply stores, which had been raided and looted. But he had enlisted in Team Space specifically to get away from his home planet, and not even speeding a flit over the hills outside Pink Skunk could ease his restlessness.

"Could you slow down?" Jodenny asked from the passenger seat. She raised her perfectly healed hand and shielded her eyes against the sun. "We've got forty-eight hours' leave, and I want to survive it mostly intact."

Myell squeezed her knee and slowed down. He would do anything for her. After the aborted hijacking he'd woken up in Sick Berth suffering from burns and a head injury. Jodenny, ensnared in cables and other debris on the Flight Deck, had been pulled out of her EV suit with broken ribs, a skull fracture, severe burns to her right hand, and pulmonary edema. It had taken her a week to wake up, and another for her to understand his marriage proposal. One of the ship's chaplains had performed the ceremony in Sick Berth, with the bride and groom in adjacent beds and Commander Vu holding Jodenny's bouquet for her.

Before the ceremony, Captain Umbundo bestowed awards and field promotions. Jodenny received her second MacBride Cross and was now Lieutenant Commander Scott. Myell was issued a Silver Star, and made a Chief Petty Officer.

"The captain should have offered you a commission," Jodenny said as they were settling into their new married quarters in T7.

He kissed her hand. "What would I do as *Ensign* Myell? Besides. Chiefs work for a living. Officers sit around and look pretty all day."

"Killing fifty-three men wasn't pretty," she murmured, her eyes damp.

"It's not that way at all." Myell pulled her tight. "The Flight staff and Commander Rokutan were already dead or dying. You saved the ship."

She still woke up screaming some nights, and he couldn't blame her. He had his own nightmares to deal with. Usually they were about crawling through a hangar of fire or being lost in the Wondjina Transport System, but every once in a while they were about Daris or the Wirrinun or the Rainbow Serpent. While Jodenny was still in Sick Berth he had driven out to his parents' farm, determined to put old demons to rest, but the place was gone. Flattened by the bank, the foundation covered over with dirt. His memories weren't so easy to bury, but when the nightmares came he and Jodenny were there for each other, to hold and comfort in any small way possible, and for that he would always be grateful.

Now, on a bright hot day with several hours of shore leave still waiting to be filled, Myell stopped the flit on a hill. The capital city of Pink Skunk, with its prefab office buildings and well-planned parkways, lay a few kilometers away, baking in the sun's glare.

"That's where I enlisted," he said, conversationally.

Jodenny leaned against his shoulder. "On your eighteenth birthday. I saw that in your record."

He had left home without Daris's permission, and spent a terrified night in the Pink Skunk bus station fearing that his brother would show up and drag him back to the farm. The stern dictates of boot camp sergeants had been pale in comparison to life at home. Team Space had fed him, trained him, and sent him down the Alcheringa, where he'd nearly gotten lost until Jodenny came into his life. He had tried to make her understand how she had saved him, but she simply insisted that they had saved each other.

Jodenny nuzzled his cheek. "Now you're brooding."

He kissed her soundly.

"Much better," Jodenny said in approval. "So, have you thought more about Wildstein's offer?"

"Was that an offer? I thought it was more like an order." A wedge-tailed eagle glided by overhead, its golden wings almost as wide as Myell was tall. The rustle of its feathers reminded him of the hiss of a snake. "I don't know if I'm the galley type."

Neither was Jodenny sure she was ready to take on Maintenance/Hazardous Materials. She would rather she and her newly minted chief—her *husband,* she reminded herself, though the wedding ring on her finger was never far from sight—spend the entire trip back to Fortune holed up in their quarters, leisurely and hedonistically enjoying the cruise. But change was a Team Space constant, and she was looking forward to getting back to work after weeks of recuperation and light duty.

Myell had his eyes on the hawk circling overhead. Jodenny asked, "Will you be happy? Staying in Team Space, married to an officer, unable to tell people about traveling through the Spheres?"

"If you're beside me, yes," he said, with no hesitation in his voice. "Will you?"

The trip back to Fortune. More personnel problems. Politics as usual, reports and paperwork, the gossiping and back-stabbing. She didn't think she would ever rest completely easy until she knew why her memory had been blocked and what had happened to Osherman and Ishikawa, but it had been weeks since she had thought about the *Yangtze*. The happiness she had found with Myell could be with her every day, as permanent a part of her life as much as anything could be considered permanent in such a day and age.

"Yes," Jodenny said. The golden hawk dipped its head, let out a sharp cry, and flapped away into the clear sky. "I will."

From Chapter One of

The STARS
DOWN UNDER

the Sequel to

THE
OUTBACK
STARS

Available March 2008

TOR® A TOR HARDCOVER

ISBN-13: 978-0-7653-1644-8   ISBN-10: 0-7653-1644-7

Betsy was the oldest house in the neighborhood, and her nighttime temperature controls were erratic. Though he meant to stay up for Jodenny, Myell fell asleep on the sofa and woke every hour or so because he was too cold, or too hot, or too cold again. When he did sleep, he dreamt of crocodiles in a deep cave, hissing and snapping their razor-sharp teeth. At oh-four-hundred he woke shaking with dread, and stumbled to the bathroom to splash cold water on his flushed face.

He went to the bedroom and burrowed into the sheets. He was just dozing off again when the wallgib beeped and Jodenny's image rolled into view.

"Betsy told me you were up," she said. "Everything okay?"

"Fine." Myell turned his head into a pillow, then turned to eye her. "Why aren't you home?"

"There was an accident with some academy students, a big mess." She was as beautiful as ever, but dark circles hung under her eyes. Her lieutenant commander bars glinted on the screen. "They borrowed a birdie for fun and crashed into the ocean. I've been fending off the media for hours. I don't think I'll be home before you leave."

He shrugged one shoulder.

"I wanted to send you off to your new job in style," she said. "I'm sorry."

Myell was sorry, too. Their last ship, the *Aral Sea*, had barely entered orbit before new duty assignments arrived in their queues. Fledgling plans for a honeymoon had been abruptly discarded. Jodenny's new position at Fleet was prestigious but demanding. Lately he'd seen more of his reflection than he'd seen of her.

Jodenny touched the gib screen, as if trying to pat his cheek. "Be kind to your students, won't you? I remember how hard it was for me to memorize everything."

"I don't think they're going to throw me in front of a classroom today."

"They should. You'll be great." A gib pinged, and Jodenny glanced off screen. "Got to go. Call me later."

"Love you," he said, but the connection was already dead.

Further sleep eluded him. He played Izim for a while, but got killed multiple times. Just before dawn he pulled on some gym clothes. He opened the top drawer of his dresser and palmed a small dilly bag. Inside were two carved totems of geckos. One had been a gift, and the other had been his mother's.

For the first time in months he tied the bag around his waist and felt its comforting weight.

Outside, the air was hot and dawn was just lightening the sky. The faux-brick homes were a bit affluent for his tastes, but Jodenny's rank had its privileges and he supposed he'd have to get used to them. At the end of the street was a steep wooded hill dotted with senior officer homes. He jogged up it, the dilly bag bouncing against his skin. The exertion left him winded but the view at the top was worth it.

"Good morning, Kimberley," he said.

The rising sun sent yellow light streaking over Fortune's capital city. Myell could see the Parliament buildings, the graceful expanse of the Harbor Bridge, and a wide, disorienting expanse of silver-blue ocean. He hated the ocean. In the center of the city stood the Team Space pyramid, blue and clean and beautiful, the hub of its interplanetary operations.

The birds had woken up, kookaburras and doves mostly, and over their song he heard the unmistakable sound of an approaching security flit. Myell kept his gaze on the city and his hands in plain sight on the railing.

"Good morning, sir," a woman's voice said behind him. "Routine security check. Everything all right up here?"

Slowly he turned. "Good morning, officers. Everything's fine."

The woman was a brunette with the insignia of a regular tech. Her nametag read M. CHIN. Her partner, Apprentice Mate H. Saro, was smaller and slimmer, and had the coiled tenseness of a dog with something to prove.

"Do you live here, sir?" RT Chin asked.

"Chief Myell. I just moved in. Twenty-four hundred Eucalyptus Street," he said.

"Chiefs don't live in officer housing," Saro said.

Myell pushed down a flare of annoyance. He reached carefully into his pocket and handed over his identification card. Chin retreated with it to the flit. Saro rested one hand on the mazer in his belt and tried to look fierce.

"Are there regulations against people taking a morning walk?" Myell asked him.

"Most people don't walk around when it's still dark out."

"Sun's up," Myell pointed out.

Saro glared at him. "And they have the common sense to exercise in the gym."

"Fresh air's better for you."

Chin returned. "Sorry, Chief. You're all clear. People get nervous when they look out their windows and see a strange face, that's all. Welcome to the neighborhood."

"But he's not—" Saro started.

"Shut up, Hal." Chin nodded briskly at Myell. "Can we give you a lift home, Chief?"

"No. I'll walk."

Saro gave him one last suspicious look before the security flit drove off. Myell started downhill. He imagined suspicious eyes watching him from every window. An hour later, after forcing down breakfast and checking his uniform for the tiniest flaws, he joined the morning crowd at the monorail station. He hung back against the railing so he wouldn't sprain his elbow offering salutes. A few curious glances came his way, but no one spoke to him or challenged his right to be there.

He didn't flaunt his Silver Star, but a lieutenant with bloodshot eyes eyed it and said, "Earn that the hard way?"

"Is there any other way, sir?" Myell asked.

The lieutenant squinted at Myell's deployment patches. "That's the *Aral Sea*'s emblem. You helped beat off those terrorists at Baiame?"

"Something like that."

The lieutenant raised his coffee cup in salute, then turned away as a train pulled in.

Kimberley's public transportation system was a hub-and-spoke design. At Green Point Myell transferred to another train and rode several stops with civilians, students, and other military personnel until they reached Water Street. Supply School was easy to find. It occupied a pierside base wedged between shipping companies and freighter lines. The flags of Fortune, the Seven Sisters, and Team Space flapped overhead, bright in the sunshine. The air smelled like fuel and vile salt water.

"Second building to the right, Chief," a gate guard told Myell. "They'll help you over there."

Once inside the steel and glass building, a receptionist took him past cubicles where RTs and civilian staff were busy socializing. The enlisted men saw Myell and got to work. The civilians were slower about it. Large vids on the walls displayed student status, lists of instructor assignments and announcements for Friday's graduation ceremony. The name of the Supply School commander, Captain Kuvik, was prominently displayed everywhere.

The cubicle maze ended in a small office where Moroccan rugs hung on the walls and handwoven baskets decorated the shelves. A bald sergeant with brown skin rose from his desk, offering a smile and a handshake.

"Bob Etedgy, Chief," he said. "Welcome back to Supply School."

"Thanks. In truth, I never came through in the first place."

"Got all your training in the fleet? Me, too." Etedgy cleared off a chair for Myell. "Don't let them hear you say it around here, but direct experience is always better than sitting on your ass in a classroom."

Etedgy had already arranged for Myell's security pass, had requisitioned a parking slot in case he ever wanted to drive in, and had put together a bright red orientation folder emblazoned with the Supply School emblem.

"You'll be meeting with Captain Kuvik at oh-nine-hundred. He meets with every new instructor, nothing to worry about there. Until then I'll take you on the guided tour. Officer training is down the street, in their own building with their own faculty and staff, so we'll skip that. I'll also get you set up with a locker down in the training room. Most of us commute in civilian clothes and change into uniform here—saves on the wear and tear, you know, and it's okay as long as it's before the students arrive. Captain's not keen on us being seen as regular human beings."

He said it with a smile, but Myell didn't think he was joking.

The classrooms were on the second and third decks of the building. Khaki-clad chiefs were already lecturing, administering tests or conducting multimedia presentations. The upper decks contained computer labs, a library, and a chapel. The mess hall was in an adjacent building, and beyond it was the gymnasium.

"So where did they stash you and your wife for quarters?" Etedgy asked. "Widen? Sally Bay? My wife and I have been on the waiting list for Lake Lu for a year."

"Nice, is it?"

"Best you can do for enlisting housing around here."

"Is that how long you've been here? A year?" Myell asked, and successfully diverted the topic.

Just before oh-nine-hundred they returned to the main building and rode the lift to the fifth deck, which offered marvelous views of the sea traffic heading in and out of port. Myell kept his gaze averted. Captain Kuvik's suite was impeccably furnished and much larger than a shipboard captain's. The walls were vidded with photos of square-shouldered graduating students, all of them ready to march off into the fleet and inflict invoices for every last roll of toilet paper.

Not that Myell thought poorly of his career track. Supply sailors didn't earn the same glory as flight crews and didn't save lives like the medical corps, but someone had to keep food, equipment, uniforms, materials, and weapons moving down the Alcheringa and throughout the Seven Sisters.

"Chief Myell to see the Captain," Etedgy announced.

Captain Kuvik's secretary, an older man with antique glasses perched on his nose, gave Myell an unfriendly look. He pinged the inner office and repeated Etedgy's words.

"Send him in," a man replied.

Myell stepped into Kuvik's office. Windows screened out the sunlight. Classical music from pre-Debasement Earth played softly on a hidden radio. Kuvik, an older man with rugged features and white hair, nodded Myell toward a chair. Five rows of ribbons were pinned above his left pocket. Some of them were for enlisted sailors only, meaning he'd worked his way up through the ranks. The office smelled like peppermint.

"Sergeant Etedgy show you around?" Kuvik asked.

"Yes, sir." The chair was hard under Myell, and a little low to the floor. "It's an impressive complex."

"The enlisted school graduates three hundred ATs a month, and we teach advanced courses to twice as many RTs and sergeants. Do the job right or don't do it at all, I tell them. I disenroll anyone who doesn't take the job seriously, and I won't have any instructors who think this is a three-year vacation after years of running down the Alcheringa."

"I don't think of this as a vacation, Captain."

Kuvik gave no indication of hearing him. "Just because Fleet assigns someone here doesn't mean you get to be in front of one of my classrooms. My instructors are role models for young ATs who need direction and guidance. You don't pass muster, I'll stick you in a basement office and make you count requisitions eight hours a day."

Myell knew all about being shoved into dead-end, tedious jobs. "I hope I pass muster, sir."

Kuvik's gaze hardened. The music on the radio rose in crescendo. Something by Beethoven, Myell thought. Or maybe not.

"I know you were instrumental in saving your ship after the insurgent attack off Baiame," Kuvik said. "That Silver Star they gave you proves that. Commander Wildstein on the *Aral Sea* speaks highly of you, and she's damned hard to please. But you also married your supervisor, Lieutenant Scott, which indicates an appalling lack of decorum and brings up serious issues of fraternization."

"No fraternization charges were filed against Lieutenant *Commander* Scott or myself," Myell said, making sure Kuvik knew her current rank.

"I'm not interested in whether your former captain had the balls to court martial you for violating regulations." Kuvik leaned forward, a muscle pulling in his cheek. "Worse than your playing house with Lieutenant *Commander* Scott is the fact that you've never undergone chief's training."

Ah, Myell thought. The true crux of the problem. He and Jodenny had discussed the ramifications of his refusal, re-hearsed possible scenarios, but he'd sincerely hoped the issue wouldn't arise.

"I was promoted in the field while recovering from my in-juries," Myell said. "Authorized by my captain on behalf of Team Space to wear the insignia and uniform, and receive all the ranks and privileges of a chief petty officer. When we ar-rived here, seven other sergeants on the *Aral Sea* were also approved for promotion."

"And those seven sergeants immediately volunteered for chief's training over at Fleet. You refused."

"Because the training is voluntary, and has been ever since the death of that sergeant on Kookaburra."

Kuvik wagged a finger. "One mistake shouldn't override hundreds of years of tradition. Initiation marks the transition from sergeant to chief. You don't just put on the uniform.

You're expected to be a leader, and being a leader means being accepted as an equal by your peers."

Myell could already picture the basement office with his name posted by the door.

"That's where we disagree, sir. A leader rises above his peers instead of hovering in the pack with them. Team Space promotes us because of who we are and what we've done, not so we can reinvent ourselves. You can do whatever you like with me, but you're not going to convince me that a month of being humiliated and bullied will make me more fit to wear this uniform."

Myell realized his voice had risen. He clamped his mouth shut. He'd given the captain enough to hang him with already.

Kuvik leaned back in his chair. The radio fell silent, and a cormorant cried out behind the windows as it swooped down toward the water.

"There are some people from Fleet in my conference room," Kuvik finally said. "They want to talk to you. Something hush-hush and very important. Any idea what?"

Myell thought instantly of the Rainbow Serpent, and of the jobs he and Jodenny had turned down in a secret underground complex back on Warramala a few months ago.

"No, sir," he said.

Kuvik rose from his chair. "Go talk to them, Chief. And if they offer you a transfer, you'd better take it. It'll be a better deal than anything you're going to get here."

TOR

Voted

#1 Science Fiction Publisher
20 Years in a Row

by the *Locus* Readers' Poll

———•———

Please join us at the website below
for more information about this
author and other science fiction,
fantasy, and horror selections, and to
sign up for our monthly newsletter!

www.tor-forge.com